AUTUMN KILLING

AUTUMN KILLING

A Thriller

MONS KALLENTOFT

English translation
by Neil Smith

EMILY BESTLER BOOKS

—

WASHINGTON SQUARE PRESS

New York   London   Toronto   Sydney   New Delhi

EMILY
BESTLER
BOOKS

WASHINGTON SQUARE PRESS
A Division of Simon & Schuster, Inc.
1230 Avenue of the Americas
New York, NY 10020

This book is a work of fiction. Names, characters, places, and incidents either are products of the author's imagination or are used fictitiously. Any resemblance to actual events or locales or persons, living or dead, is entirely coincidental.

Copyright © 2009 by Mons Kallentoft
First published in 2009 in Swedish as *Höstoffer* by Natur & Kultur.
Published by agreement with Nordin Agency.

First Emily Bestler Books/Washington Square Press trade paperback edition September 2014

EMILY BESTLER BOOKS / WASHINGTON SQUARE PRESS and colophons are trademarks of Simon & Schuster, Inc.

For information about special discounts for bulk purchases, please contact Simon & Schuster Special Sales at 1-866-506-1949 or business@simonandschuster.com.

The Simon & Schuster Speakers Bureau can bring authors to your live event. For more information or to book an event, contact the Simon & Schuster Speakers Bureau at 1-866-248-3049 or visit our website at www.simonspeakers.com.

Manufactured in the United States of America

Cover design by Anna Dorfman
Cover photo © Niklas Lindblad

10 9 8 7 6 5 4 3 2 1

Library of Congress Cataloging-in-Publication Data

Kallentoft, Mons, date, author.
  [Höstoffer. English]
  Autumn killing : a thriller / by Mons Kallentoft.
     pages cm
  Emily Bestler Books/Washington Square Press paperback original.
  1. Police—Sweden—Fiction. 2. Murder—Investigation—Fiction. I. Title.
  PT9877.21.A48H6713 2014
  839.73'8—dc23   2014017793

ISBN 978-1-4516-4267-4
ISBN 978-1-4516-4270-4 (ebook)

AUTUMN KILLING

Prologue

Östergötland, October

I s the boy in the film scared? The one running away from the camera in a world without a sky?

Is fear what we feel when we're about to lose something important in our lives?

Or was it fear I felt when I was running? When they chased me across the school playground, throwing their red-hot barbs at me, their snakelike words?

I was scared of the anger, the blows that struck without me understanding why. Were the blows my lot? Why did I arouse such anger?

I've always been most scared of loneliness. The sort that lies beyond the blows, the insults. Yet I have spent almost my whole life alone. It feels like I have been standing on my own in the middle of a desolate, rain-swept field, waiting for someone I miss to come back to me.

The skies have opened this autumn.

The rain has been tormenting the town and the fields and forests, the people. It has been raining in every possible way the clouds have managed to come up with.

The drains have been full for days. The gutters are overflowing, washing up dead beetles and drowned mice onto Linköping's streets. Rats the size of cats, with swollen, rotting white stomachs. Every person's nightmare. Young snakes are gasping for air, eager to shed their skin one more time before they drown, to live like snakes before their snake lives are over.

Who knows what else might be about to float up from the depths?

We humans are like dogs. We can be at our loneliest among other people. But we are more afraid than dogs, because we know that pain has a history, and we recognize pain when it approaches.

Those young snakes are in my blood, and they won't stop whimpering, they won't leave me alone.

Those snakes, they hiss.

They spit. Their tongues flicker beneath my skin.

The world outside is even darker than the one in these films here this evening.

The raindrops are heavy dreams against a reluctant windowpane. What am I to do?

I'm going to take back part of what is mine.

I remember Father.

But what I remember most clearly is the fear. The way he could lash out at any moment, seeking my body with his clenched fist.

My father used to hold the camera in one hand, pressing it tight to his right eye, and wave with his free hand, directing me this way and that, in his hopeless attempts to put reality right, make it the way he wanted, get it do his bidding.

But something always gets lost.

And can never be recaptured.

I know what fear is now. The feeling that this is all that can be, all that has been. That there was never any difference.

Images on the movie screen hung up in the living room. Shaky Super 8 pictures, in bleached, almost monochrome colors. I, the boy, soundless and jerky, as if only the one-eyed camera can capture my anxiety.

I saw my life unfold in those pictures. I see the same thing happening now.

Bare, cold feet drumming across dew-wet grass and cold gravel, a ball kicked high into the air, a hunched body lurching forward over a sandpit.

Then the bitterness takes over. The shame. Shoulders drooped in defeat become a person's true posture. And things like that can be inherited.

Sometimes I've felt like going straight to the heart of this evil. I've stood outside the building he lives in, under the trees, waiting.

What does the boy in the pictures, the boy who is me, want? What is he thinking, in that eternal present moment?

Does he think that the mockery is his life? The pursuit?

Mum must be holding the camera now. I'm in Dad's tobacco-scented embrace, his arms are covered with gray wool and in the background shines a black and white Christmas tree. I am crying. The whole of my two-year-old face is a picture of despair, and I'm reduced to perhaps three emotions: sorrow and panic and that wretched fear.

What's the boy thinking? The one with the puffy red cheeks?

I get a kiss on the forehead.

Father had a beard back then, as fashion dictated, and Mum looks funny in her short skirt, and now I'm happy again; for a few short seconds I am happiness.

There is a chance in the forest. Shredded by piercingly sharp rain and poisonous gray wind. An opportunity to resurrect myself, to become the person I have a right to be, the person whose life is a series of beautiful unsettling monochrome moving pictures housed in perfume-scented white sleeves.

The projector hisses behind me; my shoulders and head create a shadow on the wall at the edge of the pictures, as though I want to climb inside them and become that boy once more. Resurrect the person he could have become.

Where did the love go? The smell of tobacco. I would go to you, Father, even though you hit me. I went to you, because that was all I knew.

It must be possible to find firm ground in another person's gentleness, it must be.

Dad and I in a park. He turns away from me when I fall over. Mum turns the camera away from me, into his face, and he's grimacing. Unless that's just the way he looks?

There's no love in his face.

Only disgust.

Then the film ends.

Everything flickers. Black white, black white, jerk, jerk.

I remember the boy in the pictures.

Know what he would have been capable of.

Know what this night bears in its pus-oozing womb. Know that the young snakes have to get out, out of me, that their evil faces must be destroyed.

I can conquer my fears again through violence.

{PART I}

Lingering Love

1

Slowly, slowly into the night.

Just accelerate gently so that nothing goes wrong.

Hands shaking on the wheel, pitch black outside the car windows, the storm making the rain fly horizontally through the air, large drops merging with microscopic ones, the windshield full of black tears that no wipers could ever cope with.

Police superintendent Malin Fors can feel her heart pounding in her chest; she can see it in front of her, as black and liverish and tormented as the night outside. She is still on the forest road, and the bare branches of the trees are reaching out to grab the car, like the enraged tentacles of some prehistoric monster.

Malin takes one hand off the wheel, slows her speed, wipes her eyes, tries to convince herself that it's just rain on her cheeks.

Nothing else.

She breathes in the musty air of the car and feels nauseated.

There's a tapping sound on the metal roof of her unmarked white police Volvo. Little white bullets falling from the skies in swarms. Soon the noise is thunderous, and the hail hammering on the roof must be the size of fists, and it's drowning out the sound of the engine, screaming at her: You've made your choice, there's no going back, you've given up, Malin Fors!

Her whole body is shaking.

Janne's face dancing in front of the windscreen. Tove's.

Malin's daughter's fifteen-year-old face is alarmingly smooth, and its outline and contours drift in and out of the dark autumn night, but if Tove is trying to say anything her voice is swallowed up by the hail pounding on the roof.

And then it stops.

Only the sound of the engine, and hesitant drops on the windshield, no more than the wipers can cope with.

Malin's clothes feel wet against her skin.

She can just make out the lights of the motorway into Linköping, beacons flickering in the night, getting closer, and Malin increases her speed, thinking, I've had enough of this, get me out of here, and she sees Janne's face before her: He isn't angry or sad, just tired, and that frightens her.

It was a lovely idea: that the three of them, Janne, Tove, and Malin, belonged together, and that they could accept such a gift.

She and Tove had moved back in with Janne, to the house outside Malmslätt, toward the end of summer last year. More than a decade after the divorce they were going to try again; they felt obliged to after that crazy, scorching summer that almost cost Tove her life, when she was kidnapped by a murderer Malin was looking for.

Malin had sat in the garden that September, the garden of the house where they had lived together long before, and she had watched Tove and Janne clearing weeds and raking leaves over by Janne's old cars. She had looked at them and believed that it really was possible to start again, to create the world anew if only the willpower and foundation were there.

They had played nicely to start with. Not working too much, making dinner together, eating, loving, trying to talk, trying to say anything that might actually mean something.

Then autumn had arrived in earnest.

They had taken Tove to see a psychiatrist at the University Hospital who specialized in treating adolescents. Tove had refused to talk to her, saying there was nothing to talk about: "Mum, I'm not frightened. I'm all right. It's okay. It wasn't your fault."

"It wasn't anyone's fault."

But Malin knows it was her fault. Tove got dragged into an investigation the previous summer, and if that wasn't Malin's fault, then whose was it? If it hadn't been for her job as a detective, it would never have happened.

"People do weird things, Mum."

Malin often wished she were as rational and pragmatic as her daughter and could find it as easy to come to terms with the state of things: Tove was apparently untouchable.

The broken cars in the garden. Lids left off toothpaste tubes. Milk cartons opened the wrong way. Words tossed out into space that just bounced back, unanswered and unheard. Roof tiles that needed to be replaced. Food that had to be bought from monstrous out-of-town superstores. Guilt and regret wiped out by everyday tasks and a vain hope that the passing years had brought a level of wisdom. She recognized the irritation as it crept up on her at the start of November, like a hacksaw to her soul: the blows, the gentle yet cruel derision of love. The little boy reappeared in her dreams, and she wanted to talk to Janne about him, about who he was, or who he might be. She had lain beside Janne in bed, knowing he was awake, but her paralyzed tongue hadn't been able to form any words.

The flat in town had been rented out to some students. She worked late into the evening at the police station, and Janne made sure he had shifts at the fire station when she had days off—she had realized that, understood it, and couldn't blame him.

She had started looking into the old Maria Murvall case in her own time. She wanted to solve the mystery, find the answer to the question of what had happened to the young woman who was found raped and abandoned on a road in the forests around Lake Hultsjön, and who now sat mute and out of reach in a room at Vadstena Hospital.

Janne's patience when she lost her temper.

Which only made her more angry.

"Do whatever you like, Malin. Do whatever you have to do."

"For fuck's sake, would it kill you to have an opinion about what I should do?"

"Can't you just take a break from work when you're at home with us?"

"Janne. Never, ever, tell me what to do."

And then there was Christmas, and something about the ham, about whether they should have mild or strong mustard in the crust, and Janne had been upset when she replied, "Whatever," without actually listening to the question, and then how she had then been angry because he didn't even know something as basic as that one should use mild mustard for the crust of the Christmas ham.

He had shouted at her.

Told her to pull herself together. To try being a bit bloody nicer, a bit more normal, otherwise she could pack her things and go back to that fucking flat. He had yelled at her, telling her to fuck off, that this was all a stupid idea from the start, that he'd been asked to go to Sudan with the Swedish Rescue Services Agency in the New Year, and he had a good mind to go just to get away from her and her filthy moods.

"Bloody hell, Malin, you're not well, can't you see?"

She had waved her glass of tequila and Coke at him.

"At least I'm not so retarded that I fuck up the Christmas ham."

Tove had been sitting a few feet away from them at the kitchen table, her hands on the red cotton tablecloth, beside a new homemade decorative pin for the ham and the red plates they'd bought from Åhléns for the occasion.

Janne had fallen silent.

Malin had felt like carrying on shouting at him, but ended up just looking at Tove instead.

Her wide-open blue eyes seemed to be asking just one simple question of the mulled-wine-scented room:

Is this what loving someone means?

In that case, don't ever let me love anyone.

Malin can see the sky getting brighter above the edge of the town.

Not much traffic.

She wonders if she's got any dry clothes to change into in the flat, but knows she hasn't. Maybe something in a box in the attic, but the rest of her clothes are at Janne's.

A black car drives past her; she can't see what make it is through the fog, but the driver's in a hurry, going almost twice as fast as her.

It's raining again, and newly fallen orange and yellow leaves are drifting in front of the windshield, dancing before her like fireflies from the devil's own fire, a hearth that whispers and conjures forth evil from city and countryside alike: Come out, come out, mischief and malice, come out from your cold, flooded holes, and show us what your loveless world looks like.

Janne's pathetic excuses echo inside her head and in the sounds she hears.

No more Christmases like that one. She has promised herself that much.

"I have to go."

They had talked about it again on Christmas Day; Malin had a hangover and hadn't felt like fighting, she was just quietly furious and sad that everything was turning out the way it always used to.

"They need me there. I couldn't live with myself if I turned it down. They need my experience to set up the latrines in the refugee camp; if that doesn't happen thousands of people will die like flies. Have you ever seen a child die of cholera, Malin? Have you?"

She had felt like punching him when he said that.

They had made love one last time the night before he left.

Hard and without any warmth, and she had a sense of Daniel Högfeldt's hard body above her, the journalist she had carried on having sex with sometimes, and she had scratched Janne's back, biting his chest and feeling the metallic taste of his blood, and he hadn't objected; he seemed to enjoy being tormented by her rage.

There was steel in her that night. Hard, rigid steel.

Janne had come home a month later, and she had been immersed in her work on the Maria Murvall case, spending the weekends interviewing the officers in Motala who had dealt with the investigation.

Tove was living her own life alongside theirs. Somehow this was how things had turned out.

"She's never home. Have you noticed?" Janne asked one evening in April when they were off at the same time and Tove had gone to the cinema in the city.

Malin hadn't noticed. How could she have noticed when she herself was never at home?

They talked about seeing a counselor, trying to get some family therapy.

Several times Malin had stood with the phone in her hand, ready to call the psychoanalyst Viveka Crafoord, who had offered to see her free of charge.

But her tongue was paralyzed.

That spring Malin had watched them working in the garden again, father and daughter together, she herself merely a physical presence, her soul taken up with a complicated honor killing.

"How the hell could a father ask his son to kill his daughter? Janne, tell me?"

"Okay, no more tequila tonight."

"I hate it when you give me orders. It sounds like I belong to you."

Linköping is enveloped by ice-cold rain.

What exactly is this city, other than a cocoon for people's dreams?

Side by side, the inhabitants of the country's fifth-largest city push on with their lives. Watching each other. Judging each other. Trying to love each other in spite of their prejudices. The people of Linköping mean well, Malin thinks. But when a lot of people's lives are governed by a constant anxiety about keeping their jobs and making their wages last till the end of the month, while a minority live lives of excess, solidarity doesn't hold up. The city's inhabitants live side by side, separated by thin geographic lines. You can shout to the council flats of the sixties and seventies from the gardens of lovely villas, and call back from the shabby balconies.

Autumn is a time of decay, Malin thinks. The whole world is scared, waiting to be enveloped in the chill of winter. At the same time the colors of autumn are like fire, but it's a cold fire that only cold-blooded animals can love and take any pleasure from. The only promise held by the beauty of autumn, the leaves like flames, is that everything is going to get worse.

Her hands are no longer trembling on the steering wheel.

All that is left is the damp chill against her thin body. It's strong, my body, she thinks. I may have let everything else slip, but I haven't neglected my training, I'm strong, I'm so fucking strong, I'm Malin Fors.

She drives past the old cemetery.

She sees the reflection of the cathedral spire hit the windshield like a medieval lance ready to impale her.

What happened tonight?

What words were spoken?

What raised eyebrow, what nuance in what voice made them start again?

She has no idea; she's had a bit to drink, not much, but probably far too much to be driving this car at this moment.

Am I drunk? Adrenaline has erased any intoxication. But I'm not quite sober. None of my colleagues will be out tonight, will they?

You bastard. You pathetic, cowardly bastard, always running

away. Calm down, Malin, stop being ridiculous, stop it, no more drink, for fuck's sake stop drinking, why don't you leave, and did I hit him? Did I hit you in the kitchen, Janne, or did I just have my clenched fist in the air, pissed off at all your fucking *don'ts*?

I was flailing at the air, I remember that now, now that I'm pulling up in the car outside the front door on Ågatan.

The clock of St. Lars Church, enveloped in a brittle fog, says it's quarter to eleven. A few shadowy crows stand out darkly against the sky.

No one in sight and I don't want to think about this evening, this night. Beside the church's dark-gray stone, on the waterlogged grass, sit great piles of raked leaves. In the darkness it looks like they're rusting, surrendering their beautiful colors and letting themselves be consumed by the millions of worms emerging from the drenched ground.

You jerked back, Janne, dancing out of the way—you've had plenty of practice with worse blows than mine—and I yelled that I was leaving, leaving and never coming back.

You said, You can't drive in that state, Malin, and you tried to take the keys, and then Tove was there, she'd fallen asleep watching television on the sofa but had woken up, and she shouted, Surely you can see you can't drive like that, Mum?

You said, Calm down now, Malin, come here, let's have a hug, and I lashed out again, but again there was nothing but air where I hoped you were standing.

I pretended I'd asked if you wanted to come with me, Tove, but you just shook your head.

And you, Janne, you didn't stop me.

You just looked at the kitchen clock.

Then I ran to the car.

I drove through the blackest autumn weather and now I've stopped. I open the car door. Black tentacles tear at the gray-black sky. Open holes of fear where the starlight ought to be seeping through.

My shoes on the wet tarmac.

I'm thirty-five years old.

What have I done?

2

The key in the lock.

Malin fumbles; her hands won't obey even though they stopped shaking a good while ago.

Miss.

Hit.

Miss.

Like everything else.

The flat became vacant the previous week, but she told Janne that she'd got new tenants, another group of evangelical students. This evening's explosion, unavoidable, anticipated, postponed until it was feasible.

Malin goes inside, shaking the raindrops from her blond bob. There's a smell, a mixture of damp and detergent, and Malin can feel that the autumn has crept through the cracks in the windows and spread across the walls, floors, and ceilings.

She's shaking.

Must turn up the radiators.

Another feeling here now.

A lonely feeling. But also a feeling of something new?

The furniture is all where it should be.

The Ikea clock in the kitchen wall is still broken, the second hand lying still at the bottom of the face.

She stands in the living room, wanting to turn on the light, but she can't be bothered to press the switch. Better to slump onto the sofa in the welcoming darkness. A darkness that is all her own.

Tove.

Fifteen years old this year.

Still mad about books and top of her class, but all that has a heavier tone now, as if the game has become serious, as if time is taking its toll on her.

You're too young for that, Tove.

A few boyfriends have come and gone during the course of the year.

Goodbye, Peter. Hello, Viggo.

Can I let her go? I can't punish her with my own feelings of guilt. And she seems to be fine. Malin can see it in her daughter, the glow in her eyes, the way her girlish posture is becoming that of a woman. Malin's hopes, unexpressed: Hold your ground, Tove, you don't want to become a mother for many years yet.

Concentrate on your education.

Aren't I supposed to be giving a talk in a school sometime soon? Malin thinks. The very thought of babbling in front of a group of tired, disinterested students makes her feel miserable, so she brushes it aside.

Malin lies down on the sofa.

Feels the damp clothes against her skin.

The tequila burned out of her body now.

It feels like the evangelical students' sanctimony is still clinging to the flat, making her feel slightly nauseated.

Janne. She wants to say she's sorry but doesn't know where to start. And Tove, how can I explain to you? Could you even understand?

What do I really know about your life now, Tove? I have no idea at all, except that this flat is your home, you can move in here with me, anything else is out of the question.

Your books, out at Janne's.

I've tried sitting down beside you a thousand times over the past year, on the sofa, on your bed, asking you how you are, but the only words I get out of you are "I'm fine," accompanied, soundlessly, by "Leave me alone, Mum."

And what do I want from you, Tove?

Your forgiveness? Reassurance that everything's all right?

Can things ever be all right? That woman, the murderer, held you down on the floor with her bloody hands and was about to kill you.

And I'm the one who brought that scene into being.

There are a thousand wretched ways for it to rain. Raindrops can have any number of colors, even at night, they can take the copper of autumn leaves and make it their own; the rain can become a shower of sparks in the glow of the streetlamps, sparks like flying cockroaches.

Malin has slumped to the floor of the living room.

Watching the red, orange, and yellow cockroaches flying through the air, hearing their jaws snapping, and she forces them away, chasing them with a flamethrower, and she can smell charred cockroach corpses as she hounds them from her sight.

Nothing but mundane reality out there now.

Clouds.

Weeks, weeks of different shades of gray over her head, no blue in sight. Record rainfall and television weather forecasters talking about a flood of biblical proportions.

She found the bottle at the back of the cupboard above the microwave. She knew those buttoned-up religious types wouldn't so much as have sniffed at it. So she had left it there, consciously or unconsciously, for future use.

She drinks straight from it.

Who gives a damn if she's hungover tomorrow? It's been a quiet autumn since she caught the father and brother who planned and carried out the murder of their daughter, their sister. She'd had a Swedish boyfriend. And that was enough.

Sometimes it can actually be nice to be hungover. I'll have to come to grips with everything tomorrow, get my things from Janne. Isn't he on duty, so I won't have to see him? I'll bring Tove's things. Talk to her about moving back in.

I'm drunk, Malin thinks, and it's nice.

3

Mum.

You're so angry, Tove thinks as she pulls the covers over her head and listens to the rain clattering on the roof, hard and fierce, as if there were an impatient god up there drumming millions of long fingers.

The room smells of the country. She was just looking at the rag rugs, resting like flattened snakes on the floor, their pattern like a beautiful series of black-and-white pictures that no one will ever be able to interpret.

I know, Mum, Tove thinks. I know you blame yourself for what happened last summer, and that you think I'm bottling all sorts of things up. But I don't want to talk to a psychologist, I don't want to sit there babbling opposite some old lady. I've been chatting to other people on trauma.com instead. In English. It's as if it all gets easier when I see my own clumsy words about what happened, and about how scared I was then. The words take the fear away, Mum, I've only got the images left, but the images can't get me.

You have to look forward, Mum. Maybe you think I haven't seen you drinking. That I don't know where you hide the bottles around the house, that I don't notice that your breath smells of alcohol behind the mask of chewing gum. Do you think I'm stupid, or what?

She and Janne had remained at the kitchen table when Malin disappeared with all her rage. Janne had said:

"I hope she doesn't crash the car and kill herself. Should I call the police? Or go after her? What do you think, Tove?"

And she hadn't known what to say. Most of all she wanted her mum to come back, to rush into the kitchen in her very best mood, but things like that only happened in bad books and films.

"I don't know," she had said. "I've no idea."

And her stomach had been aching, as far as her chest, a black pressure that wouldn't let up, and Janne had made sandwiches, had told her things would sort themselves out once her mum had calmed down.

"Can't you go after her?"

And Janne had looked at her, then simply shook his head in response. And the ache had found its way up into her heart and head and eyes, and she had to struggle to hold back the tears.

"It's okay to cry," Janne said, sitting down beside her and holding her. "It's awful. It's awful, because no one wanted it to turn out like this."

"It's okay to cry," he had said again. "I'm going to."

How can I help you, Mum? Because no matter what I say it's like you're not listening, don't want to listen, like you're trapped in an autumn river full of dirty torrential water and you've made up your mind to float off into the darkness.

I can see you in the kitchen, on your way to work, in the mornings, on the sofa in front of the television, or with all your files about that Maria woman.

And I want to ask you how you are, because I can see you're feeling bad, but I'm scared you'd just be angry. You're completely shut off, Mum, and I don't know how to get you to open up.

And there's so much else that I'd rather think about: school, my books, all my friends, all the fun stuff that I feel I'm just at the start of. All the boys.

Tove pulls the covers down. The room is there again.

The ache in her stomach, her heart, is still there. But for me it's quite natural that you don't live together, you and Dad. And there'll be more fighting. Because I don't think you're coming back here, and I don't know if I want to live with you now.

A crow has landed on the windowsill. It looks in at her. It pecks at the glass before flying off into the night.

The room is dark.

"I'll be fine," Tove thinks. "I'll be fine."

Janne is lying in bed with one of the beside lamps on. He's reading a folder from the British armed forces. It's about building latrines, and it helps him to find his way into his memories, to Bosnia, Rwanda, and Sudan, where he most recently constructed latrines in a refugee camp. The memories from his time in the Rescue Services Agency mean that he can avoid thinking about what happened this evening, about what has happened and now must happen.

But the images, black and white in his memory, of people in desperate need in distant corners of the planet, are constantly shoved aside by Malin's face, her red, puffy, tired alcoholic's face.

He confronted her several times. And she evaded the issue. Yelled at him when he poured away the drink from the bottles she'd stashed away, screaming at him that it was pointless, because she still had ten bottles hidden in places he'd never find.

He pleaded with her to see someone, a psychiatrist, a therapist, anyone at all. He had even spoken to her boss, Sven Sjöman, telling him that Malin was drinking more and more but that it might not be visible at work, and asking him to do something. Sven had promised that something would be done. That conversation had taken place in August, but nothing had happened yet.

Her rage. Against herself. Presumably because of what happened to Tove. She refused to accept that it wasn't her fault, that there is evil everywhere, always, and that anyone can get in its way.

It's as if her stubbornness has led her in the wrong direction. That she's absolutely committed to driving herself as far down as she can.

And tonight she hit him. She's never done that before.

Dig deep. *Dig deep.*

Regular check-ups. Bacteria sanitation.

Janne throws the files across the room. Turns out the light.

It was pretty stupid, really, he thinks. To imagine that a bloody terrible experience could make us work together as a family. As if evil could be a catalyst for good. In truth the complete damn opposite has happened.

Then he looks at Malin's side of the bed. Reaches out his hand, but there's no one.

4

Sleepless dawn.

Axel Fågelsjö is about to get up from his leather armchair, but first he rubs his fingers over the worn, shiny armrest and stubs out his cigarette in the ashtray on the leather-topped sideboard. Then he lets his legs take the weight of his heavy yet still strong seventy-year-old body and pulls in his stomach, feeling strangely powerful, as if there were some enemy outside the door that he needs to fight with one of the many hunting rifles in the cabinet over in the apartment's master bedroom.

Fågelsjö stands in the sitting room. He sees Linköping wake up outside the windows, imagines its inhabitants in their beds, all those people with their different lives. Anyone who says there's no difference between people doesn't know what they're talking about.

The trees in the Horticultural Society Park, their crowns blown this way and that by the wind. Only gentle rain now. Not the sort of downpour that drives the rats out of the sewers. That's happened several times this autumn. And the city's pampered middle classes have been horrified by the beasts nurtured in subterranean Linköping. As if they refuse to accept that there are rats living beneath their well-shod feet. Rats with hairless tails and razor-sharp teeth, rats that will still be there long after they themselves are gone.

It's been a long time since he slept through the night. He has to get up at least three times to go to the toilet, and even then he has to stand there for five minutes before releasing the little trickle that made him so incredibly desperate to go.

But he doesn't complain. There are people with far worse ailments than him.

He misses Bettina when he wakes up at night. Only an empty white bed where she was always contours, warmth, and breath. As luck would have it, she went before the catastrophe, before Skogså slid out of his grasp.

The castle was at its most beautiful on mornings like this.

He can see the castle within him, as though he were standing in front of it, at the edge of the forest.

The seventeenth-century walls in sand-colored stone seem to rise up from the fog, more potent than nature itself.

Skogså Castle. Constructed and altered over the years according to the eccentric whims of his ancestors.

The copper roof seems to glow even when the sky is covered by low cloud, and the countless eyes of the building, the old castle's loopholes and the more recent lead windows. He has always imagined that the loopholes were watching him from a distant moment in history, measuring him against his predecessors as master of the castle. The new windows are blind by comparison, as if looking for something lost.

From this viewpoint in his memory he can't see the chapel, but it's there. Bettina isn't there, however—she had wanted him to spread her ashes in the forest at the north of the estate.

He can hear them.

The fish splashing uneasily in the black water of the moat, maybe the dead Russian soldiers, the hungry, walled-in spirits, are nipping at their gills.

Count Erik Fågelsjö.

A robber baron during the Thirty Years' War. A favorite of Gustav II

Adolf, the most brutal warrior of all, said to have mutilated twenty men in one day during the skirmishes following the Battle of Lützen. Count Axel Fågelsjö thinks, I have always felt that man's blood flowing through my veins.

In his youth he wanted to serve with the UN. But his father said no. His father, the friend of Germany, the colonel who had gone around Prussia in the thirties fawning over the Brownshirts, the castle owner who believed in a German victory long into the early 1940s.

And now?

After what had happened.

Count Erik Fågelsjö must be spinning with shame in the family vault in the chapel at Skogså, lying there naked and shrieking with utter fury.

But there's still a chance, if it weren't for that useless dandy, that bastard who came slithering down from Stockholm like a legless lizard.

Axel Fågelsjö looks out across the park again. Sometimes this autumn he has imagined he can see a man under the trees, a man who seemed to be peering up at his windows.

Sometimes he's thought it was Bettina.

He talks to her every day, has done since she died three years ago. Sometimes he goes out to the forest where he scattered her ashes, hiking there no matter what time of year, most recently through moldering fiery yellow leaves and swaying mushrooms, his dark voice like an echo between the trees, trees which seemed almost rootless, floating.

Bettina.

Are you there? I never thought you'd go first. I miss you, you know. I don't think anyone knows, not even the children, how much I love you, loved you.

And you answer. I can hear you telling me that I must be strong, not show what I feel, you see what happens if you give in. Axel, the wind whispers, and the wind is your voice, your breath against my neck.

Bettina.

My Danish beauty. Refined and unrefined at the same time. I first

saw you in the summer of 1958, when I was working as a foreman at
the Madsborg estate on Jutland, there to get some experience of farming.

You were working in the kitchen that summer, a perfectly ordinary girl, and we would swim in the lake together. I've forgotten the
name of the lake, but it was on the estate, and I brought you back
home after that summer, and I remember Father and Mother, how
they were dubious at first, but gradually gave in to your charm, and
Skogså fell to your cheerful temperament.

And you, how could you, Bettina? How dare you give in to cancer? Were you sad that our income wasn't enough to keep the castle
in good condition? It would have eaten too much into our capital, all
the millions that were needed.

I don't want to believe that. But I can feel guilty, the guilt you feel
when you hurt the person you love most of all.

Pain. You had to learn all about pain, and you told me there was
nothing worth knowing in those lessons.

The paintings on the walls here are your choices. Ancher, Kirkeby.
And the portrait of my ancestor, Erik, and all the other wonderful
fools and madmen who went before me.

You died at the castle, Bettina. You would have hated having to
leave it, and I'm ashamed before your spirit now. No matter how
gentle you could be, you could be just as hard when it came to
defending what was yours.

Most of all you worried about the boy.

Among your last words: "Look after Fredrik. Protect him. He
can't manage on his own."

Sometimes I wonder if he was listening at the door of your sickroom.

You never know with him. Or maybe don't want to know. Like
everyone else, I love my daughter, and him, my son. But I've always been able to see his shortcomings, even if I didn't want to. I'd
rather have ignored them and seen his good qualities instead, but
that doesn't seem to be possible. I see my son, and I see almost nothing but his failings, and I hate myself for it. Sometimes he can't even
seem to control his drinking.

The clock on the bureau strikes six and Fågelsjö stops by the sitting room window. Something breaks out of the darkness below, and someone walks through the park. A person dressed in black. The same man he thought he saw earlier?

Fågelsjö pushes the thought aside.

I knew it was a mistake, he thinks instead. But I still had to do it: letting Fredrik, my firstborn, the next Count Fågelsjö, look after our affairs, giving him access to our capital when my soul turned black after the cancer won. He never wanted to be at the castle, never wanted to manage the small estate and forest that were left, because it was now more profitable to take the EU subsidies for set-aside land than rent it out.

Didn't want to. Couldn't. But he ought have been able to handle the money.

He's got financial qualifications, and I practically gave him free rein.

But everyone has their good and bad sides, their faults and short-comings, he thinks.

Not everyone has enough of the predator in them, enough of the merciless power that seems to be needed in this world. Father tried to get me to appreciate the responsibility that comes with privilege, how we have to assume a position of leadership in society. But in some ways he belonged to a bygone age. Certainly, I led the work out at Skogså, I was respected in the finer society of the region, but a leader? No. I tried to get Fredrik and Katarina at least to appreciate the value of privilege, not to take it for granted. I don't know that I succeeded.

Bettina, can you tell me what I can do to make Katarina happy? And don't try that same old tune again. We had different opinions about that, as you know.

Be quiet, Bettina.

Be quiet.

Let me put it like this:

Was the bloodline diluted with you, Bettina?

He has sometimes wondered this when looking at Fredrik, and Katarina too, occasionally.

*   *   *

The green Barbour jacket sits tight across Axel Fågelsjö's stomach, but he's had it for twenty-five years and doesn't want to buy another one just because the pounds stick a bit more easily than they used to.

Things must run their course, he thinks as he stands in the hall.

We Fågelsjös have lived more or less the same way for almost five hundred years. We set the tone for the area, for this city.

Sometimes he thinks that people around here are imitating the life he and his family have always had. The first water closet in Östergötland was at Skogså, his grandfather wore the first three-piece suit. They have always shown the way, and the business and political communities understood this, even if that's all history now.

There was no invitation to the county dinner this year.

In all the years that the county governors held dinners for the most prominent people in the county, there was always been a Fågelsjö among the guests. But not this year.

He saw the picture taken at Linköping Castle in the *Östgöta Correspondent*. Count Douglas was there. The historian Dick Harrison. The director of Saab's aviation division. The head of information at Volvo. A parliamentary undersecretary with roots in the city. The editor in chief of the *Correspondent*. The chair of the National Sports Association. Baron Adelstål.

But no one from the Fågelsjö dynasty.

He pulls on his thick black rubber boots.

I'm coming now, Bettina.

The calfskin gloves. What leather!

Fågelsjö thinks that things will probably sort themselves out anyway. Hears Bettina's voice:

"Protect the boy."

I did protect Fredrik. I did what was necessary, even if, in theory, the bank could have been held responsible.

The memory of Bettina's face fades.

Maybe I should have let things go to hell with the boy, Fågelsjö thinks, as he presses the cold button of the lift to go downstairs and out into the lonely dawn.

5

No other engine sounds like that of the Range Rover: elegant yet powerful. And the vehicle responds nicely when Jerry Petersson presses the accelerator. Maybe that was how the horses of former centuries responded when long-dead counts pressed their spurs to the flanks of their sweating steeds.

No horses here now.

No counts.

But he can always get a few horses if he meets a woman who likes them; they have a tendency to like horses, women. Something of a cliché, but this cliché was also a reality, like so many others.

Petersson sees banks of fog drifting in across the fields, coming to rest beside the fir forest over to the east. The dog is sitting beside him in the passenger seat, letting its perfectly balanced body move in time with the vehicle's suspension, its eyes searching the landscape for something living to chase after, stand over, help to bring down. Petersson runs a hand through its coarse, damp fur. It smells, the dog, but it's a smell that suits the countryside, with its raw, penetrating authenticity. A beagle, a male, that he has named Howie after Howard Hughes, the Hollywood madman of the thirties who is said to have founded the modern aviation industry and who, according to legend, ended up a recluse in a castle outside Las Vegas, dependent on blood transfusions.

Petersson once read a biography of him and thought, If I ever buy a dog, I'm going to name him after an even bigger madman than me, or someone I know.

The dog's nostrils contract, open again, and its big black pupils seem to want to devour the land around Skogså.

The estate is never more beautiful than in the morning, when the approaching day seems to soften the earth and rocks. Rain is falling against the windshield and roof and he stops at the side of the road, watching some birds hopping about on the oyster-shell-colored soil, pecking for worms in the rotting vegetation and the pools that are growing larger with each passing day. The leaves are lying in drifts here, and he thinks they look like a ragged cover in a beautiful, forgotten sketch for an oil painting. And under the cover life goes on. Grubs pupating. Beetles fighting each other. Mice swimming in streams of rain toward goals so distant that they can't even dream they exist.

The dog is starting to get anxious, whimpering, wanting to get out, but Jerry soothes it.

"There now, calm down, you can get out soon."

A landscape.

Can that be a person's fate?

Sometimes when Petersson drives around the estate he imagines he can see all the characters that have come and gone in his life. They drift around the trees, the rocks and buildings.

It was inevitable that he would end up here.

Wasn't it?

Snow falling one New Year's Eve, falling so thickly it makes this morning's fog look as transparent as newly polished glass.

He grew up not far from here.

In a rented flat in Berga with his parents.

Petersson looks at himself in the rearview mirror. Starts the car and drives on.

He drives around two bends before stopping the car again. The dog is even more restless now and Petersson opens the door, letting it out first before getting out himself. It races off across the open field, presumably chasing the scent of a deer or elk, or a hare or fox.

He looks out over the field for a while before stepping down onto the soft ground. He trudges about, watching the dog running back and forth along the line of the forest, leaping into a deep ditch before reappearing, only to vanish into a pile of leaves where faded ocher-colored ones compete for attention with others that seem to be powdered with matte bronze or dull gold.

Apart from the dog, Petersson is completely alone out in the field, yet he still feels quite at ease here, in a place where everything can die yet also be born, a breaking point in people's lives, a sequence of possibilities.

He runs his hand through his bleached hair, thinking how well it suits his sharp nose and hard blue eyes. The wrinkles in his brow. Business wrinkles. Well earned.

The forest over there.

Fir trees and pines, undergrowth. A lot of game this year. His tenant farmers are coming later today, they're going to try to get a young elk or a couple of deer. Something needs be killed.

The Fågelsjö family.

What wouldn't they give for the chance to hunt in these forests again?

He looks at his arms, at the bright yellow Prada raincoat, the raindrops drumming on his head and the yellow Gore-Tex fabric.

"Howie," Petersson calls. "Howie. Time to go now."

Hard. Tough. An ice-cold machine. A man prepared to step over dead bodies.

That was how people talked about him in the business circles he moved in up in Stockholm. A shadow to most people. A rumor. A subject of conversation, something that was often the cause of admiration in a world where it was deemed desirable to be so successful that you could lie low instead of maintaining a high profile, appearing on television talk shows to get more clients.

Jerry Petersson?

Brilliant, or so I've heard. A good lawyer. Didn't he get rich from that IT business, because he got out in time? Supposed to be a real cunt magnet.

But also:

Watch out for him.

Isn't he involved with Jochen Goldman? Don't they own some company together?

"Howie."

But the dog doesn't come, doesn't want to come. And Jerry knows he can leave it be, let the dog find its own way home to the castle through the forest in its own good time. It always comes home after a few hours. But for some reason he wants to call the dog back to him now, come to some sort of arrangement before they part.

"Howie!"

And the dog must have heard the urgency in his voice, because it comes racing over the whole damn field and is soon back with Petersson.

It leaps around his legs, and he crouches down beside it, feeling the damp soak through the fabric of his trousers, and he pats the dog's back hard in the way he knows it likes.

"So what do you to want to do, eh, boy? Run home on your own, or drive back with me? Your choice. Maybe run back on your own, you never know, I might drive off the road."

The dog licks his face before turning and running back across the field and hiding under a pile of leaves, before disappearing through the dark, open doors of the forest.

Petersson gets back into the Range Rover, turns the key in the ignition, listens to the sound of the engine, then lets the vehicle nose its way along the road again into the dense, fog-shrouded forest.

He hadn't locked the castle doors when he set off on his spontaneous morning drive around the estate after waking early and being unable to get back to sleep. Who was likely to come? Who would dare to come? A hint of excitement:

I bet they'd like to come.

Fredrik Fågelsjö. Old man Axel.

Katarina.

She's stayed away.

The daughter of the house.

My house now.

He moved in their orbit a long time ago.

A crow flies in front of the windscreen, flapping its wings; one wing looks injured somehow, maybe broken.

The castle is large. He could do with a woman to share it with. I'll find one soon enough, he thinks. He's always thought, in his increasingly large homes, that he could do with a woman to share it with. But it was merely a mental exercise that he enjoyed playing, and whenever he really needed a woman it was easy enough for someone like him: Go to a bar, or call one of the numbers, and love would arrive, home delivery. Or a randy housewife in the city for a conference. Whatever. Women to share the present moment, women without any connections either backward or forward in time, women as desire-fulfilling creatures. Nothing to be ashamed of. Just the way it is.

He'd heard a rumor that Skogså was for sale.

Sixty-five million kronor.

The Wrede estate agency in Stockholm were handling the sale. No adverts, just a rumor that a castle with a vast estate was for sale in the Linköping area, and perhaps he might be interested?

Skogså.

Interested?

Sixty-five million stung. But not much. And he got more than the castle for his money. One hundred eighty-five acres of prime forest, and almost as much arable land. And the abandoned parish house that he could always pull down and replace with something else.

And now, here, on this beautiful black autumn morning, when the fog and the relentless rain and the feeling of lightness and of being at home fill his body, he knows it was money well spent, because what is money for if not to create feelings?

He wanted to meet Fågelsjö when the deal was concluded in the office on Karlavägen. Didn't exactly want to smirk at him, but rather give him a measured look, force the old man to realize how wrong he had been, and let him know that a new age had dawned.

But Fågelsjö never showed up at the meeting in Stockholm.

In his place he sent a young solicitor from Linköping. A young brunette with plump cheeks and a pout. After the contract was signed he asked her to lunch at Prinsen. Then he fucked her upstairs in his office, pushing her against the window, pulling her skirt high up her stomach, tearing a hole in her black tights, and pumping away, bored, as he watched the buses and taxis and people moving in a seemingly predetermined stream down Kungsgatan, and he imagined he could hear the sound of the great lawnmowers in Kungsträdgården.

The castle is supposed to be haunted.

The unquiet spirit of a Count Erik, who is said to have beaten his son to death when the son turned out to be feebleminded. And the Russian soldiers who were supposed to have been walled up in the moat.

Petersson has never seen any ghosts, has just heard the creaking and sighing of the stone walls at night, feeling the chill that had been stored up in the old building over the centuries.

Ghosts.

Spirits.

The castle and outbuildings were run down, so he's had everything renovated. This past year he's felt like a foreman of a building site.

Several times he's seen a black car on the estate and assumed it was one of the Fågelsjö family getting a kick of nostalgia. Why not? he reasons. Mind you, he doesn't know for sure that it is one of the family, it could be pretty much anyone, there are certainly people who'd like to visit.

He was profiled in the *Correspondent* when it became known that Skogså had a new owner. He gave an interview, mouthed humble platitudes about fulfilling the dream of a lifetime. But what good had that done?

The journalist, a Daniel Högfeldt, went for the shady-business-dealings angle, and made out that he had forced the Fågelsjö family from their ancestral home of almost five hundred years.

Whining.

Stop whining. No birthright gives anyone a lifetime's right to anything.

To this day, the article annoys him, and he regrets giving in to his vanity, his desire to send a message to the area that he was back. To recreate something that never existed: That was what he imagined he was doing.

How much damage have the Fågelsjö family done to people round here, though? How many peasants and tenant farmers and wage slaves have had to endure their bailiff's whip? How many people have been trampled underfoot by the Fågelsjös' assumption that they're better than everyone else?

Petersson hasn't taken on any employees; instead he contracts people whenever anything needs doing, and he's careful to make sure he pays them well and treats them decently.

And the story of the moat around the castle. That it was built in the early nineteenth century, long after anyone in this country had any need of a moat. Then one of the counts got it into his head that he wanted a moat, and commandeered a load of Russian prisoners of war from von Platen's work on the Göta Canal and worked them until they dropped, a lot of them dying of exhaustion. It was said that they interred the bodies in the walls of the moat when they lined it with stone, that they shut those Russian souls in for all eternity for the sake of a meaningless moat.

But sometimes it feels a bit isolated at the castle. And for the first time in his life he has felt that he could do with a friend. The security of having another living creature around him, someone who would take his side no matter what happened, who would sound the alarm if there was any danger approaching. And a dog was useful for hunting.

Is that something up ahead on the road? Howie? Back so soon. Impossible. Completely impossible.

A stag?

A deer?

No.

The rain is pouring down now, but inside the oil-smelling warmth of the Range Rover the world seems very agreeable.

Then the castle appears out of the fog, its three stories of gray-plastered stone seeming to force their way out of the earth, the leaning walls straining toward the gray sky, as if they thought they should be in charge up there. And the brighter from the swaying green lanterns he has had installed along the moat. He loves the brightness they give.

Is that someone standing on the castle steps?

The tenant farmers he's going hunting with aren't due until later on, and they've never been on time yet.

He accelerates.

He feels with his hand beside him for the dog, but the warm fur isn't there.

Of course.

Petersson wants to get there quickly, wants to hear the gravel of the drive crunch under the Range Rover's tires. Yes, there is someone on the steps.

The outline of a figure. Hazy through the fog. Unless it's an animal?

The castle ghosts?

The vengeful spirits of the Russian soldiers?

Count Erik paying him a visit with his cloak and scythe?

He's thirty feet away from the black shape now.

Who is it? A woman? You?

Can it really be that person again? Certainly persistent, if it is.

He stops the car.

Blows the horn.

The black figure on the steps moves silently toward him.

6

Gray.

The morning light is gray, but it still manages to cut right into Malin's eyes. The light is gentle, like a blunt knife found at the back of a kitchen drawer of a deceased and distant relative. She looks up, out through the living-room window. The clouds are clustered tight in different layers in front of the sun, and she can feel how her skin is swollen over swollen flesh, and she tries to look around but keeps having to close her eyes, to give her reluctant brain a rest and muffle its angry throbbing with darkness.

Her body is in a heap on the parquet floor, the radiator by her head warmer now than yesterday evening, and she can hear the water gurgling through the pipes.

An almost empty bottle of tequila beside her, the lid half screwed on, and she looks out at the flat.

Gray.

The whole of my world is gray, Malin thinks. More nuances of gray than my brain can comprehend, from the dark, leaden gray under the sofa to the almost dirty white of the walls.

And who's that looking in through the window, whose face is that peering through the fog? The contours of her guilty conscience.

Nausea. How the hell can I behave like this? A hand raised in anger.

I stink. I want to turn my face inside out so I don't have to look at myself in the mirror.

How the hell am I going to get up from here?

I want to call them, Janne and Tove, but what would I say?

That I love them?

That it's raining?

That I regret what I did?

"Zacharias! Zacharias!"

His wife Gunilla is calling from down in the kitchen with her sharp telephone-ring voice. What does she want now?

"Martin scored two goals last night," she calls.

Other women have a different voice.

Zacharias "Zeke" Martinsson, detective inspector with the Linköping Police, twists his body out of bed. Gets up, feeling that the damp in the room has made his body unnaturally stiff. Not much light is creeping past the edges of the black blind, so he knows the weather outside must still be atrocious, a perfect day for staying indoors, fix a few things that need doing round the house.

Martin.

He got an NHL contract in the end. After his success in the World Championship in Moscow they were throwing money at his agent, and six months ago he moved out to Vancouver.

Rich.

And famous.

"If you want any money, Dad, for a holiday or a new summer-house, or to come out and visit, just say. Linus is growing fast, you must want to see him."

Twelve thousand kronor.

That's how much the cheapest flights to Vancouver cost.

Each.

A hefty chunk of a detective's salary.

He's eight months old now, the boy, my grandchild. I want to see him. But getting Martin to pay for the tickets?

Never.

All those millions that the lad's earning just for entertaining a few exhausted uneducated souls. Sometimes it disgusts Zeke, just as ice hockey's affected macho bullshit always has, the way the players and coaches and fans all think they're so tough. But what do they know about real roughness, real danger, and the demands that makes of you? Have any of those prima donnas in their oversized padded shorts got what it takes if things really kick off? Sundin? Forsberg? Not a chance.

"Zeke, they're showing the goals on 4. Hurry up."

Gunilla has done the whole ice-hockey thing. All the ferrying around. Cheering him on, while he couldn't get past his dislike of the game and would rather sing with the Da Capo choir instead.

He pulls on his underwear, feeling them stretch over his thighs and balls. Standing in the darkness of the room he rubs his hand over his shaved head. The two days of stubble is sharp against his hand, but not enough for him to need to shave.

Goal.

My son.

And then Zeke smiles against his will; the lad's coping with those prima donnas pretty well. But rush downstairs?

Never.

She's not sleeping by my side. This bed is an ocean of lost opportunities.

Police Chief Karim Akbar would like to be able to put his arm round his wife, but she isn't there, he's been rejected in favor of someone else. But maybe it's better this way. For the past few years he hasn't dared approach her, scared of getting burned by her refusal.

She was always tired.

Tired after working double shifts as a social worker, when half her colleagues had emigrated to Norway to work for twice as much money for two-thirds of their old hours.

There's something I'm not seeing, Karim had often thought. But what? He had turned the feeling into an abstract problem instead of grabbing it and trying to work out what it meant or what the consequences might be. He had reflected upon how two people can spend their whole lives living side by side without ever understanding each other, and that the feeling of emptiness that both destroys you and surrounds you in that sort of relationship must be similar to what his father felt when he arrived in Sweden as an engineer, but failed to find either a job or a place in society. His father had ended up hanging from a noose made with a nylon tie in a flat in Nacksta up in Sundsvall.

Sometimes Karim has been struck by the idea that she wanted to get out. That she wanted a divorce. But if that was the case, then why didn't she say so? He was a sufficiently enlightened man not to claim any right of ownership.

But he hadn't managed to pursue the thought through to its conclusion, hadn't summoned up the energy to ask her.

And then she left. Took their nine-year-old son and moved in with another bastard social worker in Malmö.

She dared. But he knows she was scared, maybe still is.

But there's no need.

I'd never be like my compatriots, the brother and father we caught a month or so ago. They make me sick.

Divorce.

A better word for loneliness and confusion. He's tried to take refuge in work, in his new book, looking at issues of integration from an entirely new perspective, but it's slow going. Instead he has tried to come up with activities to keep their son amused when he visits.

An every-third-weekend dad. She wanted sole custody, and he gave in. It wouldn't have suited his work schedule to be a single parent every other week. And it was geographically impossible.

Bajran is with her and the other man this weekend.

In September they spent his birthday in Stockholm, and his son went with him to Götrich where he got some new suits, and he even let Bajran choose a couple of ties.

The suits are made of fine, soft wool. Cashmere. An extravagance that an upstart police chief like him can indulge himself with. That and a Mercedes.

He pulls the covers tighter around him, hearing the rain clatter on the windowsill and thinking how much he wants to move to a flat in the city, closer to everything. Lambohov is too reminiscent of Nacksta and Sundsvall.

But of course things could be worse. And Karim sees Börje Svärd's face before him, the detective's bold twisted mustache. He's on sick leave at the moment: Anna, his wife, has MS and needs round-the-clock care, help with her breathing; the illness has hit the nerves controlling the muscles around her lungs.

"She might have six months," Börje said when he applied for leave so he could be her carer.

"Take all the time you need to look after your wife," Karim replied. "There'll always be a job for you here."

And Malin Fors. Something's going to crack there, Karim thinks. But can I do anything about it? She drinks too much, but, God knows, we need her in the department.

Sven Sjöman, superintendent and head of the investigative unit of Linköping Police's Violent Crime Division, likes to think that he's coaxing the innermost secrets out of wood: its beauty, and the functional, attractive shape that lives within it.

It's an absurdly romantic notion, of course, but if having woodwork as a hobby isn't romantic, it can still be full of love.

The lathe rumbles. The sawdust sprays up onto his blue T-shirt with the logo of the Berg Lumberyard.

Sven's workshop, in a soundproof room in the basement of his house in Valla, smells of fresh wood-shavings, of varnish and polish, of sweat.

The hour he spends down here each morning is the best but also the loneliest hour of the day.

He's never liked loneliness.

Prefers the company of other people.

His wife's, for instance. Even if they don't say more than they need to each other after all these years.

His colleagues.

Karim.

And Malin. How are you doing, Malin? She hasn't had a good year, Sven thinks as he takes the rough bowl off the lathe. Then he switches off the machine and enjoys the silence that quickly fills the room.

It probably wasn't a good idea for you to move back in with Janne again. Not a good idea at all, but I could never tell you that. You have to take care of your own life, Fors. I can sometimes show you the way at work, but that's happening less and less; there's no longer much need for it.

But in life.

You reek of drink more and more. You look gray, exhausted, sad. Oh well.

As long as it doesn't get any worse. Janne, your husband, or rather the ex-husband that you're back together with, called me, wanted me to do something. He told me about your drinking, and it's certainly pretty obvious. At least sometimes. And I made him a promise. But to do what? Talk to you? You'd be furious. Suspend you? There's no justification for that. Send you to an expert? You're so stubborn, you'd refuse to go.

Getting a bit drunk is part of being a detective.

What with all the crap we see, it helps ease the pressure.

He tightens his belt. Four holes in, now, twenty-six pounds down. Better blood results. But far too many dull evening meals.

"Put your overalls on. Now. I don't want to have to tell you again."

Detective Inspector Johan Jakobsson is standing in the hall of his terraced house in Linghem. His five-year-old is in a world of her own, singing, and his words don't come close to penetrating her bubble.

Why the hell did they agree to go to the in-laws this weekend, now that he finally has a Friday off? The last thing they need is another panicky morning with a load of unnecessary aggressive words firing through the air like stray bullets.

"Can you sort Hugo out? I'll take Emma."

His wife nods and bends down for the boy's blue jacket.

"I don't want to have to tell you again."

"Do you have to get so cross?" his wife asks.

And so it starts.

"It wasn't my idea to set off for Nässjö at this ungodly hour."

"It's Dad's birthday."

"Yes, sixty-three. It's not like he can't manage without us."

His wife's mouth tightens. She's not going to dignify that with a reply, Johan thinks as he reaches for their daughter, grabbing her thin but strong arm and pulling her to him.

"Get your jacket on."

"But she won't need it in the car."

He lets go of his daughter's arm.

Shuts his eyes.

Wishes he was on call this weekend. Then he could have invented some incident, or something might really have happened.

The children. His eyes are closed, but he can still hear their voices, and it's like they become more distinct to him now, and they sound happy, full of confidence about life in spite of their sullenness, and he thinks that the thousands of hugs and kisses, the hundreds of thousands of words of praise, a million smiles and reassurances that they're loved more than anything actually work. It is possible to create happy individuals, it's simple and definitely worth the effort.

"Johan," his wife says. "Relax. We don't have to rush if you don't want to."

On the grubby, whitewashed wall in front of him there are four coat hooks. One of the middle ones is loose, dangerously close to falling off.

Waldemar Ekenberg has opened the terrace door and is taking deep drags on his cigarette. The terrace is out of the wind, otherwise he wouldn't be standing here. He'd be crouched under the extractor fan over the cooker.

He looks up at the sky. At the dense gray-white roof of the world. His morning cigarette.

There's nothing better. Even if his wife will complain that he smells of smoke when he goes back to bed.

Waldemar didn't hesitate when a temporary position in Linköping came up. He had enjoyed his earlier assignment there in connection with a gruesome investigation into the murders of teenage girls.

They didn't want him, he knew that, but they couldn't ignore his experience when all the other applicants were fresh out of Police Academy.

Fors. Sjöman. Jakobsson. Akbar. Martinsson.

Not a bad collection of cops really. A decent clear-up rate. Not too burned out.

Fors.

Completely manic, apparently much worse after what happened to her daughter, and since she got back together with that fireman.

But she's a fucking good detective. And very easy to tease.

And that can be a lot of fun.

And she's hitting the bottle. A lot of his colleagues over the years have succumbed to drink. And he's never been able to do a thing about it. Once they've fallen to the bottom of the bottle there's no way back.

Jakobsson.

Worn out by his kids.

He and his wife back in bed never had any, and that's probably just as well.

Now there's just us to worry about. They were in Thailand last winter, just the two of them, and they could take it as easy as they liked, unlike all the families with little kids in the hotel.

The love of a child. Love for a child.

You can't miss what you've never had, Waldemar thinks, taking the last drag on the cigarette.

Can you?

*   *   *

Malin is standing at the counter in the 7-Eleven on Ågatan.

Her hair is wet with rain and her underwear is cutting into her buttocks; it feels as disgusting as the bloody weather outside. She found a pair of old stone-washed jeans and a pink top at the back of the wardrobe in the flat. They must be ten years old, but they'll have to do. H&M isn't open yet, and she'll have to pick up her things from Malmslätt when she has time. That's what she's going to do: pick up her things, and Tove, and reconstruct life the way it was before they moved back in together, before she put Tove's life in danger.

A toothbrush, deodorant, toothpaste, and coffee are on the counter in front of her; the fat cashier looks sleepy as he rings up her purchases.

"Playing away?" he asks.

Playing away. Did the ice-hockey team have an away match last night?

Then she realizes what he means and feels like punching him in his fat face, but just shakes her head.

"Okay, no away match. Just a late night, I guess. When I feel the way you look, I don't bother getting out of bed."

"Just cut the crap and take the money."

The cashier throws out his hands.

"Just trying to have a laugh. That normally helps. Sorry."

Malin grabs her change and walks the hundred yards back to the flat through the rain.

Soon she's in the shower.

Water colder than the rain envelops her skin.

Driving out the evil.

Helping it freeze.

Don't think about what happened yesterday, she tells herself, just drink the coffee in the mug on the soap rack and pretend the headache pills you found in the medicine cabinet are having some sort of effect.

Her skull is thudding.

Tove can move in later this week. Maybe even tonight.

I'm working today. But nothing's going to happen that can take my mind off this damn headache, is it?

7

Göte Lindman, just turned fifty-two, runs a hand over his wet, shaved head. He's only been inside Skogså Castle once before.

At the age of eight he stood with his father in Axel Fågelsjö's study and listened as Fågelsjö dictated the terms of that summer's work, and the future, in return for them being allowed to rent an old soldier's cottage over in the far southwest corner of the estate.

"When I call, you come."

Lindman imagines he can hear the count's voice, the harshness and violence concealed in it, as he and Ingmar Johansson, a few years older than him, walk along the corridor on the first floor, looking at the bare, gray stone walls and the peculiar pictures that adorn them every fifteen feet or so.

"He's got a dog," Lindman says. "But it can't be here, or we'd have heard it by now."

"A yappy beagle," Ingmar Johansson mutters.

It's more than forty years since Lindman was here with his father.

His own dealings with the Fågelsjös were managed through the solicitor's office in the city, and thankfully he only leased land from them these days, having bought himself a farmhouse outside Bankekind.

He had been informed by a solicitor when the sale of Skogså was already a fact. His tenancy would continue as before.

They walk past room after room.

Peering in, padding about on wooden floors, stone floors, yard after yard of unused space. They had arrived in Lindman's black Saab, now parked beside Petersson's Range Rover out in the courtyard. The door to the castle was unlocked, and the alarm was flashing green. They hesitated before coming in, not wanting to upset the castle's new owner.

Petersson had appeared in Lindman's yard one day, standing next to his Range Rover with a broad smile, wearing that stupid yellow coat. The wind was blowing his mane of bleached hair and Lindman had realized that the visit could only mean trouble.

"You know who I am?" Petersson had asked, and Lindman had nodded in reply.

"Any chance of coffee?"

Another nod.

And then they had sat at the kitchen table eating Svetlana's cakes and drinking freshly made coffee, and Petersson had explained that things would continue exactly as before, but that he had one demand: When he wanted to go hunting, they would come, no matter how bad the weather was, no matter what else was going on.

"When I call, you come. Got it?"

Ingmar Johansson peers into the castle kitchen.

Copper saucepans hanging in gleaming rows from the ceiling. Even in the dim morning light they're sparkling. The entire kitchen is new, white marble on the walls and floor, shiny steel appliances, a seven-foot-long stove with ten gas rings.

But no sign of life.

No Jerry Petersson. The owner of the land that he rents, just like Lindman, is nowhere to be seen.

The call had come on Thursday evening.

"I need you here tomorrow at eight o'clock. We're going for deer. There are too many of them."

Like hell there were too many deer at Skogså. More like too few, but Petersson's voice brooked no argument. And he had been clear about the terms of the arrangement.

"It was definitely eight o'clock?" Johansson said.

"On the dot," Lindman replied.

They had spoken on the phone just after their visits from Petersson. They had agreed that it could have been much worse, he might have wanted to introduce large-scale farming to the castle estate. Petersson hadn't answered when Johansson asked him straight out about his plans for the farm, and just said he was there to talk about hunting.

"Make sure you arrive on time."

Petersson had been firm on the phone.

And here they both were.

But there was no sign of Jerry Petersson.

The steps are steep and dangerously slippery for wet boots. So they proceed carefully to the second floor, calling Petersson's name, but their voices just rebound off the bare stone. Above them, in the sixty-foot-high space above the stairs, hangs a crystal chandelier that must be several centuries old, adorned with over a hundred half-burned candles arranged in several ornate circles. On one wall hangs a mostly blue painting of a man squeezing sun cream onto a woman's back.

Panting, they reach the second floor.

"He ought to get a lift put in," Johansson says.

"Expensive," Lindman replies.

"He can afford it."

"Shouldn't we start in the cellar?"

"Sod that. He's probably got a torture chamber down there. You know, iron maidens and a single chair in the middle of the room."

"Bloody hell. I had no idea you had that sort of imagination," Lindman says.

They move through the rooms.

"So he lives on this floor," Johansson says.

"Bloody weird pictures," Lindman whispers as they emerge into a room containing several large photographs of a Christ-like figure immersed in a yellow liquid.

"Do you think that's piss?" Johansson asks.

"How the hell would I know?"

A large sculpture of a pink and purple plastic bear with saber teeth decorated with jewels and eyes that look like diamonds shines at them from one corner.

A painting of a Cambodian prisoner seems to want to chase them from the room.

The furniture looks like it was designed for a spaceship: straight lines, black mixed with white, shapes that Lindman recognizes from the interior design magazines he usually looks at when he's waiting to have his hair cut.

"Bloody hell, the things people choose to spend their hard-earned money on," Johansson says.

"Petersson? Petersson! We're here!"

"Ready for the hunt. Time to shoot some deer!"

They stop, grinning at each other, then there's a cold silence.

"Where do you reckon he could be?" Lindman asks, unbuttoning his green overcoat and wiping the sweat from his brow.

"No idea. Maybe out on the estate? Doesn't look like he's in the castle. He'd have heard us by now."

"But his car's down there. And the doors were unlocked."

"Showy damn car, that."

"Maybe, but you'd still like one."

They're both looking at a free-standing clothes rack holding ironed cotton shirts in all manner of colors.

"What do you make of him?" Johansson asks.

"Petersson?"

"No, God. Of course I mean Petersson."

Johansson looks at Lindman. At the bitter wrinkles around his eyes and mouth, at the deep furrows on his brow.

Johansson knows that Lindman lived alone on his farm for many years after his wife left him fifteen years ago. She'd been to a conference in Stockholm and came home crazy, saying she couldn't bear living on the farm anymore.

Someone must have fucked the sense out of her up in Stockholm.

But now he'd found a new one, a mail-order Russian.

"What do I think of him?" Lindman says, stretching the words. "Well, he doesn't seem to want to mess with our arrangements. Then there's this bullshit about us coming running whenever he calls. What can I say?"

Johansson nods.

"Did you know him before?" Lindman goes on.

Johansson shakes his head.

"They say he grew up in Berga. But I never read anything about his work. I don't really care about crap like that."

Johansson sees how the giant bear's eyes sparkle. Could they actually be real diamonds?

"He was pretty quick to get hold of this damn castle."

"Must have been a bitter blow for the count."

"Yeah, but it serves him right."

They stop in another of the rooms.

Looking at each other.

"Do you hear what I hear?" Johansson asks.

Lindman nods.

Outside they can hear a dog barking furiously.

Anxiously.

"He's upset about something," Lindman says. "No doubt about that."

They stand still for a moment before heading for one of the windows.

A low cloud is dissolving into fog as it drifts slowly past the window, leaving small drops of moisture on the glass.

They stand beside each other, waiting for the cloud or the fog to move. Listening to the dog, its anxious bark.

Then they look out over the estate.

The pine forest, the fir trees, the fields. Banks of fog are blocking their view down to the moat.

"Beautiful," Johansson says. "Can you see the dog?"

"No."

"Well, you can see why the count loved this land."

"I bet he's not happy in the city."

Johansson grins and looks away from the view. Down on the raked gravel in the courtyard stand the Range Rover and the car they arrived in.

Then the fog drifts away from the moat. And there's the dog, it's dark shape jerking each time it lifts its head to the sky and barks.

"That's a warning bark," Lindman says. "A deer that's fallen in the water?"

The water in the moat is black, still. The green lamps along its edge are glowing faintly.

But there's something that's not right. There's something in the water that shouldn't be there. Not a deer, Lindman thinks.

The dog looks down, then barks desperately again.

There's something yellow floating in the blackness, a vague, almost pulsating yellow circle in his gradually deteriorating vision.

"Johansson, what's that floating down there in the moat? That light-colored thing? That the dog's barking at."

Johansson looks down at the water.

Like a black snake held captive by ancient stone banks. Is that old story about the Russian soldiers true? he wonders.

Some fifty yards away, on the surface of the moat, something pale, yellow, is moving slowly to and fro, a dark outline in the water, the shape—he recognizes it instinctively, and wants to look away.

A head.

A body concealed yet still visible in the water.

Blond hair.

A face turned to one side.

A mouth.

He imagines he can see luminous fish, tiny sprats, swimming into the open mouth, a mouth that must long since have stopped gasping for air.

"Fucking hell."

"Oh shit."

"Fucking hell," Johansson repeats, unclear about what to feel or do next, only knowing that he wants the dog to stop barking. That dog will be barking in his dreams until the end of time.

8

There's something that's no longer moving.

Something that's stopped forever. Instead whatever it is that's surrounding me is moving. I don't have to breathe to live here, just like it was long ago, where everything began and I floated and tumbled inside you, Mum, and everything was warm and dark and happy apart from the loud noises and rough jolts that shook my senses, the little senses I had then.

No warmth here.

But no cold either.

I can hear the dog. Howie. It must be you, I recognize your bark, even if it sounds like you're so far away.

You sound anxious, almost scared, but what would a dog like you know about fear?

Mum, you taught me all about the fear to be found in pain. Am I closer to you now? It feels like it.

The water ought to be so cold, as cold as the heavy hail that's been firing from the skies all autumn.

I try to turn around so my face is looking up, but my body no longer exists, and I try to remember what brought me here, but all I can remember is you, Mum, how I rocked in time with you, just like in the water of this moat.

How long am I going to be here?

There's a ruthlessness here, and I see myself reflected in that ruthlessness, it's my face, my sharp, clean features, the nostrils whose flaring can scare people so, no matter who they are.

Pride.

Am I proud?

Is that time past now?

Now that everything's still.

I can float here for a thousand years, in this cold water, and be master of this land, and that's just fine.

The deer need to be culled.

The hares need to be eradicated.

People need to leave their warm, secure water.

New days need to be born.

And I shall be part of them all.

Own them all.

I shall lie here and see myself, the boy that I was.

And I shall do so even if I'm scared. I can admit it now; I'm afraid of that boy's eyes, the way the light opens the world up to him, in jerks, like the desperate bark of an abandoned dog.

9

The world comes into being through the eyes, because if you close them there are no images, and the boy is four years old when he learns to recognize his own eyes, pebble-sized deep-sea-blue objects set at perfect distance from each other in an equally perfectly shaped skull. Jerry realizes what he can do with those eyes: He can make them flash so that miracles happen, and, best of all, he can get the nursery-school teachers to give him what he wants.

His reality is still directly experienced. What does he know about the fact that on this very day, tons of Agent Orange and napalm are being dropped onto tropical forests where people hide in holes deep underground, waiting for the burning jelly to dig through the ground and destroy them?

For him, warm is simply warm, cold is cold, and the black-painted copper pipe attached to an endless, rough, red, wooden surface is so hot that it burns his fingers, albeit not in a dangerous way, but in a way that's nice and makes him feel both safe and scared: scared because the warmth in him awakens a feeling that everything can end.

A lot happens in this life.

Cars drive. Trains travel. Boats on the Stångån River blow their whistles.

He lies on the grass in the garden of his grandmother's cottage, feeling the dense smell of chlorophyll possess him, seeing how the grass colors his knees and body green. In the evenings, when the midges attack, Daddy puts a bright yellow plastic bathtub on the grass, and the water is warm on his skin and the air around him is cold, and then he runs alongside the howling grass-scented monster that gives off a sharp smell, and Daddy sweats as he pushes it across the grass. The blades sniff out the boy's feet, spraying grass cuttings from its broad maw; this isn't a game, and Daddy sees the look in his eyes but doesn't let that put him off. Daddy turns the monster, chasing the boy through the garden, crying: "Now I'm going to cut your feet off, now I'm going to cut your feet off," and the boy runs down to the edge of the forest, feels like running until the lawnmower can no longer be heard.

But inside, in the kitchen with Mummy and Grandma, his eyes work and he realizes it's best to eat buns when they're fresh, before the mold creeping up from the floor has a chance to make them taste spoiled.

Daddy comes home to the cottage after work.

With bags that clink. And then Mummy wants to sit still. She feels better after Daddy comes with the bags, Grandma too, and they are happy, but not properly happy.

The sun disappears and the heat in the black-painted copper is exchanged for a metallic smell in the chilly stairwell and multicolored glass marbles rolling in the sand of a sandpit, and then down into a hole, and someone's in the way, another boy.

Go away. You're not supposed to be there. And Jerry's hand flies up, strikes where he means it to, across the nose, and then the blood comes and the boy screams, the boy he's hit screams out loud and he himself screams, "Plaster!" not, "He hit me first." He regards himself as too good for a lie like that.

In the world of direct experience there is a dead cat in a rubbish bin by the swings in the park. He once gave that cat some cream.

There are feelings floating in the two rooms of the flat, there are questions directed at him. "Do you know that we live in Berga?" "That Daddy works for Saab, putting together planes that can fly through the air faster than words?" And he recognizes the laughter, it lacks warmth, and they sit on the orange-and-brown patterned sofa, the one they make into his bed each night, and they pour out drinks from the bottles they always have in a bag. Then they talk louder, the air turns sweet and unpleasant, and they look at black-and-white people on a screen, and Mummy can get up in a way that she can't otherwise, she can fly up from the sofa and they dance, she only does that when they've been drinking, and he likes watching Mummy dance. But then Daddy starts chasing him, he's the lawnmower trying to catch him and hit him on his arms and legs, and the boy is four years old and creeps out of an unlocked front door into the world outside that is full of life waiting to be conquered: a cat to be buried, a swing to be swung up to the sky, car and trains to be driven, people shouldn't lie in vomit and pain, shouldn't chase him anywhere.

So he screams.

He breaks things.

He draws on the walls with crayons.

He gets hold of matches and sets fire to the world, watches his wooden boat burn in the sand and feelings that he doesn't know the name of, feelings that might not even have any names, drift through the flames, and the smoldering hull rests on a desolate patch of sand enclosed by a wooden frame.

Daddy's despair. How the boy's little body flies into the radiator beneath the living-room window when drunk Daddy stumbles over him. Mummy's tired blinking eyes.

Pain which as yet is always new.

Nothing is fixed.

Nothing has set into its final form.

Perhaps that is why nothing is possible.

The boy lies in his bed at night. He is awake. In the August evening there is a hint of the first chill of autumn.

He already knows there is another world, but he doesn't think about it, he is busy living in the world of directly experienced reality.

There is no reflection as he daydreams in the darkness about killing his father. Killing him with rays that shoot from his blue-pebble eyes. He will make the lawnmower shut up.

Its blades will no longer snap at his heels.

10

The eye, as black as the water, seems to wink at Malin Fors as the head bobs in the gentle, scarcely perceptible waves.

The yellow raincoat is almost luminous in the water.

The throbbing in her own skull.

The dog barking over in the car by the edge of the forest. The sound like distant cannon fire, as if it were inside a pressure cooker.

The dog was standing by the edge of the moat when they arrived. Barking like crazy, but it didn't object when it was led to the car, just carried on barking.

Bang, bang.

What can that eye in the water see now? What was the last thing that eye saw?

The bobbing motion of the head, the little snake-like fish around it, the throbbing in Malin's own head: two things which will give this day its very own insane structure and logic.

Skogså Castle. She's driven past the end of the drive many times, but she's never seen the castle before, never had any reason to drive into the forest and out across the fields. But she's seen pictures of it in a book about Swedish castles and manor houses in her parents' apartment by the old Infection Park. A fuck-off great stone box, jam-packed with snobbery, even if there's something restrained about the building itself. The lines are straight, practically no ornamentation;

humility in the face of the dramas that have unfolded here over the years.

Malin is crouching at the side of the moat. Large, smooth rocks that must have come straight from the quarry slope steeply down into the water, the green light from the lanterns reflected in its surface. The fish down there, hundreds of them, not much bigger than sprats, blacker than the water as they move around the body.

Malin has pulled the zip of her Gore-Tex jacket right up, the hood tight around her head, three layers underneath, and still she's freezing, feeling the heavy raindrops hammering the fabric. Zeke had the coat in the car, making a comment about her ancient sweater when he picked her up, asked if she'd bought it at the Salvation Army. When he saw her jeans he grinned: "Eastern European fashion's the next big thing, is it?"

But he didn't remark upon the fact that he was picking her up from the flat, even if he must have wondered what she was doing there.

The cold helps her head to clear.

Helps her gaze focus, so she can concentrate on the corpse floating on the surface, on the blond hair, on the eye staring up at them.

Zeke by her side.

Wide awake. Curious.

"How the hell are we going to get him out?"

"We'll have to get divers from the fire brigade."

The report of the body had reached the police station at quarter past eight; Malin had heard the phone ringing when she got out of the shower, and it had an unmistakable note of urgency, as if the phone had its own consciousness and could change the way it sounded according to the circumstances.

Zeke's voice: "Some farmers have called in to say that they've found a man murdered out at Skogså Castle."

She had thrown on her clothes, and they had set off south toward Skogså. He had commented on her breath and told her she looked terrible, wondered if she'd been drinking, but she just said she'd had a couple of glasses of tequila yesterday evening, joking that he must have a very sensitive nose.

They had been the first unit on the scene, and as they arrived and parked at the edge of the forest the large castle doors had opened and out came the two men that she now knows are the tenant farmers Ingmar Johansson and Göte Lindman.

They had waited where they had been told while she and Zeke looked at the scene and led the dog away, carefully, without contaminating the crime scene. The pair had explained that they were supposed to be hunting deer with Jerry Petersson, but that he hadn't met them at the agreed time, and that they had found him, or at least what they assumed to be his body, down in the moat.

"I mean, you can't really see for sure," Johansson had said.

"But it's him," Lindman had added. "He had a coat just like that."

The corpse in the water.

Jerry Petersson.

Hotshot lawyer. Businessman. The slightly dodgy commercial lawyer who had made a fortune in Stockholm and moved back home when he got the chance to buy Skogså Castle. Malin had read the profile in the *Correspondent*.

If it really is him.

The throbbing in her head. The dog's barking. Two patrol cars had just arrived at the edge of the forest. No holding back with a suspected murder.

Jerry Petersson.

But who else could it be? Malin closes her eyes, feeling her headache, listening to the air, and she imagines she can hear the rain falling on an invisible body, someone whispering words she can't understand, words that want to make the world comprehensible, easy to understand and absorb, but they vanish before she has time to work out what they mean.

The divers arrived thirty minutes later, and now their red emergency vehicle is parked alongside Zeke's car, Forensics expert Karin Johannison's blue Mercedes, and Sven Sjöman's red Volvo. The cars are parked in a clearing on the other side of the moat, a long way from

Petersson's Range Rover and the tenant farmers' Saab. The journalists have started to appear, and they are standing in a huddle with cameras of all sizes, flashing as though they were some huge discharging storm cloud. They're shouting at the police, but are ignored.

They can smell something tasty, the reporters. Front pages. A paper-selling story that will appeal to people's desire to read about death and violence from a safe distance.

Just like some shoddy thriller, Malin thinks. Life imitating art.

None of the police or fire brigade have driven up in front of the castle.

No one wants to spoil any tire tracks, footprints, or signs of a struggle on the gravel, or whatever else Karin Johannison can find. Malin can see Karin moving round the Range Rover, taking pictures, shaking her head, wiping the rain from her forehead. Even in a yellow raincoat that woman still manages to look glamorous.

She nodded to Zeke when she arrived, and he pulled his dark-blue raincoat tighter round him.

The nod back took far too long, Malin thinks, knowing that it hides something she'd rather not know about, a truth made visible in the way that only a real hangover can give a new slant on things.

With listlessness comes clarity.

But what do I know about what they get up to? Maybe I'm just imagining it.

The firemen, the divers aren't anyone she recognizes.

Thank God. But they must know who she is, they must know all about her and their colleague Janne.

Don't think about yesterday.

Just thank God for this case. Think about the victim in the moat instead, whoever he is, however he got there. Malin watches as the divers, in their black frogmen's outfits and yellow visors, lower themselves down from the bridge over the moat on thick ropes, their bodies slowly penetrating the surface of the black water.

Karin beside her and Zeke now.

The rain is horizontal, hitting them straight in the eyes, and over at the edge of the forest, two hundred yards away, on the far side of a meadow, there are low banks of fog.

"Careful!" Karin shouts as the divers approach the body. "As gently as you can." And they fasten a sling around the corpse, give the thumbs up to a third fireman who is standing on the bridge with a winch, and then there is a whirring sound, and the body in the water starts to rise, held carefully by the divers treading water.

"What a shit morning," Zeke says.

Sven Sjöman, wearing a green raincoat, has joined them.

"So, what do we think?"

"Well, he didn't jump in of his own volition," Malin says. "Or fall in. Grown men don't often fall into water, unless they're seriously drunk or have a heart attack or something like that."

"If it is Petersson, he's somewhere around forty-five. Not many heart attacks at that age."

"No. He probably had some help."

"That's seems most likely. We'll know for sure when Karin's got the body up."

Malin nods.

"If it is Petersson, and if he has been murdered, it's every journalist's wet dream."

"Careful!" Karin calls as the rotating body is lifted clear of the water and is left hanging, feet down, the water dripping from its yellow raincoat, brown trousers, and black leather boots.

The dripping water is colored red. The yellow raincoat has been perforated by many holes, and Malin can see a number of deep injuries to the body, and a mixture of blood and water is streaming from dozens of what must be stab wounds. The blood mixes with the rain. It's raining blood, Malin thinks. So you didn't exactly fall into the moat drunk, did you?

Little silver fish are falling from the victim's mouth, wriggling like abandoned babies on their way down to the safety of the water.

Snake fish, Malin thinks.

A black eye staring right out into the rain and the thin fog that has drifted down into the moat. The corpse's other eye is closed.

You look surprised, Malin thinks. But are you really?

*   *   *

Am I surprised?

Hardly.

The water is no longer embracing me.

I am leaving your memory, Mum, and instead I'm hanging here staring down at the water, and off toward the castle, at these strangers.

I can hear and see Howie, he's barking even more fiercely now. Can he see the holes in my body? I know there are a lot of them, but I can't feel any pain, just the wind blowing through me.

Who are they, these people?

What do they want with me?

Are they the Russian soldiers from the old stories?

I'm moving slowly upward, toward a whirring noise, and I'm spinning round and round, but it's not making me dizzy, and now I'm heading toward the bridge, held by a pair of firm arms, and gradually I sink lower, my stiffening, bloody body.

A slapping sound as I touch the ground again.

I am lying on my back.

Black plastic under me. How can I know that I'm lying on my back, when I can't see or feel anything?

But I suppose that's what it's like now.

All those people standing by the edge of the moat looking at me. Who are they?

I've got my suspicions, but I don't want to believe it's true, that this has finally happened. I refuse to accept it. But there's probably no point trying to resist. And if it has happened, there are plenty of riddles to solve.

And the buzz of the lawnmower isn't here.

A woman's face in my field of vision. She's beautiful.

Then another woman.

She could have been beautiful, but right now it looks like she could do with six months' sleep; her eyes seem completely devoid of any joie de vivre.

And the way they're talking, I don't actually want to hear what they're saying, not yet.

*   *   *

"It's Petersson," Karin says as she and Malin crouch over the body lying on the bridge spanning the moat. "I recognize him from pictures in the *Correspondent* and Kalle's business magazines."

"We can ask one of the tenant farmers to identify him," Malin says. "But I recognize him too, so there's hardly any point."

Johansson and Lindman are waiting inside a patrol car. They're planning to interview them properly once they're done out here.

"Apart from the wounds he's got a large bruise on the back of his neck," Karin says. "In all likelihood, the injuries to his torso are knife wounds. Everything suggests the sort of extreme violence that you almost only see when someone loses control. You can take it for granted that he didn't inflict these wounds on himself. But I can't say much more than that out here, we need to get him back to the city to see if I can get anything else from the body. It's impossible to examine the ground out here. The rain has swept away any evidence. I might be able to find some traces of blood in the gravel, but it's far from certain."

The ambulance arrived a short while ago.

Driven by Stenlund, one of Janne's former colleagues. He waved a cheery hello and asked how Janne was, and Malin replied that he was fine.

She looks at the corpse.

The open, almost magically blue eye looks like it's trying to escape its socket, and she feels sick, wants to get up, but looks up, at Zeke instead.

"What do you think?"

"Someone stabbed him in a fit of rage, whacked him on the neck, and dumped him in the water. Or the other way round."

"Okay, from now on this is officially a murder investigation," Sven says.

Rage, Malin thinks. My hand raised against Janne, bloody hell, I was so angry, imagine if I'd had a knife in my hand, but don't think, don't think, say instead:

"We need to examine the car and the surrounding area, the whole castle and the other buildings, just to see if we can find anything. Anything that suggests a struggle, or any other evidence, come to that. Anything that looks like the murder weapon. Chances are we're looking for a knife, and a rock or something similar."

"Okay," Sven says. "We have to marshal our forces, have an initial meeting before we get going. And we need to interview the two men who found him. Call in the rest of the team. Karin, can you give the okay for us to use one of the rooms inside the castle?"

Karin nods.

A car appears at the edge of the forest.

Another of the *Correspondent*'s blue-and-white staff cars.

Everything in due course, Malin thinks, feeling her stomach contract and wanting to throw up.

Malin walks over the gravel toward the doors of the castle, thinking about the hundreds of people who must have walked that path over the years. In fear or pride, tired, or with the elation that only owning considerable property can bring.

These people are like spirits anchored to the landscape, ghosts that don't want to leave the ground and fly.

She had just closed Jerry Petersson's open eye.

Wanted him to find peace, to stop having to stare at the world with a cold, dead gaze. It's quite enough for those of us who are alive to have to see the world like that, she thought. Then she looked at him. His blank face, the exposed wounds on his reasonably toned body. Who were you? she wondered. What sort of person do you have to be to end up where you did? How did all this come to be yours? Who got so angry with you that he or she stabbed you over and over again?

Then she walked round the castle, finding a small chapel at the rear, but the door was locked. She peered in, and in the middle of the octagonal space was a raised dais that she assumed must mark the Fågelsjö family vault. Dozens of icons stared down from the walls at her, the gold surrounding the figures of Christ defying the darkness of the season, saying: "Beauty is possible."

On the other side of the castle stood two big red Stiga tractors, equipped for cutting grass, silent, as if they'd been used for the last time, their blades removed.

Malin climbs the steps up to the castle, breathing in the morning air. In spite of the nausea, she feels excited.

And that makes her ashamed. Thinks, You can feel ashamed of any emotion. Was it shame that killed you, Jerry? What were you ashamed of? If you were ashamed of anything at all. Maybe you have to be free from shame to own and live in a castle?

In the castle's entrance hall a huge chandelier hangs oddly alone up above. As if it's waiting to spread light, Malin thinks. And that painting on the wall. A man, a woman. A bit of sun cream on her back. Love? Suppressed violence. Definitely.

That picture probably cost a fortune, Malin thinks.

Muttering.

Questions.

Don't imagine I'm going to answer.

Surely you have to do something to justify your salary?

A camera clicking.

My eternity is made eternal.

I can't move. Yet I could still see Malin Fors looking at my collection of icons just now.

Maybe I can have some fun with this. Play with justice, the way I have so many times in the past.

But how can I do that? My body's full of holes. This doesn't make sense. Doesn't make sense.

Help.

Help me.

Malin Fors.

I don't recognize this fear, it's completely new.

Only you can get me out of here, Malin. That's right, isn't it?

Only you can silence this fear that I've been so desperately trying to evade. The fear that you're trying to escape too. That's right, isn't it?

11

A large black-and-white photograph of silhouetted figures in a hammock hangs on the long wall of the library. It's like the people have stepped out of the picture and just left their shadows behind.

Malin has no idea who the artist is, but it looks expensive, it has the reek of fine art about it.

The room must be thirty feet high.

Karin Johannison and two recently arrived colleagues have been through it and found nothing of interest, and now it's their meeting room.

The walls are clad in dark wood paneling and empty custom-made bookcases that probably once housed a collection of leather-bound volumes. Which authors? Rousseau? Hardly. Shakespeare? Definitely. Sven Sjöman has settled into one of the bowed white upholstered armchairs in the middle of the room. He looks tired and thin, Malin thinks, but if Sven looks tired, what must I look like?

Zeke is sitting on a jagged modern chair on the other side of the rickety metal table. He's taken off his raincoat, but there are still drops of rain on his shaven head. Waldemar Ekenberg has arrived as well and is sitting on the sofa where Malin is evidently expected to join him. Waldemar smells of smoke, his eyes dark in the gloom of the library, and his long, skinny legs seem to almost disappear in the fabric of his loose gabardine trousers.

"Sit down, Malin," Sven says, gesturing to the place beside Waldemar. "But take off that wet coat first."

Take my coat off. Does he think I'm five years old or something?

"Of course I'm going to take my bloody coat off," Malin says, and Sven looks surprised at her anger and says:

"Malin, I didn't mean it like that."

She takes off her coat and sits down beside Waldemar, and the smell of smoke from his clothes lifts her nausea to new heights.

"Jerry Petersson," Sven says. "Murdered with extreme force. We can assume that for now, until we get a more precise cause of death in Karin's report. This is the first meeting, albeit rather hastily convened, of the preliminary investigation into the murder of Jerry Petersson."

The group of detectives sits in silence.

The concentration and seriousness, the focus that's always there at the start of each murder investigation, the feeling of urgency, that they have to get somewhere fast, because they know that for each day that passes their chances of solving the case diminish.

Sven goes on: "I got the station to do a quick check. Jerry Petersson was born in 1965, and as far as we've been able to see, he only has one close relative, his father, who lives in Åleryd Geriatric Hospital. A priest and a social worker are on their way to break the news to him. We'll have to wait before we interview him. He's an old man."

Göte Lindman and Ingmar Johansson had identified Petersson a short while before out on the bridge over the moat. They weren't in any doubt, and they'd both been strangely calm.

"Any ideas about where to start?" Sven says.

The tone of Sven's voice is interested, honestly questioning, but Malin knows that he's about to carry on talking again.

"Okay," Sven says. "What do we know about Jerry Petersson?"

"A lawyer, originally from these parts," Zeke says. "Studied in Lund, but worked in Stockholm. Made a fortune and moved back here when he got the chance to buy Skogså from the Fågelsjö family. The article in the *Correspondent* suggested that they'd fallen on hard times and had to sell. The reporter also hinted that Jerry Petersson had been involved in some dodgy dealings."

"I read that as well," Malin says, remembering that it was Daniel Högfeldt who had written the article. "He must have had some serious capital to be able to buy this place. And I can imagine how bitter the Fågelsjös must have been at having to sell the estate. It had been in the family for, what, almost five hundred years?"

Fågelsjö, she thinks. One of the most famous noble families in the area. The sort of family that everyone knows something about. Without ever really knowing why.

"We'll have to question the Fågelsjös about the circumstances surrounding the sale," Sven says. "Find out which members of the family were involved."

"The family consists of a father and two children. A son and a daughter, I think," Zeke says.

"How do you know that?" Malin asks.

"That was in the *Correspondent* as well. In one of those birthday profiles of the old man when he hit seventy."

"Children's names?"

"No idea."

"That should be fairly easy to find out," Waldemar says.

"You'll have to share out the interviews between you," Sven says. "Get them done as soon as possible. I'll arrange for checks at the houses around here, and we'll put out a message in the local media that we want to hear from anyone who may have seen anything unusual in the area over the past twenty-four hours."

"If he was really rich," Malin says, "then this could have been a robbery. Someone who heard about the new millionaire in the castle and decided to have a go."

"Maybe," Sven says. "The doors were open, after all. But from what we've seen so far, nothing seems to be missing in here. And Karin found his wallet in that yellow raincoat. The knife wounds to his torso suggest the sort of violent rage you don't often see in robberies."

"No, I don't get the feeling that this was a robbery or a break-in either. This is something else," Malin says.

"What about Petersson's business affairs?" Zeke says. "If he was a bit sleazy, as the rumors seem to suggest, then there could be hundreds of people wishing him harm. People who were pissed off with him."

"That's our most important line of inquiry right now," Sven says. "We need to try to find files and business records here in the house that might indicate how to proceed. What sort of dodgy dealings was he involved in? Any former colleagues? What about his business? Did he have anything going on at the moment that might have gone wrong? We need to do a serious background check on him. There must be loads of documented evidence. Waldemar, you and Jakobsson take that. Start by searching the castle for documentation once Forensics has cleared the rooms. We also need to find out if he had any sort of will. Who stands to inherit all this? That would be very interesting to know."

"Jakobsson's not on today," Waldemar says.

"Call him in," Sven says. "And you two, Malin and Zeke, start by questioning the two men who found him."

They talk to Ingmar Johansson first.

The tenant farmer is slurping coffee on the other side of the table in the castle kitchen, running one hand through his blond hair at regular intervals, telling them how he was uneasy at first when he heard that the castle had a new owner, but that everything had seemed "fine" once he'd had the chance to talk to Petersson.

"He wasn't planning to change the terms of our lease."

"No changes at all?" Zeke says.

"No, not really."

"Not really?" Zeke wonders.

"Well, he wanted me to go hunting with him whenever he felt like it."

"And you didn't object?"

"No, why should I? It does me no good if there's too much game running around on the land I lease."

"How often were you supposed to do that?" Malin asks.

"Whenever he called."

"But how often?"

"He never said. When he called yesterday it was the first time in a long while."

"You didn't see anything odd when you got here?" Malin says, even though she asked the same thing when they first arrived at the castle. Wants to twist the truth out of Johansson with the force of repetition.

"No. I came with Lindman, and the Range Rover was parked in front of the castle. I assumed Petersson was inside the castle and would be out shortly, and when he didn't come out we went inside to look for him."

"You didn't see any other cars?"

"No."

"Were the doors to the castle open?"

"You've already asked me that. Yes. Otherwise we wouldn't have been able to get in, would we? Those doors wouldn't be too easy to force."

"You weren't here earlier today?" Zeke asks. "Or last night?"

"No, why on earth would I have been?"

Johansson's face seems to crumple, his lips tighten, and he looks at them suspiciously.

"Ask my wife at home if you don't believe me. We spent all evening watching television before we went to bed. She made me breakfast this morning."

"Do you know anything else about Jerry Petersson that you think might be of interest to us?" Malin asks.

"No, not a damn thing."

"Nothing about his business affairs?"

"Nothing."

"Did he live here alone?"

"I think so. He didn't have any staff. They say he just called people when he needed them."

Johansson pulls a face that says, That's enough questions. I've said my piece.

"You can go now," Malin says tiredly. "But we might need to talk to you again."

"You've got my mobile number," Johansson says, standing up.

Göte Lindman is a lonely man, Malin thinks as she sees his face against the white tiles of the kitchen.

A lonely farmer who's probably at his happiest when he's working a thresher or looking after his livestock, if he has any. The woman he's mentioned, Svetlana, sounded more like a piece of furniture than a life partner.

Lindman has just told them the same things they heard from Johansson. That they were summoned to go hunting, that they'd entered into an informal agreement with the castle's new owner, and that it didn't bother Lindman, because hunting was what you did in the autumn and that was when there was least work to do on the farm anyway.

"Petersson seemed like an honest man."

Lindman says the words with emphasis before going on:

"It's a bugger that we had to find him in the moat like that, things could have gone all right. I'm sure of that. Fågelsjö was an unpleasant bastard."

"Which one?" Zeke asks.

"I used to deal with the old man, Axel."

"Unpleasant, how?" Malin asks.

"His manner, well, it was . . . he really let you know who was in charge, let's put it that way."

Lindman falls silent, shakes his head, then a sudden rush of fear crosses his face.

"How did he let you know?" Malin asks.

"By raising the rent all of a sudden, for instance," Lindman said quickly.

Malin nods.

Modern castle owners. The same power relationships as always, the same oppressed tenant farmers as always, the same inferiority as always. But at the same time some people are predisposed to dislike any figure of authority.

"Do you know anything about Petersson?"

"Only that he grew up round here and made a killing in the capital."

"Do you know how he made his money?" Zeke asks.

Lindman shakes his head.

"No idea."

"Did he live here alone?"

"Only with the dog, as far as I know. What's going to happen to it now?"

"We'll take care of it," Malin says, realizing that she has no idea what they're going to do with the dog, which is still barking outside in the car.

Then more questions and answers, if they saw anything unusual on the way here, any cars, if the Range Rover was parked in front of the castle when they arrived, if he had any idea about who could have done it, and what he was doing last night and first thing this morning.

"I've got no idea who could have done it."

"I was at home on the farm. Ask Svetlana."

"You don't think I did it? Then I wouldn't have called you, would I?"

"We don't think you were involved in the suspected murder of Jerry Petersson," Malin says. "But we have to ask, we have to keep all possible lines of inquiry open, at the same time as we rule out some of the less likely scenarios."

Malin and Zeke alone in the kitchen.

The white-tiled walls make Malin think of a slaughterhouse, then a mortuary, then she imagines that the fog outside in the forest and over the fields is gunpowder smoke from a seventeenth-century battlefield.

Blood and screaming.

Amputated limbs.

Rotting vegetation and slimy mushrooms underfoot.

Men without arms screaming in sulfurous smoke from burning straw. Legless creatures, children with their ears cut off.

All the things Janne had seen in Rwanda.

"Why do you think the doors were open?" Malin asks. "The art he's got in here must be worth millions."

"Maybe he was inside when he saw someone coming up the drive, and he went out and didn't lock up behind him? That would be entirely natural, wouldn't it?"

"Or he went out for a walk or a drive, and forgot to lock up?"

"Or else he was the type who doesn't like routine chores and didn't bother to lock up, just for the thrill of it," Zeke says.

"Or else he didn't live alone. There might have been someone else in the castle when he went out."

"A woman?"

"Maybe. It's pretty unlikely, don't you think? Living in a huge castle like this out in the middle of nowhere all on his own?"

"But everyone says he lived on his own. Maybe he liked being alone?"

"Can you hear the dog?" Zeke went on.

"No. But we should give it some water."

Zeke nods.

"What are we going to do with it?" Malin asks.

"Take it to the dogs' home in Slaka."

"Or to Börje Svärd. He's got kennels, hasn't he?"

"Do you think he's up to it?"

His wife. Anna. On a respirator in the most tastefully furnished house Malin has ever seen. A good person in a bad body.

She thinks of her own flat. This kitchen alone is three times the size of the whole thing.

"We need to know more about Petersson," Malin says, thinking, We're fumbling through the autumn fog right now. But one thing is certain, he managed to do what I failed to do, get away from fucking Linköping. So why, why on earth did he come back? What sort of voices were calling him back here?

"Who do you think he was?" Malin asks.

Zeke shrugs his shoulders, and Malin wonders what dreams and desires a man like Jerry Petersson might have had. What joy and pain might he have felt?

12

What do you want to know about me, Malin Fors?

I can tell you everything, if you listen carefully enough. I know you're good at listening to voices that can't be heard, to the soundless muttering that contains certainty and possibly even the truth.

I'm not a harsh person.

I never have been, but I still had faith in harshness, I've seen all it has given me. Certainly, it made me lonely, but I chose to believe that my loneliness was a matter of choice.

I don't need anyone. I can't live with anyone. I'm not scared of loneliness.

That's what I told myself.

A car door closing.

A zip was pulled up over my face and for a moment everything went black, but then the world opened up before my eyes again. Simple and beautiful in a way it never has been before, and suddenly my faith in harshness felt like a mistake.

I'm wrong, I thought. You're wrong, Jerry Petersson.

And now we're rolling forward, the ambulance and me, and I curse myself as I lie there in that black plastic on the stretcher, bouncing up and down as the wheels try to get a grip on the gravel leading into the forest.

I'm in here.

In the cold black plastic.

I'm up here.

High up in the sky and looking down on Skogså, on Malin Fors and Zacharias Martinsson walking across the courtyard, wrapped up in themselves, on their way to Malin's car where Howie has stopped barking, his tongue hanging thirstily out of his mouth.

On that old bastard Fågelsjö in his apartment.

Where are they going, all these people? From now on?

I can see that if I want to.

But instead I glide away to other spaces, I see myself, traveling the same way I am traveling now, the same way yet so endlessly different, a body on a stretcher, a pain that I can't feel in this present now.

13

The boy is just as surprised each time he feels pain, yet it is nevertheless in that moment, when the ambulance lurches for some unknown reason and his hastily splinted broken shinbone hits the edge of the stretcher, that he becomes aware that he has a memory and that this isn't always a good thing. At that moment it causes more pain than anything he has ever felt in his life, and he is aware of it, it's as if this new pain is the sum total of all the previous pain in his life, and all of a sudden he understands his mum, but his father remains hidden to him, a pain of the soul impossible to comprehend.

Neither Mum nor Dad has been allowed to travel in the ambulance, and he can see his own anxiety reflected in the man sitting beside him, stroking his hair gently and telling him that everything's going to be all right. That June day was the start of the first UN environmental conference, the first of its kind, and the bombs are still raining down on Southeast Asia.

There's no lift in the block of flats in Berga. Their flat is on the second floor, and he knows Mum has trouble with the stairs, that she's in pain, always in pain, but he doesn't know that the ligaments in her knees are long since locked by rheumatism and that she has asked the doctors in the regional hospital to increase her dose of cortisone, and that they have refused: "Stick it out," they say, "we can't do anything."

And, in her exhaustion, she can't do anything for him, during the hours after Grandma picks him up from school and before Dad comes home from his shift on the production line.

He is balancing on the narrow railing of the balcony, and the rose bed sixteen feet below looks so soft with all the flowers, their red and pink glowing against the peeling façade of the 1950s blocks, against the unkempt lawns where the parks department staff usually lie when they have their morning beers and pass round the bottle of vodka from mouth to mouth.

He isn't scared.

If you're scared you fall.

She calls to the boy from the kitchen, too tired to get up from the chair that she had dragged to the stove where the pea soup or mutton with dill sauce or stuffed cabbage is cooking, she shouts anxiously and angrily:

"Get down from there! You'll get yourself killed!"

But the boy knows he isn't going to get himself killed, he knows he's not going to fall.

"I'll tell your dad, he'll sort you out when he gets home."

But Dad never sorts the boy out, not even when he's drunk, because he can always get away. Instead he takes him into the bedroom when he's sober, and whispers to him to scream as if he were being beaten, and that's their shared secret.

Down in the sandpit in the yard there are two little kids, and Jojje's big sister is sitting on the only intact swing hanging from the frame. All three of them are looking up at him, not worried, convinced he'll manage his balancing act.

Then the phone inside the flat rings. He wants to go and answer it, like he usually does, and he forgets he's up on the railing, and his upper body sways, first one way, then the other, he wonders if it's Grandma calling, to invite him out to the country that weekend because she forgot to ask, and the narrow iron railing disappears from under his feet. He hears Mum scream, he hears Jojje's big sister scream, then he sees the buildings and the blue early summer sky, then the rose bushes cut into his body, he hits his leg hard, and then there's a burning pain, and he tries to move but nothing happens.

He'll have to accept the consequences.

They put him in plaster up to his thigh to keep him from moving. They give Mum more cortisone so she can look after him. Dad gets the pushchair out of the cellar, and he rides in that when they go to the supermarket in the shopping center, and people stare at him as if he were a baby lying in it.

When the plaster is removed he runs faster than he ever has before.

He knows what the bags mean now. He keeps his distance whenever they appear, and Dad's bitter words reach him less and less often. He, Jerry, is a hundred steps ahead in everything, yet he still seeks Dad's embrace sometimes, even though he knows that it can close around him like a wolf's jaws, and Dad's strong fingers can become the blades of the lawnmower cutting into his body, and his words can be their honed edges: "You're good for nothing, lad."

During the last weeks of summer, his last ever in nursery school, they have to do a test.

Remember the things on a picture. Pair things together. Things like that, and he realizes what it means to be clever, the admiration it occasions in people who don't expect intelligence in anyone. But the look, those pebble-sized eyes, are still unbeatable when it comes to getting what he wants.

His schoolteacher has seen the results of the tests from nursery school. She calls out his name with a note of expectation on his first day at school, then she sees his address on the report and feels disappointed, her shoulders slump, this could be a big problem, a kid from Berga with a brain.

He's quickest at counting.

Best at writing.

Can read the most words. Sticks up his hand when no one else knows the answer, and he can see that his teacher feels distaste toward him, but he doesn't yet know why. He doesn't see the dirt on his clothes. The filth in his ears. His long, greasy hair. The holes in his sweater. He gives her the eyes instead, and something happens during the third year. She becomes his protector, takes him on, sees who he is and what he might become.

He stays out in the evenings. Creeping home, but sometimes Dad's awake.

And he does what Dad might have wanted to do in the evenings once he's quenched his thirst with wine and cheap beer. What Dad would never dare do: He hits when he says he's going to.

He hits anyone who gets in his way. He hits the head teacher when Mum and Grandma have come to school for a meeting.

But he is allowed to stay.

An exceptional talent, his teacher says.

After that he hits people when they're not looking.

He hits his way out of all the feelings, the nameless feelings that have nowhere to go in the closed circle of the backyard in Berga, the flat's two rooms, Ånestad Junior School, Grandma's various homes, and his nimble feet drum restlessly on the ground, wondering what on earth this world is good for.

14

The ambulance with the perforated body.

It's heading purposefully off toward the forest, slowly, as if anxious not to wake or upset the dead man. The dog in the car barks after the ambulance, jumping up at the window.

Standing in front of the castle, Malin can see the green lanterns swaying in the wind, and their forest-tinted light makes the gray daylight hazy. Moldering heaps of leaves at the edge of the forest. Like crumpled paper painted in bright colors by the children at a closure-threatened nursery-school. And the trees, their bare crowns watching the day's peculiar performance from their elevated position above the leaves, waving goodbye when the wind helps the branches to move.

The same questions as always at the start of an investigation. Malin poses them to herself, aware that all the others in the team will be asking the same things.

How to make sense of this?

What's happened?

Who was he, Jerry Petersson? The answer to the question of where the violence came from is always hidden in the victim's life. And death. What prompted him to return to the city and surrounding area? He had been back for about a year, but sometimes evil moves slowly.

Then the forest seems to open up before her eyes, the gaps in the trees seem to get wider, and the space is filled with a darkness teeming with shapeless figures.

Malin imagines she can hear a voice, as if all the figures were speaking with one voice, saying the same thing:

"I shall drift here for a thousand years. I shall be lord of this land."

"Save me!" the voice goes on. "I was guilty of many things, but save me, grant me forgiveness."

Then it calms down, whispering: "Why did I become the person I ended up as?"

Young snakes, pale yellow, seem to be slithering round Malin's boots. She stamps her feet but they don't disappear.

She blinks slowly.

The snakes and the shapes are gone.

An ordinary, depressing, gray, misty autumn forest. Gravel beneath her feet.

What was that all about? Am I going mad? But she isn't worried, the drinking and all the rest of it has probably just got a bit much. Then she thinks about the fact that just a few hours ago someone was wielding a knife here.

Murdering.

Killing Jerry Petersson.

She switches on her mobile again, she's had it turned off since she arrived.

Two missed calls. Both from Tove, but no messages. I ought to call her now, I really ought to.

The dog is quiet, calm. Must have lain down on the backseat.

"Malin! Malin!"

She recognizes Daniel Högfeldt's voice. He's calling to her from the driver's seat of one of the *Correspondent*'s reporters' cars.

She feels like giving him the finger.

Instead she waves at him.

"What have you got for me?"

His voice, eager.

"Forget it, Daniel," she calls.

"He was murdered, wasn't he? And it was Petersson."

"You'll find out later. Karim's bound to call a press conference."

"Come on, Malin."

She shakes her head, and he smiles a warm, gentle smile, exactly the sort of smile she needs.

Is it that obvious?

Daniel wrote the article about Petersson. Might he know something? Can't ask him now, that would be giving too much away.

She had thought that her trysts with Daniel would come to an end when she moved back in with Janne. Then one evening, after she'd sweated everything out in the gym in the basement of the police station and still felt it wasn't enough to calm her down, he had called when she was about to get in the car and go home.

"Can you come over?"

Ten minutes later she was lying in his bed in Linnégatan.

They didn't say a word to each other. Not then. Nor the next time, or the next, or the next.

He simply took her as hard as he could, and she took him in return, and they yelled out together, looked at each other, seeming to ask, What the hell is this? What are we doing? What's wrong with us?

Daniel Högfeldt looks at Malin, and can't help thinking that she looks terrible, almost so terrible that she isn't sexy anymore.

He's tried to get her to see him as more than just a body, but that hasn't been possible. She can't seem to shake her low opinion of him, assuming he only wants information about cases, when in actual fact it's her that he wants to find out more about.

She's moved back in with her ex-husband again. But how well can that really be going? When she still wants to fuck my brains out?

It's fairly obvious that she isn't happy. But if I tried to say anything she'd turn on her heel, do anything to avoid the issue.

Daniel leans back in his seat. Sees the bald detective that he knows is called Zeke go over to Malin.

Daniel closes his eyes. Gets ready to play at being the tough reporter when he tries to get something out of the other officers.

As Malin and Zeke approach the car, the dog stands up on the backseat. Its cropped stump of a tail is wagging, and it's staring greedily at the bowl of water in Zeke's hand. But when they open the doors the dog backs away. It lies down on the floor behind the driver's seat and seems to be waiting for something. Zeke gives him the water and they can hear the dog lapping at it.

"Let's get it to Börje," Malin says.

"Okay," Zeke replies.

Malin goes for the passenger seat. Zeke can do the driving.

The dog whimpers in the backseat.

Daniel Högfeldt's naked body.

What's wrong with me? Malin thinks.

The red-painted cottage sits beside the road leading up toward Skogså, not far from the turning to Linköping. The forest around the cottage opens up to give space for a field that looks more like a large vegetable patch. They've stopped on their way back to the city; something inside Malin told her that they ought to talk to the person living there, that they shouldn't leave it to the uniforms.

"The dog will be okay."

Malin has one hand on the door.

But before she can open it the door flies open.

Malin jerks back. Zeke throws himself down, already outside. The barrel of a shotgun is pointing right at them, and behind it stands a short gray-haired old woman.

"So who are you?" she croaks in a hoarse voice.

Malin backs away a bit farther, and from the corner of her eye she can see Zeke feeling for his pistol.

"Easy, easy," Malin says. "We're from the police. Let me show you my ID."

The old woman looks at Malin.

Seems to recognize her.

Lowers the gun.

Says: "I recognize you from the local news. Come in. Sorry about the gun, but you never know what you're going to get round here."

Inside the car the dog has started barking again.

"Hang your coats in the hall. Coffee? It's lunchtime, but I haven't got anything to offer you."

The old woman, who's just introduced herself as Linnea Sjöstedt, leads them into the kitchen.

The way she walks makes me look like an invalid, Malin thinks. The thought of lunch making her feel sick.

The old woman puts the shotgun down on a rustic table standing on a yellow and green, almost certainly home-woven, rag rug. An old Husqvarna stove. Collectable plates on the walls.

An old person's smell, sour but not unpleasant, and a strong sense that time will have its due, no matter what anyone might want.

"Sit yourselves down."

For the old woman the business with the shotgun is already long forgotten, but Malin can still feel the adrenaline pumping in her veins, and Zeke's clothes are wet from the grass he landed on. They watch her put an old-fashioned coffeepot on the stove and take out some blue-flowered cups.

"You can't go around pointing guns at people like that," Zeke says as he sits down.

"Like I said, you never know what you're going to get round here."

Uncomfortable rib-backed chairs, hard on the backside.

"Do you mean anything in particular?" Malin asks.

"Who knows what evil might come up with. Something must have happened, seeing as you're here."

"Yes," Malin says. "Jerry Petersson, the new owner of Skogså, has been found dead."

Linnea Sjöstedt nods.

"Murdered?"

"We believe so," Zeke replies.

"That doesn't surprise me," the old woman says, pouring out the coffee. "I haven't got any cake. It makes me fat."

"So we're wondering if you saw anything unusual yesterday, or last night, or this morning. Or anything else you thought was odd recently?"

"This morning," Linnea says, "I saw Johansson and Lindman heading toward the castle. It must have been about half past seven."

Malin nods.

"Anything else?"

Malin takes a sip of the coffee.

Boiled coffee.

So strong it makes the hairs on the back of her neck stand up.

"Sometimes, when you're as old as I am," Linnea Sjöstedt says, "you don't always know if you're dreaming or if what you see or think you see has really happened. I'm sure about Johansson and Lindman, because I'd already had my first cup of coffee by then, but could I have seen something before that? I'm not sure."

"So you did see something before that, Linnea?"

Malin is making an effort to sound serious. As if dreams really did exist.

"Well, I think I saw a black car driving toward the castle at the crack of dawn. But I'm not sure. Sometimes I dream that I've got up, and this could have been one of those dreams."

"A black car?"

Linnea Sjöstedt nods.

"Any particular make or model?"

"Maybe an estate car. It was big. I've never paid any attention to makes of cars."

"Do you rent this cottage from the estate?" Malin asks.

"No, thank heavens, my father bought it from the Fågelsjös in the fifties. I moved in twenty years ago when my father passed away."

"What about Petersson, what do you know about him?"

"He called and introduced himself. Nice young man, even if he probably wasn't always as nice as that. All that business with Goldman and so on."

"Goldman?"

"Yes, Jochen Goldman. The one who conned all that money out of that financial firm up in Stockholm, several hundred million, then fled abroad. They're supposed to have worked together. I read about it on the net. Don't you know anything, officers? That Goldman's supposed to be a really nasty piece of work."

"Nasty?" Malin asks.

Linnea Sjöstedt doesn't answer, just shakes her head slowly.

Embarrassing, Malin thinks. Put to rights by an eighty-year-old woman. But she was right, Goldman did feature in the article in the *Correspondent*, even if the focus was more on Petersson here and now, his plans for the castle and how he was supposed to have all but driven out the Fågelsjös.

But she remembers Jochen Goldman. How he emptied a listed company of money with the help of some French count, how he's spent ten years on the run, getting loads of media attention, publishing books about his life on the run, until now; for the past year or so, his crimes can no longer be tried thanks to the statute of limitations.

And none of them remembered the connection between the financial crook and their victim during their meeting in the castle?

Strange. But presumably their detective brains hadn't woken up properly by then. Just as foggy as the weather this autumn.

Irritated, Malin asks:

"What were you doing last night and this morning?"

"Inspector, do you really think I had anything to do with Peters-son's demise?"

"I don't think anything," Malin says. "Just answer the question, please."

"I got home at about four o'clock this morning. With Linköping Taxis, so you can check that. I spent last night with my lover, Anton, he lives in Valla. You can have his number as well."

"Thank you," Zeke says. "But I don't think that will be necessary. Is there anything else you think we ought to know?"

The old woman's eyes sparkle.

She opens her mouth to say something, but changes her mind before any words pass her lips.

Zeke is about to start the car. He's just patted the dog's head, talking to it, calming it down, settling it back down on the floor again. It doesn't seem to want to look at the forest and fields.

My brain isn't working properly, Malin thinks.

It wants more drink.

Goldman.

One of the biggest fraud cases in Swedish history, and he managed to stay hidden until the time limit for charges being pressed had elapsed.

And Petersson had dealings with someone like that. They've got a lot to look into, there were masses of files in several rooms of the castle, and when there's been a murder they can seize whatever they want, without the permission of the victim's solicitor. If Jerry Peters-son was in business with Goldman, how many others like him were there?

Malin looks out over the mist-shrouded field and forest and road. Thousands of different shades of gray blurring together. The wind is strong enough to send the leaves flying like flakes of copper across the green-black ground, swirling to and fro like metallic stars hanging in an absurdly low sky. In a clearing there are several ridges of deep-red leaves, like the blood pouring from Jerry Petersson's body.

Must call Tove.

Malin tries to focus her gaze, but everything is floating in front of her eyes. The rearview mirror. She doesn't want to look in it, hates her swollen features, the reason why she looks like that, doesn't want to see the shame etched in her forehead, in the tiniest corner of her face. The car seems to contract. She's having trouble breathing. Wants to jump out. Tove. Janne. How are you ever going to forgive me?

Damn.

Just give me a fucking big drink. Now. I'm pouring with sweat. I know all the things I ought to do, but I can't handle any of it.

"Are you okay?" Zeke asks.

"Fine," she replies. Forces herself to think about their heaven-sent case.

A black car in a dream? Lindman's? Johansson's? But why?

Jochen Goldman.

The entire Fågelsjö family.

Avaricious bastards in general.

I wonder which ones it's worth annoying most?

15

The very thought of going through all the files is making Johan Jakobsson annoyed. How many have they carried into the room now?

Two hundred? Three hundred?

His light-blue shirt is flecked gray with dust from all the carrying.

Johan surveys the meeting room in the heart of the police station. Burps and gets a taste of the mince he had for lunch.

The windowless room with its gray-white textured wallpaper and basic shelving was going to be their strategy room for the duration of the investigation into the murder of Jerry Petersson.

Two hard drives.

A successful working life gathered together in a corner of the police station. Grim, Johan thinks, but he is also rather glad that something's actually happening today. They hadn't even reached Nässjö and his parents-in-law when Sven Sjöman rang, told him what had happened, and asked if he could come in.

"I'm on my way. I'll be there in an hour or two."

His wife had been furious, and he didn't really blame her. She had reluctantly driven him to Skogså, then turned back toward Nässjö on her own with the children.

Even all the impending paperwork is preferable to hobnobbing with the oldies in Nässjö. They have far too many opinions about things in general, and about Johan's family in particular, for him to enjoy their company.

Everyone should mind their own business.

It was much better that way.

The files of documents and the hard drives full of more documents are all concerned with instances of people minding their own business, Johan is certain of that. Who knows what they might find here? And what might that lead to? Or else they'll find nothing. It's not against the law to have a dodgy reputation.

The files are marked by year, and occasionally by name.

So far they've only taken a quick glance at a couple of them, but Jerry Petersson seems to have been a meticulous record-keeper, and every document appears to be in exactly the right place. This won't make his and Waldemar Ekenberg's job any less wide ranging, but it will make it a fraction easier.

The names on the files.

He doesn't recognize them, apart from one: Goldman. A mocking shadow who seems to almost be a fictional character, even though he really does exist. Malin called and mentioned the connection to Goldman, and now the files with his name on are on the table in front of Johan. There must be at least thirty of them, full of the specific details of avarice.

Malin's voice. It sounded rough, in the way that only alcohol can make a voice rough. And she sounded tired and sad. She's been looking more and more tired, and Johan has often felt like asking how she is, but Malin Fors isn't the kind of person you exchange small talk about feelings with.

The door of the room flies open with an angry bang.

In the doorway stands Waldemar, weighed down by two boxes.

Files, documents, computer disks.

This is ideal for me, Johan thinks, but Waldemar sees the job as a punishment, and maybe it is on some level: Sven wants to keep their renowned loose cannon under control. His reputation is deserved, Johan has seen him use physical force to get information out of people. Once Waldemar shoved the barrel of his pistol deep into the throat of a suspect to make him tell the truth. But violence can work. In the short term. In the end it always ends up biting its own tail.

Waldemar drops the boxes unceremoniously in a corner of the room.

Stretches his back.

Huffs and puffs, mutters something about needing a fag, then he sits down on one of the chairs around the table, and Johan sees the uncomfortable back of the chair bow under his colleague's weight.

"Christ, look at all this fucking work in here."

"If we're lucky, something will come up to save us going through most of it," Johan Jakobsson says.

He remembers clearing out his parents' flat four years ago, when Dad died just months after Mum. The way he had hunted through all their papers, looking for something that he reluctantly had to admit was probably money, a banker's draft for a large sum of money, a lottery win, the only way his parents would ever have managed to get a large amount of money.

But there was no money. And he was ashamed.

"Do you believe that?" Waldemar says.

"No."

"What's to say that this Petersson wasn't a fucking crook? He could have had contacts in the underworld. We ought to check. I could head out and make a few inquiries."

"We need to concentrate on the paperwork," Johan says wearily.

Waldemar pulls out a packet of cigarettes from his jacket pocket and holds it toward Johan.

"Want one? You don't mind me smoking in here, do you?"

The room is full of retch-inducing cigarette smoke.

Smoking isn't permitted anywhere in the police station, but Johan couldn't say no. Didn't want to look like an asthmatic weakling in front of the tough guy.

Why, Johan wonders, do I give a shit what he thinks?

But I do.

They leaf through a few files at random. They've ordered extra screens from the techs so they can go through the contents of Petersson's hard drives here in the room.

Where to begin?

No idea, and Waldemar seems to think the same, saying:

"There's so fucking much of it. We need help. And it's all going to be financial stuff that I honestly won't have a clue about. Do you know about stuff like that?"

Johan shakes his head.

"Only a little."

"We need someone from Economic Crime."

"And it would make sense to do a serious search online first. See if we can find something that looks dodgy. Not least considering his dealings with Goldman."

Then Waldemar drops a black folder on the floor. He swears as he picks it up and puts it on its own on the top shelf.

Paper, paper, paper, Johan thinks.

A life as a commercial lawyer, a solicitor.

A paper-producer.

As a surreptitious criminal? You don't have friends like Goldman without being a bit suspect. Do you?

There are 1,278,989 hits on Google for Jerry Petersson. Maybe a thousand of them might be their Jerry Petersson. The name of his company in Stockholm appears in a few places. Petersson Legal Services Ltd.

Johan has checked the latest company results. Petersson seemed to have worked alone, not one single employee, not even a secretary. His accountants were named, but he needn't necessarily even have had to meet them in person. No financial results for the company since Petersson bought Skogså, just a declaration that the company was dormant. But at the same time he had started a new business, Rom Productions, to manage Skogså. Nothing unusual anywhere, from what Johan could see at a quick glance, with his limited grasp of accounting.

There are still a fair number of hits, Johan thinks, trying to ignore the sour blast of coffee and smoke that hits him in the ear every time Waldemar breathes.

They're sitting at Johan's desk in the open-plan office, at his computer, keen to get out of the cell.

A lot of the hits seem to be about a seventeen-year-old golfer from Arboga.

Several of them link Petersson to Goldman. Articles in the main business dailies and magazines. It looks like Petersson represented Goldman while he was on the run, acting as his intermediary in Goldman's dealings with the authorities and media.

A few other hits concerned with business. But no juicy stories, only boring and apparently perfectly normal business dealings.

Then Jerry Petersson's name pops up in connection with an IT company that was sold to Microsoft early in 2002. Petersson was said to be one the main backers, and as a result of the sale he made a profit of almost two hundred and fifty million kronor.

Johan lets out a whistle.

Waldemar sighs, says:

"Fuck off."

Working as a lawyer may have made you well-off, Johan thinks, but Christ, this deal made you absurdly rich.

They read about the deal.

Nothing about any disagreements. Everything seemed to have been done by the book. Nothing odd at all, only a number of happy new multimillionaires.

And then Goldman again.

According to one article from earlier this year, when his crime fell under the statute of limitations, he was living in Tenerife at the time. The article was illustrated with several pictures of a rather fat toad-like man with dark hair and sunglasses. The man was shown seated behind the wheel of a large motor yacht in a sun-drenched harbor.

"This is where we start," Johan says.

"Okay," Waldemar says. "But I still think we should ask out on the street as well."

Sven Sjöman is walking up and down in his office; he almost misses his bulging stomach at times like this, the solid, thought-inspiring mound beneath his clasped hands. Instead there's now practically nothing beneath his beige shirt and brown jacket.

Karim Akbar is standing by his desk. He's just called Stockholm and asked for support from Economic Crime.

Press conference in twenty minutes.

They've just received Karin's preliminary report.

The postmortem on Jerry Petersson showed that he died of a blow to the back of the neck from a blunt instrument, possibly a rock. The knife wounds to his torso, forty in total, were in all likelihood inflicted after Petersson's death, or after he lost consciousness from the blow to the head.

There was no water in his lungs, so he was definitely dead by the time his body was dumped in the moat. To judge by the condition of the body, death occurred some time between four and half past six that morning. He hadn't been in the water for longer than four hours at the most. Murder was the only possible explanation for the cause of death. The perpetrator could be male or female: The knife wounds were deep, but not so deep that a woman couldn't have inflicted them. The perpetrator was, to judge by the distribution and direction of the wounds, probably right-handed.

The forensic examination of Petersson's car wasn't yet complete, but the search of the gravel courtyard in front of the castle hadn't produced anything. The rain had destroyed any evidence that might have been there.

The search of the castle had yielded thousands of different fingerprints. A lot of them could be decades old, and there were no signs of obvious criminal activity anywhere. The victim's possessions appeared to be untouched. In other words, no indications that robbery was the motive. The castle chapel and other buildings were also clean.

They were in the process of draining the moat in the search for the murder weapon, because the divers hadn't been able to find anything in the sludge at the bottom. Sven was worried about the fish at first, until he accepted that they were a necessary sacrifice.

"How are you going to play this?"

Sven looks over at Karim.

"Tell it like it is. Without any details."

"The connection to Goldman?"

"They've already found that. It's on the *Correspondent*'s website. TV4 is running with it. And doubtless more to come. They're making a bloody big deal out of it."

Then Sven sees Malin's face before him. She looked worse than ever out at the castle. Red and puffy, almost old. She might well have been drinking all night. Had something happened? With Tove? She blames herself for what happened in Finspång last autumn. Or is this about her and Janne? It doesn't seem to be going very well.

"Bloody hell," Sven says finally. "Why do I have a feeling that we're only at the start of a whole load of misery?"

16

Börje Svärd is standing in the rain in his garden in Tornhagen, wearing a light-blue raincoat. From the car Malin sees him raise his hand and throw a stick between the apple trees down toward the red-painted kennel block. The two beautiful Alsatians' coats are glistening with damp as they chase the stick, playfully fighting over it with sharp, bared teeth.

Börje is a thickset man, and his waxed mustache is drooping toward the grass.

Zeke stops in front of the gate, parking behind the blue car of a district nurse. In the backseat Jerry Petersson's beagle has leaped up, not barking, just staring expectantly out at the dogs in the garden.

Börje looks over toward them. Waves them over to him, stays where he is in the middle of the garden.

The little single-story house is painted white, well maintained. Börje's wife Anna would never tolerate anything else, even though she's so weak now that she can't even breathe without help. The illness has destroyed the nerves around her lungs, and she's living on overtime at the age of fifty.

They leave Petersson's dog in the car and the Alsatians rush over to them as they open the gate.

Not wary, but welcoming, sniffing and licking, before they set off down the garden again without paying any attention to the beagle in the backseat.

Zeke and Malin go over to Börje. Shake his wet hand.

"How are you both doing?" Zeke asks.

Börje shakes his head, turns away from the house.

"I wouldn't wish what she's going through on anyone."

"That bad?" Malin says.

"The nurses are with her now. They come four times a day. Otherwise we manage by ourselves."

"Would she like to see us, do you think?"

"No," Börje says. "She hardly wants to see me. I see you've got a dog in the car? I can't imagine it's yours, Fors?"

Malin explains what's happened, who the dog belonged to, and would he mind looking after it for a while until they know if there's a relative or someone else who wants it?

Börje smiles. A smile that gradually breaks through layer upon layer of exhaustion, of grief experienced in advance.

"A bitch?"

"No. Male," Zeke says.

"That might be okay," Börje replies, then he goes over to the car, and the dog bounces about in the backseat, and a couple of minutes later it's standing at attention beside Börje while the Alsatians sniff all around it.

"Looks like he feels at home here," Malin says. "Nice and easy."

"Get back to work, I'll look after the dog. What's his name?"

"No idea," Malin replies. "Maybe you could call him Jerry?"

"That would just confuse him," Börje replies.

"We'd better get going," Zeke says.

Börje nods.

"I appreciate you dropping by."

"Look after yourselves," Malin says, then turns away.

*   *   *

The call comes at exactly quarter past two, as Malin and Zeke are parking the car at the old bus station. There's not much left of the buildings that stood on the square years ago. Now there's a parking lot surrounded by buildings from different eras. Ugly gray-paneled blocks from the sixties, well-maintained buildings from the turn of the last century, with the skeletal black trees of the Horticultural Society Park in the background.

Close to Mum and Dad's flat now. The damp, dark rooms that no one has lived in for years. The flat is pretentiously large, but it still isn't a proper apartment. Why have they still got it? So Mum can tell her friends in Tenerife that they've got an apartment in the city? Their faces are starting to fade from my memory, Malin thinks as her mobile rings again. Mum's thin cheeks and pointed nose, Dad's laughter lines and oddly smooth forehead.

A silent love, theirs. An agreement. Like mine and Janne's? A lingering love, clinging to the back of our memories, in a room to which we haven't yet managed to close the door.

The plants they think are still alive.

Dried out.

Not a single damn plant alive anymore, but what do they expect when they haven't been home for more than two years?

She pulls her mobile from the pocket of the Gore-Tex jacket.

Hears the rain drumming on the roof of the car. Zeke wary beside her.

Tove's number on the screen.

What can I say to her? Is she going to be sad, scared?

How can I talk to her without Zeke realizing?

He'll realize. He knows me too well.

"Tove, hi. I saw you rang earlier."

Silence at the other end.

"I know it all ended weirdly yesterday and I should have called back, but something's happened, and I've been busy at work. Is Dad there?"

I hit him, Malin thinks. I hit him.

"I'm at school," she finally hears Tove's voice say. She's not sad, not scared, almost sounds angry. "If you need to talk to Dad, call him."

"Of course, you're at school. I'll give him a call if I need to talk to him. Why don't you come into the city this evening and we'll have something to eat, okay?"

Tove sighs.

"I'm going to go back to the house, to Dad."

"You're going back to Dad?"

"Yes."

Another silence. It's as if Tove wants to ask something, but what?

"Well, you do whatever you want, Tove," Malin says, and she knows it's exactly what she shouldn't say, she ought to say things like: It's all going to be okay, I'll pick you up from school, I want to give you a big hug, I'll make an effort, How are you, my darling daughter?

"How are you, Mum?"

"How am I?"

"Forget it. I've got to go. I've got a lesson."

"Okay, bye then. Talk to you later. Big kiss."

Zeke looking at her sympathetically. He knows everything, absolutely everything.

"So you're living back in the city again? I wondered when I picked you up this morning."

"It's nice to be home."

"Don't be so hard on yourself, Malin. We're only human."

Tove clicks to end the call and watches her schoolmates hurrying to and fro along the corridor of the Folkunga School, sees the way the high ceiling and the dark light filtering in through the arched windows from the rain-drenched world outside makes the pupils look smaller, defenseless.

Bloody Mum.

The least she could have done is call back. She doesn't even seem to be considering coming back to the house tonight. Now the pain in her stomach is growing again, below her heart, growing impossibly large. She sounded abrupt and businesslike, it was as if she wanted to finish the call as soon as possible, she didn't even ask how I am, why did I even bother to call? She probably just wants to go and have a drink.

I know why I called.

I want her to come home. I want them to stand in the kitchen having a hug, and I want to watch.

Don't think about it, Tove.

She taps her mobile against her head.

Don't think about it.

Some twenty yards away three of the older boys are grouped around a fat younger boy. Tove knows who he is. An Iraqi who can hardly speak a word of Swedish, and the older boys love bullying him. Bloody cowards.

She feels like getting up, going over and telling them to stop. But they're bigger, much bigger than her.

Mum sounded disappointed when she said she was going back to Dad's. Tove had been hoping that would make her want to go as well, but deep down she knows that's not how things work in the adult world, everything's so damn complicated there.

Now they're hitting the boy.

Abbas, that's his name.

And she puts her pen and notepad on the floor by her locker. She pushes her way through the crowd over to the three bullies. She shoves the tallest of them in the back, yelling: "Why don't you pick on someone your own size instead?" and Abbas is crying now, she can see that, and the force of her voice must have surprised the stupid bloody idiots, scared them, because they back away, staring at her. "Get lost," she yells, and they stare at her like she's a dangerous animal, and Tove realizes why she frightens them, they must know what happened out in Finspång, what happened to her, and they respect her because of that.

Idiots, she thinks. Then she puts her arms round Abbas, he's small and his body is soft, and she pretends he's Mum, that she can comfort her with just a hug and a promise that everything's going to be all right, from now on everything's going to be all right.

Axel Fågelsjö's apartment on Drottninggatan is, to put it in estate-agent jargon, magnificently appointed, Malin thinks. But it's still only a fraction as ostentatious as Skogså Castle.

Paneling and shiny, tightly woven Oriental rugs that make her headache flare up again. Authentic, expensive, quite different from the cheap rugs bought at auction on the floors of her mum and dad's flat. The worn leather of the armchairs shimmers in the light of the chandeliers and candelabra.

And the man in front of them.

He must be about seventy, Malin thinks. And right-handed. The embodiment of authority, and she tries to stay calm, not become defensive the way she knows she always is when she meets people higher up the social ladder than she could ever get.

All this still exists.

The Social Democrats may have managed to create a superficial equality in this country for a while, but it's thin and transparent and false.

Portraits of Count Axel Fågelsjö's ancestors hang in a row above the paneling. Powerful men with sharp eyes. Warriors, many of them.

They are witness to Fågelsjö's awareness that he's better than the rest of us, worth more. Unless that's just my own prejudice? Malin thinks.

There are still big differences between people in Sweden. Bigger than ever, perhaps, because there's a professed political desire to create a blue sheen of equality, a mendacious glow, as if there's still a green shimmer of cash casting a light over the lives of the poor.

The blues say we're all equally valuable. That everyone should have the same opportunities. And then they repeat it. And it becomes a truth even if they implement policies that mean those with money in the bank keep on getting richer even in these troubled times.

The whole of society is tainted with lies, Malin thinks.

And those lies give rise to a feeling of being fooled, denied, and rejected.

Maybe that's how I feel, deep down, Malin thinks. Trampled on, without actually realizing it.

Voiceless by nature.

And if you have neither words nor anyone's ear, that's when violence is born. I've seen it happen a thousand times.

Malin looks at the portraits in Fågelsjö's sitting room, then at the stout, ruddy-cheeked count with the self-confident smile that has suddenly appeared.

New money, like Petersson's. Old money, like Fågelsjö's. Is there really any difference? And what on earth are inherited privileges doing in a modern society?

"Thank you for seeing us," Malin says as she sits down on a ridiculously comfortable leather armchair and Fågelsjö stubs out his cigarette.

Fågelsjö smiles again, his smile is properly friendly now, he means us well, Malin thinks, but with all his privileges he can probably afford to.

"Of course I'm happy to see you. I understand why you're here. I heard on the radio about Petersson, and it was only a matter of time before you came to see me."

Zeke sitting beside Malin, wary, evidently also affected by the old count's presence.

"Yes, we have reason to believe that he was murdered. So naturally that raises a number of questions," Zeke says.

"I'm at your disposal."

Fågelsjö leans forward, as if to demonstrate his interest.

"To begin with," Malin says, "what were you doing last night and this morning?"

"I was drinking tea with my daughter Katarina yesterday evening. Then, at ten o'clock, I came home."

"And after that?"

"I was at home, as I said."

"Is there anyone who can confirm that?"

"I've lived alone since my wife died."

"There are rumors," Zeke says, "that the family hit hard times and that was why you were forced to sell Skogså to Petersson."

"And who would spread rumors like that?"

Fågelsjö's eyes flashing with sudden anger, but nonetheless feigned anger, Malin thinks: No point trying to hide what everyone knows.

"I can't tell you that," Zeke says.

"They're just rumors," Fågelsjö says. "What they wrote in the *Correspondent* was nonsense. We sold the castle because it was time, it had served its role as the family seat. These are new times. Time had simply caught up with our way of life. Fredrik works for the Östgöta Bank, Katarina works in art. They don't want to be farmers."

You're lying, Malin thinks. Then she thinks of her recent conversation with Tove, and feels sick at how, against her will, she had treated it like a work conversation, how she couldn't break through and say the things that needed saying. How could you, Fors? How could anyone?

"So there were no arguments?" she goes on. "No disagreements?"

Fågelsjö doesn't answer, and says instead:

"I never met Petersson in relation to the sale. Our solicitors handled that, but I got the impression that he was one of those businessmen who want nothing more than to live in a castle. I daresay he had no idea of the work that requires, regardless of the amount of money one has to hire people to do it."

"He paid well?"

"I can't tell you that."

Fågelsjö smiles at his own words, and Malin can't tell if he's being consciously ironic and mimicking Zeke's words or not.

"I have difficulty seeing what significance the amount might have for your investigation."

Malin nods. They can find out the amount if it proves to be important.

"Had you passed the castle on to your son?"

"No. The castle was still in my ownership."

"The sale must have been upsetting for you," Malin says. "After all, your ancestors had lived there for centuries."

"It was time, Inspector Fors. That's all there was to it."

"And your children? Did they react badly to the sale?"

"Not at all. I daresay they were happy about the money. I tried to find a place for the children at the castle, but it didn't suit them."

"A place?"

"Yes, let one of them take over the running of it, but they weren't interested."

"Are you happy here?" Zeke asks, looking around at the spacious apartment.

"Yes, I'm happy here. I've lived here since the sale. In fact I'm so happy here that I'd like to be alone now, if you have no more questions."

"What sort of car do you drive?"

"I have two. A black Mercedes and a red Toyota SUV."

"That's all for now," Zeke says, getting up. "Do you know where we can find your children?"

"I presume you have their telephone numbers. Call them. I don't know where they are."

In the hall Malin notices a pair of black rubber boots. The mud on them is still wet.

"Have you been out in the forest?" she asks Fågelsjö, who has followed them to the door.

"No, just down to the Horticultural Society Park. That's quite muddy enough for me at this time of year."

When the front door has closed Fågelsjö goes down the corridor toward the kitchen.

He picks up the phone. Dials a number that he has managed to memorize with great difficulty.

Waits for an answer.

Thinks about the instructions that need to be given, how abundantly clear he will need to be for the children to understand. Thinks, Bettina. I wish you were here now. So we could deal with this together.

"The best of both worlds," Zeke says as they head back to the car.

"Sorry?"

"He lives, or would like to live in the best of both worlds."

"He's lying to us about the sale, that much is obvious. I wonder why? I mean, it's common knowledge that they'd fallen on hard times."

Zeke nods.

"Did you see how he clenched his fists when you asked about the sale? It looked like he could hardly keep his anger under control."

"Yes, I saw," Malin says, opening the passenger door of the car and thinking about the feeling she had that Fågelsjö was only pretending to be angry. Why? she asked herself.

"We need to dig deeper," Zeke says, looking at Malin, who looks like she's about to fall asleep, or start screaming for a drink.

I've got to talk to Sven. She's gone right under the ice this time.

"Let's hope that's exactly what Ekenberg and Johan are doing right now, digging deeper."

"And Karim must be basking in the glow of the flashbulbs as we speak," Zeke says.

17

Karim Akbar is absorbing the flashbulbs, his brain whirring as the reporters fire off their aggressive questions.

"Yes, he was murdered. By a blow from a blunt object to the back of the head. And in all likelihood he was also stabbed in the torso."

"No, we don't have the object. Nor the knife."

"We've got divers in the moat right now," he lies. The diving is already finished. "We may need to drain it," he says. The water is probably gone by now. His massaging of the truth is silly really, the reporters can easily check the moat, but Karim can't help it, wants to show the hyenas who decides the speed they go at.

"At present we don't have a suspect. We're looking into a range of possibilities."

The crowd of gray figures before him, most of them shabbily dressed, in line with all the clichés about journalists.

Daniel Högfeldt an exception. Smart leather jacket, a neatly ironed black shirt.

Karim can answer questions and think about other things at the same time, he's done this so often.

Is that when it's time to stop?

When autopilot kicks in?

When you start to mess about with the seriousness of the situation?

He can see himself standing in the room, like a well-drilled press officer in the White House, pointing at reporters, answering their questions evasively, all the while getting his own agenda across.

"Yes, you're right. There could be a number of people with reason to be unhappy with Jerry Petersson's activities. We're looking into that."

"And Goldman, have you spoken . . ."

"We're keeping all our options open at present."

"We're appealing to members of the public who may have seen anything interesting that night between . . ."

Waldemar Ekenberg is leaning over the table in their strategy room.

Reading one of the files about Jochen Goldman. Johan Jakobsson is slumped on the other side of the table, next to an IT expert who's installing a monitor.

"There's an address and a phone number here. Vistamar 34. Belongs to a J.G.," Waldemar says.

"Must be Jochen Goldman."

"This is from this year."

"What's the context?"

"Figures, some company."

"What's the international dialing code?"

"Thirty-four."

"That could be Tenerife, if he does live there. Vistamar. Definitely Spanish. Shall I call?"

"Well, we want to talk to him."

Johan leans back reaching for the phone, makes the call.

"No answer, but at least it rang. Doesn't seem to have an answer machine."

"Did you expect him to? We'll try again later."

"Malin's parents live on Tenerife," Johan says.

"Fucking hot down there."

"Maybe we should get Malin to make the call."

"What, you mean she should make the call because her parents live down there?"

Johan shakes his head.

"Well, you're getting to know her a bit now. She might get upset otherwise. She takes coincidences like that seriously."

"Yeah, she believes in ghosts," Waldemar says.

"Hold off from making the call. Let her do it. If it is even Jochen Goldman's number."

Waldemar shuts the file.

"I don't get most of these figures. When's the bloke from Eco getting here?"

An officer, they don't yet know who, is supposed to be coming down by train the next day.

"Tomorrow morning," Johan says.

Waldemar nods.

The Östgöta Bank at the corner of Storgatan and St. Larsgatan. Just a stone's throw from Malin's flat on Ågatan, but the two buildings couldn't be more different. Malin's block is late modern, from the sixties, low ceilings with plastic window frames installed in the midseventies. The Östgöta Bank is a showy art nouveau building in brown stone with an ornate interior.

But the rain is the same for all buildings, Malin thinks as she pulls open the heavy door and steps into the large foyer, all polished marble and a thirty-foot ceiling. The reception desk for the offices upstairs is to the left of the cashiers, who are scarcely visible behind thick bulletproof glass.

Malin and Zeke have called Fredrik Fågelsjö's mobile, but there was no answer. They tried him at home, no answer there either.

"Let's go to the bank and see if he's there," Malin had said as they drove away from Axel Fågelsjö's apartment, and now a red-haired, hostile-looking receptionist the same age as Malin is staring at her police ID.

"Yes, he works here," the receptionist says.

"Can we see him?" Malin asks.

"No."

"I see. We're here on important police business. Is Fredrik Fågel-sjö . . . ?"

"You're too late," the receptionist says neutrally, with a hint of triumph in her voice.

"Has he finished for the day?" Zeke asks.

"He usually leaves at three on Friday. What's this about?"

Never you mind about that, Malin thinks, saying: "Do you know where he might have gone?"

"Try the Hotel Ekoxen. He's normally in the bar there after work on Fridays."

"Friday beer?"

"More like Friday cognac," the receptionist says with a warm smile.

"Can you describe him to us? So we know who we're looking for?"

A moment later Malin is holding the bank's annual report in her hand. The glossy, smooth dark-blue paper feels like it's going to wear a hole in the palm of her hand.

The Ekoxen.

One of the smartest hotels in the city.

Maybe the smartest of all, situated between the Tinnerbäck swimming pool and the Horticultural Society Park, a white-plastered building that looks like a sugar lump. The hotel's piano bar has a view across the pool and is one of the most popular watering holes in the city. But not for me, Malin thinks. Way too far up its own fucking ass.

They roll slowly down Klostergatan toward the hotel through

moderate yet persistent rain. She's holding the photograph in the annual report in front of her. To judge by the picture, Fredrik Fågelsjö is about forty. His face is thin, dominated by a narrow, straight nose and a pair of anxious green eyes. He's thin, unlike his father, and the blue blazer he's wearing in the picture looks new. His shoulders are hunched, almost as if he's afraid of falling, and there's something evasive and hunted about his whole bearing.

Zeke pulls up in front of the entrance to the hotel. In the rearview mirror Malin sees a side door open, and someone steps out.

Fredrik Fågelsjö.

Is that you? Have you finished your Friday cognac?

"I think Fågelsjö just left through the back door."

A black Volvo is parked right outside the other door, and before Malin and Zeke have time to react the man they think is Fredrik has got in the car and driven off in the opposite direction to them.

"Shit," Malin says. "Turn round."

And Zeke spins the wheel, but at that moment a truck turns into the road from the other direction and stops.

"Fuck."

"I'll try his mobile again."

The truck reverses out of their way, and Zeke pulls onto the other side of the road and accelerates hard, and they head down toward Hamngatan at high speed, overtaking a rusty white Volkswagen.

"He's not answering," Malin says as they turn into Hamngatan. "I can see him," she says. "He's stuck at a red light by McDonald's."

No flashing lights, Malin thinks, no sirens. Just pull up alongside and wave him over, all according to the rule book. After all, we only want to talk to him.

Zeke puts his foot down, and they pull up alongside what they think is Fredrik Fågelsjö's car before the lights change. Hungry teenagers inside McDonald's. People defying the worsening rain and crossing the square in the background.

Zeke blows the horn, and Malin holds her police ID up to the window. Fredrik Fågelsjö, there's no doubt that it's him, looks at

Malin, at her ID, and his face takes on a look of panic when Malin gestures that he should pull over and wait for them outside McDonald's.

Fredrik nods, then looks straight ahead, seems to put his entire weight on the accelerator pedal, and his Volvo shoots away as the lights go amber, pulling in ahead of them and burning off along Drottninggatan.

Shit, Malin manages to think. Yells, "He's making a run for it. The bastard's making a run for it!"

And Zeke spins the wheel and heads off after Fredrik along Drottninggatan while Malin winds down the window and sticks the flashing light on the roof of the car.

"What the hell?" Zeke shouts. "Let command know over the radio. Get them to send more cars if we've got any."

Malin stays quiet, wants to let Zeke concentrate on driving, as Fredrik flashes past the orange building that once housed the National Bank at what must be sixty miles an hour, heading toward the Abis roundabout, past the old specialist food store.

What the hell is this? Malin thinks. Are you a panic-stricken murderer? Why the hell are you running from us?

A hundred yards ahead of them Malin sees some pedestrians throw themselves out of the way as Fredrik breaks a red light. She feels the adrenaline pumping as she shouts instructions over the radio.

"Driver refusing to stop. We're following a black Volvo . . . out toward the Berg roundabout, all available cars . . ."

Zeke swerves past a few cars that have ended up between them and Fredrik, and their speed, seventy-five now, in the middle of the city, makes Malin feel that the world as she knows it is dissolving into crazy lines and colors, and she feels violently sick now, her headache throbbing, but soon the adrenaline takes over again, and the present becomes clear and focused.

"He's turning off past Ikea, out toward Vreta Kloster," Malin yells, and the sound of the racing engine blends with the siren in a strangely exciting symphony.

Fredrik drives past Ikea's Tornby store, his car weaving as though he were drunk.

Maybe he is drunk, Malin thinks. He came out of the Ekoxen. She feels her nausea take hold of her stomach again, she feels like throwing up, but the adrenaline forces her stomach back down.

Zeke takes one hand off the wheel and presses the CD player, and German choral music, something from a Wagner opera, blasts through the car.

"What the fuck?" Malin yells.

"It makes me drive better," Zeke grins.

Fredrik is lucky with the lights as he heads across the roundabout on the E4. They pass the last blocks of flats in Skäggetorp and are out in the country, surrounded by empty fields and small farms huddled down against the wind.

The message from control is scarcely audible over the voices of the choir.

"Fågelsjö lives out on the plain, off left from Ledberg. He could be heading home."

He's pulling away, Malin thinks. "Step on it!" she yells. Could we really be getting somewhere? Did Fredrik kill Jerry Petersson? Is that why he's running?

A patrol car drives up alongside, but Zeke gestures to it to pull back, and when they reach the Ledberg junction Fågelsjö lurches left but manages to straighten the car out and continue at an ever-increasing speed out toward a small cluster of houses surrounded by thin trees, maybe a mile and a quarter farther out on the plain in the direction of Lake Roxen.

Zeke's forehead is sweating. Malin can feel him taking shallow, stressed breaths, and she pulls her pistol from its holster as the road curves toward the group of houses. A large brick villa, painted yellow, in a clump of trees. A proper upper-class mansion, and a hundred yards farther on Fredrik swings off again, down a driveway.

They follow him, and seventy yards in front of them he has stopped in front of a crooked red-painted barn surrounded by bare bushes and maples. He leaps out of the car and runs over into the barn.

Zeke pulls up behind Fredrik's car and the patrol car stops just behind them. Malin turns off the CD and the siren, and everything is suddenly strangely quiet.

Over the radio Malin says quietly: "Get out and cover us when we follow him inside the barn."

The gravel and mud outside the barn sticks to their shoes. Malin looks toward the building, feels the rain getting harder as they walk the few yards from the car to the barn door. Behind them is the villa, built in the Italian style, presumably Fredrik's home. If he's got a family, they don't seem to be in. The two uniforms have taken out their Sig Sauers, taking cover behind the car doors, ready to open fire if anything goes wrong.

Zeke beside her, both of them holding their pistols in front of them as Malin kicks open the door of the barn and shouts:

"Fredrik Fågelsjö! We know you're in there! Come out! We just want to talk to you!"

Silence.

Not a sound from the manure-stinking building.

Trying to run, Malin thinks, would be the most stupid thing you could do. Where would you go? Goldman. He stayed on the run for ten years. So it is possible. But you're hiding in there, aren't you? Waiting for us. You might be armed. People like you always have at least a hunting rifle. Are you waiting for us with a gun?

Talking to herself like that helps her stay focused, and stops the fear from taking over. Into the darkness now, Malin. Whatever's waiting inside.

"I'll go first," Zeke says, and Malin is grateful. Zeke never backs down when it comes to the crunch.

He steps inside the barn and Malin follows him. Dark, with a smell of fresh manure and some other indefinable animal waste.

There's light from one corner, opening onto a field, Zeke runs toward it and Malin follows.

"Shit," Zeke yells. "He must have gone straight through."

They rush over to the open door.

Some hundred yards away, down in the field, through the rain and fog, Fredrik is running, dressed in brown trousers and what must be a green oilskin. He stumbles and gets up, runs a bit farther, past a tree that's still got a few leaves.

"Stop!" Malin shouts. "Stop, or I'll shoot."

Which she wouldn't do. They've got nothing on Fredrik, and running from the police isn't sufficient justification for firing.

But it's as if all the air goes out of him. He stops, turns round, raises his empty hands and looks at her and Zeke, who are slowly approaching him, weapons drawn.

He is swaying back and forth.

You're drunk, Malin thinks, then shouts: "Lie down! Lie down!"

And Fredrik lies down on his stomach in the mud as Malin puts a pair of handcuffs on his wrists behind his back. A filthy green classic Barbour jacket.

He stinks of alcohol, but says nothing, maybe he can't talk with his face on the ground.

"What the hell was all that for?" Malin says, but Fredrik doesn't reply.

18

"What the hell happened?"

Zeke's hands are shaking slightly on the steering wheel as they drive back toward Linköping, past the white-tiled block of flats in Skäggetorp and the big Arla dairy in Tornby. They pass one of the *Correspondent*'s reporters' cars. Is that Daniel driving? They're utterly tireless, those vultures.

"I've no idea," Malin says. The adrenaline has dropped, her headache and angst are back, and a clearly intoxicated Fredrik is safely installed in the backseat of the patrol car. Malin didn't want him in the car with them; she and Zeke both needed time to calm down.

A van from local television news.

"But maybe," Malin goes on, "he's involved in this somehow and he got it into his head that we know, and that's why he tried to escape. And then realized how pointless it was out in the field, in all that rain."

"Or else he was just drunk and panicked when we tried to stop him," Zeke says.

"Well, we'll find out when we question him. But he could very well be our man," Malin replies, but she's thinking that there's something here that doesn't add up, that the case can't be that simple. Or can it?

Her mobile rings and she sees Sven Sjöman's name on the display.

"I've heard," Sven says. "Very odd. Could it be him? What do you think?"

"Maybe. We'll interview him when we get back to the station."

"Johan and Waldemar can do that," Sven says. "You two can try to get hold of Katarina Fågelsjö. Put her under pressure while her brother's idiotic behavior's still fresh."

Malin feels like protesting at first. Then she relaxes. If there's anyone who can get anything out of Fredrik Fågelsjö, it's Waldemar Ekenberg.

Fredrik doesn't say a word when they pull him to his feet and lead him back over the field. He maintains his silence as they put him in the patrol car.

"Okay. That's what we'll do," Malin says. "Anything else?"

"Not much. Johan and Waldemar have called a number of people and companies whose names crop up in Petersson's files. But it hasn't led to anything."

"Any signs of a lover?"

"No love at all," Sven replies.

Katarina Fågelsjö answered her phone.

Was prepared to see them, and now Malin and Zeke are heading along Brokindsleden in silence through the dim afternoon light.

They're both trying to catch their breath, to get back to their normal energy levels before they see her.

They drive past the development of detached houses in Hjulsbro.

In Malin's social studies textbook the area was mentioned as an upper-class reserve New York, but the upper class don't live here. More like the moneyed middle class.

In Hjulsbro the doctors' villas huddle together, nondescript from the outside, but large and tastefully furnished when you get inside. One of the most expensive and prestigious residential areas of the city, but still a bit feeble somehow, compared to Djursholm in Stockholm or Örgryte in Gothenburg.

As they drive through the area Malin can understand everyone who grows up in a provincial city and moves to a larger one as soon as they possibly can, a world with greater depths and heights than an ordinary, godforsaken Swedish city can offer, no matter how jumped up it is.

Stockholm.

She lived there with Tove while she was studying at the Police Academy. In a sublet one-room flat in Traneberg, and all she can remember is studying and trips to the nursery, babysitters found in the local papers, young girls who were expensive and unreliable, and the fact that Stockholm didn't have a damn thing to offer an impoverished single mother. The whole city felt shut off, as if all its opportunities and secrets could never be hers, and seemed to mock her relentlessly as a result.

The exact opposite must have been true for Jerry Petersson.

Malin had been offered a post in Stockholm several times, most recently last summer when there was a vacancy in the violent crime unit and the boss, someone called Kornman, had tried to headhunt her. He called her in person, said he was familiar with her work, and maybe she felt like expanding her territory?

Malin had a feeling they needed more women.

She'd just got the life she dreamed of with Janne and Tove, before everything went to hell. So she turned the offer down.

And now, in the car, she's cursing herself. A fresh start might be just what I need? Or would the big city break me? Mind you, a small city seems to be able to do that well enough.

Almost, anyway.

The radio is on.

She persuaded Zeke that they shouldn't listen to his choral music, and he agreed to listen to good old local radio.

The final notes of Grand Archives' "Torn Blue Foam Couch" have just faded away, and now Malin can hear the low voice of her friend, radio presenter Helen Aneman.

She's talking about their victim.

About Jerry Petersson, whom no one seems to feel sorry for, no one seems to care much about. And no one seems particularly upset about what's happened.

But somewhere there's someone who misses you, Malin thinks as she listens to Helen, and I'm going to make sure that person knows what really happened. Maybe your father, we'll deal with him in the fullness of time. You had no brothers or sisters, and your mother's dead, we know that much. Maybe a woman, or maybe even a child, even if you didn't have any of your own.

"One of the city's wealthiest sons has passed away," Helen says. "The IT millionaire, according to the rumors the criminals' friend, an exciting character that we might not get to know much about. He bought Skogså a year or so ago, the famous seat of the aristocratic Fågelsjö dynasty . . . Petersson may not have been the best-behaved person in the world, but surely he didn't deserve a fate like that? What do you think? Call in if you've got anything to say about Jerry Petersson."

A Madonna song.

"American Pie."

Zeke sings along. Maybe the song makes him think about Martin in Vancouver? About his grandchild? Or maybe they sing it in that choir he belongs to?

They're past Hjulsbro now.

The suffocating, petit-bourgeois enclave left behind.

Zeke accelerates and the car responds. They turn off.

Ahead of them she can see Landeryd Golf Club. The huge balloonlike building, home to the city's driving range.

A golfer's paradise in this autumn hell.

Where golf balls rain through the air.

19

The golf balls are whining through the air under the metal roof of the hangar-like building, several hundred yards long, bouncing high as they land.

Thirteen places.

The sound the clubs make when they strike the balls is like being hit over the ear.

A bucket of fifty balls costs two hundred kronor. An insignificant sum to anyone who belongs to any of the city's golf clubs.

Putters.

Wooden clubs.

Jerry Petersson was struck on the back of the head with a blunt object, but hardly a golf club, Malin thinks as they approach the slender, tall figure of Katarina Fågelsjö.

"I'm in thirteen. At the far end, next to the wall."

No surprise when they called to say they wanted to talk to her, she knew what had happened, but could hardly be aware of what her brother has just done.

Aggressive swings, curses, balls hitting the walls and ceiling, and the noise is like the inside of a swimming pool, and there's a similarly stale, damp smell, just without the chlorine.

People voluntarily spend the whole afternoon here, Malin thinks as she studies Katarina as she takes an apparently light and elegant swing. Her body is strong, and it's clear that she possesses the self-confidence about herself and her life that everyone with her background has, imprinted on them from the day they open their eyes and see the world for the first time.

Katarina raises a metal club, takes aim and drops her shoulder, and the club makes a fine arc down toward the ball on the tee in the Astroturf.

She must have a low handicap, Malin thinks. And she's right-handed.

Katarina must have seen them from the corner of her eye.

She stops, turns around, looks at them, and steps down from the low platform she's standing on. She holds out her hand, and Malin thinks that she must have been beautiful once, that she almost is now, with the same sharp nose as her brother, fine cheekbones, but there are too many wrinkles in her forehead, too much gray in her shoulder-length blond hair.

Bitter wrinkles. Evidence of discontent around her mouth. Sad eyes, full of a peculiar longing.

She says hello to Malin first, then Zeke.

They show their ID.

Katarina runs a hand over her forehead, and Malin thinks, She's probably only five years older than me, she could have been in the same school as me, ahead of me, the same school as Jerry Petersson. If she didn't go to a private school like Sigtuna or Lundsberg.

"Can we do this here?" Katarina asks, leaning her club on the ground. "Or shall we go to the restaurant?"

"We can do it here," Malin says. "You know why we want to talk to you? We didn't have time to say over the phone."

"Jerry Petersson. I can put two and two together."

"And the fact that your brother tried to drive away from us today."

Katarina's mouth drops open, her eyebrows rise briefly, but just a few seconds later she's collected herself again.

"My brother did what?"

Malin tells her about the car chase, how he tried to escape when they attempted to talk to him, and that he is now being questioned in the police station.

"So he was leaving the Ekoxen?" Katarina said. "He was probably worried you were going to get him for drunk driving. He's been caught before, after a friend's party three years ago, so this time he'd have ended up in prison."

Drunk driving. Driving under the influence of alcohol. I did that yesterday, Malin thinks, batting the thought aside like a golf ball.

"We caught him," Zeke says. "And he was drunk."

"Maybe he tried to escape because he had something to do with Jerry Petersson's murder?" Malin asks, hoping the direct question will provoke a reaction.

"What, my brother kill someone? Hardly."

Katarina's face is completely blank as she waits for the next question, and Malin feels tired just looking at it. It's almost five o'clock already, and even though Malin knows they need to get further with the investigation, all she wants is to be at home, having a shower, and then what?

Feel sorry for myself.

Fucking sorry.

Liquidly sorry.

Her headache has faded, but her body is screaming for more, her angst is like a fist around her heart. Have to get a grip on a hell of a lot of different things. Can I handle that?

And now this woman in front of me, stuck-up and stroppy, yet still somehow open and pleasant. Is that what they call social competence?

"So you don't believe that?" Zeke asks.

"My brother's harmless. Maybe not entirely, but he's certainly not violent."

"Can you tell us anything about him?" Zeke asks.

"He can do that better himself."

Katarina pulls another club from her bag. Looks it up and down.

"I'll get straight to the point," Malin says, thinking, Focus on Katarina herself instead.

"What were you doing last night and this morning?"

"My father was with me yesterday evening. We were drinking tea."

"He told us he left at ten o'clock. What did you do after he left?"

Katarina clears her throat.

"I went to see my lover. Senior consultant Jan Andergren. He can confirm that I was there till this morning."

She gives them a number, which Zeke taps straight into his mobile.

"I like white coats," Katarina jokes. "But you should know that he's only a lover, I've seen him a few times, and I'm not planning to see him many more."

"Why not?" Malin says, and Katarina adopts an expression that seems to say, What business is that of yours?

"Don't you know? The golden rule for affairs. More than five times, and there's a risk you start thinking it's love."

Don't put on airs just because you're fucking a doctor, Malin thinks. Don't try acting the tease with me, Katarina. I'm far too tired to put up with that.

"Did you have any dealings with Petersson?" Zeke asks.

"None at all," she says hesitantly, before carrying on in a firm voice: "Fredrik and Father looked after all that. Why?"

"The sale of the castle," Malin says. "You weren't opposed to it?"

"No. It was time. It was simply time to sell up. Time for the family to move on."

You're saying the same as your father, Axel, Malin thinks. Has he told you what to say?

"You didn't want to take over?"

"I've never had any ambitions of that sort."

The balls are still whining around them.

Pointless projectiles.

What a stupid sport, Malin thinks, as Katarina adjusts the belt of her blue trousers, checks the collar of her pink cotton sweater, and puts the club back in the bag.

"We've heard rumors that you were forced to sell because of financial problems. Is that right?"

"Inspector. We're an aristocratic family that goes back several hundred years. Almost half a millennium. We don't like talking about money, but we have never, I repeat never, had any financial problems."

"Can I ask what your job is?" Zeke asks.

"I don't work. Since my divorce I've been taking it easy. Before that I worked in art."

"Art?"

"I had a gallery specializing in nineteenth-century painting. Mainly reasonably priced Östgöta artists like Krouthén. But some more expensive ones as well. Do you know Eugène Jansson? He was my speciality, along with the female Danish national romantics."

Malin and Zeke shake their heads.

"Did you used to know Jerry Petersson?" Zeke asks.

"No."

"Was your divorce recent?" Malin asks.

"No, ten years ago."

"Children?"

Katarina's eyes darken, she seems to be wondering why this is important.

"No," she replies.

"You were the same age, you and Petersson," Malin says. "Did you go to the same school?"

Katarina stares out at the driving range.

"We were at the Cathedral School. He was in the third year at the same time as my brother when I was in the first year."

Malin and Zeke look at each other.

"I remember him," Katarina goes on, still looking out at the driving range. "But we didn't socialize. He didn't belong to my social circle. But we probably attended a few of the same parties, that couldn't be helped."

No, Malin thinks. All manner of worlds collide in high school, whether you want them to or not. People might well end up at the same parties, but that didn't necessarily mean any more than two strangers visiting the same bar today.

"So what was your gang? Zeke asks.

"A girls' gang."

"So you never saw each other socially?"

Katarina looks at them again, and a flash of sorrow seems to cross her eyes.

"What did I just say?" she says.

"We heard," Malin says.

Katarina's thin lips contract to a thin line.

"And now Jerry Petersson's sitting like some bloody Gatsby out in our castle."

Sudden desperation in both voice and eyes.

"He may well have sat there like Gatsby," Malin says. "But right now he's lying on a mortuary slab over in the National Forensics Laboratory."

Katarina turns away from them again, puts a ball on the tee, strikes at it furiously, and the ball flies off to the right.

"What sort of car do you drive?" Zeke says when she looks back at them again.

"That's my business," Katarina says. "I don't want to be impolite, but that's none of your business."

"There's something you need to understand," Malin says. "As long as we're looking for Jerry Petersson's murderer, every single hair on your backside is our business."

Katarina smiles and says:

"Okay, Inspector, calm down. Nice and calm. I drive a red Toyota, if it's really so important."

Malin turns away.

Walks out of golfing hell. She hears Zeke thank Katarina for her time. Thank god he doesn't apologize for her behavior.

"Be nice to my brother," Katarina calls after them. "He's harmless."

*　　　*　　　*

"Even if you have problems with people like that, you really have got to get a grip. You can't talk to people that way. No matter how rough you're feeling."

Zeke is in the driver's seat, telling her off as they drive out of the parking lot in Landeryd. The rain is still pouring from the sky, and the darkness of the approaching evening makes Linköping another degree less welcoming.

"I don't feel rough," Malin says.

Then she nods.

"You know what it's like. Fucking awful people like that."

And she knows that anger is a way of covering up insecurity, it's kindergarten psychology, and she feels ashamed and hopes Zeke can't see her blushing.

"She's hiding something. Just like her father," Zeke says. "And possibly her brother too."

"Yes, she is," Malin says. "Maybe it's a family trait, playing with the truth."

"Or else they just want to make our job as hard as possible," Zeke says.

They pass the villas of Hjulsbro once more, and the white blocks of rented flats with their balcony corridors opposite, on the other side of Brokindsleden. The rain is driving horizontally across the road, as if the wind and rain were trying to connect the different worlds.

"We'll just have to see if the interview with Fredrik Fågelsjö comes up with anything," Zeke says. "They're probably in the middle of it by now, if he's sobered up a bit."

20

The hands on the clock in interview room one in the basement of Linköping Police Station move silently.

One minute past six.

The grayish-black walls are covered with textured, soundproof paneling, and the halogen lamps are positioned so that they cast cones of light over the four chairs that are fixed to the floor around the oblong metal table. The chairs have only recently been fastened down, after too many suspects ended up smashing them into the walls.

A one-way mirror on one wall opens onto the observation room where Sven Sjöman and Karim Akbar are watching the people inside the room.

Johan Jakobsson is looking at Fredrik Fågelsjö. The blood test showed just under one part per thousand, but he seems to have sobered up rapidly. The look in his eyes in the dim light on the other side of the table is clear and alert. Beside Johan, Waldemar Ekenberg shifts on his chair, trying to get comfortable. Fredrik is dressed in a blue blazer and yellow shirt, and beside him sits his lawyer, a smart fellow named Karl Ehrenstierna whom Johan has met in other interviews, all of which have produced exactly nothing. We'll see, Johan thinks, maybe we can outsmart you this time.

He starts the little tape recorder in the middle of the table.

"Interview with Fredrik Fågelsjö concerning the investigation into the murder of Jerry Petersson, as well as other offenses. Friday, October 24, time 6:04 PM."

Up to now Fredrik has hardly said a word. He said yes when they asked if he wanted a lawyer present at the interview, told them Ehrenstierna's name without giving them his number, probably assumed they had it. Then he asked to call his wife, Christina, and Sven couldn't see any reason not to let him. They had enough to hold him for a number of less serious offenses, but as far as the murder of Jerry Petersson was concerned, Fredrik was so far just a name that had cropped up in the investigation. Not enough for a search warrant in conjunction with a murder investigation, but they had seized his car, which was being examined by Forensics.

"Let's start with today's events," Johan says. "Why did you try to run when the police indicated that you should pull over?"

Fredrik gives his lawyer an anxious look, as if he's wondering how they're going to direct this interview the way they want, and not fall into any traps laid by the police. The lawyer nods at him to answer.

"I got scared," Fredrik says, quickly wiping a few drops of sweat from his upper lip. "I knew I'd had too much to drink. And I didn't want to get caught for drunk driving again and end up inside Skänninge. So I panicked and tried to run. It was as if my mind went blank, and then, once I'd started, there was no going back. Ridiculously stupid. I really must apologize."

"A fucking apology probably isn't going to be enough," Waldemar says.

"No swearing, please," Ehrenstierna says, and Waldemar clenches his jaw and says:

"You could have killed innocent people. We've got you for drunk driving, obstructing police officers, reckless driving, and probably another dozen charges. Are you an alcoholic?"

Ehrenstierna says nothing.

"Perhaps you'd like to admit those offenses?" Waldemar says.

"I won't make the procedure any more difficult," Fredrik says. "And no, I'm not an alcoholic. But sometimes I drink a bit too much. Doesn't everyone? I panicked. And I'm guilty of driving while intoxicated. But that isn't the main reason why I'm sitting here, is it?"

"No," Waldemar says, leaning over the table. "The main reason we want to talk to you is the murder of Jerry Petersson."

"I don't suppose you tried to escape because you thought we were going to arrest you in connection to the murder?" Johan asks.

"My client has already explained why he tried to escape when you attempted to pull him over," Ehrenstierna says.

"I didn't even know that Petersson had been murdered. My lawyer told me a short while ago."

Ehrenstierna nods.

Then the look in Fredrik's eyes changes, and he starts talking before Ehrenstierna has a chance to stop him.

"Let me put it like this. You found the clown dead. Murdered, even. Great news, I don't mind saying so."

Fredrik's body, so tired up to now, comes to life, every muscle seems to flex.

That's cheap, Johan thinks, and looks at Waldemar with a expression that means, Keep pushing.

Ehrenstierna puts a hand on Fredrik's shoulder and says:

"Take it easy, Fredrik."

"So you wanted to see him dead?" Waldemar asks.

"My client isn't going to answer that."

"You can trust us," Johan says. "We mean you well. If you had nothing to do with the murder, then we want to know, and if you did, then we'll try to make the best of the situation. Surely you'd agree that it looks odd that you tried to escape? There's something you want to say. Isn't there?"

"My client won't be answering that either. And he has explained why . . ."

"What were you doing last night and this morning?" Waldemar asks.

"I was at home with my wife."

"Are you sure?" Waldemar says.

"Can she confirm that?" Johan asks.

"She can confirm that," Ehrenstierna says. "They were out at the Villa Italia, in Ledberg, where you caught up with my client."

"So you weren't out at Skogså?" Waldemar says.

Neither of the men on the other side of the table answers.

"We've heard that there were financial difficulties behind the sale of Skogså. Is that correct?" Johan asks instead.

"I was tired of all that crap," Fredrik says. "It was time to sell up. Father's too old, and I didn't want to take over. Nor did my sister."

"So there's nothing you want to tell us? About bad business decisions? About why you hate Jerry Petersson, the clown who took over? The man you wanted to see dead?"

Waldemar's voice is angry as he tosses the words across the table.

"That Petersson," Fredrik Fågelsjö says. "He was the worst sort of upstart, the sort who could never understand the importance of an estate like Skogså. But he paid handsomely. And if you think I had anything to do with this, good luck to you. Prove it. Like I said, I got scared and I panicked. I'm prepared to take my punishment."

"Did you know Petersson from before?"

"I knew who he was," Fredrik says. "We were at the same high school, the Cathedral School, at the same time. But I didn't know him at all. We didn't move in the same circles. We might have been at a few of the same parties. It's a small world, after all."

"So you didn't really have anything to do with each other? Neither then, nor later on?"

"Only when the castle was going to be sold. But even then I didn't actually meet him."

"I'm surprised," Waldemar says. "I thought your sort all went to Sigtuna or Landsberg."

"Lundsberg," Ehrenstierna says. "It's Lundsberg. Even I went to Lundsberg. Have you got any more questions for my client? About his education, or anything else?"

Waldemar gets up quickly, fixing his snake's gaze on Fredrik Fågelsjö's eyes.

"Tell us what you know, you bastard. You're hiding loads of shit, aren't you?"

Fredrik Fågelsjö and his lawyer jerk back.

"You were out at the castle, you wanted to pay Petersson back for taking the land away from you, didn't you? You lost your grip and stabbed him, over and over again. Confess!" Waldemar shouts. "Confess!"

The door of the room flies open, Karim rushes in, switches off the tape recorder, and he and Johan help calm Waldemar down as Sven tells Fredrik and his lawyer that the prosecutor has decided to remand Fredrik into custody under suspicion of aggravated drunk driving and aggravated reckless driving.

Ehrenstierna protests, but feebly, aware that the decision has already been taken and that he can't do anything about it here and now.

Fredrik's face is a mystery, Johan thinks, as the young aristocrat is led out of the room by a uniform.

Noble, but evasive. His anxious eyes superior now. Johan thinks, He knows we don't have anything on him. But he could very well be guilty. And from now on, he's our prime suspect.

Malin drops Zeke off outside his red-painted house.

"Take the car," he says. "But try to drive carefully."

He slams the door behind him, not in anger but in exhaustion, and walks away.

The black tiles of the house are like a reluctant drum for the raindrops.

There's a light on in the kitchen.

A Saturday at work tomorrow. No chance of getting any time off while they've got a completely fresh murder.

Sven Sjöman has called a meeting for eight o'clock. Police Constable Aronsson spoke to Fredrik Fågelsjö's wife, Christina, immediately after Johan Jakobsson and Waldemar Ekenberg finished questioning him. His wife gave him an alibi for the night of the murder, said he probably panicked when they tried to pull him over, that he sometimes drank too much but that he wasn't an alcoholic.

Malin lets the engine run in neutral, trying to summon the energy to drive off into the evening, but how, tell me how, she thinks, am I going to be able to face the hours that remain of today?

She doesn't feel up to getting to grips with anything. What happened yesterday feels unreal, as if it was a thousand years ago, if it actually happened at all.

She puts the car into first gear.

As she's about to drive off she sees Zeke open the front door and run out into the rain, she can see the raindrops almost caressing his shaved head, but it doesn't feel good, she can tell from the look on his face.

Malin winds the window down.

"Gunilla's wondering if you'd like to stay for dinner."

"But not you?"

"Don't be daft, Fors. Come in. Get some hot food. It'll do you good.

"Another time, Zeke. Say hi to Gunilla, and thank her for the offer."

Gunilla?

Wouldn't you rather have Karin Johannison in there? Malin thinks.

"Come in and have something to eat with us," Zeke says. "That's an order. Do you really want to be on your own tonight?"

Malin gives him a tired smile.

"You don't give me orders."

She drives off with the window open; in the rearview mirror she sees Zeke standing in the rain as some autumn leaves shimmer rust-red in the glow of the car's rear lights.

*   *   *

It's dark outside as she drives into the city. Damn this darkness.

What a day. A murder. A dirty great murder. A crazy car chase. An old woman with a shotgun. No time to think about all the other crap. Sometimes she loves all the human manure this city is capable of producing.

Clothes.

Must have clothes.

Maybe I could go out to the house and quickly pick up what I need. But maybe Janne would ask me to stay, Tove would watch me with that pleading look in her eyes, and then I'd want to as well.

Then Malin catches a glimpse of her face in the rearview mirror, and she turns away and suddenly realizes what she's done: She's left the man she loves, she's hit him, she put their daughter in mortal danger, and instead of helping herself move on she's flown straight into her own crap, given in to her worst instincts, given in to her love of intoxication, for the soft-edged cotton-wool world where nothing exists. No past, no here and now, and no future. But it's wrong, wrong, wrong, and she feels so ashamed that it takes over her breathing, the whole of her body, and she wants to drive out to the house in Malmslätt, but instead she drives to Tornby, to the Ikea parking lot, parks in a distant corner and gets out.

She stands in the rain and looks at the darkness around her. The place is completely anonymous and deserted, and even though it's wide open, the light from the retail boxes doesn't reach this far.

She heads over to the shopping center. Wants to call Tove, ask her for advice, but she can't. After all, that's why I'm here, because I've fucked everything up beyond hope of salvation.

She moves through the rows of clothes in H&M, grabbing underwear and socks and bras, tops, trousers and a cardigan. She pays without even trying on the clothes, they ought to fit, the last thing I want right now is to look at myself in a full-length mirror, my swollen body, red face, shame-filled eyes.

She sinks onto a bench in the main walkway of the shopping center. Looks over at the bookshop on the other side, the window full of self-help books. *How to Get Rich on Happiness, Self-Love!, How to Be the Dream Partner!*

Fucking hell, get me out of here, she thinks, as nausea takes a grip on her again.

Outside the newsagent's she sees the flysheets for both *Expressen* and *Aftonbladet*:

"Businessman Murdered in Castle."

"Billionaire Murdered in Moat."

Which one's going to sell best? The second one?

Half an hour later she's sitting at the bar in the Hamlet pub. Tucked away at the end, but still within earshot of the old closet alcoholics that make up the regular clientele.

Two quick tequilas have made her vision agreeably foggy, the edges of the world cotton-wool soft and friendly, and it feels like her heart has found a new, more forgiving rhythm.

Warming spirits.

Happy people.

Malin looks around the bar. People enjoying each other's company.

Mum and Dad. You only had one child, Malin thinks. Why? Dad, I'm sure you would have liked more. But you, Mum, I got in your way, didn't I? That's what you thought, isn't it? You wanted to be more than just an increasingly peculiar secretary at Saab, didn't you?

I've always wanted a brother. Damn you, Mum.

Tove, do you long for a brother?

Damn me.

"I'll have another," Malin says. "A double. And a beer to wash it down."

"Sure," the bartender says. "You can have whatever you want to-night, Malin."

What do I want? Fredrik Fågelsjö thinks as he huddles on the bunk in his cell, absorbing the darkness around him, running his hand over the scratched wall.

Have I ever known?

He's just spoken to his wife for the second time, just an hour ago.

She wasn't angry this time either, demanded no explanation, and instead said just, "We miss you here. Come home soon."

The children were asleep, she wanted to wake them but he said not to, let them sleep, I'd only have to lie to them about where I am.

Victoria, five years old.

Leopold, three.

He can feel the warmth of their bodies as he pulls the blanket around him to keep out the damp chill of the underground room.

He misses them and Christina. He wants to know what he wants. This room doesn't make him feel panicky. He doesn't know why he didn't answer the police's questions, why he kept quiet and lied as Father had asked him to, as if that were somehow his natural role. But he was very vulgar, that aggressive policeman. And in the car chase earlier there had been a feeling of trying to direct his own life, an intoxicating rush of adrenaline and fear.

Fredrik breathes.

Who do I have to prove anything to, really? And Father, you could scarcely bring yourself to accept Christina and her well-educated parents. God knows what you've done to Katarina.

Fredrik closes his eyes.

Sees Christina lie with the children close to her in the double bed in the bedroom in the Villa Italia.

It won't be easy, Fredrik thinks, but from now on nothing's going to come between us.

What's the bartender saying to me? Malin thinks, as she tries to keep her balance on the bar stool, not wanting to fall and lose sight of the bottles on the illuminated shelves along the wall.

There's quite a crowd behind her. She's almost drunk, but she hasn't spoken to anyone.

Then someone taps her on the back.

She turns around. But there's no one there, just her own reflection in the mirror above the bottles.

"I thought I felt someone tap me on the back?" she says, and the bartender grins.

"You're imagining things, Malin. There's no one there," and then she feels it again, sees the empty mirror, but she doesn't turn round, just says, "Stop doing that."

In her intoxication she imagines she can hear a cacophony of voices gathering into one single one, just like out at the forest around Skogså.

"I do what I want," the voice says.

"How did I end up in the water, you have to find out," it goes on a moment later. "Who had I harmed that badly?"

"Go to hell," Malin whispers. "Let me drink in peace."

"Do you miss Tove?" the voice asks.

"Tove could die," Malin yells, "do you hear? And it's my fault." She doesn't notice that the people in the pub have fallen silent, that they're staring at her, wondering why she's tossing words into thin air.

A new tap on the back.

She turns round.

"Time to go home now, Malin," the bartender says, close to her face.

She shakes her head.

"I'm okay. Give me a double. Please."

21

Malin's head rocks from a gentle blow.

Her body, if it's where it ought to be, feels swollen, and every muscle and sinew aches, and what's going on with her head?

Am I dreaming?

I'm still Malin, and the little round planets a few feet above my eyes, why do they look like the drawer handles on the cupboard in the hall?

The bed feels hard beneath me, but I still just want to sleep, sleep, sleep.

Don't want to wake up. And why's the bed so hard?

The sheet is scratching my cheek, it's blue, hard as an old rag rug, and that circle way up there looks like the light in the hall. There's a smell of newsprint, pain. Light flooding in from the left hurting my eyes, what is it that's wrong?

Go back to sleep, Malin.

Forget about today.

Gradually her gaze clears, and she realizes that she's lying on the floor of the hall, just behind the door. She must have fallen asleep there last night, so drunk that she couldn't even get to bed.

But the blow to her head?

A copy of *Svenska Dagbladet* on the floor beside her. Must be the academics' weekend subscription, and the evangelical bastards forgot to change the address when they moved. Unless it's been delivered to the wrong address.

Malin crawls up into a sitting position. She pushes away the bag of clothes that she must have managed to bring home from the pub in spite of everything.

"IT Millionaire Murdered."

The newspaper's type is restrained.

She slithers to the kitchen, looks at the Ikea clock. Half past seven. A working weekend.

If I concentrate I can still make it to the morning meeting, she thinks, but I'll have to hurry.

She gets up, comes close to falling, fainting, and there's only one solution. The bottle of tequila is still on the floor of the living room where she left it the day before yesterday. She gets the bottle, takes seven deep swigs, and by the second she can feel the aches and pains and nausea leaving her body.

A shower. Teeth-brushing, mouthwash, and I'm ready for the morning meeting.

She pulls on the jeans and long-sleeved red cotton top she bought yesterday, the damn trousers are hard to fasten, her stomach is bloated with alcohol and the red top makes her face look even more like a tomato than it already does.

She calls a taxi, they'll have to use another car for work today, she left yesterday's outside the Hamlet.

In the taxi on the way to the police station she reads the paper that the churchy students were probably missing by now.

About their case.

About lawyer Jerry Petersson, the fact that he had been murdered, a bit about his dealings with Goldman, his dubious reputation. Money, figures. Nothing they don't already know.

The taxi blows its horn. The rain is clinging to its chassis.

Her body seems to be working.

She tosses the newspaper on the backseat.

When they reach the turning into the old barracks building where the police and other authorities are based, she asks the taxi driver to stop.

"I can drive all the way to the police station," he says. "That's where you're going, isn't it? I recognize you from the paper."

"I'll get out here."

Evidently I still care a bit about what my colleagues think, Malin thinks as she slams the door of the taxi.

Outside the police station a group of reporters is standing in the rain, Daniel Högfeldt among them. Even in shitty weather like this he manages to look alert.

She goes into the station the back way, through the premises of the district court. As she walks down the corridor past the pale wooden doors of the courtrooms she imagines she can hear rifle shots. She hears them but realizes the sounds are only inside her, and she can't even be bothered to ask why.

"This is Lovisa Segerberg," Sven Sjöman says, putting one hand on the shoulder of the attractive, blond, plain-clothed woman, maybe thirty years old. "She's from Economic Crime in Stockholm. She's here to help us with Petersson's files. A qualified civil economist. And a police officer. Maybe we should introduce ourselves?"

Zeke, Johan Jakobsson, Waldemar Ekenberg, and Malin all say hello and welcome Lovisa to the investigative team.

"Take a seat," Sven says, and Lovisa sits down on an empty chair next to Malin, smiling a polite woman-to-woman smile that Malin doesn't return. Instead she looks at her clothes, how her black knitted sweater with a rosette below her chest looks fashionable, that her black wool trousers are neatly pressed, and that there's something unmistakably Stockholm about her whole appearance, and it makes

Malin feel hopelessly unfashionable and obsolete in her jeans and cheap red cotton top.

"Let's start by summing up the state of the case so far," Sven says. "Day two. You know we have a suspect in custody, Fredrik Fågelsjö, but let's start from the beginning. What else have we managed to find out about the murder of Jerry Petersson?"

The clock on the wall of the meeting room says 8:15.

The formalities and pleasantries took five minutes. It's a good thing Lovisa's here, Malin thinks. The rest of us can barely make sense of a simple tax declaration.

Sven begins by taking it upon himself to put together a timetable of Jerry Petersson's last twenty-four hours alive. Then he goes on:

"Unfortunately the examination of the crime scene hasn't given us anything definite. The rain took care of that. No bloodstains on the gravel. We've had divers searching the bottom of the moat, but they haven't found a knife or anything else that could be the murder weapon. We've drained the moat, but that didn't give us anything either. And I've just received the forensic report about Petersson's car. Nothing. At least we can rule out robbery as a motive, as we suspected yesterday. Nothing seems to be missing from the castle, and there are no signs that anyone searched through the building. And Petersson's wallet was in the inside pocket of the Prada coat he was wearing, with more than three thousand in cash. We're still checking Fredrik Fågelsjö's Volvo."

"Which is black," Zeke adds.

The fish, Malin thinks. What's happened to them? They can't have anywhere to go if the moat's been drained? I'm one of those fish. I'm drowning in the air, isn't that what fish do?

"Prada?" Waldemar says.

"Karin noted the label in her report," Sven says. "So it must be fairly smart."

Then he turns to Malin, says:

"Petersson was found by tenant farmers, Göte Lindman and Ingmar Johansson, who came to the castle to go deer-hunting with Petersson. What did they have to say?"

Malin takes a deep breath.

Recalls the conversations from memory.

She can still taste the tequila in her mouth, and wants more, but instead she gives a short summary of the interviews.

"Does anything point to them?" Sven says once she's finished.

"No," Malin says. "But we'll have to keep the option open. After all, their livelihoods are probably dependent upon those tenancies. We'll have to try to find out if the details of the contracts check out. One of them could have lost it if his whole income was threatened."

Sven nods.

"See what you can find in the files."

"They found the door open," Malin goes on. "And the alarm switched off."

She lets Zeke continue:

"Which could mean that Petersson just popped out for some reason and assumed that he'd be back inside in no time."

Waldemar snorts, says:

"So you're suggesting that could mean Petersson knew the killer? That he just went out to say hello? That he could even have been expecting the murderer?"

"That's all possible," Zeke says. "But we can't draw any definite conclusions. Maybe he went out to get things ready for the hunt and forgot to lock up, or just didn't bother."

"What do we know about the victim?" Sven says.

Petersson.

Jerry.

His face as he was lifted out of the moat, the fish in his mouth, one eye open, surprised, and Malin remembers his appearance now, sees it in a different way in her memory, how handsome he must have been, fairly formidable, no doubt, in the right setting, somewhere like lunch at Riche or Sturehof or Prinsen up in Stockholm: all the places she never went when she was at the Police Academy, the dicks in the shiny suits that she saw on the few occasions when she lost her bearings and ended up on Biblioteksgatan or Strandvägen.

Maybe Petersson was a bastard, the sort of person who thought he was better than everyone else?

Maybe.

But how much of a bastard?

Her thoughts turn to violence. She's seen people adopt it in the course of their actions. How occasionally, reluctantly, she has thought that certain people deserve the violence they suffer, as a consequence of their own actions.

But is that really true? That violence can be deserved? Of course not.

"Johan."

Sven's voice calls her back and she listens to Johan's account of what they know about Jerry Petersson: that he was a successful company lawyer in Stockholm, that he made a fortune from an IT business he invested in at the start as a venture capitalist, that he represented Jochen Goldman the con man, that he bought Skogså Castle from Axel Fågelsjö, that he grew up in Berga, was single, no children, at least none that were registered as his, and a father who had been told of his death the previous day. They hadn't managed to find out much about Jerry Petersson the person. Johan and Waldemar had spent yesterday afternoon speaking to people whose names appeared in the files, including among others Petersson's accountant in Stockholm, but they all described him as impeccable, brilliant, and, as one woman put it: "bloody good-looking."

"We've got thousands of files and documents to go through," Johan concludes. "We might be able to find some potential motives for his murder in there. So far we've been concentrating on Goldman, simply as a way of making a start."

"I can check the IT business and the tenancy agreements," Lovisa says. "That shouldn't take long." The young woman says the words with a professional self-assurance that Malin knows will be needed if she's going to be working with Waldemar.

"We've found a phone number in Spain that probably belongs to Goldman," Johan says. "In Tenerife. We tried calling once, but there was no answer. We thought maybe you could try calling, Malin."

Waldemar adds:

"It seems to make sense for you to call. What with your connections to the island," and to start with Malin is annoyed, the fact that her parents happen to live on Tenerife is no good reason for her to be the one who calls Jochen Goldman. But the irritation fades, and she thinks that Johan and Waldemar are right, they're respecting her way of working, her intuition and belief and faith that things fit together in ways that are often invisible to us.

There are scentless tracks to sniff out.

Invisible images.

Silent sounds.

Mum, Dad. Tenerife.

Goldman. Tenerife.

They don't go together, but it might mean something.

"I'll call after the meeting," Malin says.

"What about his will?" Sven asks. "Do we know anything about that?"

"No, not yet. But his father will inherit everything if there isn't one," Johan says.

Then Zeke tells them what happened when they spoke to Axel and Katarina Fågelsjö. That Katarina has an alibi, that a stressed consultant at the University Hospital had confirmed she was with him. That Axel Fågelsjö has no alibi after ten o'clock.

That both of them claimed that the rumors going around that they sold the estate because of pressing financial difficulties weren't true, that they didn't seem to have a very high opinion of an upstart like Petersson, but that they didn't appear to bear any particular malice toward him, or to have known him before the sale, even though Katarina went to the same high school as him.

"And then there's Fredrik Fågelsjö," Malin says. "The most dramatic thing that happened yesterday."

Zeke describes the car chase. Johan the interview. That Fredrik Fågelsjö claims he panicked because he had been drinking.

"We've got him in custody," Sven says. "We can hold him for a week for other charges related to his capture. We can talk to him again. Press him about the murder, even if he's being held for something else. We'll have to try to talk to him without his lawyer present. I don't think he's telling the whole truth. And I honestly don't know if he's lying about why he tried to run. He seems weak and strong at the same time. But it's extremely suspicious that he tried to escape, isn't it? For the time being, he's our main suspect.

"We need to check the Fågelsjös' finances," Sven goes on. "Dig deeper into the circumstances surrounding the sale of Skogså, see if they really had hit hard times. Segerberg, can you look into that at the same time as everything else? And we need to run an archive check on the Fågelsjös. We're already checking for Petersson."

Lovisa smiles.

Nods.

"I'm happy to work twenty hours a day until we solve this. I've got nothing else to do down here."

She says this without irony, absolutely serious, and Malin sees herself in the young officer's dedication. Admires it, but still feels like warning her that this job can consume your soul if you let it; it's a thousand times easier to take refuge in other people's misfortunes than it is to get to grips with your own, it's a thousand times easier to hide in the dark than to see your own light.

"What about their emails?" Johan asks. "Their mobile-phone records? Are we going to put in a request for those?"

"It's too soon for that," Sven says. "To get permission for that we need a more concrete connection to the murder. You'll have to make do with checking Petersson's records for now.

"What about his relatives?" Sven goes on. "Is there really no one apart from the father?"

"Looks like it," Johan says. "According to the population records."

"Girlfriends?" Malin asks. "He can't have lived out there all on his own, can he? Old girlfriends? Friends? Most perpetrators of this sort tend to belong to the victim's closest circle of acquaintances. Any lovers?"

"Not that we've found so far," Johan says.

"And no one's contacted us," Sven says. "You know how hard it is, trying to piece together someone's life story."

"Maybe he was the sort who used to pay for his fucks?" Waldemar says, and Malin's first instinct is to tell him to show some respect, but something makes her think that Waldemar might be right, in which case no one from Jerry Petersson's past would be coming forward. No prostitute would dare to identify herself in light of the sick legislation covering the subject in Sweden. A lot of men who pay for sex could actually get almost any woman they wanted. But they're still drawn to undemanding, simple sex, free from any romantic entanglement.

"The people we've spoken to only knew him professionally. He seems to have been careful to keep his private life private," Johan says.

A loner, Malin thinks. An eccentric loner in the biggest fucking castle in Östergötland. But no one, no one wants to be alone. Do they?

"He wasn't married," Sven says. "Could he have been homosexual?"

"We don't know," Malin says. "Have we spoken to Petersson's father?" she goes on. "He might know something. About Petersson's sexuality, and a lot of other things besides."

"No," Sven says. "He's only been informed of what's happened so far. Malin, you and Zeke get on with that once you've tried calling Jochen Goldman."

"So soon?" Zeke says. "His son only died yesterday."

"We can't afford to wait."

Malin nods in agreement.

Thinks with distaste about the coming visit. If there's anything that's hard to stomach when you've got a hangover, it's the smell of incontinence pads and catheters.

Åleryd Geriatric Hospital.

The last stop on the line. Maybe he's even in one of the dementia wards?

"What else?"

Sven's voice, alert.

"Malin, anything?"

He's looking at her with an expression that says he knows how hungover she is, but that he's not going to let it affect her work.

She shakes her head.

"We spoke to a Linnea Sjöstedt," Zeke goes on. "An old lady who lives in a cottage on the Skogså estate. She threatened us with a shotgun when we stopped to talk to her."

"She did what?" Sven says, and Malin sees Waldemar grinning.

"Yes, she seemed scared," Zeke says. "She said you never know what you're going to get out there. Well, she's right about that."

"She soon calmed down," Malin says. "She saw a dark vehicle leave the estate sometime late at night. Well, she thinks she did. She wasn't sure if she was dreaming or not."

"Dreaming?"

"Yes, she says she has a bit of trouble distinguishing between dream and reality."

Sven shakes his head.

"What sort?"

"She didn't know."

"We'll have to make a note of it. What does Axel Fågelsjö drive?"

"A dark-blue Jaguar," Malin replies.

A dark car.

She could have seen Axel Fågelsjö. Or Johansson and Lindman as they arrived, Malin thinks. Or someone else. One of the children? Maybe Katarina Fågelsjö has another car? Someone from Petersson's past? Goldman?

"Have we had any tip-offs from the public?"

Waldemar sounds hopeful.

But Sven shakes his head.

"We'll have to keep working on what we've got for now. And hope the general public come up with something now that it's out in the media and Karim has put out an appeal."

"The *Correspondent*'s gone big on this today," Johan says. "The national media too. Murder, car chase, Fredrik Fågelsjö in custody."

"Anything we don't already know?" Sven asks.

Johan shakes his head.

"We're bound to get something about his business dealings," Lovisa says. "Even if it's anonymous. That's if there's anything there."

"If he was a bit shady, then he could have had contacts in the underworld here in the city," Waldemar says. "You're sure you don't want me to ask around among my contacts?"

"You just want to avoid the paperwork," Sven says with a laugh. Then he's serious again. "For the time being, you prioritize the paperwork, understood?"

Waldemar nods in response.

"Malin," Sven goes on. "Call Goldman. See what he has to say, if that really is his number."

Malin closes her eyes.

Fredrik Fågelsjö trying to run.

A body dumped in a moat. By Fredrik? Maybe, maybe not.

In some ways Petersson's going to be left in the black water forever.

Together with the dozens, maybe hundreds of other ancient souls, shackled in stone and time, Malin thinks. Caught in their own misfortune, their fate impossible to escape or come to terms with.

Loneliness runs like a red thread through human history, Malin thinks. It's the underlying note of our stories.

22

Tenerife.

Like a poem, a sketch within Malin.

Scorched mountains, slumbering volcanoes, an eternally shining sun above a muddle of houses. Swaying palm trees, sunbeds in long rows along the beaches, pools casting glittering reflections on mutated liver spots, cancer forcing its way through the skin and on into the bloodstream, and in a few months the dreams are over, those dreams of eternal life in the sun.

Fraying pictures from her parents' paradise.

The flat she knows her mother thinks is far too small, maybe that's why she and Tove have only ever been invited out of politeness, because Mum thinks the place she's found for herself in the sun is too meagre?

Maybe Mum just wants to be left in peace. Ever since I first learned the word I've had the feeling that you're avoiding me, that you're pulling away. Are you ashamed of something, Mum, but don't want to admit it? Are you trying to avoid me so you don't have to see yourself in the mirror? Maybe it's okay to do that with grown-up children, but not the way you did with me when I was four, when I somehow worked out that that was what was going on.

And what would we say to each other, Mum? Malin thinks as

she sits at her desk, surfing between various articles about Jochen Goldman.

On several sites he's described as the worst con man in Swedish history. It still isn't clear how many millions he got away with when they emptied Finera Finance of all its assets. And by the time it was uncovered Jochen Goldman had fled the country and his bourgeois roots on the island of Lidingö, the wealthy enclave on the edge of Stockholm.

He managed to elude the police, and Interpol.

Jochen Goldman, seen in Punta del Este in Uruguay.

In Switzerland.

In Vietnam.

Jakarta. Surabaya.

But always one step ahead of the police, as if they didn't want to catch him, or else he had his own sources inside the force.

Jerry Petersson had been his lawyer. His intermediary in his dealings with the authorities and media at home. Goldman had written two books during his ten years on the run. One book about how he emptied the business and claimed he had every right to do so, then another about life as a fugitive, and to judge from the reviews Jochen Goldman had tried to portray himself as a capitalist James Bond.

But a long way short of that sort of nobility, Malin thinks.

Before Goldman carried out his heist, he spent three years in prison for fraud. At the same time he was also convicted of making unlawful threats, actual bodily harm, and extortion.

Pictures of him on the run.

A sharp nose in what was otherwise a round face, slicked-back hair, playful brown eyes, and blond hair down to his shoulders. Big yachts, shiny sports cars made by Königsegg.

Then, once his alleged crimes relating to Finera Finance had passed the statute of limitations, he popped up on Tenerife. A report in the online version of the business daily, *Dagens Industri*, shows a smiling, suntanned Goldman beside a black-tiled pool with a view of the sea and the mountains. A shimmering white house in the background.

Mum's dream.

This is what it looks like.

White-plastered concrete, glass, maybe a garden with scrupulously neat plants and bulging armchairs to lean back in and forget all the denial and bitterness.

Finally she comes to an old report in the business weekly, *Veckans Affärer*.

The tone is vague, hinting that Jochen Goldman may have got rid of people who got in his way. That people who had done business with him had disappeared without a trace. The article concludes by pointing out that these are rumors, and that the myth of Goldman survives and grows precisely through such rumors.

Malin takes out the note with the number that might be Goldman's.

Nods to Zeke on the other side of the desk.

"Okay, I'm going to call our shadow now."

Waldemar Ekenberg is drumming his fingers on the desk in the cramped meeting room. He fiddles with his mobile, lights a cigarette without asking the newcomer, Lovisa Segerberg, if she minds, but she lets him smoke, carries on calmly reading a summary that she's found in one of the black files.

"Restless?" Johan Jakobsson says from his place.

"No problem," Waldemar says. "But I'm running out of cigs."

"They sell them in the canteen over in the courthouse, don't they?"

"That's shut on Saturdays. I saw they had a special offer on boxes of ten-packs down at Lucullus. Can I have fifteen minutes to pop down there?"

Johan smiles.

"Is that really a good idea? We need all three of us here, Waldemar. Come on, what the hell."

"You know how I get if I haven't got any cigs."

"You can cadge one off someone, can't you?"

"Fuck, the air in here is terrible."

"Maybe because you smoke," Lovisa says from her chair.

"Go on, then," Johan says. "But watch yourself, Waldemar. Watch yourself."

"I'm only going to buy cigs," Waldemar says with a grin.

The Spanish number is engaged the first time Malin dials, but the second time the phone is picked up on the fourth ring, and a nasal, slightly hoarse voice says:

"Jochen, who is this?"

A voice from Tenerife. Clear skies, sun, a bit of a breeze. And no fucking rain.

"My name is Malin Fors, I'm a detective inspector with the Linköping Police. I was wondering if you had a moment to answer a few questions?"

Silence.

For a few moments Malin thinks Jochen Goldman has hung up, then he clears his throat and says with an amused chuckle:

"All my dealings with the authorities go through my lawyer. Can he contact you?"

The cat after the mouse.

The mouse after a bit of string.

You miss the game, Malin thinks. Don't you?

"That's just it, the lawyer Jerry Petersson, the man who represented . . ."

"I know what's happened to Jerry," Goldman says. "I manage to read the papers down here, *Malin*."

And you've still got your contacts, Malin thinks.

"And you know why I want to ask you a few questions?"

"I'm all ears."

"Were you in Tenerife on the night between Thursday and Friday?"

Goldman laughs, and Malin knows the question is banal, but she has to ask it, and it's just as well to get it out of the way.

"I was here. Ten people can confirm that. You can't think I had anything to do with the murder?"

"We don't think anything at this point in time."

"Or that we had a difference of opinion, Jerry and me, so that I sent a hit man to get my revenge? Forgive me if I can't help laughing."

"We're not insinuating anything of the sort. But it's interesting that you should mention that."

Another silence.

Flatter him, Malin thinks. Flatter him, then maybe he'll drop his guard.

"Looks like you've got a pretty nice house down there."

More silence. As if Goldman is looking out over his property, the pool, and the sea. She wonders if her flattery makes him feel threatened.

"I can't complain. Maybe you'd like to visit? Swim a few lengths in the pool. I heard you like swimming."

"So you know who I am?"

"You were mentioned in *Svenska Dagbladet*'s article about the murder. Someone googled you. Doesn't everyone like swimming? I'm sure you look good in a bathing suit."

His voice. Malin can feel it eating into her. Next question:

"So there were no problems between you and Jerry Petersson?"

"No. You need to bear in mind that for many years he was the only person who stood by me and took my side. Sure, he got paid well for it, but I felt I could trust him, that he was on my side. I regard him, or rather regarded him, as one of my best friends."

"When did you stop regarding him as one of your best friends? Recently, or earlier?"

"What do you think, Malin? Recently. Very recently."

"In that case, I'm sorry for your loss," Malin says. "Will you be coming up for the funeral?"

"When's it going to be?"

"The date hasn't been set yet."

"He was my friend," Goldman says. "But I've got other things to do apart from grieve. I don't believe in looking backward."

"Do you know of anyone else who might have had any reason to want to harm Jerry Petersson? Anything you think we should know?"

"I mind my own business," Goldman says. Then he adds: "Was there anything else?"

"No," Malin says, and the line goes quiet, and the fluorescent light above her head starts to flicker, as though it were flashing Morse code from the past.

One of your best friends, Jochen?

What do you know about friendship and trust?

Nothing.

But what do I know?

Not much, I have to admit, but there's one thing I do know, and I've known it since the very first time we met:

I wouldn't want to be standing in your way if you thought you'd been let down.

I felt drawn to you from the start. I was appointed to represent you when you were accused of beating up one of the partners in the business, when he had a heart attack. And I realized I enjoyed your company, basking in the reflected glory of your Jewish chutzpah, your cheekiness. It was like you gave the finger to everyone who got in your way, no matter who they were.

But friends, Jochen?

Come off it.

You could well be the only person I've met in the last few years who's actually frightened me.

Neither of us was, or still is, in your case, the sort who paid the slightest attention to friendship. That sort of thing's for queers and women, isn't it?

Your ruthlessness. Your contacts.

We were both smart. But maybe you got the better of me in the end? Or did I get the better of you? Maybe we did have a sort of friendship, the sort where two people devour each other's souls, getting close to the other and seeing themselves reflected in each other's shortcomings and successes, making them their own. Maybe it was that rarest sort of friendship, truly equal, and therefore so fragile? Why cling to something when there's not really anything to lose?

Two men.

Our paths crossed, we were fated to meet, and we had in common the fact that we weren't going to let anything or anyone stand in the way of what we wanted. But you were more stupid and more courageous than me, Jochen, and I had more money than you, but what did that matter? I was envious of your ruthlessness, even if it sometimes scared me.

Jochen, I see your suntanned body on the shiny chrome sunbed beside the black chlorinated water.

I see Malin Fors at her desk.

She has her head in her hands, wondering how she's going to get through the day. Then she thinks about me. The way I was lying face-down in the moat, dead, I've accepted that now, and the sight of me there, or being lifted up through the air with my body punctured by senseless brutality won't leave her alone, but it gives her something to think about, and that makes it irresistible to her.

Violence offers her some resistance. She hopes it can tell her something about who she is.

She needs me. She suspects as much.

Or else she already knows all too well. Just as I know what the boy suspected when the rays of the low autumn sun hit his eyes.

23

The light pulsates in the eyes of the boy who owns the playground of Ånestad School.

The previous week the retirement age in Social Democratic Sweden was lowered to sixty-five, and a few months ago the Mariner 10 spacecraft flew past Mercury and sent pictures of the lonely planet back to earth.

Here and now, in the school playground, in the sharp rays of the sun, the verdant foliage of the birch trees rustles, and the boy runs after the ball, catches it with one foot, spins around, and then kicks the white leather ball, and the ball shoots off toward the fence where Jesper is standing, ready to fend it off, but something goes wrong. The ball hits his nose, and the blood that gushes out of his nostrils a moment later is a deeper, livelier red than the color of the bricks in the walls of the low school building.

Eva, the teacher, saw what happened and rushes over to the boy. Yelling, she grabs his arm and shakes him before comforting the crying Jesper. She seems to want to scold rather than offer comfort, and she shouts right in the boy's ear: "I saw that, Jerry, I saw that, you did that on purpose," and he gets dragged away, he knows he didn't hurt anyone on purpose, but maybe he ought to, he thinks as the door of the classroom closes and he is expected to wait for something, but what?

Jesper.

A doctor's kid from the villas of Wimanshäll. His dad's evidently the sort of doctor who cuts people up.

The boy already knows that they treat the kids from the villas differently from him and the others from the blocks of flats in Berga.

It happens in the little things they think nine-year-olds don't notice: who gets to sing the solo at the end of year assembly, who is suspected of misbehaving on purpose, who gets most attention and praise in class.

So a girl sings in the gymnasium, two boys play the flute, and he doesn't recognize any of them from the place where he lives, and all of them apart from him are dressed in white, and all of them apart from him have their parents there.

But he doesn't feel lonely, feels no shame, he's figured out that shame, even if he doesn't understand the word itself, is pointless. That he isn't like Mum or Dad.

Unless he is, really? When he stands in the second row on the penalty line of the handball court and is expected to sing songs decided by others for people he doesn't care about, is he not like Mum and Dad then? Doesn't everyone want him to be like his parents then?

Maybe he did aim for the nose after all?

Enjoyed watching the blood gush out from stupid Jesper's nose, like it had been cut by the blades of a lawnmower?

There, in the gym hall, he actually knows nothing about the world, except that he is going to make it his.

He spends all summer drifting around the backyard on his own. He spends many summers doing this.

Mum has long since given up.

She developed an allergy to the cortisone they pumped into her to help the ache in her joints, and becomes stiffer and stiffer in a whimpering, corrosive pain that is gradually wearing away the woman she once was to the sum total of mute fury. Grandma has had a stroke, the cottage has been sold, Dad accepted a severance package from Saab and has drunk the last of the pay-off during the autumn. They had no need for his skills when they went over to production of the Viggen. He could have got work as a cleaner, or in the canteen, but wasn't it better that he took the money, and looked ahead, to the future?

Dad likes the company of the Parks Department workers. The lawnmower, with its comfortably sprung seat. The blokes in the Parks team don't judge him, they don't judge their own.

And the boy longs for the end of the summer holidays, for football training to start again. There are no differences out on the pitch. On the pitch he decides. On the pitch he can be a bit rougher, and what does it matter if the boy from Sturefors falls badly and breaks his arm?

He has friends. Like Rasmus, who's the son of a sales manager for Cloetta chocolate. They moved here from Stockholm, and one evening the boy is around at Rasmus's when Rasmus's dad has business colleagues there for dinner, and his dad asks Rasmus to show the guests that he can do forty push-ups in a row, and someone suggests a competition. And then they are lying there on the parquet floor of the living room, him and Rasmus, doing push-ups alongside each other, and he goes on and on, long after Rasmus is lying flat on the floor and their audience are shouting: "Enough, enough, point taken, young man."

Rasmus's dad says: "Rasmus, he's not too good at school. But Jerry's supposed to be pretty smart." Then he sends Rasmus to bed and the boy has to leave, and he is eleven years old and is left standing in the cold autumn evening outside the sales manager's rented villa in Wimanshäll looking up at the vibrant starry sky.

He goes home. The windows of the blocks of flats are like closed eyes, their bodies black shapes against the dark sky.

Mum is asleep in bed.

Dad is asleep on the green sofa.

Beside him a pizza box and half a bottle of Explorer Vodka. The flat stinks of dirt.

But this isn't my crap, the boy thinks as he creeps into bed beside his mother, feeling the heat from her sleeping body.

24

At quarter past eleven Waldemar Ekenberg pulls up outside a rundown workshop in Tornby industrial estate.

It has finally stopped raining, but the low, drifting clouds almost seem to be licking the shabby corrugated roof, where large flakes of red-brown plastic paint are flapping in the wind.

There is no sign above the two large black garage doors, but Waldemar knows what's concealed inside: a car-mechanics workshop where no cars are ever repaired. The entire thing is a front for laundering money from various criminal activities. But the man behind it, Brutus Karlsson, is a smart bastard that they've never managed to get for anything worse than actual bodily harm.

Waldemar gets out of the car.

Walks calmly toward the workshop and knocks on one of the doors, hears steps approaching within.

It makes sense to use someone like Brutus, use him to get information. Several times he's actually pointed Waldemar in the right direction, when they've had a case involving one of his competitors. Brutus's honor among thieves goes no further than people on the same side as him.

"Open up!" Waldemar shouts. "Open up!"

Brutus will recognize my voice, he thinks, and there's a mechanical sound as the door slides up.

"You?" Brutus says. "What the fuck do you want?"

The man in front of him, in jeans and a leather jacket, is short but broad-shouldered, and Waldemar knows perfectly well that there's violence in that body. There are rumors that Brutus was behind several severe beatings in the underworld. Among other things, he's suppose to have crushed the spine of some bloke from Poland.

Brutus's face is broad, and there's a scar across his nose that doesn't sit well with his blond hair.

"Can I come in."

A question, yet not a question.

Behind Brutus in the shabby garage stand three men of Slavic appearance. They're all wearing Adidas tracksuits and seem to have very little to offer society.

Waldemar steps inside.

The garage door closes behind him.

In the center of the workshop stands a table surrounded by six chairs. There are a few tools on a workbench, but there's no smell of oil or petrol, just damp.

Waldemar thinks it's best to get straight to the point.

"Jerry Petersson," he says. "Does that name mean anything to you?"

Brutus looks at him.

"And who the hell is that?"

"You know who," Waldemar says, taking a step closer to him.

The three Slavs move closer, their eyes darkening, and Waldemar sees one of them clench his fists.

"So you come waltzing in here with your arrogant pig's attitude, asking about some fucking bastard?" Brutus says.

"Jerry Petersson."

"I know who he is. Don't you think I read the papers?"

"Well?"

"Well what?"

Waldemar takes a quick step forward and takes a firm grip of Brutus's jaw with one hand.

"Stop playing so fucking tough, you little shit. Do you know if Jerry Petersson had any dealings with anyone on your side of the law?"

The Slavs hesitate, waiting for a signal from Brutus, and with his free hand Waldemar pulls his pistol from the holster beneath his jacket.

"Okay, okay," Brutus says in a slurred voice. "I can assure you of one thing. Petersson had nothing to do with anyone on this side anywhere round here. If someone like him had been involved, I'd have known about it. Let go, for fuck's sake."

And Waldemar lets go, takes a step back and puts his pistol back in the holster, and as he is snapping it shut he realizes his mistake. One of the Slavs flies at him, and Waldemar feels a fist hit him over one eye, and he falls to the filthy gray-painted floor of the workshop. The three Slavs hold him down, their breath smells sourly of garlic, and all he can see is their unshaven cheeks.

Brutus's scarred face above Waldemar.

"Who the fuck do you think you are? Coming here like this. Throwing your weight about. Do your colleagues even know you're here?"

And Waldemar feels fear grip his stomach, no one knows where he is, anything could happen now.

"They know where I was going. They'll be here if I'm not back within an hour."

Brutus gestures with his head, and the Slavs let go of Waldemar.

"Get up," he says.

Then Waldemar is standing facing him, the Slavs in a circle around them.

An arm flies out and Waldemar ducks instinctively, but the blow hits him on the cheek. Then another, to his left eye.

"What the fuck are you doing, beating up a cop?" Waldemar shouts.

"Listen," Brutus says. "I've got enough shit on you to get you put away. I can dig out a dozen men you've beaten up in the course of your duties."

Two quick punches.

A burning pain and Waldemar spits, realizes he has to get out of there, have a cigarette.

"Fuck off now, pig," Brutus says, and behind him Waldemar hears the door rattle, and thinks, fucking hell, how long before I can retire?

Malin and Zeke have picked up the car from outside Hamlet, and now they're waiting outside a room in Åleryd Geriatric Hospital while the nurses change Åke Petersson's incontinence pad.

Zeke didn't ask about the car, and Malin was glad he didn't, the last thing she wants is a stern lecture.

From inside the room they hear groaning but no whining, no cross words. The walls of the corridor are painted white, stenciled with pink flowers. A clock with a white face and black hands sticks out from the wall. It says 2:20, and Malin can feel the pizza she's just eaten at the Conya pizzeria churning in her stomach. But the fat has soothed her hangover, and she can't feel any grimier than she already does. Must go to the gym, she thinks. Sweat all the crap out.

Thank god Zeke hasn't mentioned what she told him yesterday, about leaving Janne again.

The smell here.

Ammonia and disinfectant, cheap perfume and excrement, and the odor that slowly dying old people give off.

A man in a wheelchair is staring out at the rain through a window at the end of the corridor. It stopped a while ago, but not for long. How much can it actually rain?

Then the door opens. A young blond nurse shows them in. In the bed, its top end propped up, sits a thin man with a chiseled face, and Malin thinks that he looks like his son, his dead son, and what would have happened if Tove died, if she had died in the flat in Finspång more than a year ago?

Everything would be over.

But in the man's watery gray alcoholic's eyes there is no grief, just loneliness. He has one hand clenched into a stroke victim's claw, his right hand, so maybe he can still talk, but what if he's mute, what if he has trouble distinguishing dreams from reality? What do they do with the conversation then?

One of his eyes, on his lame side, seems blind, fixed in its socket, a broken, rigid camera, only capable of filming black.

"Come in," Åke Petersson says as the other nurse leaves the room. One corner of his mouth droops when he talks, but it doesn't seem to affect his speech.

"You can sit over there."

By the wall is a worn green sofa. Brown curtains cover the window, shutting out the season.

It's uncomfortable, and Malin looks at the framed photographs on the table beside Åke, the woman, young and beautiful, then older with eyes weary from life.

"Eva. Taken by rheumatism. She died of an allergic reaction to the cortisone when she was forty-five. She took all that she had in the house, must have hoped her allergy to the medicine had gone."

Jerry.

Your mum. So she died. How old would you have been then? Ten? Fifteen?

"That's when I stopped drinking," Åke says, and it's as if he wants to tell them his whole life story, relieved that somebody finally might want to hear it. "I pulled myself together. Stopped working for the parks, got some training in computers. Got a job doing data entry."

"Sorry for your loss," Zeke says.

"We would have preferred to wait," Malin says. "But . . ."

"He was my son," Åke says. "But we didn't have much contact over the last twenty-five years."

"You had a falling-out?" Malin asks.

"No, not even that. He just didn't want anything to do with me. I never understood why. After all, I stopped drinking when he was sixteen."

Did you hurt him? Malin wonders. Was that why?

"Maybe I wasn't the best father in the world. But I never hit the lad. Nothing like that. I think he just wanted to get away from everything I stood for. I think he felt that way even when he was a child. He was better than me, to put it bluntly."

"What was he like as a child?" Malin asks.

"Impossible to handle. Did crazy things, got into fights, but he was good at school. We lived in a rented flat in Berga, but he went to the Ånestad School with all the doctors' kids. And he was better than them."

"What was he like toward you? And you to him?"

The words literally pour from Åke.

"I worked a lot when he was a kid. A hell of a lot. That was when things were going well in the aviation industry."

The old man twists in the bed, reaching for a glass from the bedside table and drinking the transparent liquid through a straw.

"Do you know if he had any enemies?"

Zeke's voice is soft, hopeful.

"I knew no more about his life than I read in the papers."

"Do you know why he bought Skogså? Why he wanted to move back here?"

"No. I called him, but he hung up every time he heard it was me."

"Anything that might have happened when you were still in touch?"

The old man seems to consider this, his pupils contracting, then he says:

"No. Of course he was an unusual person, the sort people used to notice, but nothing special ever happened. I really didn't know much about his life even back then. When he was at high school. Before he moved to Lund. He never used to tell me anything."

"You're sure of that?" Malin asks. "Try to remember."

The old man closes his eyes and sits in silence.

"Could he have been homosexual?"

Åke remains calm when he replies:

"I can't imagine that he was. I seem to remember him liking girls.

When he was at high school there were several girls who used to phone the flat in the evenings."

"What was Jerry like in high school, generally?"

"I don't know. He'd pretty much turned his back on us by then."

"So Jerry moved to Lund?"

"Yes. But by then he'd broken off all contact."

"What about before that?"

But Åke doesn't answer her question, and says instead:

"I did my grieving for Jerry a long time ago. I knew he'd never come back to me, so I got all the sadness out of the way in advance, and now he's gone all I've got is confirmation of what I already felt. Strange, isn't it? My son is dead, murdered, and all I can do is revisit feelings I've already had."

Malin can feel that her marinated brain isn't keeping her thoughts in order, and they wander off to Tenerife, to Mum and Dad on the balcony in the sun, the balcony she's only seen in pictures.

And pictures, black and white, emerge from her memory, she's very young and wandering round the room asking for her mum, but Mum isn't there, and she doesn't come home either, and she asks Dad where Mum's gone, but Dad doesn't answer, or does he?

Strange, Malin thinks. I always remember Mum as being there, yet somehow not. Maybe she wasn't even there?

Tove.

I'm not there. And she feels acutely sick, but manages to control the gag reflex.

Then she forces herself back to the present, and stares at the wall of the room. A shelf full of books. Literary fiction, by famous difficult authors: the sort Tove devours and which she can't stand.

"I started reading late in life," Åke says. "When I needed something to believe in."

*   *   *

Dad!

Dad, Dad, Dad!

What would I need you for? To raise my hand against?

You know why Mum took the cortisone, the pain in her body ended up as pain in her soul.

You dragged yourself up from that green sofa for your own sake, not mine, and what did you get up for? Sitting and programming the simplest sort of code, the only thing your pickled brain could handle.

I see you there in bed, your cramping stroke-paralyzed half-body is like a physical embodiment of the muteness that always characterized your side of the family, those taciturn, useless men.

You tried to contact me, Dad. But I wouldn't take your calls. What would we have said to each other?

Would we have spent Christmases in Berga eating cheap sausages? Meatballs, Jansson's Temptation, pickled herring ad nauseam?

You stopped trying to contact me.

Certain doors have to be closed for others to open. That's just the way it is. But at the same time: Is there anything more exciting than a locked door?

I had been hoping you'd get in touch when I moved back to the city. When I bought the castle. I could have had you driven out there, I could have shown you my home.

Someone else could have come too.

There's something tragic about you now, as you tell the nurse to angle the blinds so you can look out at the rain. You speak to her nicely, with a meekness you've learned to express perfectly.

You look out into the room.

One eye blind after the stroke.

You blink.

As if you can see something you could never see before.

Is it me you can see, Dad?

25

The phone in her hand shaking. The living room of the flat dark, as if darkness could subdue her nerves.

I'm scared, nervous about calling my own daughter. I've spent two days being scared to talk to her. Is that really true?

The third ring cuts off. Crackling. Fragments of a voice.

"Tove? Is that you?"

"Mum!"

"I can hardly hear you, the line's really bad for some reason."

"I can hear you."

"Hang on, I'll go over to the living-room window, you know reception's a bit better there."

"Okay, Mum, go to the window."

"There, can you hear me any better now?"

"I can hear you better now."

"Are you coming over this evening?"

"It's already evening, Mum. I'm out at Dad's."

"So you're not coming?"

"It's a bit late."

"Maybe tomorrow, then."

"I've arranged to meet Filippa tomorrow. We're going to the cinema. Maybe I could stay over afterward?"

"I think I'll be at home. But you've probably read in the paper about the man who was found out at Skogså. So I might have to work. But you'd be okay here on your own, wouldn't you? I might have to come out to the house and pick up a few clothes and things."

"Let's talk tomorrow, Mum."

Then Tove hangs up, and Malin looks out of the living-room window at the rain that seems to be trying to whip God out of the church over there.

Tove.

It's as if there's a great chasm between what I ought to do and what I'm actually doing. She wants to call Tove again, just to hear her voice, try to explain why she is the way she is, does what she does, but she doesn't even know why herself.

And Tove wanted to end the call quickly, she didn't pick up Malin's remark about maybe coming over tomorrow.

Why?

Does Tove think I'm going to go back?

Could that be it?

Maybe she's had enough of me? Is she holding back to protect herself?

In the gushing water in the gutter outside, bloated bodies float past. Shiny, covered in silvery drops, with teeth that glow white in the darkness.

Where do all these rats come from? Malin thinks. From the underground caves where we try to conceal all our human shortcomings?

Then she thinks about her conversation with Tove, how people can avoid talking about the things that matter to each other, even though the world they share is collapsing. How a mother and daughter can do this. How she herself has never even spoken to her own mother like that.

*   *   *

The rest of the day had been fairly hopeless for her and Zeke. There had been another press conference, in which Karim hadn't given the vultures anything at all.

But Lovisa Segerberg, Johan Jakobsson and Waldemar Ekenberg had had a good day in their stinking strategy room.

In a way that struck Malin as miraculous, Lovisa had managed to dig out information that proved that the Fågelsjö family had indeed fallen upon hard times, and that was why they had had to sell Skogså to Jerry Petersson.

They met up inside the windowless room full of documents and files. The entire investigating team, including Sven Sjöman and Karim Akbar.

It was almost four o'clock, and during the course of the day Waldemar had managed to injure his face in a way that none of them wanted to ask about. One eye was swollen shut and dark blue, and his cheek was vivid shades of blue and lilac.

"I walked into a fucking lamppost when I was going to get cigarettes," Waldemar said, but everyone in the room knew that wasn't true, and Malin thought that he'd finally been given a taste of his own medicine.

Waldemar looked considerably more worn out than usual when he declared: "Only two days into this investigation, and I'm already sick of this paperwork Hades."

They had all laughed at the expression.

Paperwork Hades.

A kingdom of death for paper, and a hell on earth for police officers.

Malin had told them about her conversation with Jochen Goldman, how he had seemed almost amused by her call, then they had talked about Petersson's father.

Then sudden seriousness when Lovisa started talking.

"I've got hold of the records of transactions Fredrik Fågelsjö conducted at the Östgöta Bank during the year before last. Evidently he picked up a lot of stock options, risked a lot of money, and most of them went against him."

"And?" Zeke asked, and Malin was glad he asked the question.

"He lost a great deal of money. Far more than he invested. But the day after Skogså was sold, the debts were all written off."

"So you're saying that Skogså was sold to cover up the mistakes?" Karim said.

Lovisa nodded.

"Probably, yes."

"So old Axel Fågelsjö can't be very happy with his son," Malin said.

"I doubt it," Lovisa said. "I can't find any definite proof of it, but he might have had power of attorney to do what he wanted with the family's money."

"He does work at the bank, after all," Sven said. "He'd have had plenty of opportunities to conduct his own affairs."

"Doesn't that go against good banking ethics?" Waldemar asked.

"Only if you're a broker yourself," Lovisa replied.

"He's an advisor," Zeke said. "It said so in the annual report."

"Well, now we know that it isn't just a rumor that the Fågelsjös were in financial difficulties," Sven said. "That backs up our suspicions against Fredrik. Now we know for certain that he could have been angry, possibly even furious, that the family lost Skogså, and maybe he took that anger out on Petersson. We also know that in all likelihood he was the reason the family lost the estate. Of course we'll have to interview him about it tomorrow morning. But there's not really any reason to question the other members of the family about this, is there? They've just been withholding the truth to protect the family name, and they'd probably just close ranks, so we'll wait until we've got something more concrete. I know we all think they're hiding a lot from us, but for the time being we're just going to have to try to uncover their deepest secrets without actually talking to them. If we do find anything, then any future interviews will be all the more effective. And maybe Fredrik Fågelsjö himself will reveal something. He might be softening up down there in his cell."

And Malin thought of Fredrik, maybe lying curled up on his bunk, alone, in the way that only a murderer can be alone.

But she has trouble believing that.

Then Sven again:

"Have we dug out anything else?"

"No," Waldemar said, and Lovisa and Johan agreed.

"We'll keep going with the tenancy agreements and the IT company. Petersson doesn't seem to have had a will."

"Well, good work so far," Karim said, and it struck Malin that the divorce seemed to have taken all the fight out of him, and she knew he shared her sense of loss, that he longed for his wife and son, that he was trying to find an opening back to everyday life, a crack to crawl through.

Malin has sat down in the living room.

She's resisting, just as Åke Petersson must have done. The most sensible thing would be to pour the remaining contents of the bottle of tequila down the sink out in the kitchen, but she can't bring herself to do that.

You never know when it might come in handy. Now, perhaps?

I should have told Tove to get a taxi. Any other mother would have done anything to see their daughter.

But not me.

I let the conversation run into the sand, I couldn't handle it.

How did Tove sound? Disappointed, alone? Neutral? Keeping her distance? She didn't actually want to come.

Have I given in to my fear now? Malin wonders. Have I realized that I can't keep you safe forever, Tove?

You can actually die, beloved daughter.

I learned that last autumn.

And that's why I daren't love you, look after you, because I'm so damn scared of that pain, just the thought of it makes me want to wipe out my own consciousness.

What's wrong with me, unable to deal with the most basic genetic love of all? Tove, I understand if you hate me.

I should have asked to talk to Janne. Checked if I could pick up my things.

But out of all the possessions she has out in the house in Malmslätt, the only ones she misses are the files relating to the case of Maria Murvall. She would have liked to have them with her now, spread out across the floor, trying to fit reality into a system, construct a pattern, a structure that would explain all the mysteries, make all the subtleties look obvious, a solution to a riddle that explains her to herself.

But maybe it's just as well that the files are out in Malmslätt.

Because it must be a hopeless case.

Jerry Petersson.

Jerry.

A rented flat in Berga, maybe no bigger than mine, possibly even smaller. Did he hit you? Did he? When he was drunk? Or did he just frighten you? I hit Janne. The same thing? No. Hitting a child is different, isn't it? And your mother, was she drugged up with all her painkillers? Did she take the cortisone to put an end to it all? And you watched all this happen, not the subdued drama I had out in the villa in Sturefors, with Mum and Dad living in silence, all the words that should have been said but that remained unspoken, the way Mum avoided me without me even realizing, how all I wanted was her embrace, but it was never open to me. It's possible to hit someone without actually doing so physically.

We both made it to Stockholm, Jerry, but your driving force must have been much stronger, more focused than mine, because mine had no focus at all really, did it? You hit a home run, while I hit a punching bag in the gym. Drinking. But there's not really much difference.

You broke away from your father. My own break with my father was slow and painful, but with Mum it occurred at the start of my adult life.

Or earlier? Had Mum broken with me from the start?

Malin wants to stop thinking, so she turns on the television. The evening news is coming to an end, and she doesn't know if they've covered her case tonight, but they must have had something about it. The final item is some footage from a courtroom somewhere in the USA, an antiabortion activist shooting a doctor who carried out abortions in his clinic.

She turns off the television.

An early night.

Her whole body is itching with nerves, and she lies down in bed, but the only color she sees when she closes her eyes is the dark brown color of the tequila, endlessly enticing.

Then she opens her eyes.

Fredrik Fågelsjö.

The look of fear on his face. His body under the blanket on the bunk in his cell. Were you just scared? Or did you actually give in to your fury and kill Jerry Petersson?

If your poor business sense cost your family the castle, then your father must despise you, hate you. Maybe your sister Katarina feels the same, but she's still your sister. Malin feels her stomach contract, in a gentle but painful longing for the brother or sister she never had.

And Jerry Petersson. Who pops up in the middle of the family scandal and is later found dead in a moat that is said to house the unquiet spirits of Russian soldiers. Jochen Goldman.

People who are said to have disappeared. Murdered.

Ruthlessness and inadequacies.

Malin closes her eyes again.

Waits for sleep, feeling her consciousness drift away inside itself, and soon the world outside is just one electrical impulse among many for her memories to navigate by.

The world outside the window gradually disappears, turning into a crackling sound, and she hears someone whisper, wonders, Who's trying to tell me something?

Is it the voice from the forest, from the bar in the Hamlet?

The figures aren't there, don't want to show themselves, and in the borderlands between sleep and waking Malin gets a sense that he, or they, or whoever it is, is afraid for their own fate, afraid to entertain the idea of their own pain.

Then she sees a lawnmower in the beginning of a dream, moving across grass, and she sees it from the perspective of the blades.

Not a manual rotary mower like her dad had, but a red Stiga chasing a pair of filthy feet across dew-wet grass. She sees the blades lick the boy's ankles, hears a voice shout: "Now they're going to eat up your feet, now they're going to tear your little feet to shreds."

The images in the dream are black and white, but the machine and the blades are red, and the noise of the engine and the petrol fumes blur her thoughts.

Then the boy stops. Lets the mower's blades run over his feet.

Malin wants to see the boy's face, but he keeps looking the other way.

Then he runs, on bloody stumps now, he takes aim and drifts right out of her vision.

26

Malin Fors has dreamed a dream about a person who is a mistake, not an unwanted person, but a mistake. She can't remember the person, she can't even remember the dream, but its narrative is inside her like a slow earth tremor as she stands in front of the counter of freshly baked bread in the Filbyter patisserie, which has started opening on Sundays to fight off the competition from the cafés out at the Tornby shopping center.

Empty fridge. Waking up hungry. Toiletries, clothes, and that was where her shopping spree had ended.

Zeke on his way there for a quick breakfast before the morning meeting in the station. Sunday like a normal Monday when they're dealing with a case of this size, Saturday working yesterday, Sabbath working today.

Two days since they found the body, no chance of any time off while the investigation is still in its infancy.

She should really have had the day off today. Come up with something to do with Tove. Going to the pool, anything. Maybe even picking up her wretched things, talking to Janne, they could have had lunch together, Sunday steak and cream sauce.

That could have worked.

Couldn't it?

That whole life feels like a mockery. And she wishes that Janne would call and shout at her, but he hasn't even done that. Should I call and shout at him because he hasn't called to be cross with me? Or to criticize me for ignoring Tove? But he must realize that I'm working today, the papers are full of the case.

She sits upstairs, with her three cheese rolls and a large mug of coffee, looking out at the desolate square, where a transparent, persistent rain makes all the shop signs pale, and only a few pigeons can bear to face the day, pecking away just as they always seem to.

She's finished one of the rolls by the time she sees Zeke's shaved head appear over by the stairs, and he smiles as he sees her, calling to her:

"You look a hell of a lot better today. And that top suits you."

"Shut up," she says, and Zeke smiles:

"You know I'm only concerned about you. And that is a nice top."

Malin adjusts the pale-blue top she's wearing, one of her new purchases from H&M. Maybe Zeke's being serious, she must have looked like a pig in that red top yesterday.

He's arrived empty-handed, and she wonders if he's not going to have anything, but at that moment her mobile rings. Sven's name on the screen. He sounds anxious:

"Malin, we've had a call from someone who says he's Petersson's lawyer. Says he wants to meet one of us. Sounded like he's got something to tell us."

Zeke's face opposite her, watchful now.

"So the lawyer has a lawyer?" Malin says.

"Had, Malin. They all have."

"And where is he?"

"A Max Persson, office at number 12 Hamngatan, close to Trädgårdstorget."

"So he's there on Sunday morning?"

"He is."

"What about talking to Fredrik Fågelsjö?"

"I'll deal with that myself. Without his lawyer. Just a polite conversation in his cell."

"Okay, we'll talk to Petersson's lawyer. We're at Filbyter having breakfast. We can skip the morning meeting."

"Yes, not much has happened since yesterday," Sven says.

"Anything else at all?" Malin asks.

"Nothing," Sven says. "And no tip-offs either."

"Let's see what secrets the lawyer's got for us," Malin says.

"Fingers crossed."

"Our secrets are what make us human," Malin says. "Isn't that what you usually say, Sven?"

Sven laughs as he hangs up.

Max Persson's office is on the top floor of a yellow brick building from the fifties. Outside the room is a terrace where a couple of abandoned wooden chairs are fighting a losing battle against the wind and rain, and Malin can almost see the varnish disintegrating in the autumn weather.

Malin and Zeke are each sitting in a red armchair. Max Persson is sitting in majesty on an office chair on the other side of a gigantic glass-topped desk.

A pink Oriental rug on the floor.

Garishly colored paintings on the walls, silhouettes made with what looks like spray paint. The man behind the desk is a similar age to Jerry Petersson when he died. He's wearing a shiny gray suit, the cheapness of which is accentuated by a pink tie on a pale-blue shirt.

Max Persson seems to think a lot of himself, Malin thinks.

A clown of a lawyer.

But very good-looking.

Clearly defined features, prominent cheekbones.

"We understand that you were Jerry Petersson's lawyer?" Zeke says.

"Well, that's not quite right. But I did help Jerry with the purchase of Skogså, with drawing up the contract. It gets quite complicated when you're dealing with such a large, special property."

"So you weren't his lawyer?"

"Absolutely not," Persson says.

And Malin suddenly realizes that Persson wants to tell them something confidential, and that he doesn't want Jerry Petersson to look like his former client, because then he could be accused of breaching his code of confidentiality as a lawyer.

"Jerry," Malin says. "Were you friends?"

"Well, not friends as such. We studied together down in Lund, and I ended up here in Linköping, which was his home city of course."

"So you go way back?" Zeke wonders.

Persson nods.

"And there's something you want to tell us?" Malin says.

Persson nods again.

Then he starts talking.

"Like I said, I helped Jerry when he was buying Skogså. I met Axel Fågelsjö and his children when I was out inspecting the property, and I have to say that they seemed extremely bitter about the sale. Not that they said anything specific, but the whole time I got the impression that they didn't want to sell. Don't ask me why."

"Had you heard anything about financial difficulties?" Malin asks. "Did the Fågelsjös say anything?"

"No, but, like I said, I got the impression that they were forced to sell, and that they didn't really want to. And that impression was reinforced by what happened last week."

Persson, evidently taking great delight in everyday drama, lets what he is about to say hang in the air.

"Well?" Malin prompts.

"Well, at the beginning of last week Axel Fågelsjö approached me. He wanted to buy back the castle and estate. He was prepared to pay twenty million more than they got for it. He was adamant. I took the offer to Jerry, but he just shook his head, had a good laugh, and told me to turn down the old man's offer."

Lies.

A family estate that no one wanted to sell. Trying to run from the police. Dealing in stock options. "It was time." Not a chance. This had nothing to do with a way of life that had become outdated.

The thoughts are flying through Malin's head and she thinks about Axel Fågelsjö, his powerful figure and his magnificent apartment.

Maybe they ought to concentrate more on Axel than Fredrik? Who knows what the old man might be capable of?

"How did Fågelsjö take Petersson's reply?"

"He was furious on the phone. Utterly furious. I almost thought he was going to have a stroke. It sounded like he was throwing things."

Malin looks at Zeke, who nods back at her.

"Do you know anything else about Jerry Petersson that you think we should know?"

"We didn't have a great deal of contact," Persson says. "Not even after he moved back here. Jerry was a lone wolf. He always was, even back in Lund. Quite brilliant, he got away with doing maybe a fifth of the studying the rest of us had to do, but he still finished on top. He didn't need other people the way we mere mortals do. He never seemed to be searching for someone to love, he was looking for people who could be useful to him. People like me."

"We've been having trouble finding friends and acquaintances," Malin says.

"You won't find any," Max Persson says. "Friendship wasn't Jerry's thing."

They're standing in the doorway of the building housing Max Persson's office. It's pouring with rain now, the drops drumming on the ground like a plague of locusts ready to destroy everything in their path.

Not a soul in sight.

The city paralyzed by the season.

"So, a frustrated Count Axel Fågelsjö," Zeke says.

"Who loves that land," Malin says.

"And who wanted it back, but he couldn't have it."

"Because Jerry Petersson refused to sell."

"As if he owned the man's soul," Zeke said.

"And Fredrik Fågelsjö, who gambled the castle away," Malin says. "Maybe he wanted to put everything right? And if Petersson was out of the game, the family could buy back the castle. But where have they suddenly got the money from, the money behind Axel Fågelsjö's offer for Skogså? I'll call Sven, maybe he hasn't got around to talking to Fredrik Fågelsjö yet."

The door to the cell opens.

Fredrik Fågelsjö is sitting on his bunk with a cup of coffee in his hand, reading a copy of *Svenska Dagbladet*.

"Can I come in for a few minutes?" Sven Sjöman asks. He looks at Fredrik, at the way his shoulders seem to be weighed down by an invisible force, and the skin around his eyes seems to have become chapped during his time in the cell. His eyes seem to be pleading for alcohol, the way that Malin's do sometimes. I'll let you have what we know in tiny portions, Sven thinks.

"Ehrenstierna isn't here."

"I just want to ask a couple of questions," Sven says. "If that's okay?"

"Okay."

Fågelsjö seems tired, as if he's already given up on something, Sven thinks, or as if he's in the process of giving up on something.

He sits down beside him on the bunk's mattress, detecting the smell of urine from the shiny stainless-steel toilet.

"A lot of people here at the station have problems with alcohol as well," Sven says. "There's no shame in it."

"I haven't got a problem," Fågelsjö replies.

"No, but no one here would look down on you if that were the case."

"Good to know."

"We know about your dealings in stock options," Sven goes on.

Fågelsjö doesn't reply.

Sven looks round the cell, at how bare it is.

"You've got children, young children. And a wife. Do you miss them?"

"Yes. I do. But you're not letting me have any visitors."

"Not us. The prosecutor. Is everything okay with your family?"

"Everything's fine."

"That's good. My wife and I have been married thirty-five years, and we still enjoy each other's company."

"I got scared. I panicked," Fågelsjö says. "I didn't want to spend time in Skänninge. Missing such a large chunk of the children's lives. Can you understand that?"

Sven nods, moves a bit closer to him.

"What about your father? He must have been pretty mad about your financial affairs?"

"He's always been a bit mad," Fågelsjö says with a smile. "He was angry."

"And yet you all told us that it was time to sell?"

"If you come from a family like ours, you do anything you can to protect the family name."

"Perhaps that was what you were doing?" Sven says. "Going out to Skogså that morning to get your revenge on Jerry Petersson for taking the castle away from you? I promise you, it will feel better if you tell us."

"I'm not even going to dignify that with a denial," Fågelsjö says. Then he adjusts the newspaper in his lap with an exaggerated gesture. "If you'll excuse me?"

"Then last week you tried to buy back the castle."

Fågelsjö raises his eyes from the paper with a look of surprise.

So you know about that? he seems to be thinking.

Sven nods.

"We know. Where did you get the money from? As I understand it, you gambled away the family fortune, and plenty more besides."

"We got some money," Fredrik says. "But it isn't my place to explain how."

"Not if you don't want to," Sven says. "And Petersson just laughed at your father. Did you want to show your father how strong you were, Fredrik? Did you just want to put everything right, I can imagine it must be difficult having a father like that, and now you just wanted to put everything right, so you went out there that morning and killed Petersson. Is that how it was? And you lost control? It will feel better if you . . ."

Fågelsjö leaps up from the bunk. Throws the paper at the wall, shouting:

"I didn't do anything! I didn't do anything!"

27

Rented flats.

The logo of Stångå Council on the notice board by the front door.

Malin didn't notice the housing association sign the first time they were here, took it for granted that a man like Axel Fågelsjö would own his own apartment.

What sort of contacts would you need to get a rented flat on Drottninggatan with a view of the Horticultural Society Park? Either way, I live in a rented flat, Axel Fågelsjö lives in a rented flat.

The building's lift is broken, so Malin and Zeke have to take the stairs up to the apartment on the fourth floor.

Malin is out of breath.

Feeling sick, but if you feel sick as often as I do, she thinks, then feeling sick becomes a natural state. She knows why her body is protesting, alcohol functions just like any other drug, when your body wants more it lets you know, protesting noisily that the pleasure fuel had stopped flowing. Her body is taking last night's abstinence as an insult.

Taking flight in drink.

Breathing, deep, breathless breaths, and she loses count of the number of steps, and she tries to concentrate on the Fågelsjö family instead.

They were forced to sell.

It wasn't time.

Maintain the façade.

And they wanted to buy back the castle.

But where did the money come from? Sven has just called. Didn't manage to get it out of Fredrik, who had lost vast amounts. And Petersson had merely laughed at Axel Fågelsjö's proposal.

How to proceed?

Get your son to kill Petersson so you can buy back the castle and land from the dead man's estate, at whatever cost? Or kill him yourself in a fit of rage?

Malin looks at Zeke, can see he's thoughtful as they pant their way upstairs in their dripping raincoats, knows he's thinking the same thing as her, he's not stupid, and through the windows of the stairwell they can see the rain hammering down, large drops, small drops, all about to be smashed on the tarmac below.

But are the Fågelsjös, father and son, murderers? Malin feels uncertainty wrench at her stomach, an uncertainty bordering on disbelief.

They are standing outside Axel Fågelsjö's apartment.

Zeke nods to her, says: "Let's see what he's got to say."

Malin rings the bell, and they hear it ring on the other side of the heavy brown-painted wooden door, then footsteps, and they glimpse an eye peering through the peephole before the footsteps go away again.

Malin rings again.

Twice, three times. Five minutes, ten.

"He's not going to open up," Zeke says, and turns away.

Axel Fågelsjö has sat down in his leather armchair, looking into the fire crackling in the hearth, feeling its heat against his feet.

They're here again, the police.

It was bound to happen.

Do they know about the financial affairs yet? Fredrik's mess?

Maybe even the attempt to buy back the castle? They must, Axel Fågelsjö thinks. And they're stupid enough to put two and two together
in the most banal way possible.

But sometimes the truth is banal, often the most banal thing
imaginable.

Like when Fredrik told him; he was sitting in this very chair,
albeit out at the castle, and he had felt like ripping the head off his
offspring, saw his son lying on his back whimpering like a worthless
cockroach, and he had no choice but to get a grip on things himself.

Bettina, I did what I had to, what I promised you.

I stared at myself in the mirror, looked at the portraits on the wall,
saw the derision in my forefathers' eyes, the love in yours. I saved our
son. But the feeling in that room, impossible to get around:

You're no son of mine. You can't be.

They hadn't spoken to each other for a month. Then he had
phoned Fredrik, summoned him, and his son had wept at his feet
again, clinging onto the doorframe like a wretched beast.

Derision and shame.

Love can encompass those feelings as well. But if we don't take
care of each other, who else is going to?

I promised your mother that I would love you, look after you,
both of you, on her deathbed. Did you hear? Were you eavesdropping outside her sickroom that last night? That's the only thing that
has ever made me weak, Bettina, your illness, your blasted suffering,
your terrible torment. And I trusted you, Fredrik. Against my better judgment. And now you've been so damn stupid, driving your
car while you were drunk and trying to escape the police. Drawing
everyone's attention to us when there was no need. You should have
stopped the car, taken your stupid punishment. We can deal with
things like that. But sit there in your cell and feel the consequences
of your actions. Your children, my grandchildren, I don't recognize
myself in them. But perhaps that's because of their mother? That
woman has never liked me, no matter how I've tried.

Fredrik.

Maybe it would have been better if you were retarded?

The police, that strong, intelligent, worn-out woman and him, that obviously tough man, I didn't let them in. If I'm going to tell them anything else, they'll have to force me with all the means at their disposal.

Fredrik and Katarina.

You do whatever you like now, don't you? Don't they, Bettina?

Well, let's see what happens. Even if Fredrik tells them everything, what will those police officers do with the information? Even if they both seem to be made of sterner stuff than you, beloved, derided son.

Katarina.

I don't need to worry about her. She does as I say. Always has done. She's the accepting sort.

Axel Fågelsjö gets up. Goes over to the window overlooking the Horticultural Society Park. Is that someone standing under the bare trees in the rain?

Is someone standing there looking up at me? Or do my eyes deceive me?

Fredrik Fågelsjö has asked to see Sven Sjöman.

Has asked him to sit down on the bunk in his cell again, and says in a voice full of resignation:

"You don't have to believe me, but I had nothing to do with the murder of Jerry Petersson. I don't think anyone in the family did. But this is the story, as I see it."

Fredrik takes a deep breath before going on:

"When Father got depressed after Mother's death, I was given access to the family fortune, to take care of day-to-day expenses. That made sense, because I work at a bank and know about finances."

Fredrik falls silent, as though he were having second thoughts.

"What do you do at the bank?" Sven asks. "You're a financial advisor, aren't you?"

"I work with business customers. We're often involved when small businesses around here change ownership. I work with the financing of that."

"Do you enjoy it?"

"Well, it may not be quite what I used to dream about," Fredrik says. "But it's a decent bank job, considering that it's in Linköping. Anyway. Mum's death hit Father hard. He gave me power of attorney to look after the finances until he felt better."

"And you started to get involved in stock options?"

"Yes," Fredrik says, leaning back against the wall of the cell, and then he started to explain about the poor condition of the castle, about his father's relatively weak finances, about his mother's death, and how he started dabbling in options until everything got out of control once he had access to the family fortune, but he had meant well.

Fågelsjö's voice starts to fade and Sven wonders if he's about to start crying, but if that's the case he manages to hold back his tears.

"So Father was forced to let the right sort of people know that Skogså was for sale, and that was when Petersson popped up. Him, of all people. It was only thanks to my and Dad's contacts at the bank that we were able to stave off bankruptcy until the deal was concluded."

"The bank had no responsibility?"

"No, I conducted all my dealings with the family fortune as a private individual. It was simply hushed up. And Father sold Skogså to save me from bankruptcy. He promised Mum on her deathbed that he'd look after me and Katarina, no matter what it cost. And that's what he did."

"It must have been hard," Sven says.

"It was hard for Father," Fredrik replies, leaning forward. "But for me? I was just worried about Father. That might be hard to understand, but it's the truth. Father *is* Skogså."

"And after that? More recently? You tried to buy back Skogså, didn't you?" Sven asks.

"Yes."

"How? Where did the money come from?"

"We came into an inheritance. The Danish side of the family. An elderly countess who had been a successful industrialist left enough of a fortune that even we inherited a very large sum of money."

"And then you decided you wanted to buy back the castle?"

"Petersson just laughed at Father's offer."

"Did you confront Petersson yourself?" Sven asks, and Fredrik seems to hesitate before replying.

"I'll be completely honest. I was there the evening before Petersson was found murdered. He let me in, and rejected my offer in no uncertain terms. He asked if I'd like a glass of cognac in the rooms where I'd grown up. His smile was so arrogant that I'd have killed him happily, but I didn't."

Fågelsjö pauses, folds his hands on his lap.

"Mind you, I should have," he says eventually.

"So you think you should have killed him?" Sven asks.

"Yes," Fågelsjö says. "I should have. But how often do we ever do what we ought to?"

"What car were you driving when you went out there?"

"My black Volvo. The one you've got impounded."

"Your wife said you were at home when we spoke to her."

"She was trying to protect me. That's natural enough, isn't it? Trying to protect your nearest and dearest?"

What we ought to do?

Hesitation, hesitation. That's one of the many differences between me and you, Fredrik Fågelsjö. I never hesitated.

You people are so conceited.

What do we need people like you for? You try to lay claim to all the traditions of our world and believe that your heritage and wallets can solve all your problems, but you still don't understand the ultimate power: saying no to money, no matter how large the amount.

I took great pleasure in laughing at the old man's offer. In offering you a cognac.

How did you treat me? How do you treat each other? How do you think it feels to have forty stinging, open wounds in your soul?

Were you the person who came to me that morning, Fredrik? Scared and weak as you are, you tell your story. Where's the nobility in that, in your story?

You were muttering.

The police officer almost embarrassed, but you didn't notice that.

You wanted to prove to your father that you could increase your fortune. That you could, in front of your computer screen, do what your forefathers used to on the battlefields of old.

And you, Malin, what is it that you ought to do?

28

Ought to call Tove.

I'm her mum, Malin thinks.

Maybe she can come this evening.

It's already long past lunch by the time Zeke and Malin go through the swinging doors into the police station.

The open-plan office is Sunday empty, the rain like a never-ending wall outside the windows.

Ought to, ought to, ought to call Tove, but I've had my mobile switched off for hours now. I'm longing to get down to the gym.

How can I bear to let you out of my sight now, Tove? It was impossible for the first ten months after the catastrophe in Finspång. I was like a leech, at least that's how it must have felt for you. To protect you, or to calm my own fears? My sense of guilt?

Malin sits down at her desk and switches on her computer, and Zeke does the same. It isn't long before Sven Sjöman comes over to their desks. He tells them what Fredrik Fågelsjö has just said.

"Could he have done it?" Malin asks.

"Who knows? Maybe they had a fight? And he killed Petersson by mistake?"

Malin looks at Sven, at the doubt that has started to take shape in his eyes. Maybe Fredrik isn't their man? She knows Sven must have considered this. But she also knows that he will carry on regarding Fredrik as their prime suspect until there's any evidence to the contrary.

"If Fredrik murdered Petersson when he was there on Thursday evening, the timings don't fit," Malin says. "According to Karin, the body had only been in the water for a couple of hours, four at the most. And he had been dead for a maximum of five hours, so since approximately four o'clock that morning. And Forensics haven't found any traces of blood in Fredrik's car, which they certainly ought to have done, because the perpetrator must have been covered in blood. The fact that the gravel in the tires matches the gravel out at Skogså is explained by the fact that he admits to having been there the previous evening, but it doesn't tie him to the murder. Unless he's lying about the times, of course."

"Do you think he could have gone back the following morning?" Zeke asks.

"I don't know, but his wife has given him an alibi and we can't force her to testify against her husband. She might just be trying to protect her family."

"I got the impression that he is telling the truth," Sven says. "But you never know. He could have gone back. The dark car that old Mrs. Sjöstedt saw could have been his, even if she wasn't quite with it."

"Who knows what he might have done?" Zeke says.

"Yes, to appease his father," Sven says. "He seems to be a real patriarch. Fredrik seems almost to forget that he has a family of his own when you talk to him about his father."

"A search warrant?" Zeke asks. "To help us get a bit more clarity?" Sven shakes his head.

"We simply can't get a search warrant for Fågelsjö's home in connection with the murder at the moment. He's in custody for other reasons, and Ehrenstierna would put a stop to that at once. If we did search his house in connection with those other offenses, we wouldn't be able to use anything we found in any eventual murder prosecution."

"What about Katarina Fågelsjö?" Zeke says.

"We can interview her again," Malin says. "That feels like a natural next step."

She hears herself say the words, even though all she wants is to get down into the gym and beat the shit out of the punching bag.

"Have we got her address?"

"Yes," Sven says, "we've got it."

Malin switches on her mobile.

No new messages.

Then she dials Tove's number, but gets straight through to voice mail.

Where are you? Malin thinks. Tove? Has something happened? And she sees the beast looming over Tove, and feels that she herself is the beast.

Tove, where are you?

"It's Mum here. Where are you? You have to realize that I worry. Call me when you get this."

Tove lets herself be swallowed up by the darkness of the cinema. Filippa is sitting beside her and they're both gawping at how handsome Brad Pitt is. She likes silly films, lots of kissing and cuddling and people in love in a nice way. Books are a different matter entirely, she likes the ones that everyone else thinks are difficult.

She tries not to think about Mum.

Doesn't want to think about the fact that she's probably not coming back to them, and about what she's decided to do herself.

How can I tell Mum about it? She'll be sad, she'll go crazy, maybe do something really stupid. But like Dad said, I can't live with her at the moment, not with her the way she is, when she can't cope without a drink.

And then there's what Dad is going to do today. Does he have to do it so soon?

Brad Pitt smiles.

His teeth are white.

Tove wants to sink into that whiteness, wrap it around all her feelings, leaving just the nice things.

Waldemar Ekenberg runs one hand over his ever more swollen bruises, and puts the other on Lovisa Segerberg's shoulder, giving it a proper squeeze as he says:

"I bet you've got softer bits on your body, Segerberg. Haven't you?"

Lovisa feels like standing up and screaming at this evidently severely socially handicapped hillbilly cop to drop the sexist remarks, but she knows his type all too well: macho officers, of all ages, who can't help making the most bizarre, insulting comments to and about female police officers.

Once she raised a similar issue with her boss, but she had just shaken her head and said:

"If someone as attractive as you wants to be in the police, you'd better be prepared for a whole load of comments. Try to take it as a compliment."

Lovisa is having trouble seeing the hand squeezing her shoulder as a compliment, and without saying anything she slides from his grasp and puts the papers in her hand on the desk.

She, Waldemar, and Johan Jakobsson have spent all day in paperwork Hades. And have only got through a fraction of the material.

But there's one thing they can say with certainty: The tenancy agreements were legitimate, and the IT business seemed to be entirely aboveboard. Petersson appeared to have got his fair share of the money, no more, no less. He had merely invested in the company, not acted as its legal advisor, so there was no question of bias. They hadn't found a will, and during the course of the day Johan had made another twenty pointless calls to everyone from commercial lawyers whose names cropped up in the files to the carpenters, electricians, and other workmen who had been employed by Petersson out at Skogså. No one had anything interesting to say about him. He seemed to have managed all his business dealings in an irreproach-able manner.

The clock on the yellow textured wallpaper says 2:25.

Lovisa looks at Johan, the more pleasant, soft-spoken officer of the two she's been set to work with. Competent and inoffensive.

Evidently Waldemar is also competent, and at lunch over at the National Forensics Laboratory she noticed how the other officers treated him with the respect the police usually reserve for officers who really know how to make things happen.

"Time's getting on," Waldemar says, settling down at his place at the table, in front of a screen showing the contents of Jerry Peters-son's hard drives in neat folders.

"I can't think straight," Johan says. "So much fucking paper."

"The only thing I can see that could have a direct connection to the case," Lovisa says, "is the company Petersson owned with Jochen Goldman. The one dealing with the books and the income from in-terviews with Goldman. The company accounts look terrible. Maybe there's more money somewhere, or else the interest or capitalization value of Goldman's celebrity status was a lot higher."

"Capitalization value," Waldemar says. "You sound like a right nerd."

"We'll mention it at the next meeting," Johan says.

"The morning meeting first thing tomorrow," Waldemar says, and Lovisa thinks that no one could be less suited to paperwork than him.

Katarina Fågelsjö, dressed in dark jeans and a pink tennis shirt, is leaning back in a sofa that Malin knows comes from Svenskt Tenn and costs a fortune. The fabric of the sofa was designed by Josef Frank, old-fashioned black tendrils snaking through leaves in strong autumn colors against a pale-blue background.

A fortune, she thinks. At least by my standards, and then she thinks how badly she fits in with this room, conscious of how cheap her H&M jeans look, her woolen sweater, how vulgar her sports socks are, and how scruffy she is as a whole compared to Katarina Fågelsjö. Malin feels like creeping along the walls, taking up as little space as possible, but she knows this won't do, so she'll have to hide her insecurity behind brusqueness.

A fragile wooden table in front of them, three cups of coffee that neither Malin, Zeke, nor Katarina has touched. The whole room smells of lemon-scented detergent and some expensive, famous perfume that Malin can't place. Paintings on the walls. Classical, but with the same aura of quality as Jerry Petersson's artworks. A lot of portraits of women by windows in bright light, women who all seem to be waiting for something. One painting in particular, of a woman by a window facing the sea, takes Malin's interest. She reads the signature: Anna Ancher.

Through the large living-room windows Malin and Zeke can see the Stångån River flowing gently past, the raindrops forming small, fleeting craters as they hit the surface. On the other side of the river large villas clamber up the slope toward Tanneforsvägen, but it's regarded as much smarter to live on this side of the river, closer to the center.

As far as Malin can tell, Katarina lives alone in the large, modernist villa from the thirties beside the Stångån, and she's in a more obliging frame of mind now than she was at the driving range.

"Go ahead," she says with a smile. "I'll answer as best as I can."

"Did you know that your father tried to buy back Skogså from Jerry Petersson?" Zeke asks.

"I knew. And I didn't approve."

"Why not?"

"That's a closed chapter for me. We have everything we could possibly need anyway. But obviously I couldn't stop him trying. Jerry Petersson was the rightful owner of the castle. That's all there was to it."

"And your brother?" Malin asks, looking at Katarina, the way she seems to be struggling with something, and if Malin asks open questions she might start talking, revealing some secret that could take them forward.

"He would probably have liked to see the castle bought back."

"Were you angry with him because of his investments?"

"So you know about that?"

Katarina acts surprised.

"Naturally, it was a mistake that Father gave my brother access to the family capital. He's never been particularly talented. But as to whether I was angry? No. Do you know about the Danish inheritance?"

Malin nods.

"Do you think we got Petersson out of the way because he was the only thing standing between us and getting Skogså back?"

Malin looks at Zeke, he's gazing out of the windows, and she wonders what he's thinking about. Karin Johannison? Maybe, maybe not. You've got a wife, Zeke, but who the hell am I to criticize anyone else? We share our secrets, Zeke.

"You could have told us all this out at the golf club," Malin says.

"At the driving range," Katarina corrects with a shrug.

"Why do you think your brother tried to get away from us?"

"He was driving under the influence. He couldn't even handle a month in prison. He's the timid sort. Like I said."

"Do you live here alone?" Malin asks.

"Yes. I've lived alone since the divorce."

"No children?"

"No. Thank God, I almost said."

"And your lover? The doctor. Does he usually stay here?"

"What's that got to do with you?"

"Sorry," Malin says. "Nothing. It's nothing to do with us."

"There's no love there," Katarina says. "Just really good sex. A few more times. The sort of thing a woman needs every so often. You know what I mean, don't you?"

*   *   *

A text message from Tove.

"Got your message. Was at the cinema."

Of course.

She was going to the cinema.

What should I reply?

She replies: "Great! Now I know."

No: "Are you coming around later?"

Zeke behind the wheel. On the way to her flat to drop her off.

Can't deal with anyone but herself tonight. If that.

Skirts.

Tops.

Sandals.

A photograph album.

Malin's life in a big heap on the hall floor when she went into the flat.

Bags and boxes full of her clothes, shoes, books, and things. Neatly piled up, and when Malin realized what was in front of her in the flat she felt like crying, and she sat down on the hall floor, but however much she tried to squeeze out some tears, none came.

My things, the person I am. No, not the person I am, more like a receipt for the pointless person I've become.

Janne had turned up with her things from the house during the day, using her spare key to get in, then dropping it through the mailbox afterward. She would have liked to pick up her things herself, would have liked them to be at home when she went, him and Tove, and they would have asked her to sit down at a ready-laid table and would offer her some hot stew that would take the edge off all the chill and rawness, the thirst and confusion.

Now, instead, this pile of life. In this shitty-fucking-tiny-musty-raw-damp-lonely flat.

Did Tove help Janne? Have they turned against me in tandem?

But what can I expect? I hit him. In front of Tove. How the hell could I? Am I any better than the father and brother in that honor killing?

God, how I miss you both. I miss you so much it crosses every boundary and you disintegrate and are replaced by something else.

But why isn't Tove here? Tove, where are you? Your things? You could have brought it all at once, couldn't you?

Malin sits with her back to the front door.

She has a bottle of tequila in her hand, but isn't drinking. Instead she's pulled out the files about the Maria Murvall case from the bags Janne left.

She reads.

Sees Maria Murvall sitting on the floor, like her, in another room. Alone, excluded, shut off, numb to the point of nothingness, maybe scared beyond the bounds of what the rest of us call fear.

Malin twists and turns all the facts in the case, as she's done hundreds of times before.

What happened in the forest, Maria?

What were you doing there?

Who could hurt anyone the way he or she or it hurt you, where does that malice come from? Where do the sharp, living branches that ate their way into your genitals come from? The electrically charged spiders? The cockroaches with sharpened jaws that ate their way up your legs?

Evil is like a torrent, Malin thinks. Like tons of clay sliding down a hillside in a merciless autumn storm. A flood of death and violence wiping out every living thing in its path, leaving a desolate landscape behind it, ash lying in heaps on the ground, and we, the survivors, are forced to eat each other to survive.

Wrath summoned back. Set free.

Malin gets up, leaving the files and things in the hall. She goes into Tove's room, sees the unmade bed, wishes Tove were lying there again, and she starts to cry when she realizes that that bed, in many ways, is empty for good now, that she may never pick Tove up from the sofa in front of the television and carry her to bed, that the child

Tove was has vanished, replaced by the young woman who measures everything around her, who evaluates and tries to stay as far as possible from any obvious pain. A person who doesn't sleep a sleep of innocence.

In Malin's dream, damp and darkness and cold become one and the same. They merge into a black light and in the center of that light is a secret, or possibly several secrets.

I loved, says a voice. Search in love. I hit, says the same voice. Search in the blows, a third voice says in the dream. Young snakes, chopped to pieces by lawnmower blades, move before her eyes, crawling out of the sewers in streets whose names she doesn't know.

Then the voices fall silent, the mutilated young snakes vanish.

29

Malin.

This house is associated with you, Janne thinks as he stands in his kitchen, sipping a glass of cold milk and eating slices of salami. Outside the night is its own master, full of all the demons he has encountered in his life.

Malin, Janne thinks. It's lonely out here in the forest without you, but these old wooden walls can't contain the pair of us. The bed with my mother's crocheted bedspread isn't wide enough.

The house smells of damp and nascent mold, spores sent out in the night like silent malaria mosquitoes.

Muteness.

Like a soundless animal, that's what it's like, our love. That's what you're like, Malin, and I can't handle it anymore.

You've always accused me of running, and I certainly have, I've taken refuge in the care of others, people who needed me in Rwanda and Bosnia, and most recently in the borderlands of Ethiopia and Sudan. I was there last winter.

They called me again last week, the Rescue Services Agency, but I turned them down, I've done my bit, I'm going to stay and deal with my life, the way it looks right here, right now.

You're the one who can't deal with it, Malin, and as long as you aren't prepared to look inside yourself I can't help you. Tove can't help you. No one can help you.

But that's over now, Malin. It doesn't matter that you hit me. Nor that you did it in front of Tove. She'll survive. She stronger than us. Smarter. That's not what this is about.

I'm here in my house, and you're welcome to visit, but not to move back in. It's time for us to cut the chains of this love, and the still, soft desire that we've been tumbling around in for so long.

What is there beyond that love?

I don't know, Malin. And that fills me with comfort and fear.

Tove.

It got confusing for Tove in the end.

You want me to call you, don't you? If only to shout at you. It would never occur to you to call me. You're too proud for that, though I don't think you realize it. But we're beyond phone calls now. I promise to watch over you as best I can, but now that you seem to have made up your mind to follow the path straight down into the darkness, there isn't much I can do, is there?

Your boss, Sven, he called me today. I told him we've split up again, said that I was worried about you, just like him, and he said he might not have realized just how much you'd been drinking earlier this year, that he's thinking of sending you on a short trip so that you can clear your thoughts. That's a good idea, I told him. Because I can't reach you, I said. You just get angry if I try. And he understood, and I told him our relationship is over, that it was easier to be straight with him than with you, that I probably couldn't say it like that to you, to your face. That I should probably keep my distance.

And do you know what he said, Malin?

He said: "I promise to keep an eye on her. Trust me," he said, and he's the sort of man you're happy to entrust with the things you care about most.

I can live with the fact that you raised your hand against me. With the pain and sorrow of that. But not Tove's look of confusion.

She needs security now, Malin, confidence that this world is good, and means us human beings well, because even if she can look after herself it's our duty to spare her from evil, to give her faith in goodness. That's what this is about.

And I can hear you snort.

But that's how it is. You don't have to have any faith yourself, you just have to convey the idea of faith.

I don't know how many nights I've lain awake and sweating in a soaking-wet bed after dreams about people's cruelty to one another. I've had thousands of nights like that, Malin, but I still haven't lost my faith.

But I know when it's time to move on.

I know when the darkness of night threatens to become the only thing that exists.

That's why I came over with your things today, Malin. I knew you wouldn't be at home. I carried the boxes upstairs on my own, I took my jacket off and laid it over your things so they wouldn't get wet in the rain on the way from the car.

So that you would understand what I could never say.

Dad! Dad!

Tove knows she's screaming in the dream. This is the dream she most often has, and in the chat rooms the others have tried to persuade her not to be scared of the dream but to welcome it as a chance to learn to live with what happened last summer.

The masked figure above her.

She herself immobile.

Dad's and Mum's voices close, yet still too far away, as the woman approached her with darkness and violence and a desire that everything should end so that everything could begin.

Together with the others she had tried to understand the woman who wanted to kill her. Tried to understand where her anger and evil had come from, and when Tove felt she understood, the fear had vanished and she learned to accept the dream.

Dad! Dad!

And he comes, saves her from deep inside the darkness together with Mum. Light streams into the room and if her screams were to reach her lips in this dream he would rush the thirty feet from his bed to hers. He'd wake me up, save me from the fear.

Mum.

You're in the dream too.

You're standing back.

It looks like you're in pain.

How can I help you? I see your torment, maybe I even understand it. Is it because you think you've lost me? Is that why you've turned away?

Because you have become your own pain.

Your own fear.

Karim Akbar has got out of bed, taking deep breaths in the empty, dark room, and all he can smell is himself. The house lacks other smells these days. It feels inadequate, with its sensible, early-eighties architecture, like a wine that has matured poorly, and its bad sides have taken over. Edginess, rawness.

He's thought of selling the house. Getting a flat in the city, but he hasn't been able to summon up the energy.

His wife gone.

His son gone.

In Malmö. With her new man, the one she met on that council course for social workers in Växjö.

Karim had thought he was about to kill her when she told him, but she was sensible, took him out for lunch, and even then, when she had asked him to have lunch with her, he had known what was coming.

It was two years since his wife had met him, the pure-blood Swede, in the same line of work as her.

Karim's own career is in the balance.

Today he had a call from a headhunter in Gothenburg.

A job at the Immigration Authority in Norrköping, just one down from the very top of the tree, but he's not sure.

Do I want to be responsible for sending people back to the hell-holes of the world? They want me as a figurehead. An immigrant face to appear in the media. To unsettle them.

But something new has to happen.

The case they're working on at the moment.

Jerry Petersson. Fågelsjö. Goldman.

All these privileged people who can't get along, can't live along-side each other with their tasteless wealth. But maybe, Karim thinks, the violence comes from somewhere else? The tenant farmers? Who knew what resentments they might harbor toward their landlord? Differences in wealth always lead to violence sooner or later. As history demonstrates.

Someone mentioned in the will, if we ever find one? Anything is possible.

Shame.

Shame is always involved.

According to a lot of people with his background, his wife had committed the ultimate sin and he should have had her killed.

And that's what his instinct told him.

At first.

He can admit that to himself. But is there anything more loath-some than that father and brother they picked up in that latest so-called honor killing, who killed their own daughter and sister?

I'm not that primitive, Karim thinks.

He took a step back, gave up there and then in the restaurant, let her go, taking the boy with her, never discussed any other pos-sibility, and gave her what she wanted for her share of the house. He convinced himself that was what he wanted, to be broad minded and magnanimous in the midst of betrayal.

Karim goes over to the window and sees that the rain has stopped. But for how long?

He shouts out in the house.

His wife's name. His son's.

His former wife's name.

Any love is better than loneliness, he thinks.

Lovisa Segerberg is lying awake in her room at the Hotel du Nord. The walls are so thin that she can feel the damp and cold outside trying to find their way into the room, and she hears a freight train rumbling through the station just a couple of hundred yards away.

Gloomy. But not dark enough to sleep.

The linoleum floor, a thin mattress from Ikea, nothing but a shower in the shabby bathroom. But I don't need anything else, Lovisa thinks. She spoke to Patrik at eleven o'clock. He was still awake, up working, and he asked about the case she was working on, but she couldn't be bothered to explain, just told him she missed him, and that she didn't know how long she'd be staying in Linköping.

Kiss, kiss.

Goodnight, darling, and she can feel him in the room in the same way that she felt him during their first night together. Warm and present and real. They're getting married next summer. Will have a wonderful life together. Not mess it all up like all the other poor bastards seem to. Like Malin Fors seems to have done, according to the talk in the station. She stank of alcohol today, stale drink, but no one seemed to care, or at least no one said or did anything if they did. But what do I know about what goes on behind the scenes?

What a gang, Lovisa thinks. Waldemar. The idiot. Sexist. But not really dangerous. And Sven Sjöman. The commanding officer every policeman dreams of having.

She looks up at the ceiling. Thinks:

Patrik, where's your body now, where is whatever it is you are when we're not together?

Zeke has got up alone.

It's still dark outside the windows of his detached house, and in the garden the trees and bushes resemble burned-out, prehistoric skeletons.

He sips his coffee.

Thinks about Malin.

This past year has taken its toll on her.

He thinks that he's going to have to keep an eye on her, that he probably can't do much more than that. Give her chewing gum so the others don't notice the smell. Stop her from driving. He can see her alone in her flat with a bottle of tequila.

Maybe I ought to talk to Sven, Zeke thinks, he's thought about doing that before, but Malin would regard any conversation like that as a serious betrayal. She'd think he had gone behind her back if she ever found out about it, and maybe the trust between them would be gone for good.

But she's drinking way too damn much.

Her demons are snapping at her heels.

Your heels are bleeding, Malin, Zeke thinks, noting that it's started to rain again.

It's a long time since he gave up smoking. But this morning he really feels like having a cigarette.

He closes his eyes; Karin Johannison's body, her soft hard warm body is there. What the hell are we playing at really? And in the bedroom Gunilla lies sleeping. I love her, Zeke thinks. So much. Yet I'm still capable of lying to her face.

I have to go to the toilet and throw up afterward. But I can do it. And I do.

Waldemar Ekenberg is standing on his terrace in the garden, smoking.

The rain is pattering on the corrugated plastic roof and dawn is slowly breaking over Mjölby, and the sky looks almost the same color as the bruise on his cheek.

He told his wife what had happened. As usual when he talked about the rough side of the job she didn't get worried, just said: "You never learn."

In his thoughts he curses all the paperwork. He's still shocked at the amount of paper and documents one single person can produce in the course of a short lifetime. And he's just as fed up of the amounts of money all that paper shuffling can produce.

Smoke thick in his lungs.

Where's the justice in a paper shuffler like Petersson living in a castle, when ordinary, decent workers end up practically on the street when factories and workshops close down? Hundreds of thousands of jobs lost in Swedish industry. What happens to the blues' false promises of solidarity then?

What's going to happen to them, the workers?

The less intelligent.

He stubs his cigarette out in the coffee tin half-full of sand.

Thinks:

What about me, what would I be doing if I wasn't a cop? Maybe I'd be a security guard at some supermarket, accused of using excessive force on a difficult customer.

"Walle! Walle!"

His old woman shouting indoors. Best see what she wants. Without her, I'd be nothing but my own stupid self.

Johan Jakobsson is lying stretched out in bed, his children on either side of him, having got home from their grandparents early yesterday evening.

His wife asleep alongside.

A blessed harvest, he thinks, listening to his wife's breathing. That's what his family is. He thinks of her, and the way they apologized to each other, the way they always do.

They're best friends, through thick and thin.

What's a good friend worth? he thinks.

As much as a family? As much as a father?

No. But almost.

30

Early morning.

The world gray-blue like a newborn infant outside the windows of the open-plan office.

Sven Sjöman looks out over the empty chairs and desks, breathes in the smell of paper and lingering sweat. The light from the fluorescent tubes overhead merges with the gray light from outside. Sven thinks about how many detectives he has seen come and go through the course of his career. Malin is one of the best, possibly the best of them all. She understands about listening to the silent voices of an investigation, weaving together the choir of hunches and words into a clear truth.

But it's taking its toll on her.

The conversation with her husband, or ex-husband, yesterday. Janne. A decent fellow. He called again, worrying about her.

I'm worried as well, Sven thinks. But now I've finally had an idea about what I can do without her realizing that I'm trying to help her. If she suspected she'd be furious. Maybe refuse to go. But at least Janne thought it was an excellent idea.

Everything seems to affect Malin badly right now. Everything's on the surface and gets scorched by the slightest touch.

Johan, Zeke, Börje, Waldemar.

Börje at home with his wife, the next attack of her MS will in all likelihood mean death.

It's taking its toll on Börje. But Börje doesn't seem to be affected by everything the way that Malin is. He seems to have an ability to take pleasure in what he has with his wife, in what he has had.

Waldemar. He's going to go mad in that room full of paper. But I can probably use his questionable talents. I'm not in favor of the way he conducts police business, his brutality, but I'm not so stupid that I can't see the value of it at times. That's why I didn't veto his transfer from Mjölby. God knows where he got those latest bruises, but he doesn't complain, and if you work the way that Waldemar does, you have to take the knocks.

Petersson. Who knows what might be lurking under his unturned stones? Give people a whiff of money and they're capable of almost anything.

Sven pulls in his stomach, sighs, thinks about his brother, self-employed, when he was about to start another business, and how he guaranteed the loan himself and had to sell his house in Karlstad to repay the bank when the business went bankrupt.

Several years later his brother got rich when he sold his next company. Sven asked for his money back, and they were standing on the terrace of his brother's house, and his brother replied, with a blank look on his face: "That was business, Sven. You took a gamble and you lost. Let's not get apples and pears mixed up now."

Sven stayed to dinner, that evening.

But he hasn't spoken to his brother since then.

He opens the *Correspondent* on his desk. The speculation in the paper points in the same direction as their own. The Fågelsjös, Goldman. Business.

Money, fraternity.

Who could have got so angry or upset or disappointed with Jerry Petersson that he ended up in the castle moat, beaten to death and stabbed, among the walled-in prisoners of war?

*   *   *

The others look as tired as me, Malin thinks as she looks round at the detectives who have gathered for the first meeting of the week in the preliminary investigation into the murder of Jerry Petersson.

The time is 8:30.

Johan Jakobsson has dark rings under his eyes. Waldemar Ekenberg is ragged from smoking, Lovisa Ekenberg looks like she slept badly in her hotel; they probably have lousy beds in the Hotel du Nord down by the station. Sven Sjöman is the only one who looks alert. Karim Akbar is sitting listlessly at the end of the table, but his shiny gray wool suit is as well pressed as usual, and the pinkish-red tie has been chosen with care.

Silence has descended on the room. The sort of silence that can occur in a room full of detectives searching their minds for a sense of where to go next, waiting for something that is hidden to reveal itself before their eyes.

They've been through the Fågelsjös' lies about their finances, that Fredrik Fågelsjö had lost money on bad investments and had to sell up. And that they had come into an inheritance and tried to buy the estate back, but that Petersson had turned down the offer, in spite of it being a good deal. That Axel Fågelsjö had refused to let Malin and Zeke in, but that Katarina had spoken to them, and that Fredrik had spoken openly and admitted that he had gone out to see Petersson the evening before the murder, but claimed that nothing had happened apart from him confronting Petersson and demanding to be allowed to buy the castle back.

"If he was there the previous evening, he can't have killed Petersson then, Karin's reports says he died in the early hours of the morning and that the blow to the head killed him outright," Sven said. "From what we know about Petersson's last twenty-four hours, he doesn't seem to have met anyone apart from Fredrik. He only made one call on his mobile, and that turned out to be to his cleaner. A Filipino woman with a solid alibi, and who hadn't been there for a week."

"If Fredrik did kill him," Malin said, "then he must have gone back the next morning. But his wife has given him an alibi. But we've got no way of knowing, that could just be a married couple's alibi."

"And the Filipino cleaner?" Waldemar asked. "Could she have any crazy relatives?"

"Aronsson's spoken to her," Sven said. "She's clean as a whistle. Anyway, if that were the case, surely he'd have been robbed."

Then they went through the rest of the case, but there wasn't much new to report.

"We've checked Petersson's emails," Johan said. "And we received the log of telephone calls from Telia late yesterday. Both his mobile and landline. But we haven't found anything unusual there, apart from the two calls from a phone booth out at Ikea."

"Is that so unusual?" Karim asked.

"No, but they're the only calls where we don't know who made them, and of course pretty much everyone has a mobile these days."

"Which phone booth was it?"

"One out in the parking lot," Johan replied.

"Is it covered by any of the security cameras?"

"I'm afraid not, I checked. There's no camera there. And the calls were made several months ago, so there's next to no chance of finding any witnesses."

Karim breaks the silence that has followed the run-through:

"Any tip-offs from the public?"

"It's been remarkably quiet," Sven says. "I thought we'd get loads of calls about the things Petersson got up to, but maybe he was just the sort who left satisfied customers and people behind."

"Do people like that actually exist?" Zeke asks.

"No," Waldemar says.

"And we haven't found the murder weapon," Sven says.

"Where do we go from here?" Karim asks.

"Well, the team in Hades will keep digging, trying to find out why the company Jochen Goldman and Petersson ran between them wasn't more profitable," Sven says. "Malin and Zeke can try to talk to Axel Fågelsjö. Bring him in for questioning if he puts up a fuss. After all, it isn't that incredible that someone in that family killed Petersson so they could buy back the castle from his estate."

"Do you think they could have paid someone to do it?" Malin asks.

"Unlikely," Sven says. "But that did occur to me, even if there's no evidence to suggest it."

Malin nods.

"Petersson's father stands to inherit everything," she goes on. "Unless some unknown child or a wife pops up abroad."

"People have been killed for less," Waldemar says, and in his voice Malin can hear a longing, but she can't grab hold of the feeling lurking at the back of Waldemar's wishes.

Just as well, she thinks, looking at his bruise, which has turned orange and yellow round the edges, like an autumn leaf.

Sven picks up the phone on the third ring.

"Number unknown" on the display, yet the call has come straight through to his phone, bypassing reception.

The open-plan office is noisy now. The morning calm has gone, and the place stinks of coffee.

Police officers in uniform and plain clothes hurrying back and forth, talking into headsets, looking busy, stressed.

"Sjöman."

"Sven Sjöman?"

"Yes."

"Yes, hello. This is Peter Svenungsson from Interpol up in Stockholm."

"Hello."

"I read on the net about Jerry Petersson, that he's been murdered."

"That's right. A couple of men found him in the moat of the castle where he lived when they were about to go hunting."

"I've got something that might interest you."

"Go ahead. We're grateful for any information."

"I'm sure you know that Petersson was Jochen Goldman's lawyer while he was on the run. We only ever came close to catching Goldman once, we got a tip-off that he was in Verbier in Switzerland. The coffee was pretty much still warm in the pot when the local gendarmes got there, but he managed to get away again."

"And?"

"Petersson gave us the tip-off. He called and told us where Goldman was."

Sven can feel his heart skip a few beats.

"Bloody hell."

"He didn't give an explanation, and he was aware he was breaking his oath of confidentiality, but we promised he could stay anonymous."

"Thanks," Sven says. "Great. When did this happen?"

"Three years ago this autumn. I remember it well. It was just before Goldman's second book came out. If you want my opinion, I think you should check Jochen Goldman bloody carefully. If anything of that sort's actually possible with that slippery bastard. He's probably capable of waiting years for revenge until the right opportunity arises. And of course we all know the rumors about what he's capable of."

Sven is sitting on the edge of Zeke's desk, pushed up against Malin's.

"So you think Goldman might have found out that Petersson gave him away and wanted revenge?" Malin says, thinking that Sven seems to want to say something else, but won't let it out.

"That could fit," Zeke says.

Sven nods.

"Goldman isn't the sort to move on stoically and forget a betrayal. Don't you think?"

Tenerife, Malin thinks. And sees her mum and dad on their balcony. Cardboard cutouts, figures in an advertising brochure selling a happy retirement.

Sun, heat.

No clouds, no frost, no darkness, rain or hail.

Just light.

Just a beaming, wonderfully carefree life after victory. As the evangelical bastards who rented her flat might have put it.

31

Sven has left Malin and Zeke alone at their desks.

"We need to have another word with Goldman," Malin says. "Confront him. See what he says."

"Call him," Zeke says.

Malin dials the number. The phone rings ten times, no answer. She shakes her head.

"He could have sent someone," Zeke says. "We need to find out if any known hit men have been active."

"The book," Malin says. "Didn't Segerberg say in the meeting that Goldman's book had sold badly? Worse than expected? And if they were partners in the business, they would have shared the profits."

"So you think Petersson wanted to shop Goldman to create a bit of a buzz about the book? So it would sell better?"

"Maybe. Sven said that Interpol got the tip-off just before the second book was published."

"But why would he do that? He was already rolling in money," Zeke says.

"A lot is never enough," Malin says. "And business is business. You know, the basic principles."

"Like Fredrik Fågelsjö," Zeke says. "He made a profit to start with, then wanted more, then lost it all."

"Greed," Malin says. "That's killed a lot of people."

Books, books, books.

Was it greed that killed me?

Don't ever go into publishing if you want to earn money.

We printed the second book ourselves, published it through a small company because we thought that would sell better than the first, and why give the money to anyone else? We were as naïve about the book as parents about their children.

But the bastard bookshops hardly ordered any copies, and I used my own money to print fifteen thousand copies, and we needed some serious media attention.

So I called that police officer.

Tipped them off.

But Jochen got away. Presumably tipped off in turn, but I was never worried about him finding out. The detective I called was reliable. And I could always deny it, say that one of Jochen's closest associates must have betrayed him, because there were still a few of us who knew where he was, in spite of everything.

Shoddy, I know.

But there were articles about Jochen, about how close the police had come to catching him, and the book started to sell, only five hundred copies had to be pulped in the end and we made a small profit.

In business I only had one principle: the bottom line. Practically anything was permissible if it helped a deal go well.

Business is business.

If I couldn't earn money from Jochen Goldman, what would I want with him? Really? There's nothing more fleeting than friendship.

But I also know what his anger and self-assurance make him capable of, what doors they can open.

*   *   *

This time Axel Fågelsjö lets them in, invites them to sit down in the sitting room while he goes off to the kitchen to get coffee and cake.

The panels on the walls shine as if they've just been varnished.

I wonder if Fågelsjö has ever seen so much as a picture of a plastic baseboard, Malin wonders as the thickset man comes back with a full tray in his hands.

"I knew you'd be back," he says, serving coffee and shop-bought cinnamon buns. "I'm sorry I didn't tell the whole truth."

"Why did you lie to us about the sale of Skogså, when you didn't actually want to sell?" Zeke asks.

"That's obvious, isn't it? It looks fairly compromising for the family, no doubt about that. For Fredrik."

"But the fact that you lied doesn't make it any less compromising," Malin says.

Fågelsjö's goodwill vanishes. Malin sees his face close up, as if the air were going out of his round, pink cheeks.

"And Fredrik," Malin says. "Why do you think he tried to get away from us? When we only wanted to talk to him."

"He was scared he'd end up in prison," Fågelsjö says. "He panicked. No more, no less."

"So you don't think he was out at Skogså on the morning of that Friday, then? We know he . . ."

Axel heaves himself to his feet and stretches to his full height, shouting, throwing the words at them in a fury, drops of coffee and cake crumbs flying through the air.

"What the hell gives you the right to come here and stir things up? You have absolutely no evidence of anything!"

Zeke's steel eyes. His gaze boring deep into Fågelsjö's eyes.

"Sit down, old man. Sit down, and calm down."

Fågelsjö goes over to the window facing the park and lets his arms drop to his sides.

"I can confirm everything that Fredrik has told you, that I tried to buy back Skogså. But we had nothing to do with the murder. You can go now. If you want anything more from me, you'll have to call me to an official interview. But I promise you, there would be no point in that."

"How did it feel, when he turned you down?" Malin asks.

Fågelsjö stays by the window.

"Were you angry with Fredrik?" she goes on, and can see a silent rage taking over the count's body, and she thinks: you're not the one who should be angry, Jerry Petersson should be angry, and then she remembers what it was like at high school. There were people like Jerry Petersson there when she was at the Cathedral School, working-class boys who were bloody smart and talented and good-looking, who moved in the smart circles without ever truly being admitted to them, and she remembers that she thought those boys were rather tragic. She kept her distance from all that, she had Janne, but she still daydreamed of belonging to the innermost circle of the lovely, smart, and self-proclaimed important students.

"What were you really doing later that night?" she asks aggressively. "Well? Did you go out to Skogså to kill Petersson? Or to persuade him once Fredrik had failed? And it all went wrong? And you ended up killing him?"

The words are firing out of Malin.

She wants to lash the old man with her questions, scare the truth out of him. No fucking way I'm going to retreat from someone like you.

"Or did you pay someone else to do it?"

"Go now," Fågelsjö says calmly. "The same way you came. I'm tired of this damn Petersson."

But I'm not tired of you, Malin thinks.

In the stairwell on the way down they meet a reporter and photographer who Malin knows are from the *Aftonbladet* evening tabloid.

"Good luck with him," Malin whispers after the vultures. "Screw him properly."

*   *   *

Sven Sjöman is eating the salad his wife put in his lunchbox that morning.

Crab sticks and rocket.

An artificial fishy smell hits his nose, reminds him of ammonia. He's alone in the staff room, hungry at eleven because he got up so early. The ugly metal chairs look as uncomfortable as they are, and along the long wall of the room hangs a hideous tapestry of Linköping's skyline on an autumn day like this one. Disproportionately large crows fly around the spire of the cathedral, and on the roof of Linköping Castle sits a misshapen gray cat.

Salad is rabbit food.

Not food for a day like today. Today's real root-vegetable weather. Mash, and shiny, fatty pork belly.

He's told Karim about the call from Interpol, and that Malin tried to call Goldman again.

Sven takes a last mouthful of the salad.

Thinks, What's best, a short, happy life, or a long, miserable one?

At that moment he finally makes up his mind that a trip will do Malin good, even if it's questionable that the state of the investigation justifies it. He'll ask Karim to talk to her about it. That way she won't be suspicious.

Waldemar Ekenberg walks over to Malin and Zeke as they sit at their desks eating sandwiches they bought at the Statoil petrol station on Djurgårdsgatan.

"Did you get anything out of Axel Fågelsjö?"

Malin shakes her head.

"There's something there," she says. "Something."

"You think so? Your female intuition?" Waldemar says.

Malin gives him a weary look.

"I wouldn't mind eating my sandwich in peace," and as she says this Karim Akbar comes over to her desk.

He puts a hand on her shoulder, nods to Zeke and Waldemar, before saying:

"Malin, what would you say to a trip to Tenerife? Have a chat with Jochen Goldman?"

Malin closes her eyes. Lets Karim's suggestion sink in.

Sun.

Heat.

Mum, Dad, far away from Tove, Janne, all that.

"What do you say? Put some pressure on him? He's bound to be there," Karim says.

"I'll go," Malin says quickly. "Is this Sven's idea? Because he thinks I need to get away? That's it, isn't it?"

"You're paranoid, Malin. The investigation requires you to go. And a bit of sun would do you good," Karim says. "Anyway, you've never been down to visit your parents, have you?"

Malin looks at Karim suspiciously. Give him a stare that warns him that that's none of his business.

"Is Janne home?" he goes on, and there's an odd note in his voice, as though he's dealing with a formality, and it annoys Malin.

She thinks she knows what he's getting at.

"Tove can stay . . ." and then she stops herself. Karim doesn't know that they've separated, and he doesn't need to know. Unless he does know already?

"Janne can look after Tove," she says in the end.

"Good," Karim says. "I'll sort out a ticket for tomorrow. Make sure you're packed. And be careful. You know what people say about him."

Malin on her own beside the coffee machine in the staff room. Holding her mobile. Wants to call Tove but knows she's at school now, in a lesson, but she has to see her before she goes.

Wants to call Janne. But what would she say? She has to let them know she's going. Call Daniel Högfeldt and ask for a serious after-noon fuck session? Creep off to the Hamlet and have a stiff drink? Either of the two last ideas sounds wonderful. But she has to work, then pack.

Should I call Mum and Dad? Let them know I'll be there tomor-row? Given their attitude to surprises, I'd cause chaos down there. But I ought to phone anyway. I'll have to see them, even if I don't want to, I haven't told them about the separation, that Tove's still living out at Janne's, that she hasn't moved back in yet, unless Janne's said something, they might have called the house, Dad does that sometimes, but Janne wouldn't have said anything, would he?

It'll be nice to get away from this dump for a few days.

In one way, she thinks, you can see Jerry Petersson as the ultimate product of Linköping, where the inhabitants lose their roots in their desire for money and ridiculous material status. Look at Mum, she's never managed to get a home where she feels she belongs, I don't think she has, Malin thinks, and then she thinks about Janne's house, the flat, and it hurts, and she brushes the thought aside, refuses to admit to herself that she's like her mother in so many ways. Instead she thinks about the fact that you can see Jerry Petersson as the arche-typal class traitor, someone who doesn't know his place, who wants to become something he can never be. A handsome dog that will never win any competitions because he doesn't have the right pedigree.

I hate the Fågelsjö family, she thinks. Everything they stand for. But I can't bring myself to hate them as individuals. And she sees Katarina Fågelsjö on her sofa, her eyes, and she wonders where the sorrow in them comes from? Childlessness. Something else?

Malin picks up her coffee and sniffs the black liquid before head-ing back to her desk.

"You didn't get me one?" Zeke says, looking at Malin's cup.

"Sorry," Malin says, sitting down as Zeke lumbers off toward the staff room.

Malin enjoys the hot coffee, feeling the liquid sting her mouth, before she is brought back by Johan Jakobsson's voice.

He's holding a bundle of papers toward her.

"Just got this from the ladies in the archive," he says. "It turns out that Jerry Petersson was involved in a car accident when he was nineteen. One New Year's Eve. After a party. He was a passenger, in the front seat. The two in the backseat didn't get off so lightly. One boy was killed, and a girl suffered serious head injuries."

Malin can't remember ever hearing any reports of the accident; presumably she was too young to notice when it happened.

"And do you know what makes it all the more interesting?" Johan says.

Malin throws out her hands.

"The accident happened on Fågelsjö's estate."

PART II

Rain from a Cloud That Will Never Return

Östergötland, October

Eggs hatch.

Blind baby snakes peer out. More and more and more. They make my blood boil.

But let me start here: Let's pretend there's a film.

A film about a person's life, where every moment is captured from an illuminating angle.

My film isn't black, white, or a thousand colors. It's matte red and sepia-tinted, a slow journey through numbing loneliness.

I see thousands of people in the images.

They flicker past but never return. Nothing and no one stays, it's the loneliest of lonely films.

There's no disgust in the people's faces, merely, at best, a lack of interest. Most of them don't see me. I am a person in the form of air, like a fading outline in a shifting landscape. I once had something to cling to, but I've taught myself to be free. But did I ever actually manage it? Maybe I just tell myself I did so that I can bear to go on.

And now? After what's happened? Him, I don't want to say his name, floating in the cold dark water. I have no illusions about forgiveness or understanding.

But the rage was wonderful. It was as if the snakes left me, ran out of my body and left me calm and powerful. It really didn't matter what direction it was aimed in, but to say that he didn't deserve it is wrong. I can do it again if need be, if only to experience once more that feeling of something evil disappearing out of me, the snakes calming down, and me, the person I could have been, should have been, there instead.

It was within me, the violence. And it comes from you, Father, you're the man in the pictures, you're hunting me, beating me, you don't care about the others hunting me, beating me, making me the least significant person in the world, and no one, no one cares, no one comes to my rescue.

Except him. He comes.

The pictures shift.

I have a friend. A proper friend. He saves me.

Sometimes I work this autumn, in spite of what's hunting me.

I can feel the warm breath of destruction against my neck. No matter what I do, I must protect myself, it's the only way for us to survive.

They're hunting me now, trying to find out who I am. But I shall evade them, it must be my turn now. I don't regret anything, after all, I've simply restored a form of order. I possess both the fear of the hunter and that of the hunted. In some ways I long for the violence to give me the feeling of calm again, even if I know that's wrong.

I am all the nuances of loneliness that exist in the world, all the quiet, soundless fear.

Father.

You're rushing round with your camera, a cigarette glued to your free hand. You raise your bitter, scarred hand with nicotine-yellow nails. Strike nimbly at the body lying on the ground. I don't want to be that body.

But you don't exist, Father. In a way, I can put even that injustice right. I have been waiting beneath the trees, outside the doors of the heart of evil. Maybe this is my time, after all.

You boys who hate me without me knowing why, without you knowing why. You do not exist.

And then you are gone, you, my rescuer, my friend.

Just like everyone else, you have disappeared.

32

Viva Las Palmas. Viva Las Palmas.

The ZZ Top song pops into Malin's head as she comes down the steps from the plane and heads toward the bus waiting to take her and the other passengers to the arrivals hall.

The sun is sharp, and the early afternoon light cuts into her eyes, her throat feels dry, and the air is hot on her far too thick sweater. It smells of heat here, sweet and cooked, as if the world were being slowly steamed.

She starts sweating at once.

It must be eighty-five degrees.

Palms sway alongside gigantic hangars, scorched grass stretches out between the runways, and through the sun-haze Malin can make out a jagged volcanic mountain.

Viva Las Palmas. Vegas. It's all just a great big game, throw the dice and see where you end up.

But she isn't even in Las Palmas, she's at Tenerife Airport, and it strikes her that all these damn islands are the same.

Soon a gaggle of squawking vacationers is jostling her in the bus, an exhausted mother holding a sleeping two-year-old in her arms, a gang of teenage boys, already seriously drunk, yelling an IFK Norr-köping football chant.

The bus starts, and the cargo of sweaty humanity inside jerks, trying to stay upright even though there isn't enough space to fall over.

Tiredness and sated longing seeping from people's pores.

She called Mum and Dad yesterday and could hear the panic in Dad's voice, no doubt exacerbated by Mum's presence. "What? Coming tomorrow? For work? What sort of work would bring you down here? So you'll be staying in a hotel? Good, no, I don't mean that, but we haven't had time to get anything ready, come over for dinner once you've checked in. Pick you up? Tomorrow at two o'clock? Ah, we've got a teeing-off time booked at the Abama. You should see the course, Malin, the best on the island, it's practically impossible to get a round there."

The bus stops.

Malin gets out, pulls her single heavy case toward the exit.

Outside.

The warmth is suddenly nice, pleasant again now. Not too hot, not too cold, and it's nice to escape the blasted rain and hail, fired by an angry wind at defenseless faces.

"Taxi, madam?" "Limousine?"

A long line of taxi drivers is waiting under a white concrete roof.

They're leaning against their cars, cigarettes dangling from the corners of their mouths, and don't seem terribly interested in driving her to Playa de las Américas, wherever the hell that is.

She manages to pull the piece of paper out of the front pocket of her skirt, getting even hotter from the effort, and reads the name of the hotel.

She says the name to the taxi driver she assumes is first in line for a customer, but he gestures toward his colleagues.

A short, fat, bald man farther back in the queue of cars raises his arms and waves her over.

"Taxi?"

Malin nods, and the man takes her case and dumps it unceremoniously in the trunk of his white SEAT.

She gets in the back.

No air-conditioning.

Her top and skirt stick to the black vinyl seat, and she realizes that the taxi driver is looking at her expectantly in the rearview mirror.

"Where to?" he says.

"Hotel Pelicano," Malin says, and the taxi driver frowns anxiously, as though he were suddenly worried that she might not be able to pay.

Twenty minutes later Malin is sitting on an unsteady bed in a small room with small windows in one corner, where a medieval air-conditioning unit is groaning worse than ten decrepit fridges. The gray paint is peeling from the walls, and the yellow plastic floor is covered with cigarette burns.

Rebecka, the new girl in reception at the police station, had booked the hotel, and Karim must have given her an extremely low budget.

There were bars full of prostitutes on either side of the hotel, and it must be at least a mile and a quarter down to the beach at Playa de las Américas, which they drove past on their way here. There was no lobby to speak of, just a shabby desk where an equally shabby man in his midforties with greasy hair checked her in with the declaration: "Room already paid for."

Malin gets up from the bed.

She's longing for a swim. But the hotel hasn't got anything remotely resembling a pool.

She goes into the bathroom, which is actually pretty clean, but nothing can hide the smell of sewers. A shower cubicle, no bath, and she wants a shower before going to see the local police. They know she's coming, have offered their assistance.

Malin looks at her face in the mirror.

She conjures up Tove's face, and thinks that she's more like Janne really. She called Tove yesterday, had thought about driving to her school and waiting for her after her last lesson, to take her home and make some food, have a chat, tuck her in, all the things she ought to be doing, but she called instead, afraid that she wouldn't be able to leave if she met Tove, if she held her in her arms.

She said she had to go away for work, just a couple of days, and Tove snapped:

"Now you're doing what Dad does, Mum, going off when everything gets difficult."

"Tove, please," she heard herself say, and there was something liberating in pleading with her fifteen-year-old daughter, and Tove fell silent, then eventually said:

"Sorry, Mum. Go. I realize it might be nice to get away."

"It's work."

"Where are you going?"

Malin hadn't planned on telling her. Didn't want to.

"Tenerife," she said.

"But that's where Grandma and Grandad live! I want to come too!"

"You can't, Tove. I've got to work. And you've got school."

Eighteen months ago Tove would have insisted, maybe shouting down the phone, but now she just kept quiet.

"Did you help Dad move my things?" Malin asked.

"No. He didn't want me to."

Then, after another silence:

"So you'll be seeing Grandma and Grandad?"

"I don't know. Well, we've agreed that I might go and see them tomorrow."

"You've got to see them, Mum."

"I'll say hello from you."

"Give Grandad a hug and tell him I miss him. Give Grandma a hug as well."

Then she calls Janne's mobile, hoping to get voice mail, and she does, and leaves a message about going way. He hasn't called back, so she assumes he doesn't care.

Malin goes back out into the room, takes all her clothes off, thinking that even if the air conditioner sounds way too loud, at least it works. Then she gets into the shower and turns it on, genuinely surprised at the strength of the water pressure, and lets the water run down her face and body.

She didn't drink anything on the plane.

And it's lucky there's no minibar in the room.

Then Tove comes into her mind again, and Malin wonders why she hadn't just turned up at the flat or at the station, why she hadn't insisted on meeting, or even suggested meeting, and she feels the muscles around her rib cage contract as she realizes that Tove feels the same ambivalence as she does. You've worked out that keeping your distance makes you feel better, haven't you, Tove?

She pretends to hug Tove. The hot water of the shower is Tove's warm body.

I'm your mum, and I love you.

The police station is more than half a mile away, but Malin decides to walk, wearing a thin white dress and a pair of white canvas shoes.

She walks past big hacienda-style villas behind tall, white-plastered walls, newly built row houses and run-down blocks of flats with laundry drying in the windows. She passes hotel complexes where huge pools sparkle behind thin hedges of tropical plants she doesn't know the names of. A thousand pubs and bars and restaurants screaming out their offerings: FULL ENGLISH BREAKFAST, SWEDISH MEATBALLS, PIZZA, GERMAN SPECIALITIES.

She wants to look away.

She hopes that Los Cristianos, where her parents live, is a bit more upmarket, with a few more redeeming features than the tourist ghetto of Las Américas.

The police station is in a cubelike three-story building on a small square lined with sidewalk cafés. The sea, shimmering blue in the afternoon light, is visible at the end of a street leading off the square.

Where is everyone? Malin thinks. On the beach?

She pushes open the stiff door of the police station and steps in.

No chairs on the speckled floor of the entrance hall, just a notice board on one wall with posters showing the faces of terrorists.

Behind bulletproof glass sits a young uniformed officer. He's smoking, gives her a dismissive glance, as if he gets her sort in here all the time.

He must think I'm just another stupid tourist, Malin thinks. Probably thinks I've been mugged by Russians. Unless he thinks I'm a prostitute? Would he think that?

Malin goes up to the glass, holds up her police ID.

The policeman raises his eyebrows in an exaggerated, Latin gesture.

"Aah, Miss Fors, from Sweden. We've been expecting you. Let me call for Mr. Gomez, who will assist you. He'll be right out."

33

Waldemar Ekenberg slams the car door shut, and Johan Jakobsson rushes after him through the rain, in under the porch of the red-brick block of flats in the district of Gottfridsberg. The area was built in the forties, small flats with a lot of rooms, perfect homes for all the families who moved to the city to work for Saab, NAF, and LM Ericsson.

Will this rain never end? Johan thinks, then for a few seconds the rain turns to snow inside him, to scentless chill, and he reflects upon the fact that we're only at the start of the darkness, November, December, January, February, March, dark months that rip the souls from people's bodies, kids kicking up a fuss on the hall floor, refusing to put their overalls and boots on, protesting against the itchy hats pushed down on their heads.

This morning had been really shit.

The kids both had furious tantrums, God knows what got into them, and his wife was still cross because he hadn't gone to Nässjö with them.

It was a relief to come to work.

A huge damn relief.

And now he watches as Waldemar taps the code into the keypad beside the door, pushes it open angrily as if he's annoyed at this whole wretched autumn, and then they're standing together in a stairwell that smells of damp, looking around, as if there were something there apart from peeling gray-green paint, a list of names, and a staircase made of speckled stone.

"Fucking hell," Waldemar says, and Johan can't tell if his colleague means the stairwell or the weather, but he guesses that Waldemar means the weather and says:

"Yes, and we're only at the start of it."

Jonas Karlsson.

Third floor.

"Right at the top," Waldemar says, and Johan thinks that his swollen, closed eye tells you all you need to know about how brutal Waldemar can be.

Thirty seconds later they are standing in front of a gray-brown door, listening to a doorbell ring inside, then footsteps as someone slowly approaches the front door.

Jonas Karlsson. He was at the wheel in that car accident they found in the archive. Jerry in the car, on the Fågelsjös' land, as it was then. A young man named Andreas Ekström died, and girl named Jasmin Sandsten was handicapped for life.

Nice to get away from the paperwork, Waldemar thinks.

Sven Sjöman this morning: "Dig about in that accident. See if it stirred things up, it's happened before."

People's pasts, Johan thinks. Shackled to them, walled up inside their memories.

Jonas Karlsson.

What happened on that New Year's Eve almost thirty years ago was by all accounts an accident, but how much must you have regretted it since that night? Do you feel responsible for a young man's death, a young woman left severely handicapped? And, if so, what has your life been like since then?

The door opens.

A man with thinning hair and a bulging gut under a wine-red

lamb's-wool sweater looks at them wearily, doesn't say hello, just gestures them in with his right hand.

Puffy cheeks, but a sharp nose, and Johan thinks that seventy pounds and twenty years ago Jonas Karlsson was probably pretty good-looking. A faint smell of alcohol on his breath.

"Take your shoes off. You can sit down on the sofa," and Jonas seems to enjoy giving them orders, there's a force in his voice that's lacking in his bearing.

"I need a piss, then I'll be with you," and Jonas disappears into the toilet as Waldemar and Johan sit down on the white sofa in the living room, feeling the blue-and-white striped wallpaper closing in on them.

Neat and tidy. But not much furniture and a big flat-screen television.

A typical bachelor pad, Johan thinks, and if their files are accurate Jonas ought to be forty-three years old, but he looks considerably older, tired and worn out. In one corner sits a liquor cabinet, its door ajar, an ashtray with a few cigarette butts on the table, but no pervasive smell of smoke.

"Do you think he drinks?" Johan asks.

Before Waldemar can answer they hear Jonas's voice:

"I drink far too much when I'm on a binge. But I hold it together." Then he sits down in front of them on an armchair by the window looking out onto the inner courtyard, the black and apparently dead branches of some birch trees swaying crazily in the wind and the intermittent rain. There's a bookshelf full of DVDs, VHS tapes, and boxes of Super 8 films with illegible handwritten labels.

"Do you live here alone?"

"Yes."

"No family?" Waldemar asks.

"No, thank God. So you want to talk about the accident?"

"Yes," Waldemar says. "But first: Do you wank with your right hand or your left?"

"What?"

"You heard."

"I'm right-handed, if that's what you want to know."

"You've heard what happened to Jerry Petersson?" Waldemar asks.

"I read about it in the paper."

"We're working on a fairly broad front at the moment," Johan says. "So we're checking most people who've ever had anything to do with Jerry Petersson."

"I didn't know Petersson," Jonas Karlsson says. "Not then, and not afterward either."

"So how come you were in the same car that New Year's Eve?"

"We were heading back into the city. I'd borrowed Dad's car and Jerry asked if he could have a lift. That's how I remember it. And I had space in the car. So why not? He offered me a hundred kronor, seemed desperate to get away from there."

Exactly the same as in the file about the accident. Jonas says the same things today as he did twenty-four years ago.

"The party took place on the Fågelsjö estate, in some sort of parish house?" Johan asks.

"Yes, in a parish house that they built as a gift to the church, I think."

"And Petersson wanted to leave the party. Why do you think that was?"

"I've got no idea. Like I said: I didn't really know him. It was cold and late. I suppose he just wanted to go home."

"Did you know the Fågelsjö kids, do you still know them?" Waldemar asks.

Jonas shakes his head.

"God, no. They were really stuck-up. I was in the parallel class to Fredrik Fågelsjö, and he was the one organizing the New Year's party. Sometimes he used to invite me and some of the others to make up the numbers."

Johan nods.

"And Petersson, was he friends with either of the Fågelsjö kids?"

"No, I don't think so. In some ways he was more like me. An ordinary working-class kid who was allowed to join in sometimes."

"And you weren't friends, you and Jerry?"

"No, I said that."

"And the others in the car? Were they friends with Jerry?"

"Andreas Ekström was in Jerry's gang. Jasmin Sandsten probably had a crush on Jerry, that's probably why she wanted to come. I think most of the girls had a crush on him."

"So you think Jasmin Sandsten had a crush on Jerry Petersson?" Johan asks.

"I don't know. All the girls seemed to be crazy about him. That's what he was like."

"Jerry's gang?" Waldemar says.

"He just had a lot of friends," Jonas Karlsson says, rubbing his top lip with one hand. Strange, Waldemar thinks. We haven't found a single person who describes themselves as Petersson's friend.

"But he wasn't friends with the Fågelsjös?"

"No, not as far as I know. There was a group of rich kids, no one else was let in except when they wanted to make up the numbers."

"Can you tell us about that evening?"

Waldemar is making an effort to sound friendly, establish trust, and Johan is surprised at how genuine it actually sounds.

Jonas clears his throat and seems to gather his senses before he starts talking again.

"Like I said, Fredrik Fågelsjö had organized a New Year's Eve party. I got invited, and was allowed to borrow Dad's car to get there, as long as I promised not to drink. After midnight I wanted to go home, piss-ups like that are no fun if you're not drunk as well."

"No, they certainly aren't," Waldemar says.

"And as I was about to leave Jerry Petersson came over with Jasmin Sandsten and Andreas Ekström and asked for a lift. Andreas squeezed into the backseat with the girl and Jerry sat in the front, and the rest is history. I was driving sensibly, but we still slid in the darkness and snow and ended up rolling over into a field. We had seat belts in the front, but not in the back, and they got tossed about like they were in a centrifuge before being thrown out of the rear window. Andreas died of head injuries, and Jasmin . . . well, she still isn't right."

"The others had been drinking?" Waldemar says.

"It was New Year's Eve."

"Did anything particular happen at the party?"

Jonas Karlsson shakes his head.

"Do you think about the accident much?"

Johan says the words slowly, and he sees Jonas's face tense and his pupils expand.

"No. I've put it behind me. It was an accident. I was cleared of any responsibility, and I didn't feel that anyone blamed me for it. But sure, sometimes I think about Andreas and Jasmin."

"Were you friends with Andreas and Jasmin?"

"Only superficially. We went to the same parties. Talked between classes."

"Did you have any contact with Petersson over the years?" Waldemar asks.

"Nothing. Not a thing. I haven't spoken to him once. But it looks like things went well for him. No doubt about that."

Waldemar rubs his knees, fiddling restlessly with his fingers.

"Is it okay if I smoke?"

Jonas nods.

"If you let me have one."

"Can I ask what your job is?"

"I'm a nurse. I work nights in the X-ray department."

"You never married? No kids?"

"No, that's not my thing."

And the room fills with suffocating smoke, and Johan has to force himself not to cough before asking:

"Do you feel guilty?"

Jonas looks surprised at first, then thinks before he says:

"Sometimes."

"What about the parents? Were they angry with you?"

"I think they all accepted it was an accident, that things like that happen. I don't know. I think Andreas's parents managed to move on. I got that impression at his funeral."

"Was Jerry at the funeral?" Johan asks.

"No."

"Fredrik Fågelsjö?"

"No, are you kidding?"

"What about Jasmin's parents.

"She was left a vegetable," Jonas Karlsson says. "I heard her dad took it hard. I think they got divorced."

Johan doesn't reply, looks out of the window, thinks about the father who lost his daughter that New Year's Eve, sees his own daughter running through the house out in Linghem.

In a flowing white dress.

A daughter whose soul vanishes in a snow-covered field one night. A daughter who doesn't stop breathing, and instead faces decades of suffering. What sort of emotions might something like that bring to life?

Zeke Martinsson puts his head in his hands, trying to shut out all the sounds of the police station. The noise and beeping that fills the open-plan office sometimes makes him so crazy he can't think.

Malin in Tenerife.

Must have landed by now. What are the chances of her seeing her parents? God knows.

Zeke has just spoken to Axel and Katarina Fågelsjö about the accident. Sven Sjöman had already spoken to Fredrik Fågelsjö about it, in the presence of his lawyer. All the members of the Fågelsjö family say they can hardly remember the New Year's Eve when the accident took place, it's all in the past, and none of them ever gave any thought to the fact that Jerry Petersson was the surviving passenger. Not when he popped up as a prospective buyer for the castle, and not when he was murdered.

As Axel Fågelsjö expressed it over the phone, "The people in the car were a long way outside our closest, central circle of acquaintances. The children used to invite them sometimes to help fill the rooms."

Of course they remember. Of course they remember that Jerry was the passenger.

As Katarina put it, "I don't remember that party at all. I have no memory of it whatsoever, it's all a blank."

There's something that doesn't fit here, Zeke thinks. He can feel that it's important. But how?

Too much.

Too little.

Skogså.

Always their castle, their estate.

A car spins off the road one New Year's Eve, and one young person dies, another is terribly injured. One of the people in the car, one of the survivors, is found dead many years later in a moat on the land which now belongs to him.

"It's all a blank."

You're lying, Zeke thinks. There's nothing like death to make people remember things.

34

I'm crawling over the snow toward her, I think she's dead, she's not moving and I'm going to bring her back, I'm going to, I'm going to blow air into her lungs and bring her back to life. There's blood trickling from her ears, and the whole world, all the business of New Year's Eve, is ringing inside me and I hear nothing, but I see, and the car's headlights are flickering, pumping out their dead light that makes it look like Jerry is moving in slow motion, he's running through screaming black-and-white images, and the cold is here and a silence, a black silence that I know will follow me for the rest of my life.

Jasmin, was that your name?

Andreas? Where is he? Jerry is standing next to me as I crawl forward, he's yelling something but I can't make out what. I want to listen to him, show myself worthy of being his friend, there's nothing I want more than to be his friend.

I hold your head in my arms, Jasmin, and the snow around you is stained gray with gray blood, and why doesn't this night have any sound, any color? Not even the blood has the strength to be red.

And what's Jerry shouting? What is it he's shouting?

He wants something. And now I remember, how the words shot through the car, drive slower, slow down, and the world spun around,

around, around, breaking into a thousand different sounds, and the screams stopped, and I was hanging upside down in the silence and looking at the steering wheel, at Jerry, who was fiddling with a tape, and then I fell and started crawling.

I thought I could see someone standing above Andreas's body.

A being with the colorless color of fear.

And Jasmin in my arms. She's breathing. How do I know that? Jerry is standing beside me, screaming, "She's breathing, she's breathing," and slowly, coldly, as if through cotton wool, his words reach me, he's screaming, looking at me with his relentless blue eyes, he wants something, he really does want something.

In a way that I will never want anything again.

I can drift back to that field now. It lies there still and pale in the rain and mist, in this raw cold that confuses even the voles that live there.

I'm not about to tell anyone about that evening, that night. About love and decisiveness and death and the white snow and the delicate trickles of blood running from a girl's deaf ears, the blood that spread out beneath her like a soft pillow of the finest velvet.

I was angry.

Disappointed, but determined to push ahead with the life that was mine. I would become the most ruthless of all ruthless people.

I'm drifting higher now.

Looking at Skogså from above. I can see Linnea Sjöstedt's little cottage, she's sitting inside waiting for a death that won't come to her for a long time yet.

The snow sails through the air in its perfect flakes, hardly bigger than motes of dust.

I used, I use my blue eyes.

I am standing in a field, a few square yards of the boundless, outstretched world that is mine, of the vastness of space that is now mine.

A boy ceases to be a boy, as the snow and rain come to rest on the ground.

Who was I, as I stood on the steps in front of a school building just a few months before, feeling the muted rays of the late-summer sun stroke my cheek?

35

The boy, as he still is, stands on the steps of the Cathedral School in the late-summer sun, warm as the memory of his mother's cold hand.

The boy doesn't smoke like so many of the other students of Linköping's most prestigious high school. But he still stands on the steps, holding court, sees his people around him, learning each day how to manipulate them into doing what he wants, thinks that there's nothing wrong with that, because the others don't know what they want.

Then come the boys and girls from the large farms, the estates and castles throughout Östergötland, and it doesn't matter what he says or does, or how much the others look up at him, those people treat him as if he were air. They might talk to him and about him, but there's always a sense of amusement, of distance, in what they say and do, the fact that they let him exist, yet somehow not.

He wants to be able not to give a damn about them, not to want their favor, but he can't help himself, he tries to be amusing on the steps, in class, in the refectory, but it doesn't get him anywhere.

There are closed societies in that school.

For the castle and estate boys, for doctors' kids with family trees, but not for kids from Berga with a mother dead from rheumatism and a pointless father studying in adult education, of all fucking things.

He, the most handsome and smart of all, ought to be an obvious member of the Natural Science Society, or Belles Lettres and Tradition, which, even though it's where the poetic nerds hang out, is still full of status and validation.

Fuck you.

And the parties. The ones they hold and where they invite everyone except him. His brilliance threatens them, frightens them.

But Jerry merely sees a closed door.

A door that will be opened.

At all costs. And if the boys, with all their silly names and houses and cars, are ridiculous, it's a different matter with the girls. The castle and estate girls with their fine-limbed bodies and soft blond hair framing their narrow faces and even narrower lips.

There's something beautiful, irresistible, in the way they move, and they all move toward the boy, like almost all girls do, but while the others allow themselves to be moved by his blue eyes, the nice girls look away at the last moment. The well-bred girls know who the boy is, where he comes from, they know he's a sight worth seeing, a source of amusement rather than a person to be taken seriously.

But there is one girl, the most beautiful of the well-bred girls, who sees who he is beyond the person that he is, who sees the formidable boy he really is, the man he will become, and the life he will be able to offer.

She dares.

And so one evening, after an annual school competition and the party that followed, they make their way down to the Stångån as it winds through Linköping, and they lie down together on a mattress in an abandoned pump house, and she is naked beneath him, and her body is white, and he fills her with his warm hard fleshy soul, and they both know they will never get past this moment, the feeling of this instinctive love, how their unconscious can let go of all doubts and simply relax in the sweat, pain, explosion, and a space free from fear.

Then a New Year's Eve.

White snow falling from a black sky on a blood-stained field.

A boy screaming the words that make him a man.

36

The sea is shimmering in shades of blue that Malin has never seen before, and the sun appears to see its task today as erasing the boundaries between the elements. Malin can feel her dress sticking fast to her lower back as the warm wind wraps itself around her body in a soft, undemanding embrace.

She looks at her showy surroundings.

The pool terrace has been built on a cliff some hundred yards above a deserted beach of black sand.

The pool.

Lined with black mosaic, and Malin thinks a swim would be nice as she looks at the man in the water, swimming length after length without paying any attention to the visitors who have just arrived.

The terrace must be at least four hundred square yards, and Malin and Inspector Jorge Gomez, wearing a crumpled beige linen suit, are sitting under a parasol at a teak table toward the edge of the terrace. On the other side of the pool, in front of the enormous cubelike house, two big-chested blondes are lying on sunbeds, tapping at their mobile phones and adjusting their outsized sunglasses, while three gorillas in jeans peer out of a living room whose large glass doors have been opened onto the terrace.

A modern castle, Malin thinks. A secluded setting, but only six miles or so from the clamor of Playa de las Américas.

A modernist dream.

White and steel, with the sun to heat it. This must have been the sort of thing you were dreaming about, Mum?

The man in the pool carries on swimming, and small waves spread out to the black edges of the pool, running over, and one of the big-chested blondes gets up and waves across to them, and Gomez waves back.

He drove Malin out here, not saying much, only that they were aware of Jochen Goldman's questionable past but that there were a lot of far worse crooks on the island, people who really had been convicted of murder and didn't just have a dodgy reputation, and that they naturally left him alone seeing as there was no current warrant for his arrest.

"He's not one of the noisy ones," Gomez said in broken English. "Not like the Russians. We keep them on a short chain."

"Do you think he'll let us in?"

"If he's home, I expect he will."

Ten minutes later they were standing outside the gates, the black SEAT in neutral, as a male voice said over the loudspeaker, "Drive up to the house, and someone will meet you there."

They were met by a young woman wearing a dress, and she showed them to the table on the terrace and said before disappearing inside the house, "Mr. Goldman will be with you shortly."

Doing the crawl.

Water.

Goldman in the pool.

One arm in front of the other. And Malin sees the muscles in his arms working, feels how much she wants to get in the pool, feel her own body fight against the water, forcing back the pleasant, soft barrier it constitutes.

*   *   *

The muscular yet still fat body is full of energy as the suntanned Jochen Goldman heaves himself out of the pool, accepts a towel from one of the gorillas, then heads toward them with a smile and wet, bleached hair.

The towel around his neck. A heavy watch on one wrist, skin the color of bronze and a thick gold chain around his neck. His teeth whitened, unnaturally bright for a man of forty-five who, in all likelihood, hasn't led the most sedate of lives. A murderer? The sort of man who gets rid of people? Impossible to tell.

Malin feels no fear of him. She feels something else.

Goldman stops thirty feet away from them, puffing out his bulging stomach, drying his hair with his right hand before fastening the towel around his waist.

He holds out his hand to Malin.

She takes it, and the handshake is as firm as his smile feels untrustworthy, and Malin sees that he must have had several bouts of plastic surgery during his years on the run, he has just a few wrinkles around his eyes, and cleaner features and a more pointed nose than in the old pictures from the papers. Goldman sits down in a chair beside them, and one of the gorillas comes over with a pair of sunglasses with diamond-studded frames, and Malin smiles, saying; "Nice sunglasses," then she introduces herself:

"Malin Fors, detective inspector with the Linköping Police. We spoke on the phone. This is my Spanish colleague Jorge Gomez," and Gomez nods toward Goldman, who raises his head slightly in return.

"I'd be grateful if you could take off the sunglasses. So I can see your eyes when we talk."

"They're from Tom Ford. You've got taste," Goldman says, taking off the glasses. "So you were the one who called about Jerry?"

You know it was, Malin thinks, and Goldman smiles in amusement.

"And now you've come all this way just to have a chat with me."

Malin realizes that nothing in the world will make Goldman tell her more than he's already decided to say, so she gets straight to the point.

"We have reason to believe that you knew that Jerry Petersson once tried to give you up when you were on the run."

Another smile, and his brown eyes sparkle against the sun as he says:

"Of course I knew that. I found out through my source in Interpol. I only just got away that time."

"Did you want revenge?"

"No, I got away, didn't I? And why would I want revenge now, several years later? I've never trusted Jerry completely. He wasn't the type who inspired total confidence, and in a situation like mine it made sense to take precautions."

"But you said you were friends?"

"We were. I still had more confidence in him than most people."

Malin nods.

She can see the drops of water slowly drying on Jochen Goldman's skin, as he leans back, legs wide apart, shamelessly making the most of the day as though it were his last.

"He wanted to sell books," he goes on. "His greed was amusing. He had just cashed in several hundred million from that IT company, but he still couldn't help himself trying to increase the sales of the book."

Out at sea a large cruise ship had appeared on the horizon.

The busty blondes had disappeared from the terrace now.

All that was left were the watchful eyes of the heavies from inside the living room.

"You have a good life here."

"I work hard. But I'd like to have a woman here."

"You've got several," Malin says.

"But no one like you."

Malin smiles, feels Goldman's eyes on her, and she wonders if she should adjust her dress, the wind has blown it up, but she leaves it where it is, she doesn't usually take advantage of that, but this time she makes an exception. For herself, or to confuse Goldman?

I don't care, Malin thinks, looking down at her skin.

Gomez is holding his mobile, and it buzzes as a text arrives.

"So you're saying you weren't even angry with Petersson?"

"No. If you don't expect loyalty, you don't get disappointed by betrayal. Don't you think?"

"I don't know," Malin says, and she sees Janne in the hall of his house the first time he was about to go to Bosnia, the evening before his departure, and how she tried in vain to stop him from packing his camouflaged rucksack.

"It's true."

"Did you carry on doing business with him?"

"Oh yes."

"Even though you didn't trust him?"

"He didn't know that I knew. And one thing you need to understand, Malin, is that sometimes Jerry Petersson was exactly the sort of man you wanted on your side."

"Why?"

"He had certain qualities. A ruthlessness that could be exploited."

"What do you mean by ruthlessness?"

Goldman raises his eyebrows, to indicate that he isn't going to answer.

"How did you get to know each other?" Malin asks instead.

"It was when I got into trouble on one occasion. My usual lawyer at the same firm was on holiday. I liked him at once. And when he set up his own practice, I went with him."

"Do you know why he set up on his own?"

"He scared the others."

"Scared them?"

"Yes, he was much smarter than them, so they had to get rid of him."

Malin smiles. Goldman strokes his stomach and flares his nostrils like Tony Soprano.

"Is there anything you think I should know? About your business dealings? About Jerry?"

"No. Surely you should do some of the work for yourselves?"

Goldman smiles.

"So you didn't decide to get your revenge in retrospect, you didn't send a hit man?"

Goldman grins at Malin as if she herself were a hired killer, but a welcome, anticipated one.

He puts on his sunglasses and tilts his head so that the sharp sparkle of the jewels' reflections hits Malin's eyes and she has to squint.

"Don't bore me, Malin. You're better than that. Anyway, if I did do that, I'm hardly likely to tell you."

Malin turns her face to the sea.

Thinks about Tove.

Wonders what she's doing now.

Thinks about Mum.

About Dad.

About the fact that he's probably looking forward to her visit later that evening.

"Take a walk with me," Goldman says. "Let me show you the grounds."

She follows him down a steep flight of steps that winds down toward the beach.

He's still wearing his swimming trunks, and his brown body shines in the sun as he tells her about the Spanish architect who designed the house, that he has also designed a house for Pedro Almodóvar in the mountains outside Madrid.

Malin says nothing.

She lets Goldman talk, thinks that they're out of sight of the gorillas now and that Gomez is probably still sitting up on the terrace, talking into his mobile.

Goldman asks if she's read his books, and she says no, then realizes that she probably should have.

"You haven't missed anything," he says.

He jumps down onto the black sand of the beach, rushes down to

the edge of the water so as not to burn his feet on the hot sand, and
Malin sits down on the bottom step, takes off her canvas shoes, then
runs down to the water as well.

"Take your clothes off. Have a swim. I can get a swimsuit for you.
You have no idea how wonderful it is to lie on this beach and feel the
salt crystallize on your skin."

"I can imagine," Malin says, and against her will she wants to lie
on this sand with Goldman beside her, looking at him, at the misdi-
rected energy that forms him.

He throws a stone into the water. It bounces across the surface.

"That stone," he says, "that's what I felt like for ten years."

"Self-inflicted," Malin says. "And you were richly rewarded for it."

"You're harsh," Goldman says.

"A realist," Malin replies. "Did Jerry Petersson ever mention a car
accident he was in once?" she goes on.

Warm water between her toes, a little bubbling, frothing wave
rolling over the black sand.

"It was when he was in his late teens, people died."

Goldman stops.

Looks at her, and she can't see his eyes behind the sunglasses,
but she realizes that he is about to tell her what they came down to
the beach for him to say, what she has unconsciously been expecting him to say if she treated him like an ordinary person.

"He bragged about it once. One New Year's Eve in Punta del Este.
That he was the one driving the car, that he was drunk, but managed
to persuade someone else who was sober to say he had been driving.
Jerry was proud as punch about it."

37

You're babbling, Jochen.

What you told her about the accident: I have no memory of any New Year's Eve in Punta del Este. Do I?

I see you standing on the terrace of your newly built castle looking out across the sea.

Of course I wanted to give you up.

Like a cowboy film, John Wayne on the run, escaping from the Apaches through a canyon on the border between Texas and Mexico.

I'm drifting away from you now Jochen, leaving you there with your restlessness; you haven't managed to escape that yet.

Swim a few more lengths of your shimmering black moat.

You should know that where I am now there's no restlessness, only curiosity and fear and a thousand other feelings that I don't know the names of. I don't have to keep other people at a distance, I don't need a moat.

I'm finally free from angst and shame.

But you aren't, are you, Malin?

Malin looks at the hotel room.

It's hot now, the air-conditioning shut off automatically when she left, and the smell of mold is more noticeable. She's taken all her clothes off and is lying on the bed, wishing she'd been booked into a hotel with a pool, would love to feel cold water embrace her body.

Instead she looks at the gray-green patches of damp on the ceiling and waits for Zeke to answer his mobile.

It's four o'clock, he ought to answer now.

And there comes Zeke's hoarse voice in her ear.

"Malin. What are you up to? How are you?"

"I'm lying in the shabbiest hotel room I've ever stayed in."

"How's the weather?"

"Sun. Hot."

"Have you seen Goldman?"

"Yes."

"And?"

Suddenly there's agitated shouting from one of the bars, then disco music pumping out at full volume.

"A disco?"

"A bar full of prostitutes," Malin says.

"Exotic," Zeke says.

"I was about to say that Goldman claims Jerry Petersson was driving the car that New Year's Eve, not Jonas Karlsson. According to Goldman, Petersson was drunk and persuaded Karlsson to say he was driving to avoid prosecution."

Silence over the line.

"Bloody hell," Zeke finally says. "Do you believe him? Or is he playing with us?"

"Impossible to say. But we can use it. Put Karlsson under a bit of pressure."

More screaming from the prostitutes.

"Have you spoken to him yet?"

"Yes. Jakobsson and Ekenberg went to see him. Now they can go and do it all over again."

"The Fågelsjö family?"

"They claim they hardly remember the accident."

"They remember," Malin says. "No doubt about that."

Zeke is silent for a moment, and Malin thinks about Gomez's offer of a beer just now, and how she said no even though her body was shrieking for a cold beer or preferably something even stronger.

But she resisted.

Then Zeke goes on:

"Waldemar and Johan will have to talk to Karlsson again in light of this new information. And we need to talk to the relatives of the others in the car. That's still a possibility. Karlsson may have been trying to get money out of Petersson. One of the relatives might have found out the truth, and God knows what that could have stirred up. Stabbed forty bloody times."

"Talk to the Fågelsjös," Malin says.

"Will do," Zeke says. "Fuck knows where this shit's going to take us. Have you called home, to Tove?"

None of your business, Malin thinks. I haven't wanted to call because Tove's at school, isn't she?

"Never mind that now," Malin says. And hears how it sounds. "Sorry," she adds.

"No problem, Malin," Zeke says. "But you have to realize that this case isn't more important than your own daughter."

Shut up, Zeke.

"Someone's knocking at the door," Malin says. "Probably house-keeping. I've got to go."

Zeke hangs up.

No knock at the door, she just wanted to end the call.

Jerry, Malin thinks. Jerry. If it was you driving that night, you locked it away in a little black safe and threw away the key, didn't you? Only took it out when you were having a pissing contest with Jochen.

I never take my secrets out, Malin thinks, because I don't know what they are. And you, Jochen, you don't want to know what your real secret is, do you? You think everything can be controlled, that you can make the world do whatever you want.

She closes her eyes.

Feels anxiety coursing through her body.

I'm tired of feeling so miserable, she thinks. Angry and scared. Why have I got the same look in my eyes as Katarina Fågelsjö?

Mum and Dad in a little while.

Golf clubs swinging against a blue sky. The worst nonactivity of all.

This case, Malin thinks. It's dragging me back to the growth ring right at the center of my trunk.

Malin's fallen asleep. Lying defenseless with her arms above her head, like a child who knows instinctively that her mum will never leave her.

She's dreaming about a man in a suit sitting in a futuristic office chair behind a mahogany desk in a room with large windows facing onto a busy street. The man is wearing a gray suit, and he has no face.

He is talking to her. She wants to put a stop to it but doesn't know how.

"You're lying quietly on the bed," he says. "In your shabby room, and deep down you wish you could lie there all evening, all night, but you know you have to wake up, you have to go out, and soon you'll get in the shower, try to shake off all your emotions before heading right into the middle of them.

"You've come down here to this overdeveloped island to discover my secret, how I ended up with all those stab wounds in my body. And I'm grateful for that," the man says.

"But you're more interested in your own secret than mine."

"Do you imagine you're going to find it at your parents'" this evening? Don't hope too much, Malin. Wouldn't it be better to go home? Stop drinking and look after your daughter? But you can't even manage that. That's how weak you are.

"It's much easier to concentrate on me.

"With me, you can glimpse truths and completely avoid having to deal with yourself.

"Have a drink, Malin.

"Drink, Malin.

"It'll make you feel better."

Then the man and the room disappear. Only his voice remains.

Malin can hear his voice inside her, whispering:

"Drink, drink, drink."

And in her sleep she wonders where the voice comes from. Is it a gentle plea from her own body for calm, for release from the sadness, longing, and fear?

She wakes up and the voice disappears, but the feeling of it lingers in the room.

She gets in the shower.

Fifteen minutes later she's sitting in a shabby bar looking at her reflection in a chipped mirror.

The glass of tequila half full, the cold beer glass alongside misted up.

Mum.

Dad.

Here I come. But I should have brought Tove with me. So you could see her. The most beautiful of all beautiful things.

"He's not home this time either," Waldemar Ekenberg says as they try ringing on the door of Jonas Karlsson's flat for the third time in a day.

"And he hasn't got a fucking mobile."

"Where could he be?" Johan Jakobsson says.

"No idea."

Johan looks at the door.

Solid and closed, in a way that suggests it wants to keep its secrets. They were here two hours ago, after Malin's call to Zeke, and Jonas Karlsson wasn't at home then either. Nor was he at work at the hospital.

Back at the station they've had police constables looking for the parents of the girl and boy involved in the car crash. Both couples had divorced now, but still lived in the city.

Evening now. We can't disturb them this late for something this flimsy, Johan thinks. But tomorrow we'll have to.

I'm not looking forward to tomorrow, he thinks, as he turns on his heel and heads down the stairs, away from Waldemar, away from Jonas Karlsson's flat.

38

Reluctant loss has an address.

Number 3, Calle Amerigo.

The two quick tequilas and beers have done their job.

Malin's hands rest easily on her bare legs. She's wearing a short white skirt and a pink blouse, not too creased even though they've been packed away in her case.

The clock on the dashboard of the taxi says 7:25. Dad's words over the phone:

"Come at half past seven, we're sure to be back from our round by then."

The taxi feels its way out of Playa de las Américas along a road that follows the sea, the worst of the noise and commotion is left behind, replaced by a residential calm. Hastily constructed hotels no longer line the shore, just equally quickly built blocks of flats where the careful decor of the balconies indicates pensioners.

Mum.

They spent a long time looking for a flat by the sea, but they were too expensive.

In Los Cristianos the taxi swings off toward the mountains, where increasingly tall white-plastered blocks scramble up ocher-colored cliffs.

I haven't seen my parents for three years.

Have I missed them?

Sometimes, maybe, when I hear Dad's voice over the phone and he asks me to come down and visit, or when he's been going on about the plants.

Mum.

I might have spoken to you ten times, and even then we only asked each other about the weather.

Have I missed you in Tove's life? You, Dad, you've asked after her, of course you have. But you haven't really cared, not properly.

That's why I was able to move to Stockholm on my own with her and attend Police Academy, because I felt that you weren't there, not for me, and not really for her.

Has Tove missed you?

Malin tried to call her a short while ago, but there was some problem with the line.

Of course Tove has missed her grandparents. Janne's mother and father are long since dead, hardened smokers that they were.

Malin is tipsy from the tequila. She feels she can be honest with herself in the taxi.

The buildings here. Storage space for people.

What's this scorched bastard volcano island got, apart from heat and a flight from responsibility?

"Come at half past seven."

Malin shuts her eyes.

"We'll be back from the golf course by then."

The lift stops on the fourth floor, and the chipped metal doors glide apart, and Malin wants to close them again, run from the house, and get a taxi back to the airport and get the first plane back up to the darkness and rain and cold.

She heads toward the door in the stairwell that must lead to her parents' flat.

Warmer back home than here. The white, marble-like stone on the walls and floor of the landing seem to create a peculiar chill, a sort of cold she's never experienced before, and she's eight years old and standing outside the house in Sturefors, it's cold and it's raining and she's lost her key and she can hear Mum inside the house. Mum knows she's standing out on the steps and is freezing and crying and wants to get indoors, but she doesn't open up, angry that Malin has lost her key.

Malin standing outside the door.

The door in Tenerife.

I'm going to turn back.

Maybe they aren't home.

But she can hear the familiar voices through the door, first talking to each other in a normal conversational tone, then shouting at each other, and she's lying in her bed in the room she lived in as a girl, listening to them shouting in the bedroom at the other end of the house, and there are cold autumn nights, winter nights, spring nights, and summer nights, and she doesn't understand what they're saying and she's seven eight nine years old and doesn't understand the words, but she knows Mum and Dad are shouting things that change everything forever, the sort of things that change the direction of life, whether or not anyone realizes it.

And now, outside this door, Mum and Dad's words fall silent in her memory. Did they even exist, those words? She can only remember herself in the darkness. How everything was quiet and she lay there waiting for life to start.

Rattling.

Malin jumps back.

She doesn't have time to see the shadow over the peephole in the door, and Dad is suddenly standing in front of her, suntanned and jolly and happy to see her. His face is rounder and he looks well, and he pulls her to him, takes her in his arms and gives her a long hug without saying a word, and in the end Malin says:

"Dad, I'm having trouble breathing."

And he lets go of her. Steps aside. Says, "Let's go in and see Mum," and Malin goes into the flat, sees the furniture and rugs they brought down from Linköping, how badly they match the new Spanish hacienda-style furniture.

"How are you?" Dad asks as he follows her into the living room.

"Fine," she replies, and out on a balcony with a view of the Atlantic she sees her Mum facing away from her, against the strange glow from the streetlamps. Mum is sitting at a table in a pink tennis shirt, her hair still a blond bob, and Malin wonders what her face looks like.

Wrinkled? Alert, angry, or just older?

Mum doesn't turn around, and soon Malin is standing beside her on the balcony, hearing Dad's voice say: "Here she is!" and now Mum notices her, and Malin thinks that her face looks like it always has, only browner, with the same pinched expression in spite of the smile on her lips.

Mum gets up.

Air-kisses my cheeks.

"Have you been drinking, darling? You smell like you have. And you do look a bit puffy."

And without waiting for a reply she goes on:

"It's lovely that you're here, darling. Wonderful. It's about time. We've bought the best paella from a place on the way back from Abama, oh, you should see the course there! What a course! Henry, get your daughter a glass of wine, would you? There, now sit yourself down," and Malin sits down opposite her mother on her parents' balcony in Tenerife and she doesn't know whether to look at her mum, around the flat, or out to sea.

"So what are you *really* doing here?"

Mum is drinking her wine quickly and nervously, and Malin is taking great gulps from the glass Dad has just put in front of her, and she wonders if this is what visiting your parents is like when you're an only child whom they haven't seen for three years. Then Malin takes another deep gulp of wine and thinks that there aren't any rules for this sort of thing, no accepted standards of human behavior, and she wishes Dad were here, but instead she can hear him doing something in what must be the kitchen.

Mum opposite her, with her question hanging in the air.

"A case I'm working on," Malin replies. "It led here. So I came down."

And any other person would have continued to ask about the case, wondering what it was about, what the connection was that meant a detective inspector from Linköping was prepared to take a five-and-a-half-hour flight down to Tenerife.

But Mum starts talking about the golf course.

"You see, it's in Abama, the most exclusive resort on the whole island, and it costs an absolute fortune to play even if you can actually get a tee-off time, but they held a lottery for slots at the Swedish Club and what do you know, we won! You should see the first hole, we were there with Sven and Maggan . . ."

Malin pretends to listen.

Nods.

Inside she is telling Mum about Tove, how Tove is, that she's growing up. She tells her about Janne, that they've separated and that she's very upset about it and sometimes doesn't know what to do with herself, and "if you mishit the ball there it can fly out to sea, and you lose three strokes and then the whole round is ruined," and Malin tells her that she can see that she's making a mess of everything, that she wants to drink, that she's drinking too much, she drinks like a fish, and that deep down she's already admitted to herself, but only herself, that she's a fucking alcoholic but that there's no way she's ever going to admit that to anyone else, and she nods happily when Dad pours her some more wine, and suddenly plates appear on the table alongside a shop-bought paella in an aluminium tray with three langoustines perched on top of the yellow rice.

Darkness has fallen.

And Malin can hear hesitant, distant music from the pubs down by the shore and she listens to it as Dad says:

"Help yourself, Malin."

And she stretches out too quickly and knocks her wine over.

Damn.

"Oops," Dad says. "I've got it."

"Still as clumsy as ever!" Mum says, and Malin feels like getting up and leaving, but she doesn't move.

*   *   *

Malin can hear her mother chattering away to one of her friends on the phone in the living room.

Dad with his calm face opposite her, he almost seems to think it's a relief that Mum's left the table.

The paella is all gone.

It was good, Malin thinks, in spite of everything.

Mum's been talking about golf, about hairdressers, about the rising price of food, about the fact that the flat may not be that big but its value has gone up, about some yoga class she's just started going to, all this and much more, and then the phone rang and she went to answer it. Now Dad asks:

"How are things with Tove?"

The wine has gone to Malin's head.

"She's starting to get grown up."

"Like you've been for a long time."

You're smiling at me, Dad.

"And with Janne?"

He must know that we've separated.

"It's okay. We couldn't make it work. No point trying, really," and just as Dad is about to respond to what she's said, Mum appears in the doorway, saying: "That was Harry and Evy. They're coming over. They're keen to meet our clever detective inspector daughter."

No, Malin thinks. No.

And Dad looks at her, says: "You know what, Malin? Why don't you help me clear the table, then we can take a stroll down to the shop and get some ice cream before they get here?"

"Yes, you do that," Mum says. "My feet ache. We must have walked at least twelve miles today. How many sixty-seven-year-olds can do that?"

Malin drains her wine glass.

Makes sure she gets the last drops, but Mum doesn't seem to notice how thirsty she is.

39

The freezer case and air-conditioning of the little supermarket are groaning.

The shopkeeper greeted Malin's dad like an old friend, and Dad had a long conversation with him in almost fluent Spanish. Malin didn't understand a word of what they were saying.

"Ramon," Dad says. "Nice bloke."

And now he says:

"What do you think? Vanilla or chocolate? You'd rather have chocolate, wouldn't you?"

"I'd rather have a beer in the bar next door."

He gets a tub of chocolate ice cream from the freezer before turning to face her, the front of his pale-blue shirt speckled with yellow from the paella, and Malin sees now that his hair is much thinner than when they last met.

"We can do that if you like, Malin," and the next minute they're sitting in the bar, in lingering eighty-five-degree heat under a whirling fan in the ceiling, and Malin wipes the condensation from her glass and thinks that the feeling is the same here as back home in the Hamlet or the Pull & Bear. The walls of the bar are covered with blue tiles, decorated with white fish caught in nets.

Dad takes a deep gulp of his beer and says:

"Mum doesn't change."

"So I see."

"But somehow it's easier down here."

"How do you mean?"

"There's less pretending."

Malin takes a mouthful of beer and nods to show that she knows what he means, then she takes a deep breath.

"You've been having a tough time," he says.

"Yes."

"Anything you want to talk about, love?"

Do I want to?

What would we say to each other, Dad? And the fish on the tiles, half of them have their eyes closed, as if they're in a dark moat, and she feels like telling him about her dreams, about the boy in them, tell him and find out who he is, find out what's hidden in the darkness in those dreams.

"I've been dreaming about a boy," she says finally.

"A boy?"

"Yes."

"A little boy?"

Dad is quiet, drinks some more.

"Did Mum ever go away when I was little?" Malin goes on.

"The ice cream's melting. Shall we go back?" he says.

"Dad."

"Some things are best not spoken about, Malin. Some things are just the way they are and you have to accept it. You're pretty good at not letting anyone get too close. You always have been."

"What's that supposed to mean?"

"Nothing," he says. "Nothing."

Malin empties her glass in four large gulps before she gets up and leaves a five-euro note on the bar.

She and Dad stand beside each other on the pavement. Cars go past and the noise of people's voices merges with unfamiliar music.

"You've got a secret, you and Mum, haven't you?" Malin says. "Something you're not telling me, even though you should."

Dad looks at her and he opens his mouth, moves his mouth and tongue, but no words come out.

"Tell me, Dad. I know there's something I need to know."

And he looks like he's about to say something, then he looks up at the balcony of the flat, and Malin can just make out the figure of her mother up there.

"The secret. There is a secret, isn't there?"

And Dad says:

"We'd better get back up with the ice cream before it melts. Our friends will soon be here." Then he turns and walks away.

Malin doesn't move.

"I'm tired, Dad," she says, and he stops, turns back toward her again. "I'm not coming back up. I'm going to go back to the hotel."

"You have to say goodbye to Mum."

"Explain to her, will you?"

And they stand there facing each other, fifteen feet apart. They look at each other for almost a minute, and Malin is waiting for him to come over to her and give her a hug and force everything that stings and burns away from reality.

He holds the ice cream up.

"I'll explain to Mum."

Then Malin sees the back of his shirt. Pale-blue and sweaty in the dim light from the bar, the shop, the streetlamps, the stars and the half-moon.

What are you doing here?

Jochen, do you usually come here? Is that you, sitting over at the bar, showing off your bronze skin?

What's she doing here?

They seem to be wondering, the men sitting by the counter around the podium where the naked girls are dancing in blue fluorescent light. She's in one of the bars opposite the hotel. She can crawl home from here.

Lesbian?

I don't give a damn what you think, Malin thinks. I don't give a damn that each shot of tequila costs thirty euros and that the girls keep disappearing with men behind a curtain.

African women.

Balkan girls.

Russians.

Many of them must have ended up here after being threatened with violence. How many of them are going to end up like Maria Murvall?

But now they're dancing, their oiled skin shining as they spin listlessly around the poles with their eyes empty of emotion.

Malin downs her fourth tequila and at last the room, the girls, the men around her start to lose their edges and blur together into a single warm, calm image of reality.

I can sit here okay, Malin thinks.

This bar is my place.

She raises a finger and calls the bartender over.

He fills her glass and she puts money on the bar. She knows that as long as she pays, she'll be allowed to drink, and if she ends up falling off her stool they'll carry her out into the street and tuck her out of the way so she can sleep it off.

But I'm going to cling to this planet, she thinks.

Then she closes her eyes.

Tove's face. What's she doing now? Is the beast there by her bed, about to strangle her? Do drowned sewer rats wants to nibble the skin from her sleeping body? I'm coming, Tove, I'll look after you.

Janne's face. Daniel Högfeldt's. Mum's, Dad's.

Away with you all. Do you even wish me well?

Away.

Maria Murvall. Mute and expressionless, yet still so clear. As if she's chosen to withdraw from the world to avoid seeing the darkness.

Jerry Petersson. Trying to move in the moat, clamber out, but the green spirits are holding him down, the fish, but also the worms and crabs and eels and aggressive black crayfish eating away at his body, falling from his mouth and empty eye sockets.

Jochen Goldman's body. Is he going to come after me now? Am I in his way? Am I going to end up as shark food?

I don't care.

The Fågelsjö family's self-awareness and bitterness. A car rolling over and over like a huge snowball on a cold, snowy New Year's Eve.

Dark-colored cars.

Eyes that see, but notice nothing. The world disappears and becomes soft and malleable, simple and easy to understand, to like.

Drink, drink, drink, says the voice. Drink. It'll make you feel better, everything will be fine.

I'm more than happy to listen to that voice, Malin thinks.

40

*Y*ou should see them now, Malin.

What are their names, your colleagues? Waldemar? Johan?

They're standing in the morning chill with Jonas Karlsson outside the building he lives in, asking him to go in, saying they have to talk to him, that he didn't tell them the truth about what happened on that fateful New Year's Eve.

You see, Malin, I'm keeping an eye on what you're all doing.

It hasn't been such a great morning for your colleagues. The prosecutor has ordered that Fredrik Fågelsjö be released from custody, he's received a request from the lawyer, Ehrenstierna, which convinced him that Fågelsjö was unlikely to commit any further offenses, and that he would remain at your disposal. "We can't hold such a prominent member of the local community for a whole week on relatively minor offenses."

But you police still suspect him.

New Year's Eve. When will that snow stop falling? When will those lawnmower blades fall silent?

Was I the one driving?

What was I doing at Fredrik Fågelsjö's New Year's party? I don't want to remember, but it was one of those things people do, Malin, when we both want something yet somehow don't, when we want to demonstrate our sovereignty, yet have to let go of it in order to get something.

Jonas is scared now.

I can feel it when I position myself just an inch away from him. He knows that time has caught up with itself.

Jonas was on his way to work when the police came back. He tells them he spent the whole of the previous day at the racetrack out in Mantorp.

Maybe he was the one driving after all?

Jochen is capable of playing with anyone just for the fun of it. Without all those games his life is pointless.

Now the door to Jonas Karlsson's block of flats closes.

Waldemar's hand on his shoulder as they disappear inside the building. And I am with you, Malin, beside your sleeping head 34,052 feet up in the air.

Secrets, Malin. You used to love secrets when you were a little girl, and now you're obsessed with them.

The plane is moving through the atmosphere. You're sleeping a dreamless sleep and you could do with it, you had to stop the taxi on the way to the airport so you could leap out and empty the previous day from your stomach.

Are you incorrigible, Malin?

You look so exhausted as you sit there leaning against the cold concave window, deaf to the roar of the engines. I actually feel like stroking your cheek, Malin, and that's probably all you want, isn't it?

Sinking into human warmth.

Sensing that it exists somewhere beyond the cold stones of the moat.

Jonas Karlsson has sat down on the sofa in his living room. Johan Jakobsson is sitting opposite him in an armchair while Waldemar Ekenberg walks restlessly up and down the room. The coffee table is covered with empty bottles and a squashed wine box, and the sour smell of drying alcohol stings their nostrils. But apart from the mess on the table, Jonas's flat is clean.

Waldemar's long frame is shaking, his voice deep and colored by a hundred thousand cigarettes.

"You lied to us," he says, and Johan feels his voice make him shiver: the catch at the end of the words in spite of his local drawl, in spite of the smoker's hoarseness.

Jonas seems to have capitulated already, ready for the storm that's coming his way now.

"I didn't . . ."

"Shut up, you soppy git!" Waldemar shouts. "Of course you fucking lied. Jerry Petersson was driving the car that New Year's Eve. Not you."

"I . . ."

And Johan wants to tell Waldemar to take it easy, to show a bit of consideration, but he stays silent. There's something about the atmosphere in the room that he finds irresistible, against his will.

"If you tell us the truth, there won't necessarily be any consequences for you," Johan says. "It was so long ago . . ."

"I wasn't the one . . ."

And Johan looks into Jonas's scared eyes, sees that he realizes that everyone around here, either by media or rumor, will find out his story and whisper it behind his back.

Then Waldemar raises one hand, tenses his open palm, and lets it fall hard across Jonas's mouth, and Jonas screams, and blood trickles from a cracked lip.

Waldemar leans over him.

"Do you want more? Do you?"

"I . . ."

Another blow whines through the air, hits the back of Jonas's head, throwing him forward into the coffee table.

"Well?"

"I wasn't the one driving!" Jonas Karlsson yells. "It wasn't me. Jerry, Jerry, Jerry!"

*   *   *

Malin's woken up.

Her brain somehow shut off by the buzz of the plane, the constant rumble of the engines, and the noise of the young children two rows in front. She has a retired couple next to her, suntanned, they've evidently spent a long time in the sun and could have been her parents. They smiled at her when she woke up, opening her hungover, bloodshot eyes.

The tin of Heineken in front of her is half empty. It's calmed her body down, stifled the nausea.

An excursion to the heat.

But only physically. I want to get away, she thinks. She sees Jerry Petersson in the moat, his body drifting this way and that from the regular yet uneven movement of the water.

Looks like you were a bastard, Malin thinks. A real bastard. So why on earth do I care?

And then she hears a voice in the depths of her throbbing skull.

What else would you care about instead, Malin? Everything you ought to but can't quite get to grips with?

"Okay, you're going to tell us what happened."

Waldemar Ekenberg's voice is calm but commanding, and the words conceal the threat of further violence.

Waldemar has sat down beside Jonas Karlsson on the sofa, handing him a roll of toilet paper he's just got from the bathroom, and Johan leans forward in his armchair and says:

"Tell us the truth now. Jerry's dead. He can't do anything to you now."

And Jonas Karlsson clears his throat, looks up and starts to talk, with a piece of toilet paper stuck to the cut in his lip.

"Jerry was at the party when I got there. I think he got a lift with someone else. At half past one Jerry wanted to go back into the city, and I offered to drive him and the others. We went out to the parking lot where I'd left the car. Fredrik Fågelsjö had gone up to the castle with the people he wanted to carry on the party with, and we weren't among them."

"So you were friends, you and Jerry?"

"I was one of a lot of people in his gang. Friends? He didn't have any friends. He could make you think you were his friend, sure. And I wanted to be his friend. I admired him, he was the sort of person you wanted to be, the sort you wanted to like you, at any price."

"So you admired him. Then what?"

"The four of us, me, Jerry, Andreas, and Jasmin, were going to drive back to the city. When we got to the car Jerry announced that he wanted to drive. He was wound up about something, he'd been in a bad mood all evening. He got really aggressive when I refused at first. Shouting and screaming. So I threw him the keys, said, "You drive then, if it's so fucking important," and I got in the passenger seat and put my seatbelt on, and Andreas and Jasmin got in the back, but they must have been too drunk to remember their belts."

"What was Jerry upset about?"

"No idea. He always had loads of secrets."

"So you set off."

Waldemar puts his arm round Jonas's shoulders.

"Jerry really put his foot down."

"You didn't get very far."

"We must have been doing sixty or seventy when we hit the bend. The wheels lost their grip, and I remember thinking we were fucked, then the car was rolling over and over into that snow-covered field, and it was like being inside a washing machine full of brilliant light, then everything stopped and it all went quiet. After a bit I saw Jerry hanging upside down beside me, he was struggling to get free, and he undid my belt, and if he was drunk before, the adrenaline must have cleared his head completely."

Johan can see the scene in front of him.

The two young men staggering round in the snow, trying to protect themselves from the wind and the driving snow, then seeing the bodies farther off in the field.

"We saw them. Andreas and Jasmin. They were lying in the field."

"Did you go over to them?"

"Yes. Blood was trickling from Jasmin's ears, but she was still breathing."

"But you realized Andreas was dead?"

"I think so."

"What next?" Waldemar asks.

"Jerry grabbed me by the arms and said, 'I'm going to get nailed for this, I was drunk, but if we say you were driving I might get away with it.' He looked at me with his big blue eyes and I realized I'd never be able to say no to him. And I thought, What's the point of Jerry's life being ruined? He said, 'If we say you were driving, the police will write it off as just an accident caused by ice, because you're sober."

"So you agreed?" Johan asks.

"Yes."

"Just like that? That sounds too straightforward to me."

"Jerry could be extremely persuasive. And he promised me all sorts of things before the police and the ambulance arrived. He promised to be my friend, and there was nothing I wanted more, it was like a dream come true. And he promised to give me money if he ever got rich."

"Did he become your friend?"

"No, he moved to Lund, didn't he?"

"Did you ever get any money?"

"No."

"Did you ever ask?"

"No. It was so long afterward when articles about his businesses started to appear in the papers."

Waldemar snarls his words:

"You never tried to blackmail him when things started to go well for him? Or when he moved back here? You never threatened to tell the truth?"

"No. What did I stand to gain from that? If the truth came out then everyone in the city would know I'd lied, and I'd just look pathetic. I could even have been charged."

"So aren't you?" Waldemar says. "Pathetic, I mean?"

Jonas laughs nervously.

"That's exactly what I am," he says.

"It never occurred to you that the parents had a right to know what really happened?"

Jonas gestures toward the bottles on the table.

"It occurs to me every day."

"So you never tried to get any money from Jerry? You didn't go out to see him that night? And then it all went wrong?"

"That night I was around at a couple of friends,' we were drinking till the early hours. You can call them."

"You bet we're going to call them," Waldemar says.

Jonas wriggles out of Waldemar's grasp. Gets up and stands in the middle of the room.

"Jerry Petersson wasn't like other people. And everything he promised me that night, he didn't do any of it. But to this day I still think I did the right thing. Andreas was dead. Jasmin handicapped for life. They knew what they were doing when they got in the car, even if they were drunk. They were mature enough to understand the consequences of their actions. No one blamed me, it was written off as an accident, and accidents happen. So why ruin Jerry's life? In other people's eyes, you never escape something like that."

"You mean driving while drunk and causing the deaths of other people?" Johan asks.

"That's exactly what I mean," Jonas says, pulling the piece of toilet paper from his lip, which starts bleeding again.

41

The windscreen-wipers are working frantically to keep the rain off, to keep the view clear.

The clock on the dashboard says 1:35.

Through the windscreen Malin can see fields and clumps of woodland, red-painted houses, and the whole world up here seems to be covered with a dull ash.

Not so much as a single swim on Tenerife. No water for her burning body.

But she does feel a bit better now. The alcohol has cleared her blood enough for her to be able to drive from Norrköping to Linköping. She feels like going straight to the Folkunga School and storming into whatever lesson Tove is having and just hugging her. It's almost a week since she fled the house after hitting Janne while she was drunk. Almost a week since the body was found in the moat.

The heat of Tenerife. The rain and cold. She's put on the thick sweater with the Norwegian pattern that she took with her for when she got back.

But Tove will have to wait.

She's spoken to Zeke. Got the latest updates about the case: that Fredrik Fågelsjö has been released, that Jonas Karlsson has admitted

Jerry Petersson was driving, but that he had an alibi for the night and morning of the murder.

Malin has got the address of one of the parents of the boy who died that New Year's Eve, a woman called Stina Ekström living in Linghem.

"I can stop off on my way back," she told Zeke.

"We could meet up there."

"I'll do it on my own. Don't worry."

"How was Tenerife?"

"Hot."

"Your parents?"

"Let's talk again once I've spoken to Stina Ekström, if she's home."

Malin puts the radio on. As she gets closer to Linköping she manages to find the local station.

She recognizes Helen Aneman's soft, sensual voice. It's been years since they last met, even though they live in the same city. They talk on the phone sometimes, agree that they should meet, but nothing ever comes of it.

Acquaintances rather than friends, Malin thinks as she listens to Helen talking about a dog show taking place in the Cloetta Center that weekend; then, as Helen's voice disappears, music spreads through the car, and Malin feels her stomach clench. Why this song, why now?

"Soon the angels will land . . . Dare I say that we have each other . . . ?"

Ulf Lundell's voice.

Janne's body close to hers. Ridiculously romantic, the way they used to dance to this song in the living room of the house after sharing a bottle of wine with Tove sleeping on the sofa, untroubled by the music.

Linghem.

The sign scarcely visible through the rain-sodden air.

Of all human nightmares, losing a child is the worst.

I was allowed to keep you, Tove, Malin thinks.

A car rolling into a deserted, frozen winter field.

The knock on the door.

"I'm sorry to have to tell you . . ."

Malin turns off toward Linghem, driving past a football pitch and a church. A solitary man in a hooded jacket is standing beside a headstone in the small, walled churchyard with a bunch of flowers in his hand; it looks like he's talking to himself.

The small row house furnished with pine furniture.

Crocheted cloths on polished wooden surfaces, and on the cloths Swarovski crystal figurines, an impressive collection, Malin thinks, as Andreas Ekström's mother puts a pot of fresh coffee on the living-room table.

There are seven framed photographs on a bureau.

A toddler grinning from under his fringe in a nursery-school picture. A picture taken on a football pitch. End of school. A well-built teenager on a beach somewhere. Short hair ruffled by the wind, and a few feet out in the water stands a man who could be Andreas Ekström's dad.

"Now you know what he looked like," Stina Ekström says, sitting down opposite Malin on a matching wine-red velvet-clad armchair.

Similar pictures of Tove at home on the chest of drawers in the bedroom.

"He looks like a real charmer," Malin says.

Stina smiles in agreement.

How old are you? Malin thinks.

Sixty?

The woman in front of her has short fair hair, gray at the temples, and the wrinkles around her thin lips reveal years of smoking. There's a smell of smoke, but Malin can't see any ashtrays or cigarettes. Maybe Stina has succeeded in giving up? Somehow managing to hold the cravings at bay?

Black jeans.

A gray knitted sweater.

Eyes that have got used to days coming and going, that there really aren't any surprises. It's not tiredness I can see in her eyes, Malin thinks, it's something else, a sort of calm? No bitterness. A sense of being at peace, can that be it?

Stina pours the coffee with her left hand, then gestures toward the plate of homemade buns.

"Now, what on earth can the police want with me?"

"Jerry Petersson."

"I thought as much. Well, of course I read the papers."

"He was there when your son died."

The look in Stina's eyes doesn't change. Is this what grief looks like when you've come to terms with it?

"He was in the passenger seat. He was wearing a seatbelt and got out okay."

Malin nods.

"Do you think about the accident much?"

"Not about the accident. About Andreas. Every day."

Malin takes a sip of coffee, hears the rain pattering on the window several feet to her left.

"Did you live here then?"

"Yes, we moved here when Andreas was twelve. Before that we lived over in Vreta Kloster."

Malin waits for Stina to go on.

"I was angry at first," Stina says. "But then, as the years passed? It was as if all the anger and grief finally gave way, that nineteen years with Andreas was still a wonderful gift, and I think it's pointless grieving for things that never happened."

Malin can feel her heart contract, as though squeezed by a huge fist, and how her eyes start to tear up against her will.

Stina looks at her.

"Are you all right?"

Malin coughs, says:

"I think it must be an allergic reaction."

"I've got two other children," Stina says, and Malin smiles as she wipes the tears from her eyes.

"Did you feel any hatred toward the lad who was driving?"

"It was an accident."

Malin sits in silence for a few moments, then leans forward.

"We've received information which suggests that Jerry Petersson was behind the wheel that night, and that he was drunk."

Stina says nothing, nor does the look in her eyes change.

"He's supposed to have persuaded Jonas Karlsson to say . . ."

"I understand," Stina says. "I'm not stupid. And now you're wondering if I knew, or found out about it, and decided to go and murder . . ."

"We don't think anything of the sort."

"But you're here."

Malin looks into Stina's eyes.

"I lost a lot that night. My husband and I got divorced a few years later. We couldn't talk about Andreas, and in the end it was like there was nothing left except silence. But regardless of who was driving, there's no anger left, no hatred. The grief is still here, but it's just one of the many background notes that make up a life."

"Was there anyone else who was particularly upset?"

"Everyone was upset. But it's a long time ago now."

"Andreas's dad?"

"He can answer that himself."

Zeke is with him now, out in Malmslätt.

"What about the Fågelsjö family? Did they pass on their sympathies?"

"No. I got the impression they were trying to pretend it never happened. Not on their land, and not after a party organized by their son."

Malin closes her eyes. Feels bloated and nauseated.

"Can I ask what you do for a living?" she goes on. "Or are you retired?"

"Not for another four years. I work part-time at a day center for people with learning difficulties. Why do you ask?"

"No reason, really," Malin says, getting and holding out her hand over the table.

"Thanks for seeing me. And for the coffee."

"Take a bun with you."

Malin reaches for the plate, takes a bun, and soon the soft dough is filling her mouth.

Cinnamon. Cardamom.

"Aren't you going to ask what I was doing on the night between Thursday and Friday last week?"

Malin swallows and smiles.

"What were you doing?"

"I was here at home. I spent half the night chatting on the Internet. You can check my log if you need to."

"That won't be necessary," Malin says.

Stina gets up and leaves the room. She comes back with a pack of chewing gum.

"Take a couple," she says amiably. "Before you meet your colleagues."

Malin parks the car outside Folkunga School.

She switches off the engine, hears the rain almost trying to force its way through the bodywork, puts her hands on the wheel and breathes in and out, in and out, pretending that Tove is sitting next to her, that she can throw her arms round her and hug her hard, so hard.

Malin stares at the entrance, the broad steps leading up to the castle-like building with doors that are three times the height of the pupils themselves. The mature oak trees around the school are trying desperately to cling to the last of their sunset-colored leaves, and seem to think that the world will end if their leaves go.

You're in there somewhere, Tove. Malin doesn't know her timetable. What lesson would she have now? Swedish, math? All she has to do is go in and ask at reception, then find the classroom and take Tove out for coffee and a hug. But I reek of drink, don't I? Unless the chewing gum has helped?

I hope Tove comes out during her break. Then I can see her, run up to her, maybe say sorry, or just look at her from here in the car. Maybe she'll come over if I manage to see her. But she probably won't come out in the rain.

I'm going in.

Malin opens the car door and puts one foot on the ground, sees a few students cross the schoolyard, their shadowless motion framed by the windswept oaks, as old as the school itself.

She pulls her foot back. Closes the door. Puts her shaking hands on the wheel, willing them to stop, but they won't obey. She takes deep breaths. Needs a drink. But she manages to hold the thought at bay, with all her strength.

There. Now the shaking has stopped.

She pulls out her mobile, dials Tove's number. Voicemail clicks in.

"Tove, it's Mum. I just wanted to let you know I'm home again. I thought maybe we could have dinner together this evening. Can you call me back?"

Malin turns the key in the ignition, and the car's engine drowns out the rain.

She closes her eyes.

Inside her she sees a huge stone castle towering up through thick autumn fog.

Not Skogså.

Another castle. A building she doesn't recognize.

She lets her gaze settle over the moat.

Full of swollen, naked, white corpses, and small silvery fish gasping in the air. And a pulsating sense of fear.

42

Zeke runs across the parking lot toward the entrance to the police station. The damp is running down the old ocher-colored barracks, which has been given a new lease of life as the home of the city's police, courts, and the National Forensic Laboratory.

He swears to himself about this fucking bastard weather, but knows there's no point in cursing the forces of nature, it's utterly pointless and gets you nowhere.

In the rain his thoughts go to Martin.

In the NHL. The lad already has enough money to be able to relax in the sun until his dying day.

And the grandchild I've hardly seen.

What am I up to?

Andreas Ekström's father, Hans.

Only fifteen minutes since I left.

An angry old man in an old, run-down house. All hell broke loose when Zeke said that Jerry Petersson had probably been driving the car when his son died.

Hans Ekström got up from the chair where he was sitting in the kitchen and shouted at Zeke that that was all crap, and he wasn't about to let some bastard show up and stir that all up again now that he'd finally managed to put it behind him.

Hans had refused to answer any questions after that, but to judge from his reaction, what Zeke told him came as a complete shock.

Which meant he had no reason to murder Jerry Petersson. Unless Hans was a really good actor. A right-handed one at that.

Hans had concluded by cursing the Fågelsjö family: "They couldn't even be bothered to send flowers to the funeral."

They could have done that, Zeke thinks as he opens the door to the police station; evidently the new automatic doors aren't working, the rain and damp have probably got into their mechanism and stopped them working.

Malin.

Zeke sees her sitting at her desk, and she looks so tired, utterly exhausted. If the sun had been shining down in Tenerife, it sure as hell hadn't been shining on her.

A shadow of a person.

Is that what you're turning into, Malin?

He feels like going over and putting his arm round his colleague, telling her to pull herself together, but knows she would only get angry.

She looks up and catches sight of him, doesn't say anything, just looks back down at the papers on her desk again.

Zeke turns and goes upstairs to Sven Sjöman's room.

He'll just have time before their meeting.

Sven is standing by the window, looking out at the main building of the University Hospital and its eastern entrance. The white-and-yellow panels covering the ten-story building are shaking in the wind, seem to want to let go and fly across the city, coming down to land in a more bearable site.

Zeke takes a few steps inside the room.

"Don't say anything to Malin," he says. "She'd never forgive me for going behind her back, but you can see the way she is. She's drinking way too much."

Sven shakes his head.

"This conversation stays between the two of us. I'm glad you've mentioned it, because I've been giving it a lot of, well, a lot of thought."

Sven turns around.

"She's not holding everything together," Zeke says. "I can't bear to see it. I've tried . . ."

"I'll talk to her, Zeke. The trip to Tenerife was partly an attempt to give her a bit of breathing space."

"You should see her now. It doesn't exactly look like she spent her time in a luxury spa."

"Maybe the trip was a stupid idea. We'll have to see how it goes," Sven says. "You're making sure you drive when you go out together?"

Zeke nods.

"I drive pretty much all the time."

He pauses.

"I'm sure what happened in Finspång last year hit her hard," he goes on.

"It did," Sven says. "But who wouldn't be badly affected by something like that? I don't think she can understand that. Or accept it."

The clock on the wall of their usual meeting room says 3:37.

The investigating team is all there.

Windows here, unlike in paperwork Hades.

No children in the nursery playground, but Malin can see them through the windows, running about the rooms, playing as if this world was altogether good. A red and blue plastic slide. Yellow fabrics. Clear colors, no doubts. A comprehensible world for people who grab life with both hands and live in the present.

The people in here, Malin thinks, are the exact opposite.

Karim Akbar's face is composed, his body seems to have been taken over by a new sort of middle-aged seriousness, on the verge of exhaustion.

Autumn is wearing us down, Malin thinks. We're turning into characters in a black-and-white film.

Zeke, Sven Sjöman, Waldemar Ekenberg, Johan Jakobsson, even young Lovisa Segerberg from Stockholm seem ready for a long break from anything involving police work and rain.

The investigation.

Right now it looks like it's in danger of rusting solid, like the entire city.

Lines of inquiry.

Snaking back and forth across our brains like the lights on a communal ski track.

Suspicions. Voices. All the people and events that emerge when they lift the stones that made up Jerry Petersson's fairly short life.

Sven is standing at the whiteboard at one end of the room. On the board he has written a list of names in blue marker.

Jochen Goldman.

Axel, Fredrik, and Katarina Fågelsjö.

Jonas Karlsson.

Andreas Ekström and Jasmin Sandsten's parents.

Then a row of question marks. New names? New information? Anything that can help us move on?

Malin takes a deep breath. Looks across at the children in the nursery. Hears Sven's voice, but can't bring herself to say anything.

Fragments from a meeting:

Her own account of her trip to Tenerife.

That Jochen Goldman is ambiguity personified.

Her encounter with Andreas Ekström's mother. The others listen attentively. Lovisa tells them that she is steadily working through the files and contents of Jerry Petersson's hard drives, but that it would take at least five specially trained police officers to do it at anything like an acceptable rate, and Karim saying, "We don't have the resources for that." They still haven't found a will, nor anything like a blackmail letter, nor even anything remotely suspicious. They've spoken to several more of Petersson's business contacts, but the conversations haven't produced anything.

And Waldemar and Johan tell them about their latest conversations with the Fågelsjö family, and how they claim that they can hardly remember the accident, and that they managed to get hold of Jasmin Sandsten's father, Stellan, at work out at Collins Mechanics, but that the conversation gave them nothing except that he had an alibi for the night of the murder. They hadn't yet had a chance to talk to Jasmin's mother; she and her daughter were evidently at a rehabilitation home outside Jönköping.

Zeke on his meeting with Hans Ekström.

Grief.

A dead child.

So many years later, perhaps it doesn't matter much who was driving and whether or not they were drunk.

A child, a cherished child, is dead. Or, possibly even worse, a living death.

Guilt.

Fundamentally meaningless. But can the anger ever end? Forty stab wounds, years of fury unleashed.

Sven quickly explaining the prosecutor's decision to release Fredrik Fågelsjö. Then: "We'll have to keep an eye on him," empty words, and he knows it. They don't have the resources to keep an eye on him.

"Contacts," Waldemar snarls. "Who knows what that bastard Ehrenstierna's got on the prosecutor?"

And Malin thinks about her own work.

The inquiries.

Maria Murvall.

The violence and the hunt for the truth that she imagined might be able to comfort those left on earth when their relative was drifting about in some sort of bright, radiant sky.

"Did you check your contacts in the underworld?" Sven asks Waldemar.

"Looks that way, doesn't it?" Waldemar says, and the others laugh cautiously. "I checked. But it doesn't look like Petersson had any connections there."

And she hears Sven saying that they'll have to keep digging through Petersson's life, try to follow the threads of the inquiry as doggedly as possible. Following the lines they already have.

"We," she hears Sven say, "are at a stage in the investigation where everything just seems to be spiraling downward. We might make a breakthrough, or we might get hopelessly stuck. Only hard work can help us now."

Listen to the voices, Malin whispers quietly to herself.

"I'm going to Vadstena to talk to Jasmin's mother."

"Söderköping," Sven says. "You can go tomorrow, you and Zeke."

"I'd like a word with you, Malin."

Sven's voice had sounded formal, authoritative outside the meeting room, and now she's going up the stairs beside him to his office, and he closes the door behind them and tells her to sit down.

Carved wooden bowls on a white pedestal. Malin knows Sven has made them himself.

She's sitting in front of him, with him behind his desk with his familiar furrowed face, although Malin can't quite come to terms with the new wrinkles that have appeared since he lost weight.

There's a stranger in front of me, and he's talking to me, he's worried about me. Don't worry, Sven, I'm doing enough of that myself, can't you just leave me alone?

"How are you feeling?"

"I'm fine."

"I'm not so sure."

"I'm fine. Tenerife was great."

"So it was good?"

"Yes."

"Did you get a bit of sun?"

Malin nods.

"And you got to see your parents?"

"I met them. That was nice."

"I've been—and I still am—worried about you, Malin. You know that."

Malin sighs.

"I'm okay. Everything's just a bit much at the moment. I've split up with Janne and things haven't settled yet."

Sven looks at her.

"And the drinking? You're drinking too much, that much is obvious just from looking at you. You . . ."

"It's under control."

"That's not what I'm hearing and seeing."

"Has someone talked to you? Gone behind my back? Who?"

"No one's said a word. I've got eyes of my own."

"Zeke? Janne? He's perfectly capable of . . ."

"Be quiet, Malin. Pull yourself together."

After Sven's stern words they sit in silence facing each other across the room, and Malin knows Sven wants to say something else, but what could he say? It's not as if I've turned up drunk at the station.

Or have I?

"Has Zeke said anything?"

"No. I've got eyes of my own."

"So what now?"

"You carry on working. But think very carefully before you drive. Let Zeke do the driving. And try to pull yourself together. You've got to."

"Can I go now?" Malin asks.

"If you like," Sven says. "If you like."

43

"Mum?"

"Tove? I've been trying to get hold of you."

"I was at school."

Shall I say I was outside? Will that make her happy? Or sad because I didn't go in?

"Are you coming tonight? Did you get my message?"

"I'm going to the cinema."

"Don't you want to hear how it went at Grandma and Grandad's?"

"How did it go?"

"Tove, please."

"Okay."

"Will you come around after the cinema? You've got to. I want to see you. Can't you tell?"

"It'll be late after the cinema. It's probably best that I get the bus back to Dad's."

"I can make us some sandwiches."

"I've got all my things out there. I mean, I do kind of live there."

"It's up to you."

"Maybe tomorrow evening, Mum."

"You know you can live at my place as well. That used to work."

Tove is silent at the other end of the line.

"Do I have to beg, Tove? Can't you come around?"

"Do you promise not to drink if I come?"

"What?" Malin says. "I only have the occasional drink. You know that."

"You're incredible, Mum, you know that? Completely messed up."

And Tove clicks to end the call, and the words linger like nails on her eardrum. Malin wants to get rid of them, shake them out of her ears and hear other, warmer words instead, words that conjure up a different reality, one where she doesn't lie to her daughter as a way of lying to herself.

Then she sees the monster looming over Tove, ready to kill her, and the monster turns its masked face toward Malin and smiles, whispering: "I'm giving you what you want, Malin." And at that moment she knows that she drinks largely because she was given a valid excuse when Tove came close to losing her life, that she had the chance to create an internal construction that justified her giving in to her greatest passion: intoxication, the soft-edged world without secrets, the world where fear isn't a feeling but a black cat that you can stroke and whose claws never rip any burning holes in your skin.

Look at me. Poor me. She wants to smash herself into pieces, but most of all she wants to down a glass of tequila.

Where am I?

I'm standing at the entrance of the police station and I'm wondering where to go, Malin thinks as she looks out into the darkness, watching the raindrops turn into gray splinters in the orange glow of the streetlamps, as the old barracks change color in the autumn darkness, turning mute gray instead of matte beige. It's just gone seven o'clock. The paperwork surrounding her trip to Tenerife kept her working late.

Malin doesn't move.

Makes a call on her mobile.

He answers on the third ring.

"Daniel Högfeldt here."

"Malin."

"So I can see from the screen. It's been a while."

"You know how it is."

"And now you want to meet up?"

"Yes."

The doors glide open and three uniformed officers walk past her with quick nods.

"I don't take much persuading. Can you come round in half an hour?"

Yes."

She can already feel him inside her as she ends the call.

And exactly thirty-five minutes later Malin is kneeling on all fours on his bed in his sparsely furnished flat on Linnégatan and holding onto the thin metal bedstead as he pumps hard and deep into her and she screams out loud, and he is hot and hard and unknown and familiar all at the same time.

He's like a whip inside me, she thinks.

His hands are sharp barbed wire on my back. She wants to shout; Faster, deeper, you bastard, farther in, harder, and it's as if he can hear her thoughts because he thrusts harder into her each time his body moves and he digs his nails into her neck and she can feel his sweat dripping like cold rain down through her skin and into her flesh and bones and soul.

Don't resist.

Explode instead.

Let consciousness disappear in pain and beauty, let the little snakes with their many and varied faces retreat to their darkness.

He's lying on his back beside her on the gray sheet and his toned body stands out against the closed venetian blind. He's talking, his voice is calm and clear, with all its hardness and warmth intact, and she tries to understand what it is he's asking her.

"So you've split up?"

She's lying beside him and hears herself reply, with breathless, drifting words.

"It wasn't working. I ended up hitting him."

"It never works. How could you believe it could?"

"Don't know."

"What about the Petersson case? Are you getting anywhere? If I were you, I'd take a good look at Goldman."

"Sod the case, Daniel."

His hoarse laughter. And she wants to creep next to him, lay her arms round him, but it's as if he's not really there beside her, unless it's her capacity for closeness that doesn't really exist.

"Shall we go another round?" His hand on my thigh, but I can't feel it, and his neutral words seem to contain a desire to express something else, as if he had actually been waiting for me, as if he thinks it might somehow be possible to discover something together.

Wasn't that what we were just doing? Malin thinks.

Then she stands up, gets dressed, and he watches her silently.

"You're going?"

Idiotic question.

"What do you think?"

"You can stay. I can make some sandwiches if you're hungry. You look tired, maybe you could do with someone making a fuss over you for a while."

"Don't talk crap, Daniel. I can't think of a worse suggestion."

"Go on, then. The Hamlet's probably still open."

"Shut up, Daniel. Just shut up."

Zacharias Martinsson has pushed Karin Johannison's skirt high up over her stomach, he's pulled off her white nylon tights and carried her through the laboratory in the basement of the National

Forensics Lab and put her down on her back on a stainless steel workbench.

She is writhing before him and he is eating her, absorbing her moisture and sweet scent and taste, and he hears her groaning, is that the tenth, the twentieth time now?

Gunilla back at home. No doubt waiting with the evening meal when he called to say he had to work late, that he probably wouldn't be home until eleven at the earliest.

He tries to bat away the image of his wife alone in the kitchen at home, but it refuses to budge.

He found a reason to pay Karin a visit once last autumn, and she made time for him, leading him down to the laboratory to show him something, and it just happened. They had both been longing for it, and she whispers. "Now, come inside, come in, Zacharias," and he lifts her down onto the floor, pulls down his trousers, and he's hard and she's warm and soft and pliable, and she looks at him, whispers "My neck's sweaty, lick the sweat from my neck."

Maria Murvall's face in front of Malin.

The photo of the bruised rape victim's face is lying on the parquet floor of the living room, and she twists and turns the image of her own obsession.

Maria.

Your secret.

Preserved within you.

Within your silently screaming body in the white room of Vadstena Mental Hospital, tomorrow I'm going to another hospital, to another mute person.

The bells of St. Lars Church strike ten, and Malin wonders if Maria is asleep now, and if she is asleep, what would she be dreaming of?

Tove.

Probably on the bus with her friend now.

She won't come here. And who can blame her, the way I've been behaving? I pleaded with her, and she's probably like everyone else deep down. If they catch a glimpse of weakness, they take the chance to show their own power.

Did I really just think that, about my own daughter?

Malin stops midthought, feels shame take a sucking grasp of her body.

Thrust the thought away.

Who was she going to the cinema with? A boy? How can I let go after what happened? The evil disappears, diminishes in memory over time. Only a hesitant electricity remains as a vague fear, doesn't it? A fear that can excuse anything.

I don't understand all this. I don't understand myself.

And Janne. His warmth like a vanishing dream deep inside a memory. She doesn't want to talk to him, doesn't want to ask for forgiveness. What sort of person am I? she wonders. Capable of feeling such derision toward my own love?

Malin goes out into the kitchen and gets the bottle of tequila from the cupboard above the fridge.

Half left.

She raises the bottle to her lips.

What's this autumn doing to you, Malin Fors? To all of you?

Where is it going to take you?

Look where it took me.

Something you should know: Sometimes I've felt Andreas close to me, I've been able to feel his breath, free from any heat or cold or scent. I haven't been able to see or hear him, but I know he's both near me and as far away as he can get.

Jasmin's here too, part of her.

Should I be scared of them?

Do they wish me harm now?

My world is white. Theirs may be black or gray and cold as the night when the car rolled into the memory of both the living and the dead.

You can't find out my secret, Malin, and if you did it probably wouldn't help you. There's power in secrets.

My secret?

Uncover it if you want to.

Follow the trail all the way out into loneliness and fear.

Maybe I can have forgiveness then.

If there's any reason for it.

Forgiveness.

The word zigzags through Janne's head as he makes a sandwich for Tove, and he looks over at the kitchen worktop where Malin stood screaming just a week ago, where she raised her hand and hit him.

Can you spread forgiveness over time?

How can we approach forgiveness, Malin and me? Because somehow it's as if we can only do one thing together: feel that we have some sort of debt to each other, that our lives are nothing but an insult, an inadequacy, an injustice that needs to be apologized for.

Have we grown too old, Malin?

How long must an apology be allowed to work between people like us? Twelve years. Thirteen?

Tove likes liver pâté with pickled gherkins.

She's sitting watching television upstairs.

Curled up in its glow.

At home here.

You're going to want me to apologize for her making that choice, Malin. Aren't you?

She's been to the cinema with her friend Frida.

Seems to steer clear of boyfriends, hasn't really had one since Markus. Since Finspång.

"The sandwiches are ready, Tove. Do you want herbal or ginger tea?"

No answer from upstairs.

Maybe she's fallen asleep.

*   *   *

Tove leans back in the sofa and zaps through the channels.

Desperate Housewives. Some reality show. A football match. She ends up watching a documentary about an artist who's made a sculpture of one of the people who jumped from the World Trade Center, a woman falling to the ground. The sculpture was going to be placed where the towers stood, but people said it was degenerate. Unworthy.

As if they refused to accept that there were people who were forced to jump from the buildings.

She takes a bite of her sandwich.

She couldn't handle going to see Mum. Not tonight. Tonight she just wants to sit in the darkness and watch television, hear Dad doing whatever he's doing downstairs.

And the sculpture on television.

A crouching bronze figure. Slight in the wind, just like in the real world. It looks like you, Mum, Tove thinks. And she wants to go down to Dad, ask him to take her home to Mum's, see how she is, maybe stay there with her. But Dad probably wouldn't want to do that. And maybe Mum would be cross if they just showed up like that.

Her mobile buzzes.

A text message from Sara. Tove taps a reply as the television shows a close-up of the sculpture's frightened face, its shimmering bronze hair floating in the wind.

44

Zeke Martinsson looks at the clock at the top corner of the screen.

8:49. Still relatively calm in the station, everyone must be busy somewhere else. No morning meeting today, they went through everything in enough detail yesterday, everyone knows what they've got to do.

Malin should have been here long ago. They ought to be well on their way to Söderköping by now.

Where are you, Malin?

Down in the gym? Hardly.

Has something come up to keep you away? Doesn't seem likely.

Did you feel like giving in to the pain yesterday?

To drink?

Gunilla wondered why he got home so late, even though he'd called to say he'd be working. He stood in the kitchen and lied straight to her face without a moment's hesitation, and without managing to feel any shame. Instead he felt sorry for her, for having a man who could betray her without hesitation after so many years of marriage. And he had fallen asleep quickly, imagining Karin Johannison's thighs around him.

Zeke looks around at his colleagues. Some in uniforms. Some without. Focused yet somehow aimless. What do you all want, really?

Malin doesn't know what she wants, yet she still does it every day. Here, in this open-plan office she gets straight down to the task of trying to make people believe that no harm can come to them.

So where are you, Malin? Zeke's phoned three times, twice on her mobile and once on her landline, but no answer. Maybe she's at Janne's?

No answer at Janne's either.

Högfeldt?

Too complicated. I don't know anything about what they get up to.

"Where's Malin? Shouldn't you be in Söderköping by now?"

Sven Sjöman's tired, somehow compressed voice as he calls from the lift door.

Zeke gets up.

Gives Sven a look, and Sven frowns and looks like he's thinking that she might have messed up badly, maybe we should have taken her problems even more seriously?

The two detectives meet in the middle of the room.

Look at each other.

"I think she's at home," Zeke says.

"Let's go," Sven says.

Zeke rings Malin's doorbell and hears the angry signal on the other side of the door.

Sven standing silently beside him, wearing one of the force's dark-blue padded raincoats.

No talking in the car.

What would they say?

Zeke rings again.

Again.

Sven opens the letterbox and peers in, and the sound of heaving breathing, a sleeping person's movements, seeps out to the stairwell.

"Have you got a skeleton key?"

"I keep one on my key ring," Zeke says.

"She's lying on the hall floor."

Zeke shakes his head, suppresses the instinctive anxiety gripping his stomach and focuses on action.

She's breathing.

Asleep.

Could be injured.

"Give me the key," Sven says, and a few seconds later the door is open and they see Malin on the hall floor, a white T-shirt pulled up above her navel, little pink hearts on her underwear.

No blood.

No bruising, no wounds, just the sound of heavy, longed-for sleep and a strong smell of alcohol.

An empty tequila bottle.

The *Correspondent* next to her head.

They kneel at her side, look at each other, no need to ask the question that's going through both their heads.

What are we going to do now?

Turn off the rain. It's too cold. And it's drumming on my skin in a bloody annoying way, and what on earth's that, so cold against my legs?

I don't want anything to do with this, and who are those people talking?

Janne.

Yell:

"Daniel, fucking stop doing that!"

Fucking stop.

And the drops keep drumming and they're icy cold and what am I doing outside with no clothes on in this weather and what are they saying?

Sven. Zeke.

What the hell are you doing here?

"Hold onto her."

"Sit still."

Fabric against my body. Zeke's face, his shaved head, and he looks focused, Sven, are you there, and I see the bathroom now, the shower, I can feel it against my head and shit, shit, the water's cold, and I see them now, both of them, I'm sitting in the bath and they're showering me and my T-shirt's clinging to my body and my underwear, the stupidest pair I've got, they hardly even cover the hair down there, and just stop . . .

"Stop it, I know what your fucking game is!"

She flails with her arms.

Tries to force the showerhead away.

Drops.

But the liquid ice, the small sharp needles batter her, forcing her back.

"Let me sleep, you bastards!"

The dressing gown is warm against her skin and the coffee slipping down her throat is hot. Her head is throbbing, and Malin wonders if she's seeing double, with two Svens and two Zekes, and she wants to scream out loud, or drink more, but the look in their eyes holds her back.

Sven on a chair by the window. Zeke standing by the sink, looking first at the broken Ikea clock and then at a pigeon that settles on the windowsill for a few seconds before flying off toward the church tower.

Say something.

Tell me off.

Tell me I'm a bloody awful person.

A weak-willed drunk, just someone else who can't resist the slightest internal demon.

Call me a shit. An asshole.

But neither of her two colleagues says anything.

They've forced her to take two aspirins and two hydration tablets, and now she knows they're expecting her to finish the coffee.

They go out into the hall, she can hear them talking. Hears Sven say: "I'll keep an eye out, keep her on her feet, we can't manage without . . ."

Zeke: "She needs a detox clinic."

Is that really what he says? I must have heard wrong. He'd never say something like that.

They come back. They stand beside her in the kitchen without speaking.

And when the coffee is finished Sven says:

"Get some clothes on, then you and Zeke get over to Söderköping. You've got a job to do."

Somehow Malin has survived the drive, she has no idea how, and now, just before lunchtime, she and Zeke are standing in a room with flowery wallpaper in Söderköping's rehabilitation home. In front of them sits Ingeborg Sandsten in a deep-red armchair. Beside her lies Jasmin Sandsten in a blue wheelchair, and under a leaf-green blanket they can see her spastic body, twisted by years of involuntary muscle spasms. One of her brown eyes is open, the other closed, and her gaze betrays no sign of conscious life. Jasmin Sandsten breathes in heavy rattles and sometimes lets out a growling sound, and every time the sound escapes from her mouth her mother reaches over and wipes the saliva from the corner of her mouth with her right hand.

A window in the background. A bare, wind-tormented tree, a desolate canal path that seems to be waiting for summer visitors on bikes and the canal company's old white-painted passenger boats full of American tourists.

A mother who has never strayed from her daughter's side, Malin thinks, feeling a deep respect for the two strangers in the room. Even if Jasmin doesn't know what's going on around her, she must know that she hasn't been abandoned. Do you know, Malin thinks as she looks at the girl in the wheelchair, that you've got pure love on your side? Your mother is what people ought to be like. Isn't she?

If Tove had ended up like this.

What would I have done? I can't even bear to think about it.

"We should have been in Tenerife," Ingeborg Sandsten said, laying her thin hands on her equally thin thighs. "At the Vintersol rehabilitation center, but they turned us down at the last minute when they found out how badly handicapped Jasmin is. So we came here instead. This is very nice too."

Malin's first thought is: "What a coincidence. I'm just back from there," but that would have been an insult to the mother and daughter who never made it.

Ingeborg Sandsten's face is thin and lined, showing signs of never-ending exhaustion, and the woman's tiredness makes Malin feel more alert.

"I've looked after Jasmin since the accident. I get money from the council to be her carer."

"Can she hear us?" Zeke asks.

"The doctors say she can't. But I don't know. Sometimes I think she can."

"Our colleagues spoke to your former husband yesterday," Malin says.

"He's still angry."

"Has he spoken to you? Have you heard what we suspect happened on the night of the accident?"

"Yes, he called me."

"And what do you think?"

"It might be true, but it doesn't make any difference, does it?"

"You didn't know anything about that?" Malin asks.

"I see what you're getting at. I didn't know. And I was here with Jasmin all last week."

Then the growl from Jasmin as her face contorts in unimaginable pain. She must have been very pretty once upon a time. Ingeborg wipes her grown-up daughter's mouth.

"Did Jasmin know Jerry Petersson before the evening of the accident? Do you remember?" Malin asks, aware that she's fishing, casting out nets and hooks, trying to catch underwater voices.

"I don't think so. She'd never mentioned him. But what do any of us know about the lives of teenagers?"

"And the Fågelsjö youngsters? Did she know them?"

"She was in a parallel class to Katarina Fågelsjö. But I don't think they were friends."

"So you didn't know anything about what happened that night?" Zeke asks again. "That it might have been Jerry Petersson driving?"

"What do you think?" Ingeborg Sandsten says. "That Jasmin might have told me?"

Two dozen heavy raindrops hit the windowpane like a salvo.

"Deep inside her dreams Jasmin remembers what happened," she goes on. "Deep, deep inside."

The car pushes through the waterlogged landscape of Östergötland. Gray, lifeless forests, lonely gray fields, gray houses.

Zeke's hands firmly gripping the steering-wheel.

Malin takes a couple of deep breaths.

"It was you who asked Sven to talk to me, wasn't it?" she asks.

Zeke takes his eyes from the road for a moment. Looks at her. Then nods.

"So are you angry now, Malin? I had to do something."

"You could have said something to me directly."

"And you'd have listened, would you? Sure, Malin, sure."

"You went behind my back."

"For your own good."

"You go behind a lot of people's backs, Zeke. Think about what you could lose."

Zeke takes his eyes from the road again. Looks at her before his hard green eyes fill with warmth.

"Nobody's perfect," he says.

"Birds of a feather flock together," Malin retorts, then the sound of the car engine takes over and she swallows some saliva to suppress the lingering nausea.

Her mobile rings when they're about six miles from Linköping. A number Malin doesn't recognize. She takes the call.

"This is Stina Ekström. Andreas's mum."

"Hello," Malin says. "How are you?"

"How am I?"

"Sorry," Malin says.

"You asked if I remembered anything particular about the time leading up to the accident. I don't know if it means anything, but I remember one of Andreas's friends from when he started high school. Anders Dalström. He and Andreas were friends, it started when we moved to Linghem and he started secondary school. I seem to remember that Andreas looked after him. But they didn't see so much of each other when they started at different high schools. I remember him from the funeral. It looked like Andreas's death hit him hard."

"Do you know where he is now?"

"I think he still lives in the city. But I haven't seen him for a long time."

"So they were friends?"

"Yes, in secondary school out here."

Then Stina falls silent, but something stops Malin from ending the call.

"We were angry back then," Stina goes on. "Jasmin's parents were angry. We'd both lost our children, in different ways. But anger doesn't get you anywhere. I've learned that all we have in the end is how we treat our fellow human beings. We can choose. To empathize, or not. It's as simple as that."

45

Follow the voices of the investigation, Malin.

Follow them into the darkest of Östergötland's forests if that's where you hear them whispering. Snatch at every straw in the really hard cases.

The dense forests around Malin and Zeke are suffering from the same loss of color as the sky, as if the whole world has been adapted for the color-blind. The leaves on the ground are black here, they've got none of their burning colors left. The smell of their decay almost seems to make its way inside the car, pungent and simultaneously ominous.

Then she sees the little single-story house in a patch of woodland a few miles south of Björsäter, its rust-red color almost seething in the persistent rain and dead afternoon light.

The investigation's latest voice belongs to Anders Dalström. Malin doesn't yet know how he fits into the case.

Follow the voices of the investigation until they fall silent.

Then you follow them a bit further, and sometimes you might get a reward in the form of a connection, a context, the truth.

That's what people want from us, the truth, Malin thinks.

No more, no less.

As if the truth would make them any less afraid.

They stop the Volvo in the raked gravel drive in front of the house. A red Golf is parked outside a workshop. If Skogså was a box, Malin thinks, you could fit thirty houses like this one inside it.

On the front door is a handwritten sign with Anders Dalström's name. The door opens, and in front of them stands a man in jeans and a Bob Dylan T-shirt. His face is thin, but his nose is stubby and his cheeks covered with acne scars.

"Anders Dalström?" Zeke asks.

The man nods, and his long black hair moves in the wind.

"Could I have a glass of water?" Malin asks when they enter the shabby kitchen. Dalström smiles: "Of course."

His voice is hoarse and gruff, wary but still strong and friendly. He hands Malin a glass with his right hand.

Concert posters from EMA Telstar cover the walls of the kitchen. Springsteen at Stockholm Stadium, Clapton at the Scandinavium in Gothenburg, Dylan at the Ice Hockey Hall in Stockholm.

"My gods," Dalström says. "I never quite made it."

Malin and Zeke are sitting on an old-fashioned kitchen sofa, slowly drinking freshly brewed hot coffee.

"You play?" Malin asks.

"More when I was younger," Dalström replies.

"You wanted to be a rock star?" Zeke asks, and Dalström sits down opposite them, takes a deep gulp of coffee, and smiles again. The smile makes his snub nose look even smaller.

"No, not a rock star. When I was younger I wanted to be a folk singer."

"Like Lars Winnerbäck?" Malin asks, remembering the sold-out concert she attended at the Cloetta Centre when the city's most famous son came back to perform.

"I'd have liked to be Lars Winnerbäck. But it never took off."

You're still waiting, aren't you? Malin thinks.

"I've got a studio over in the workshop. I built it myself. Record my songs in there. But not that often these days. Work takes it out of me."

"What's your job?"

"I work nights at the old-people's home in Björsäter, so I'm knackered all day. I worked last night, and I'm on again tonight."

Malin had begun their conversation by explaining to Dalström why they were there, and what they had found out about Jerry Petersson and the night of the accident, and what Andreas's mother had told them. Maybe I should have held back, she thinks now. But her brain is too slow for that, and there are no reasons at all to suspect Dalström of anything.

"Did you have any success?" Zeke asks. "With your music?"

"Not much. In high school I used to get asked to play at parties, but that stopped after graduation."

"Did you know Jerry Petersson back then?"

"Not at all."

"You weren't at the same school?"

"No. He and Andreas were at the Cathedral School. I went to Ljungstedt."

"So you didn't know Jerry?" Malin asks.

"I just told you that."

"What about Andreas? His mum said you were good friends."

"Yes, we were. We used to stick together. Look out for each other."

"How do you mean?" Malin asks.

"Well, we did stuff together. Used to sit next to each other in class."

"Did you grow up together?"

"We were in the same class in Linghem. From year seven, when Andreas moved there."

Malin sees herself in the school playground in Sturefors with her classmates, most of them scattered across the country now. She sees the bullies, the boys who made a habit of attacking anyone with an obvious weakness. She can still remember the bullies' names: Johan, Lass, and Johnny. She can still remember her cowardice, how she wanted to tell them to stop, but for some reason she always found an excuse not to.

"But you grew apart when you started high school?"

"No."

"No?" Malin says. "That's the impression I got from Stina Ekström."

"We still saw each other. It's a long time ago. She must have forgotten."

"But you weren't at the New Year's Eve party?"

Zeke's voice hoarse, as rough as the rain outside.

"No. I wasn't invited."

Malin leans over the kitchen table. Looks calmly at Dalström. He seems to be trying to hide his face with his thin black hair.

"His death hit you hard, didn't it? It must have been tough, losing a friend."

"That was when I was most involved in music. But sure, I was upset."

"And now? Do you have many friends now?"

"What have my friends got to do with this? I've got more friends than I have time to see."

"What were you doing on the night between last Thursday and Friday, and on Friday morning?" Zeke asks as he puts his coffee cup on the table.

"I was at work. You can ask the staff nurse, I'll give you the number."

"We have to check," Malin says. "It's part of the routine."

"No problem," Dalström says. "Do whatever you have to do to get hold of whoever killed Jerry Petersson. Okay, it sounds like he was a bastard, and if he was driving that night then he deserved some sort of punishment. But getting murdered? No one deserves that, not for anything."

"So you knew?" Zeke says.

"Knew what?"

"That Petersson was driving?"

"I had no idea. You just told me. She did."

"Have you got the number of the hospital where you work?" Malin asks as she glances at Zeke and drinks the last of her water.

Darkness has fallen over Linköping by the time Zeke drops Malin off outside her door in Ågatan.

Light is streaming out of the Pull & Bear pub, the noise filtering out to the street, and in just a few seconds I can be standing at the bar with an oak-aged tequila in front of me.

"Go upstairs now," Zeke calls before he pulls away. Standing in the doorway Malin checks her messages on her mobile: one from Tove, saying that she's going back to Janne's. It's been a week since we last saw each other, Malin thinks. How did that happen?

Malin called the staff nurse at Björsäter old people's home on the way back, and she confirmed Anders Dalström's alibi, checking the roster to see that he had been working that night.

Malin lowers her mobile, steps out into the street, and looks at the pub's sign, radiating a soft, warm, enticing glow. Her hangover is still lingering in her body with undiminished force, and is now exacerbated by vast amounts of regret and longing and desire, but she still wants to go into the pub, sit down at the bar and see what happens.

Then the familiar sound of her mobile ringing.

Dad's name on the screen.

She answers.

"Hi, Dad."

"So you got home okay?"

"I'm home. I've been working today and yesterday."

"You realize Mum wondered where you got to?"

"Did you explain?"

"I said you got a call about work and had to rush off."

White lies.

Secrets.

So closely related.

"How are things with Tove?"

"She's fine. Waiting for me up in the flat. I'm just outside at the moment. We're about to have some supper, egg sandwiches."

"Send her my love," Dad says.

"I will, I'll be back with her in a minute or so. I've another call, I've got to go, bye."

Malin puts the key in the lock.

Opens the door.

Post on the floor. Advertising leaflets from various discount warehouses.

But beneath the leaflets.

A white A4 envelope with her name written in neat capital letters in blue ink.

No stamp.

And she takes her post into the kitchen, tossing the adverts on the table, takes out a kitchen knife, opens the envelope, and pulls out its contents.

Pictures.

Loads of pictures.

Black-and-white pictures, and Malin feels herself going cold, then fear gives way to anger, which soon turns back into fear again.

Dad outside their block in Tenerife.

A grainy picture of Mum on the balcony.

The two of them in the aisle of a supermarket, pushing a trolley.

Dad on the beach. On a golf course.

Mum in a terrace bar, alone with a glass of wine. She looks relaxed, at ease.

Pictures that look like they've been cut from a Super 8 film.

Pictures taken by someone spying, documenting, stalking.

Black-and-white pictures.

A message.

A greeting passed on.

Goldman, Malin thinks. You fucking bastard.

46

Sven Sjöman leans back in the wine-red leather sofa in the living room of his villa, pointing at one of the photographs that are spread out on the tiled coffee table. The grandfather clock in the corner has just struck eight, the sound echoing perfectly from the case he made himself. Hand-woven rugs on the floor, large, healthy potted plants hiding the view of the dark garden.

Sven looks at Malin, who is leaning forward in the Lamino armchair opposite him.

She called him, and he told her to come around at once.

The photographs on the table. Carefully laid out with pincers. Sven's finger in the air.

"He's trying to frighten you, Malin. He just wants to scare you."

And Malin gives in to panic:

"Tove. What's to say they're not going to go for Tove?"

"Calm down, Malin. Calm down."

"It can't happen again."

"Think, Malin. Who do you think's behind these pictures? What's the logical answer?"

She takes a deep breath.

In the car she tried to think clearly, force her fear aside.

She ended up back at her first instinct:

"Goldman."

Sven nods.

"This," he says, "plainly isn't something we can ignore. But I don't think you need to worry. It's just Goldman playing one of those games that he obviously loves so much."

"You think so?"

"Who else could it be? It must be Goldman. He's playing with us, enjoying the fact that he can scare you. And all the pictures are from Tenerife."

"But why?"

"You've met him, Malin. What do you think?"

Jochen Goldman by the pool. The sea and the sky in competing shades of blue, his body down on the beach, the way you were playing with me, getting me where you wanted me. And here: the rain like castanets on the plastic roof of Sven Sjöman's porch.

"I think he's bored. He just wants to show who's in charge."

Sven nods.

"But if there's any truth in the rumors about what he does to people who get in his way, we have to be careful. Take this seriously."

"But what can we do?" Malin says in a resigned tone of voice.

"We'll send the pictures to Karin Johannison. She can check for fingerprints and see if they can find anything else. But I doubt they'll find much."

Sven pauses before going on:

"You don't think it could be anyone else? Someone you put away who wants to cause trouble?"

In the car on the way to see Sven, Malin had thought through who might want to get back at her. There were a lot of names, but no one she thought would go as far as coming after the police officer who caught them.

Murderers.

Rapists.

Muggers.

A biker gang? Hardly.

But it would make sense to check if anyone had been released and was putting some sort of warped plan into action.

"Not that I can think of," Malin replies. "But we should check if anyone I put away has just got out."

"Okay, we'll do that," Sven says, and his wife comes into the room, says hello to Malin and asks:

"Would you like a cup of tea? You look half-frozen."

"No, thanks, I'm fine. Tea stops me from sleeping."

And Sven chuckles and his wife gives him a curious look, and Sven says, "Just a private joke," and Malin laughs, feeling it's the only thing she can do.

"I'd like a cup," Sven says, and his wife disappears into the kitchen, and when she's gone he asks Malin how she is. He asks the question slowly, in a voice Malin knows he wants to sound both sympathetic and hopeful, and she replies:

"I had a bit of a slip-up last night. I'm sorry you had to see me like that this morning."

"You know I ought to do something?"

"Like what?"

Malin leans farther forward over the table. Asks again:

"Like what, Sven? Send me to rehab?"

"Maybe that's exactly what you could do with."

And Malin stands up, hissing at him angrily:

"I've just had a threatening letter containing pictures of my parents taken in secret and you're talking about rehab!"

"I'm not just talking about it, Malin. I mean it. Pull yourself together, or I'll have to suspend you and get you checked in for some sort of treatment before you can come back to work. I've got strong grounds to force you to do that."

Sven's voice without any softness now, the boss, the man in charge, and Malin sits down again and says:

"What do you think I should do with Mum and Dad?"

"It might do you good, Malin. Get you back on track again."

"Should I tell them?"

"Think about it. Once this case is cleared up."

"Can we ask the police in Tenerife to keep an eye on them? And on Goldman?"

"That's what we'll do, Malin."

"Do what?"

"Wait and see, as far as you're concerned. As for the rest, we'll contact the local police on the Canary Islands. I presume you've got a contact there?"

Malin feels the last remnants of the day's nausea leave her body. Rehab.

Over my dead body.

Got it, Sven?

Not a chance in hell. I was just a bit down. I'm dealing with it, you've got to believe me, Sven.

A hand on Sven's shoulder, a cup of tea on the table in front of him.

"Your tea, Earl Grey, extra strong, just the way you like it."

The rain is tapping stubbornly at the car roof.

Her stale breath fills the car as she pulls out her mobile and brings up Jochen Goldman's number, but there's no ringing tone, just a bleep followed by a message in Spanish, presumably saying that the person cannot be reached, or that the number is no longer in use, or something equally bloody irritating. Malin clicks to end the call, puts the mobile phone on the passenger seat, and wonders if it's her or the damp air making the car smell of mold.

She starts the car.

Won't tell Dad. Or Mum.

She drives home to her empty flat, hoping that she'll be able to sleep.

Malin can't sleep. Instead she looks out of the window, at the rain drawing jerky lines on the night sky.

Her body is warm under the covers, calm, not screaming for alcohol or anything else. She dares to allow the extent of her longing for Janne and Tove into the room.

She pulls the covers over her head.

Janne is under there. And Tove as a five-, six-, seven-, eight-, nine-year-old, every age she has ever been.

I love the idea of our love. That's what I love. Isn't it?

A knock at the window.

Forty feet above the ground.

Impossible.

Another knock, the familiar sound of glass vibrating slightly.

She stays where she is. Waits for the sound to stop. Is there something rustling out there? She pulls off the covers. Leaps the several feet to the window.

Rain and darkness. An invisible body drifting above the rooftops?

Drink. Drink.

The words throbbing in her temples now. And then the knocking at the window, three long, three short, like a cry for help from some distant planet.

Am I the one crying out? Malin wonders when she's back under the covers a few seconds later, waiting for more knocking that never comes.

I'm a long way away from you now, Malin.

But still close.

You know who was knocking, don't you? Maybe it was me, unless it was just your alcohol-raddled brain playing tricks on you.

Drink, Malin.

Darkness is snapping at your throat and you've shown yourself to be weak.

If only for alcohol, money, or love.

I myself gave up on love on that New Year's Eve. After that I focused all my attention on money. I knew even then, there in my student room in Lund, where I can see myself huddled over my law books, that money was the only way I would ever find love. That's why I so eagerly ran my fingers over the thin, soft paper of those law textbooks.

47

The young man taps his finger against the silken paper of the law textbook.

He's got plugs in his ears to shut out all the noise of his corridor in the block for students from Östergötland in Lund. He uses his implacable blue eyes to photograph the pages of the book. Look, see, memorize. Law is the simplest of subjects for him, words to fix in his memory, and then use as required.

He is in Lund for three years. He doesn't need any longer to accumulate the points and the marks he needs to serve at the district court in Stockholm. Three years of forgetfulness, to suppress the narrowness of a city like Linköping, of a school like the Cathedral School, of a life like his has been.

Of course they are here as well, people with surnames that are inscribed with quill pens in the House of Nobility, but less notice is taken of them here.

He scales the façade of the Academic Association's handsome building one night. Down below the girls stand and scream. The boys scream as well. He travels to Copenhagen to buy amphetamines so he can stay awake and study. He smuggles the pills beneath his foreskin, smiling at the customs officials in Malmö.

He keeps to the edges of the carnival that takes place during his second year. He arrives late at pubs and bars, shows his face, fueling the rumors about who's the smartest of all the smart students, about who gets the prettiest girls.

He is merely a body in Lund. Yet also whispers and guesses. Who is he, where does he come from, and one evening he beats up a boy from Linköping in a carpark behind one of the student union buildings. He told anyone who wanted to know who Jerry Petersson really was: a nobody. A nobody from a nothing flat in a nothing area of a nothing city.

"You know nothing about me," he screams as he stands over the prostrate boy who is no more than a black shape in the light of a solitary streetlamp. "So you won't say anything. You let me be whoever I want to be. Otherwise I'll kill you, you bastard." He leans over, picks up a piece of metal from the ground, holds it like a knife against the boy's throat, screams: "Do you hear this, do you hear them? Do you hear the lawnmower, you bastard?"

He learns all about the female gender. Its softness, its warmth, and that they're all different and can be transformed in different ways, and that they can act as his chrysalis and give birth to him time after time after time.

He learns what physical longing means as he lies in his student room and dreams about the woman who should have been his, the woman he still dreams will one day be his.

Those dreams are his secret.

The secret that makes him human.

48

It's getting closer, Malin.

You can feel it in your black dream, spun of secrets.

People who can't make sense of their lives, who never get to grips with their fear. Crying for help with mute snake-voices.

Condemned to wander in misery.

They're all in your dream, Malin. He's there, the boy.

Malin.

Who is that, whispering your name?

The world, all human life, all feelings cremated, all snakes slithering around the bloated hairless rats in the overflowing gutters of the city.

Only the fear remains.

The most ashen gray of all feelings.

I want to wake up now.

Maria.

I fell asleep far too early.

Wide awake, Fredrik Fågelsjö thinks as he looks at the bracket clock on the mantelpiece, how its black marble pillars seem to melt into the black stone of the open hearth. The clock is about to strike half past eleven.

Raw weather outside, dry heat in here. Lake Roxen raging wildly just a few hundred yards away.

The fire is crackling, the logs shimmering in tones of orange and glowing gray, the whole room smells of burning wood, of calm and security.

He turns the cognac glass with an easy hand, raising it to his nose and inhaling the aroma, the sweet fruit, and he thinks that he will never drink anything but Delamain. That the last thing he will drink in his life here on earth will be a glass of Delamain cognac.

It was good that Ehrenstierna could use his contacts. Those nights in the cell were terrible. Lonely, with far too much time to think. And he realized something, it came to him as that stuffy old superintendent was going on about his family, about Christina and the children. He realized that the money and Skogså and all that crap really didn't matter at all. He's got all that matters here, and Christina, their socially unequal love, and the children, are everything. What they have works, even if Christina has never got on with Father, even though she's become one of them as the years have passed.

The children. He's neglected them to get what he thought he wanted, what Father wanted.

I'll have to cope with a month in Skänninge Prison next summer. I can do it. I know that now.

Christina and the children are staying with his parents-in-law. It was arranged long ago, and no time in custody would change that, they had agreed on that. But he would stay at home. Enjoy the Villa Italia in the autumn darkness.

They ought to be home soon.

Fredrik loves the peace and quiet of the villa on an evening like this, but he'd quite like to hear the sound of the car pulling up now.

Hear the children rush up the steps in the rain.

Their footsteps.

*   *   *

Fredrik pours himself another cognac.

They're still not back, and he wants to call his wife but holds back the urge. They've probably just stayed to watch a film, or they're playing a game, one of those common parlor games that his mother-in-law, terrible woman, loves.

The castle.

It's part of a dead man's estate now, belongs to Petersson's father. The police haven't tracked down any other rightful heirs, but they've still got the money, thanks to some old bag in a branch of the family that they've never had anything to do with. Money that's leaped out of their history.

Father's going to make an offer.

The natural order restored.

Because who should live at Skogså if not us? Even if it isn't really that important, it's ours. And we need to pass it on.

Jerry Petersson.

Someone who moved out of his class. Who didn't know his place, who never knew his place. That's the simple way of looking at it, Fredrik thinks.

He was drowned in his own ambitions.

A solicitor named Stekänger is in charge of his estate. A good, quick offer and the matter will be dealt with, if Petersson's father accepts it. If he refuses, we'll raise the offer a little. The land is ours, and no kids except mine will get to play there, I feel that very strongly, against my own inclinations.

Then I'll get to grips with the farming. Grow crops for biofuel and make the family a new fortune. I'll show Father I know how it works, that I can create things and make them happen.

That I can be ruthless. Just like him.

That I'm not just a bank official who's only good at losing money, that I can carry the family into the future.

Fredrik feels his cheeks burn as he thinks of the stock options, the losses, and how incredibly stupid he has been.

But now there's money again.

I'll show Father I'm good enough to have my portrait on the wall at Skogså. And once I've shown him, I'll tell him that his opinion of me doesn't mean anything, that he can take his portrait and go to hell.

Fågelsjö gets up.

Feels the parquet floor sway beneath his feet as the cognac goes to his head.

He sits down again. Looks at the picture of his mother, Bettina, beside the clock. Her gentle face enclosed by a heavy gold frame. How Father has never been the same since she went. How he seems almost lost, left behind.

Fredrik was eavesdropping outside his mother's sickroom at the castle during her last night of life. Heard how she made Father promise to look after him, their weak son.

His mother wasn't at all like that female detective who arrested him out in the field after he tried to get away from the police in the city, yet Fredrik finds himself thinking about her for some reason.

Malin Fors.

Quite good-looking.

But trashy. Bad taste in clothes and far too worn out for her age. She's got that cheap look that all country girls from poor families have. What distinguished her from others like her was that she seemed completely aware of who she was. And that it bothered her. Maybe she's intelligent, but she could hardly be properly smart.

Are you going to be back soon?

The old villa seems to have secrets in every corner and the damp and rain are making the house creak, as if it's trying to send him a message in Morse code.

Then Fredrik hears something.

Is that the car pulling up, his wife's black Volvo? The clock strikes. Of course, it must be them. The children are probably asleep in the car now; if they were going to be spending the night with her parents Christina would have called.

He gets up.

Walks unsteadily out into the hall where he opens the double doors.

The rain is driving against him, but he can't see any sign of a car in the drive.

Solid darkness outside.

And the rain.

Then a pair of car headlights come on over by the barn.

Then they go off again.

And on again, and he can't see the car well enough to see what model it is, but it looks like it's black, it is, and he wonders why his wife doesn't drive right up to the house in weather like this, maybe the damp has caused engine trouble, and he steps out onto the porch and waves, and the headlights flash again, over and over again. His wife and children. Do they want him to run over with an umbrella? Or is it his father? His sister?

Flash.

Flash.

Fredrik pulls on his oilskin.

Opens the umbrella.

Flash.

Then darkness.

He heads through the rain toward the car, which now has its lights off, maybe fifty yards away.

Darkness.

He can almost feel his pupils expand, his eyes working feverishly to help his brain make sense of the world, as if the world disappears without the right signals.

He should have switched on the garden lights. Should he go back?

No, carry on toward his wife and kids.

He's approaching the car.

His wife's car.

No.

Tinted glass, impossible to see through.

Something moving inside the car.

An animal?

A fox, a wolf?

A quick sound from whatever it is that's moving.

And Fredrik goes cold, his body paralyzed, and he wants to run like he has never run before.

It's only a dream, Malin thinks. But it never seems to end.

Fear only exists in the dream.

Something knocking deep inside me.

The fire, the fire I shall one day go into, is nothing to be afraid of.

I've given in. And that frightens me.

What I am, is my fear. Isn't that right?

PART III

The Carefree and the Scared

Östergötland, October

The film doesn't stop just because I want it to.

It's endless, and the images become more and more blurred, indistinct, gray, as their edges smolder.

No matter what happens, they won't catch me.

I shall defend myself.

I shall breathe.

I won't hold back any of the rage. I shall let the young snakes, the last of them, leave my body.

I have to admit that it felt good this time. It wasn't a sudden outburst like the first time. I knew what I was going to do. And there were a thousand reasons. I saw your face in his, Father, I saw all the boys in the schoolyard in his face. I undressed him like they undressed me, I pretended I was laying him on an altar of young snakes.

It made me calm, the violence. Happy. And utterly desperate.

The darkness is getting thicker now, the raindrops are balls of lead crashing onto the ground, onto the people.

It's my turn now. I'm the most powerful.

No one will ever again be able to turn away from me. And who really needs those pigs with their traditions, names, the sense of superiority they acquire at birth. The pictures flicker, black and white with pale yellow numbers. The story of me, the one firing out of the projector, is approaching its end now.

But I am still here.

Father embraces me again in the pictures, and he's thin, and Mum won't survive the cancer for much longer. Come to me, son, stand still so I can hit you.

I have a friend.

It's possible to escape loneliness, captivity. The strangers and the fear, all the things that are unbearable. Life can be a blue, mirror-calm sea.

Money.

Everything costs.

Has a price.

The boy sitting in the garden in the pictures on the white projector screen doesn't know that yet, but he has a sense of it.

Money. It should have been my turn.

Father, you have no money. You never have had. But why shouldn't I? Your bitterness isn't mine, and maybe we could have done something together, something good.

But things went the way they went.

A rented flat, a row house, feeble little abodes.

I am running alone through the garden in the pictures. The devil take anyone who creates loneliness, and the fear that comes with it.

The devil take them.

Boys. Living and dead, men with skins to try to fit into.

Then the reel ends. The projector flashes white. Neither the boy nor the man is visible any longer.

Where should I go now? I'm scared and alone, a person who doesn't exist in any pictures. All that is left is the feeling of young snakes crawling beneath my skin.

49

The solicitor Johan Stekänger speeds up and puts the windshield wipers on full, and they flap like hens with their necks wrung over the windshield in front of him.

The Jaguar responds to his commands, and they glide past the bus in plenty of time to avoid a sad black Volvo Estate.

The heated seat is warming his ass agreeably. It's particularly rough outside at this time of the morning. The car still smells new and fresh of chemicals, and the gray interior undoubtedly matches the season.

The art on the walls of the castle, every wall covered by pictures that don't seem to be of anything at all, but which he understands are worth a great deal.

Hence the idiot in the tweed suit in the seat next to him, a Paul Boglover, sorry, Boglöv, an expert in contemporary art, down from Stockholm to document and value Jerry Petersson's art collection.

Boglöv is presumably hoping he'll get the chance to sell the rubbish, Johan Stekänger thinks as they pull up in front of the castle, beyond the bridge over the now empty moat.

He hasn't said much.

Maybe he's picked up on my dislike of him, Stekänger thinks.

That was actually one of the reasons why he moved back to Linköping after studying in Stockholm. The people here were more homogeneous, and you hardly ever saw any queers on the city's well-kept streets. He's always had trouble with queers.

The clock on the dashboard says 10:12.

An estate inventory of the most grandiose variety, the largest he's ever dealt with. There'll be a hefty fee at the end of it, that much is beyond question.

So it was worth putting up with an art-loving queer from the queer metropolis.

He can't stand me, Paul Boglöv thinks as the ill-mannered solicitor in the cheap green suit and the blond hair hanging down over his collar taps the code into the alarm panel beside the main door of the castle.

But why should I care what he thinks?

Backwoods bigot.

"Well, welcome to the splendor of Skogså."

"Bloody hell!"

The words are out of Boglöv's mouth before he can stop them, and when he finally manages to tear his eyes from the enormous painting on the wall of the entrance hall he sees the philistine solicitor beside him grinning.

"Really? Valuable?"

"It's a Cecilia Edefalk. From her most famous series."

"Doesn't look like much if you ask me. A man rubbing sun cream on a woman's back. I mean, he could have rubbed it into her front!"

I'm not going to respond to that, Boglöv thinks.

Instead he takes out his camera, photographs the painting, and makes some notes in his little black book.

"There's stuff like that in almost every room."

Boglöv goes from room to room, taking photographs, doing calculations, and reacting with childish surprise, and with each room the feeling of making a great discovery grows within him. Was this what it felt like when they discovered the Terra-Cotta Army in China?

Mamma Andersson, Annika von Hausswolf, Bjarne Melgaard, Torsten Andersson, a fine Maria Meisenberger, Martin Wickström, Clay Ketter, Ulf Rollof, a Tony Oursler head with the lights switched off.

Impeccable taste. Contemporary. Must have been bought during the last decade.

Did Jerry Petersson choose the works himself?

A feeling for quality. That's something you're born with.

And the philistine.

His idiotic comments.

"Looks like an ordinary photograph if you ask me."

About the little Meisenberger.

"A bit of glass with holes in."

About the Ulf Rollof above the bed in what must have been Petersson's master bedroom.

Art worth thirty million kronor. At least.

Almost all the rooms have been checked when Boglöv gets a glass of water in the kitchen and reads through his notes, checking the pictures of the works in his camera.

It's all in the eye.

Petersson, or someone else, must have had a perfect eye for art.

You're moving through my rooms.

You gawping, him mocking.

You don't know what you're about to find, what I've just seen.

There's a reason I was drawn to art, that much is true.

But I'm not going to talk about that now, Malin Fors will have to guess her way to it.

I was overwhelmed by art. I got so much more out of it than I expected. At first I couldn't afford it, but it didn't take long.

In my pictures I saw, I see, all the feelings I don't have names for. Just look at the perforated glass above my bed. At the beauty and pain

in it. Or at Melgaard's fist-fucking monkeys, their poorly disguised ter-
ror at what they are, what they have become, the love they left behind
somewhere.

Or at Maria Meisenberger's empty human shadows. Like sins you can
never leave behind.

"There's a chapel as well," the philistine says. "It's got some Jesus
pictures in gold. Do you want to see them?"

Icons, Paul Boglöv thinks. He doesn't even know they're called
icons, but he can't mean anything else, can he?

"Where's the chapel?"

"Behind the castle, down by the forest."

Boglöv puts his glass down on the draining board.

Outside the Lord of Rain is in full command, the day dark even
though it is only just midday.

They walk quickly around the castle. The chapel is located alone
and abandoned on the edge of a dense forest of fir trees.

A key in the philistine's hand.

Icons, Boglöv thinks. I wonder if Jerry Petersson had as much
taste when it came to them?

"Looks like it's unlocked," the philistine says.

And they open the doors to the chapel.

They glide open slowly, creaking.

A dull light through glassless openings.

And they both let out an endless scream when they see what's
lying there naked, almost draped across the raised slabs marking the
site of the Fågelsjö family vault.

50

Death has no smell here. The stench of decay that meets Malin doesn't come from the corpse but from the forest surrounding the chapel.

The ground is waterlogged but doesn't seem able to flood.

Fredrik Fågelsjö's body is naked.

Malin knows it is, even though it's already lying on a trolley in a black bag designed for the purpose of transporting and concealing corpses.

She's standing at the entrance to the Skogså chapel, trying to escape the rain that the wind is driving toward her, looking at the gilded pictures of Christ on the walls, the halos around the head of the Son of God, a halo that no one yet living seems to possess this autumn.

The vultures are being kept at a distance. She could see the expectation in their eyes as she walked past them. Their little BlackBerrys ready for notes, the starved cameras, their instincts aroused, finally something has happened again. Daniel isn't there. Perhaps he's on his way.

Sven Sjöman and Zeke beside her, silent and focused, thoughtful.

Fredrik Fågelsjö.

Murdered. Like a sacrifice on the family vault.

An autumn sacrifice.

But for what? And by whom?

The three detectives want to take the connection to Jerry Petersson's murder for granted, but they know that they can't. No stab wounds this time, but a clear message nonetheless: a naked body on a grave.

They have to keep all their options open in the investigation, there's no guarantee that the two murders are linked just because they almost share a crime scene or because the victims have a shared history. Who knows what meandering pathways violence takes? Malin thinks. Dead ends, dark and lonely. The methods are clearly different, but it's a myth that a murderer always kills in the same way.

The solicitor and the art expert.

They were in quite a state when Malin, Sven, and Zeke arrived an hour or so ago, but they had had the sense not to go too far inside the chapel before pulling back cautiously from the immediate vicinity.

The reason why they were there was obvious. And they hadn't seen or heard anything.

No reason to detain them.

Karin Johannison and her two male colleagues from the National Forensics Lab are searching the scene, looking for fingerprints, picking up things invisible to the naked eye and putting them in plastic bags.

Karin on the subject of Fredrik Fågelsjö once his body had been put inside its black plastic bag:

"He appears to have died from a blow to the head. The wound looks like it could have been inflicted by a hammer. It struck him cleanly, so it isn't possible to say if the perpetrator is right- or left-handed. No other obvious signs on the body, no violence against the genitals as far as I could see from a quick look."

"Was he murdered here or moved here?" Malin asked.

"In all likelihood he was moved here. There are definite signs of blood by the entrance. Even if his clothes are missing, I think he was undressed here. The fibers we've just found on the floor look like the ones I found on the body when I first checked it."

"So murdered somewhere else, but undressed here?"

"Probably, yes."

"What about why he was brought here to the chapel, to this grave?"

"Memorial stone."

"Same thing. What do you think about that?"

"That's not my area, Malin. I don't think anything."

"And the way he was killed?"

"It must have been a very hard blow."

"In anger?"

"Maybe. But the murderer didn't lose control, because then you'd expect more than one blow."

And now Karin Johannison makes a sign to her colleagues.

The two men carry Fredrik's body out of the chapel.

What are you trying to say? Malin thinks as they pass her.

What do you want to tell us?

The family vault in front of her.

Fredrik Fågelsjö gambling away the fortune, the family estate. Is this your father and your sister getting revenge? But why would they do it now, when the family has just inherited a lot of money and in all likelihood will be able to buy back the estate from Jerry Petersson's father? Or was it the family that got rid of Petersson and now had to get rid of Fredrik because for some reason he can't keep quiet or knows too much?

Or is this something else entirely? Does Fredrik have any connection to Goldman? It feels like a hell of a long shot. Or did Fredrik play a bigger part in the tragedy of that New Year's Eve, did he do more than just arrange the party? Or has Fredrik been murdered because he murdered Petersson?

Why is all this happening now? If Jochen Goldman is somehow behind it all, it may simply be because he hadn't got round to it before now. Who knows how much someone like that might have to tidy up from his past? Maybe he's sent a lot of people to the bottom? Sent a lot of photographs?

Unless these murders aren't connected at all? What enemies did Fredrik have? The tenant farmers?

Jerry, Fredrik. Did anyone have a reason to hate both of you?

The icons on the walls seem to glow, as if encouraging her to carry on.

In spite of the cold and rain, in spite of all the crap, Malin feels her brain starting to work again, trying to make sense of the possibilities presented by a double murder.

Her detective's soul kicks in again.

There are no doubts, no grief anymore. Just focusing on a mystery that needs to be solved.

"Shall we go inside the house and run through what we've got?"

Sven's voice doesn't sound tired but expectant, as if his police officer's soul has come to life.

"Good idea," Zeke says, turning away from the scene of violent death.

Malin, Zeke, and Sven are standing in the castle kitchen, going through the options, everything that Malin thought out in the chapel and a few more possibilities besides.

"Different methods," Sven says. "But I still think we're dealing with the same murderer."

Malin nods.

"There are too many connections between the murders. The location, the victims' histories. I'd be astonished if it weren't the same perpetrator."

"Maybe the first murder was committed out of rage, and the second planned?" Zeke ponders.

"Unless Fredrik committed the first murder and was himself murdered in revenge," Sven says. "We simply don't know. But the chances are that we're dealing with one and the same murderer."

"And we can write off the parents of the kids in the car crash," Malin says. "They had no reason to want Fredrik dead. If they wanted to kill him for organizing the party, they'd have done so long ago."

They mention Jochen Goldman, agree that the connection is a long shot, but that they can't dismiss the possibility entirely.

The three detectives are silent for a while, considering all the possible scenarios, sensing how elusive and multifaceted the truth is.

"You two go and tell Axel Fågelsjö," Sven goes on. "Johan and Waldemar can inform Katarina."

"And question them. We'll handle the old man," Zeke says. "After all, they could well have had something to do with this."

"True enough," Sven says. "They might have wanted Fredrik out the way because of his business dealings, or they could be guilty of Petersson's death and he was on the point of cracking and talking."

Malin shakes her head skeptically, but says nothing.

"And we'll have to take a closer look at Fredrik's life. His dealings with the bank," Sven says. "Maybe he didn't only lose his own family's money? He could have enemies. More work for Johan, Waldemar, and Lovisa in Hades."

"What a bloody mess," Zeke says. "How the hell are we going to get anywhere with all this?"

"They can check all the business stuff in Hades. A bad deal seldom occurs in isolation," Sven says, then he gives Malin a sympathetic look that annoys her and makes her want to say, "Stop worrying so fucking much. I'll be fine," then she thinks, What if I'm not, what if I can't hold on? What happens then? And then the indistinct concept of rehab pops into her head like a small firework.

"And we'll have to talk to Fredrik's wife," Zeke says. "She hasn't reported him missing."

"You do that," Sven says. "He might have told her he was going somewhere. Any other thoughts?" Sven goes on. "The car crash?"

"Dubious. But we have to ask ourselves why he was laid on the family vault naked," Malin says. "Almost like a sacrifice."

"Do you think the murderer's trying to tell us something?"

"I really don't know. Maybe he or she is trying to make us believe that there's something to tell. Get us to look in a particular direction.

Possibly toward the Fågelsjö family themselves. It's all been in the papers, after all."

"You mean it could be someone in the family who wants to be discovered?"

Zeke, questioning, beside her.

"More the opposite," Malin says.

"How do you mean?"

"I don't know," Malin says. "It just feels like there's something here that doesn't make sense."

"You're right about something not making sense. Well, we'll have Karin's report tomorrow, and we'll take it from there," Sven says. "And we need to map out Fredrik's last twenty-four hours alive. We haven't exactly got very far with Petersson. Unless there really isn't anything to fill in that we don't already know about, apart from his encounter with the murderer."

"So how do we think Fredrik got here?" Zeke asks.

"Forensics are going to have a look for tire tracks around the castle. See if they can find any that don't match the solicitor's car. There's nothing to suggest that anyone's been inside the castle. The alarm was on when they arrived. Well, go and see Axel Fågelsjö now. Before the media announce it."

"It's already out," Zeke says.

Cars from the *Correspondent* and local radio. The main national broadcaster, SVT. TV4. Local television news.

Overeager vultures. Even if they don't mention any names, the victim's relatives can always put two and two together, and no one should find out about a death through the media.

Still no Daniel out there.

In his place an older reporter that Malin, oddly enough, doesn't recognize, and the photographer, the young girl with dreadlocks who Malin knows takes good pictures. What is it she's trying to capture here?

Death?

Violence? Evil. Or fear.

Whatever you do, don't take any pictures of me. I look like a pig.

Sven's mobile rings.

He hmms a few times beside them. Hangs up.

"That was Groth in Forensics," he says, turning toward Malin. "The examination of the pictures of your parents didn't come up with anything, I'm afraid."

Malin nods.

"Shit," Zeke says quietly. He was furious when he found out about the pictures this morning. "Couldn't the pictures have something to do with all this?"

"Somehow it all fits together, doesn't it?" Malin says. "It's just a question of how."

Malin leaves the kitchen and goes out into the main hall, stopping once more in front of the huge painting of a man rubbing sun cream into a woman's back.

Thinks that the picture is beautiful and tawdry at the same time.

She feels something as she looks at it, but she can't put her finger on what.

Sven walks past her.

She says: "I'd like Zeke and me to deal with Katarina Fågelsjö."

"Okay, if you think that's a better idea," Sven says. "Waldemar and Johan can talk to Fredrik's wife instead. But start with his father. And not a word to the bloody media."

51

Axel Fågelsjö is standing quietly in front of the sitting-room window. The fog that drifted in when the rain stopped is obstructing the view of the Horticultural Society Park; the naked trees are like thin silhouettes of bodies, and Fågelsjö seems to be looking for something, as if he has a feeling that someone down in the park is watching him from a distance and was just waiting for the right opportunity to attack him.

It was as if he knew why they were there, as if he knew what had happened, and while they still were in the hallway he said "Out with it, then!" to Malin and Zeke, as if he had spent all night waiting for them. They asked him to go through to the sitting room and take a seat, but the old man refused: "Just say what you've got to say here," and Malin sat on a worn old rococo stool by the door and said straight out:

"Your son. Fredrik. He was found dead in the chapel at Skogså this morning."

The terrible meaning of the words blew away her insecurities.

"Had he killed himself? Hanged himself?"

And in Fågelsjö's face, in the pink confusion of wrinkled skin stretched over fat, Malin saw a hardness, but also something like clarity.

I despised my son. I loved him.

He's dead, and perhaps now his sins can be forgiven. His sins against me. Against the memory of his mother. His ancestors.

And, deep in his shiny pupils, grief, yet still somehow hidden behind layer upon layer of self-control.

"He was murdered," Zeke said. "Your son was murdered."

As if he wanted to provoke a reaction in Fågelsjö, but he merely turned away, went into the sitting room and over to the window where he is now standing, his back to them as he answers their questions, apparently unconcerned by the circumstances. Malin wishes she could see his face now, his eyes, but she is sure there are no tears running down Axel Fågelsjö's cheeks.

"We can tell you the details of your son's death if you want to hear them," Malin says. "We know a fair amount already."

"How he was found, you mean?"

"For instance."

"I'll be able to read about it in the paper soon enough, won't I?"

Malin still tells him what they know, without going into any great detail. Fågelsjö remains motionless by the window.

"Did Fredrik have any enemies?"

"No. But of course you know that I wasn't happy with him after the financial debacle."

"Anyone who might be trying to get at you?"

Fågelsjö shakes his head.

"What were you doing yesterday evening and last night?" Zeke asks.

"I was at Katarina's. We were talking about the possibility of buying back Skogså from the estate. Just her and me. It was late when I walked home."

Father and daughter, Malin thinks. They're together on the night when Fredrik, the brother, the son, is murdered. Why?

"Nothing else you think we should know about Fredrik? Any other business deals that might have gone wrong?"

"He didn't have that level of authority at the bank."

"No?"

"He was a middleman."

"Could he have had anything to do with Jochen Goldman?"

"Jochen Goldman? Who's that?"

"The embezzler," Zeke says.

"I don't know of any Goldman. But I can't imagine Fredrik had anything to do with an embezzler."

"Why not?"

"He was too cowardly for that."

Malin and Zeke look at each other.

"What about Fredrik's wife? What was their relationship like?"

"You'll have to ask his wife about that."

"Do you want us to arrange for someone to come and be with you? We'd prefer not to leave you alone."

Fågelsjö snorts at Malin's words.

"Who would you send? A priest? If you don't have any more questions you can go. It's time to leave an old man in peace. I need to call an undertaker."

Malin loses patience with the old man.

"I don't suppose your family had Jerry Petersson killed, and then Fredrik was on the point of cracking up and confessing? So you murdered him?"

Fågelsjö laughs at her.

"You're mad," he says.

And Malin realizes how much it sounds like a conspiracy theory.

"We're going to see Katarina now," Malin goes on. "Perhaps you'd like to call her first?"

"You can tell her the news," Fågelsjö says. "She stopped listening to me long ago."

Malin and Zeke takes the stairs back down, their steps echoing in the stairwell. Halfway down they pass a black cleaner washing the steps with a damp mop.

"He's a cold bastard, that one," Zeke says as they approach the door.

"He can shut off completely," Malin says. "Or rather, shut himself in."

"He didn't even seem upset. Or the least bit curious about who might have killed his son."

"And he seemed even less concerned about Fredrik's wife," Malin says.

"And his grandchildren. He didn't mention them at all," Zeke adds.

"Presumably he's too old for rage," Malin says.

"Him? He'll never be too old for that. No one gets that old."

Axel Fågelsjö has sat down in the armchair in front of the open fire.

He clenches his big, spade-like hands, feels his eyes well up and the tears run down his cheeks.

Fredrik.

Murdered.

How could that happen?

The police.

No one to talk to, the fewer words spoken, the better.

He sees his grandchildren running through the living room out at the Villa Italia, chased by Fredrik, then they run on through the pictures inside him, children's feet running across the stone-floors of the rooms of Skogså. Who are the children? Fredrik, Katarina? Victoria? Leopold?

I want my grandchildren here with me, but how can I approach her, Bettina? His wife, Christina, she's never liked me, nor I her.

And really, what would they want me for?

The truth, Fågelsjö thinks, is for people who don't know any better. Action is for me.

You're a widow now.

Your two children fatherless.

Johan Jakobsson looks at the woman sitting in front of him on the sofa in the large living room of the Villa Italia, hunched up and tear-streaked, yet still radiating a sort of faith in the future. She must be financially secure, and Johan has seen this before in women with children when he arrives to break news of their husband's deaths, the way they immediately seem to focus all their energy forward, onto the children, and the work of limiting the damage to them.

Johan leans back in the sofa.

Christina Fågelsjö looks past him, toward Waldemar Ekenberg, who is sitting on a stool by the grand piano, rubbing the bruise on his cheek.

Christina has just explained that she decided to spend the night at her parents with the children after drinking wine at dinner. That she often ate dinner with the children at her parents without Fredrik, "they've never got on very well, Frederik and my parents," and that her parents can confirm that she was there.

"You didn't call home?" Waldemar asks.

"No."

"And he wasn't here when you got home?" Johan asks, and he is struck by the idea that Christina could have murdered her husband to get a share of the recent inheritance before it was spent trying to buy back Skogså.

A long shot, he thinks. The woman in front of him is no murderer. And the inheritance must have gone mainly to Axel. But she does appear to be right-handed. Along with practically everyone else.

"I assumed he must be at the bank."

"Did he have any enemies?" Waldemar asks, and it strikes Johan that it's just the right moment for that question, phrased in that way, and reluctantly he has to admit that he and Waldemar work well together as police officers. He is convinced that Christina is telling the truth when she replies:

"Not that I know of."

"His father? His sister?"

"You mean because of the debacle?"

Christina shrugs her shoulders.

Waldemar strikes one of the keys of the piano gently. Light in Christina's eyes.

"I know we've asked before," Johan says. "But do you know why he tried to escape from us? Could it have . . ."

"We talked about it the day he was released. He got scared, panicked. Anyone might have done in those circumstances."

"Do you think it occurred to him that driving under the influence of alcohol is illegal as well as dangerous?"

"Sometimes he thought he was above that sort of thing. Sometimes rules were meant for other people."

"What was your marriage like?" Johan goes on, and Christina answers without thinking.

"It was a good marriage. Fredrik was a generous man. The Fågelsjö family are good at love."

And at the moment Christina says the word "love," two small children run into the room, a little girl and an even younger boy. The children rush over to their mother, talking at the same time:

"Mummy, Mummy, what's happened? Mummy, tell us."

"Mum? Is that you? It's a bad line."

Tove.

It's not yet half past two and it's already starting to get dark over on the horizon beyond the jagged, shredded Östgöta plain. Malin is sitting in the Volvo with Zeke, on their way to Katarina Fågelsjö's address.

She wants Tove to say she's coming around this evening, that she'll stay the night in the flat in the city and not out at Janne's.

They drive past Ikea, the carpark full at this time of day, and at the petrol station near Skäggetorp people are filling their shiny, well-kept cars. She looks at the spot where she parked when she went to buy clothes and seems to see two men gesturing to each other beside a car.

Malin blinks.

When she opens her eyes again the men are gone.

Down by the river and the Cloetta Center the new high-rise block is going up, the Tower, a miniature skyscraper, a pointless piece of showy architecture so that another of the city's vain property developers can stamp his name on Linköping's history.

"Mum? Is that you? I can't really hear you."

"I'm here," Malin says. "Are you coming home this evening? We can do egg sandwiches."

"Maybe tomorrow?"

And mother and daughter talk, about how they are, what they've been doing, what they're going to do.

Malin hears her own voice, but it's like it doesn't really exist. As if Tove's voice doesn't exist. And this absence of voices forms a loneliness which forms itself into an inadequacy which forms itself into grief.

The car pulls up outside Katarina's modernist villa down by the river; fallen apples are still lying under the trees, and only now does Malin see the decay, that the house needs plastering and that the entire garden could do with being cleared out and maybe replanted.

Malin and Tove hang up.

The windshield wipers are working frantically.

Their movement makes the shape of a heart, Malin thinks. Painted hearts, rubbing sun cream into a woman's skin.

Signs of love that were never interpreted.

And she knows which question to ask Katarina Fågelsjö.

52

As if she had been waiting for this to happen.

Katarina is sitting in front of Malin and Zeke on the sofa from Svenskt Tenn. Her face betrays no dismay, no grief, no despair.

She has just had news of a death.

Your brother has been murdered.

And Katarina seems to shrug her shoulders, brush herself off, and move on. He was still your brother, Malin thinks, in spite of his shortcomings.

Malin looks at the Anna Ancher painting on the far wall, the woman at a window facing away from the viewer. She reminds me of your father, Katarina, by the window facing the Horticultural Society Park, as if they're both trying to hide their faces at all costs, to avoid having to reveal what they feel.

Is that what you're supposed to do? Pretend the world outside, any feelings, don't exist? Or is there something else you're hiding?

She hears Zeke asking questions and Katarina answering.

"Yes, Father was here. He went home. I went to bed. No one can verify that. Is that necessary?

"I didn't kill my own brother, if that's what you're thinking. We're not behind either of the murders. Matter closed. Enemies? Fredrik was harmless. He didn't have any enemies. Yes, the day my father dies I'll inherit almost everything now, but I've had everything I need for a long time."

The irony sharp as a razor blade as Katarina says these last words. Zeke runs out of questions.

Katarina folds her hands in her lap, letting her fingers rest on each other on the blue silk of her knee-length skirt, and Malin thinks that she has that gentle restlessness you only see in women who have no children, a mournful longing that finds expression in an edginess, a chronic nervousness and sudden attempts at warmth.

Katarina frowns, and Malin thinks that a single feeling can define a person's life if it's sufficiently strong, make that person want to live in that feeling, even though it will never return.

Another painting on another wall. A woman on her own in blue, facing a misted window, impressionistic. She's longing for something, Malin thinks.

"You and Jerry Petersson," Malin says. "You went out together, didn't you?"

And Malin can hear how hard, inadequate, and clumsy her words sound, and she sees Katarina's face contort before she says:

"Surely now's not a time for fantasies, is it, Inspector?"

I see you leave Katarina's house, Malin, then I see you enter the police station.

You're trying to validate your own shortcomings in those of other people, aren't you? You want so badly to believe that your own pain can be eased simply because other people feel a similar pain.

That's arrogant, Malin.

But you're good at dragging things out into the open, I have to admit that. You dare to follow your instincts, the traces of feelings lingering in the air, the way in which we human beings breathe each other's love.

We are parasites on each other's love, Malin. Trying to shift it to where we want it to be, trying desperately to understand what it wants with us. What are we to do with all the love, friendship, fear, and despair?

Did you expect Katarina to answer your question?

Or that I would whisper the answer as I drift, my mouth just an inch from your ear?

I don't think so.

No victories are won so cheaply.

You can do better than that, Malin.

Now you've gone to see your boss, Karim Akbar.

He doesn't mention it to you, but he's just turned down a job he was offered at the Immigration Authority. Nor will he say that he feels good, standing there looking out over the innards of the police station, and the detectives he realized he appreciated more than he could possibly have imagined while he was thinking about the job offer.

Karim is also thinking about a book he's in the middle of writing, about immigration issues, work on which has been very slow for too long.

And then there's you, Malin.

What are we going to do with you?

What are what are we going to do with all these lives that are stuck inside themselves?

The paperwork Hades in the police station feels more claustrophobic than ever.

Lovisa Segerberg, Waldemar Ekenberg, and Johan Jakobsson have been over at the Östgöta Bank to fetch files and computers from Fredrik Fågelsjö's office, as well as his personal computer and other documents from out at the Villa Italia.

It's half past three.

Outside in reception the vultures are waiting for some sort of statement, but apart from a press release confirming the name of the victim they haven't been given a thing. Karim is refusing to hold a press conference, wants to let the investigation proceed in peace, as he just said in the staffroom.

Johan rubs his eyes, thinking about his wife, who's probably at home playing with the kids now.

Fredrik Fågelsjö's father.

Jerry Petersson's files. They haven't even got through a tenth of Petersson's papers yet, and now there's a whole new set from a new murder.

In spite of their silence, television and radio news are featuring the murder heavily. There are profiles of both Jerry Petersson and Fredrik Fågelsjö. Naturally the *Correspondent* has the murder as the lead item on its website, a lengthy article written by that journalist that Johan is convinced Malin is having a relationship with, or at any rate fucks sometimes. He's written that the second murder might perhaps have been avoided if the police had been more efficient in solving the first. Was he even out there at the castle?

Waldemar is sitting at the end of the table sipping a cup of coffee. Strong and black, and he looks bored out of his mind. Huffing and puffing, he doesn't seem to want to get down to work. Lovisa, on the other hand, is concentrating on Fredrik's computer, clicking from one document to the next. Maybe she's hoping to find a connection between Jochen Goldman and Fredrik?

Then Waldemar gets up and goes over to stand behind Lovisa, and starts massaging her shoulders, saying:

"You like this, don't you?"

Lovisa stands up.

Turns toward Waldemar. Says in an ice-cold voice:

"Don't fucking touch me. I don't give a damn how many young female officers you've sexually harassed in your time, but you don't fucking touch me. Understood?"

Waldemar backs away.

Throws out his arms with a grin.

"Calm down, love. No sense of humor?"

"I've had an email from Interpol in Stockholm," Sven Sjöman says as he heads toward Malin's desk.

The beginnings of a headache. Withdrawal, Malin thinks. But no hangover at least.

"Jochen Goldman left Tenerife," Sven says. "Three days ago."

"Where's he gone?" Malin asks.

"Stockholm, via Madrid. But no one knows where he went after he landed at Arlanda."

"So it could have been him who put the pictures through my letterbox?"

"Unlikely. But he might have got someone else to do it. Maybe simpler for him to arrange direct from Stockholm."

"So he was in the country when Fredrik Fågelsjö was murdered," Malin says.

"We haven't got any connection at all between them so far, but we'll see what the files throw up," Sven says.

"We haven't got anything on him at all," Malin says. "He's got every right to do whatever he likes. Maybe those photographs are just part of a warped game."

"I still don't get it, though," Sven says. "Why would Goldman want to come to Sweden right now?"

"Who knows?" Malin says. "But I'm convinced Goldman is behind those pictures. It can't be anyone else. Aronsson just gave me the results of her search: No one I've put away who might want revenge has been released recently."

Sven pulls in his stomach and reminds her that they have a case meeting in five minutes.

"We really need to start making some progress here, Malin. The vultures in reception are demanding quick results."

Tired detectives around a conference table.

Words flying through the air, summaries, new ideas. A criminal investigation that's treading water, where every conversation and exchange risks leading their work in an emotional direction rather than a logical one.

The playground of the nursery empty.

Sven Sjöman summarizes the state of the investigation.

"We're still going through Petersson's files. Nothing unusual so far, no other relatives or significant figures in his life. We still haven't found the murder weapon, in all likelihood a knife.

"We need to keep digging into Petersson's relationship with the Fågelsjö family, especially Fredrik and Katarina. We also need to find out more about his dealings with Jochen Goldman. And we're still looking into the circumstances surrounding the car crash."

Then Sven falls silent.

Looks at Lovisa Segerberg.

"Anything new?"

She shakes her head.

"Nothing so far."

"There's so much fucking paperwork," Waldemar snarls. "It doesn't feel like we're getting anywhere."

"If you feel stuck, dig even deeper," Karim says, and Malin thinks it sounds like he's trying to convince himself rather than his detectives.

"We need to start making some progress here," Karim goes on. "We haven't got anywhere yet."

"You're right about that," Malin says.

"The media are going crazy. We've got a press conference in two hours."

"Those pictures you received, of your parents. We're assuming that Goldman's behind them," Sven says, and Malin tries not to listen as he goes on about the photographs.

Then he runs through the state of the investigation into the murder of Fredrik Fågelsjö, about Axel and Katarina Fågelsjö's questionable alibis, and the fact that Fredrik's parents-in-law have confirmed his wife's alibi.

"Most murders occur within families," Waldemar says. "And Axel and Katarina have plenty of reasons for wanting to get rid of the black sheep of theirs after he fucked up their finances. Maybe they were worried poor little Fredrik would crack and give them away?"

"Do you really believe they did it?" Malin asks. "Murdered their own son and brother? No matter what the reason?"

"Even if Axel and Katarina didn't do it themselves," Waldemar says, "they could have arranged for it to happen. That goes for both murders."

"But why such a grandiose gesture?" Zeke asks.

"To divert attention away from themselves," Waldemar says.

"We just need to do more work here, into every aspect, this feels like our main line of inquiry right now," Sven says. "Try to work out what they've been up to recently, what calls they've made, to start with."

"Email?" Johan says.

"We'd need to seize their computers for that," Sven says. "We'll start with their mobiles. We've got enough grounds for that now."

"It's too early for computers," Karim adds. "After all, we've got nothing concrete on them at all."

"We spent today checking the neighbors closest to the castle again," Sven says, "and around Fredrik's house. Chances are he was there on the evening he was murdered. But no one saw anything. Linnea Sjöstedt didn't bother with her shotgun this time round."

The detectives laugh.

"And Karin's report?" Zeke goes on.

Sven nods.

"She was quick. It's just arrived, even though she said it would be tomorrow at the earliest. Fredrik died of a blow to the back of the head. A blunt instrument, a rock, something like that. A hard blow, but not hard enough to rule out the perpetrator being a woman. And, as she said at the crime scene, it's impossible to tell if the perpetrator is right- or left-handed. Not much blood loss, but the blow caused severe internal bleeding in the brain that would have made him lose consciousness immediately. Time of death sometime between ten o'clock on Thursday evening and two o'clock Friday morning, which basically gives Axel and Katarina Fågelsjö alibis, unless they're involved in this together. Axel's supposed to have left his daughter's at two o'clock that night."

"Goldman," Zeke says. "He could have been there."

Sven pauses before going on:

"Fredrik was in all likelihood undressed in the chapel after his death. The body was free from soil and dirt, which suggests that he wasn't undressed elsewhere. But we haven't found any clothes. Karin found the same fibers on the body as on the floor of the chapel. These could have come from the perpetrator's clothing, probably an ordinary pair of jeans."

"Can Karin say if he was killed there?" Zeke says.

"The blood found in the chapel is Fredrik's, but it's impossible to tell if the blow was dealt there or somewhere else."

"So," Malin says, clearing her throat, "what you're saying is that someone might have beaten Fredrik to death at his home and driven the body to the chapel. Or that Fredrik could have been murdered somewhere else and then taken to the chapel. Or that someone might have abducted him and taken him to the chapel, and killed him there?"

"Yes."

"Unless he was in the chapel or out at the castle of his own free will," Malin says, "then got taken by surprise by someone there. Or he arranged to meet someone there. That gives us several thousand possible scenarios. I presume Forensics have checked the Villa Italia?"

"Forensics found no evidence of violence either in the villa or in the surrounding area," Sven says. "But there are plenty of stones in the farmyard that could have been used to hit him over the head. Seeing as it's been raining for ten hours solid, any traces of evidence have been washed away."

"What about at the castle, around the chapel?" Zeke asks.

"The door was unlocked," Malin says. "And the Fågelsjö family had access to the keys, of course. But the murderer could have used the victim's keys, if he had them on him."

"We haven't found any keys," Sven says. "We'll have to ask Christina if she knows where her husband's keys are."

"The crime scene may have been free of forensic evidence," Malin says, "but it's still got a story to tell. He was laid on that vault like a sacrifice. A family sacrifice? Could it be some sort of ancient Nordic way of restoring family pride?"

"Hence the focus on the surviving Fågelsjös," Karim says.

"But what if someone's trying to get us to concentrate on the Fågelsjö family?" Malin says, to put into words the doubts she felt when at the crime scene.

"You mean, to protect themselves?" Zeke asks.

"That's stretching it," Waldemar says. "What if Fredrik murdered Petersson, and someone wanted revenge for his murder? Who would have any interest in avenging Petersson's death?"

"His father," Johan says.

"But he's old and hardly capable of orchestrating something like that," Malin says.

"So who actually liked Petersson?" Sven says.

"No one, as far as we can tell," Zeke says.

"I think Katarina liked him," Malin says.

And the other detectives in the room fall silent, looking expectantly at Malin.

She throws out her arms.

"It's just a hunch, okay? Let me think about it a bit more. I want to break out of the circles we seem to be stuck in."

"Try to uncover the facts, Malin," Karim says. "We haven't got time for hunches."

Malin tries to focus on the whiteboard, on Sven's notes, make some sense of the words, pen strokes, colors.

But any sense of context eludes her, this entire investigation is like a palette full of mixed-up paint, a gray mess.

"Neither of them seems to have been Mr. Popular, exactly," Zeke says. "Fredrik was a failure. And if you ask some people, Petersson was a little piglet turned big swine."

There you sit in your depressing room, trying to uncover the truth.
Me, a big swine?

I might have been a big swine once upon a time, if you mean that I was ruthless in business.

But where do you think my ruthlessness came from?

Why did I scare the other partners of that smart law firm to the point where they kicked me out, even though I brought in more money than anyone else?

Why did I lose the popularity contest?

The man standing alone in an office on Kungsgatan, close to the smart social hub of Stureplan, feeling the breeze from the newly installed air-conditioning against his face, doesn't care about that. In all respects except one, he's looking to the future.

53

Jerry feels the cool air stroke his cheeks. Below him, on the other side of the polished office windows, Kungsgatan snakes down toward Stureplan in the late-summer sun. In Humlegården red lawnmowers are moving over tired grass, their blades in his dreams like bearers of all he thinks he has left behind. The blades force him onward, give him no time to rest, but he knows that at some point he will have to stand up to them.

He is standing here for the sake of money, at least that's what he thinks, unless it's because having an office here makes a good impression when he's standing at the upstairs bar of the Sturehof. He doesn't know, and he doesn't care.

The boxes from the move haven't been unpacked yet, and he has just had a call from his first client at Petersson Legal Services Ltd. Jochen Goldman wanted help setting up an endowment insurance in Liechtenstein.

This room. Its fine lines, free from dirt, the opportunity it gives him to create his reality himself. The sofa in the corner upholstered in shiny white fabric.

Clients come and go through the room. People and buses and cars hurry past in all seasons along Kungsgatan, a young man, little more than twenty years old, sits before him and explains an idea, an opportunity, an advanced piece of technology that might come in useful in the new economy.

Jerry is amused by the young man and gives him and his idea two million kronor, and three years later, a year after Foreign Minister Anna Lindh was murdered, the company is sold, and the man in the room on Kungsgatan is several hundred million kronor richer.

A bigger flat at the top of a turn-of-the-century building at Tegnérlunden, where the art comes into its own, is all he treats himself to. He could have bought it long before, but never actually got around to it until now.

A balcony railing to balance on in his memory, the park like a mirage of the life that was once his, swallows which fly close yet so far from their shadows.

Sometimes he thinks he sees her in other people. Her hair, way of moving, a smell in the NK department store one Saturday. He keeps himself up to date about her life, there are ways, but he never approaches her. He thinks that what he feels will disappear as the years pass, but it doesn't. It gets deeper and deeper.

Instead he gets to know all of them.

The superannuated gold diggers of the Sturehof, their tragic, slack genitals, the Russian whores out in Bandhagen, the casual fucks that seem to pop up all over the place, body to body, hard and quick, arms tied to a bedstead, maybe. Sometimes he pretends that they are her, gives them her face, but he no longer knows what she looks like, she's become a hazy memory.

Then an acquaintance phones, the estate agent who helped him with the flat in Tegnérlunden, to tell him that a castle southwest of Linköping is for sale—wasn't that where you're from?—thought he might be interested.

The memory becomes clear again.

Sweeps through his body.

He stands in all the rooms which have been his and feels all the cold hands which have ever caressed his cheeks or chest. He feels that he has always been on his way there: That is where I shall go, maybe one black autumn night full of fluid darkness. But I shall get there.

54

Axel Fågelsjö has dug out a photograph album from the old oak cupboard in the dining room, and now he is sitting in his leather armchair, going through the plastic sleeves with their black-and-white pictures.

Bettina with the children in her arms in front of the chapel, before they went to school.

Katarina with a beach ball down by the lake.

Fredrik looking anxious beside one of the strawberry fields.

A staff photograph. Men and women who worked for me. And that great oaf of a man, the one who drove the tractor into the chapel door, and we had to have a new one put in.

Fredrik and Katarina running over a meadow toward the forest in one picture. You took that picture, didn't you, Bettina?

Is he with you now, Bettina? Is Fredrik with you?

He shuts his eyes. Feels more tired than he has ever done before. Wishes Fredrik were here with him. Talk to him. Say something nice.

Then his head empties, all his thoughts stop, and for a moment Axel Fågelsjö believes he's about to die, that his heart or some blood vessel in his brain has given up, but he can feel himself breathing. He wants to open his eyes, but they stay shut.

He seems to hear Fredrik's voice:

"I can see you in the armchair in the sitting room, Father.

"See myself in the pictures in the album. And I can say that I miss those days, when I was little and didn't yet know what burden history lays upon people like me.

"I was little then, but I remember the staff in the photograph.

"That you called them—farmhands and maids.

"And how violent you could be toward them.

"You're alone now, Dad, but you don't realize it.

"Buy back Skogså. Install yourself there once again.

"Sit here in your apartment for now and look around, look at Mum and me and Katarina in the photographs.

"You'll never understand that the only three things that matter are birth and love, Dad.

"The third?

"Death, Dad. Death.

"That's where I am now. Do you want to come with me?"

And with that the voice is gone, and Axel Fågelsjö's thoughts fill his mind once more and he wants to call the voice back, but knows it's gone, never to return. What remains are the pictures. Like a broken film, they stretch out through the album.

You can't hear me, can you, Father? You can't see me, Fredrik, you can only see me as a photograph. Are you even sad? Or are you just mourning your own inadequacies, your inability to understand yourself?

It's not too late yet, Father. You've got Katarina. You've got the grandchildren, and Christina would be happy to let you into her and their lives, if only you take the first step and let her know that she really is good enough.

You won't get any invitations with your elbows.

You have to be bigger than your own instincts. You have to be adult about it, otherwise you're on your own. You have to realize that we, your creations, are the people we are, and that there's nothing you can do about it.

And Father.

There's one thing you should know: I always tried to do my best.

I'm drifting behind you, Fredrik, you're just as confused and basically alone in death as in life.

The mist is closing in around the forests, the city, and the castle.

What is it that's happening in that obscurity? In the gaps between what we see and hear?

In the police station Lovisa Segerberg and Waldemar Ekenberg are threshing on through the files and digital documents, trying to find out who we were, what might be hiding in the remnants of our lives.

Zeke Martinsson is talking to his son Martin over the phone.

They don't have much to say to each other, but he asks about his grandchild.

Johan Jakobsson has gone home to his children and his tired wife.

Karim Akbar has just had an argument with his ex-wife on the phone.

Sven Sjöman is eating the last of the year's pickled gherkins from the garden, looking at the woman he has spent his life with and still loves.

Börje Svärd is trying to pull a stick from Howie's mouth out in his garden, while in the large bedroom inside the house his wife Anna clings to life as hard as she can, the tubes of oxygen hissing beside her bed.

I am so close to you now, Fredrik, drifting. Has it ever occurred to you that you could have taken my side that afternoon, that evening, that night?

You can see Malin Fors down there.

She's happy.

Tove is with her in the flat. She's finally made it, at last. They're about to eat dinner, pizza. She's staying over.

Mother and daughter. Together. The way it should be.

55

Tove came in the end.

She's sitting opposite Malin at the kitchen table. Malin's tired from work, from thinking, from drinking and not drinking, tired of all this damn rain. Can you make me feel a bit brighter again, Tove?

You're more beautiful than I've ever seen you before. You are the only thing in my life that's pure, clear, unsullied. When you called to say you could come for dinner I yelped with joy down the phone and you shut me up, seemed to think I was embarrassing.

Tick tock.

The Ikea clock still marks the seconds, even though the second hand has fallen off, and the faulty lamp above the worktop flickers every twenty seconds.

How can Tove look older, more grown up, in just a week?

The skin stretched over her cheekbones, her features sharper, but her eyes are the same, yet somehow unfamiliar. Age, her relative age, suits her.

"I've missed you," Malin says, and Tove looks down at her pizza, takes a sip from her glass of water.

Takeaway pizza.

Didn't have the energy to go shopping, had nothing in the flat, and Tove likes pizza, she really does.

Tove pokes at the mushrooms.

"Something wrong with the pizza?"

"No."

"You normally like pizza."

"There's nothing wrong with it."

"But you're not eating."

"Mum, it's too fatty. I'll get spots, and I'll get fat. I had one on my chin last week."

"You won't get fat. Neither your dad nor I . . ."

"Couldn't you have made something?"

And Tove looks at her as if to say, I know what you're doing, Mum, I know what it's like being grown-up, don't try lying to me, or convincing me that you can handle it.

Malin pours some more wine from the box she bought on the way home the other day. Third or fourth, no, fifth glass, and she can see Tove wrinkle her nose.

"Why do you have to drink tonight? Now that I'm here, like you wanted?"

Malin is taken aback by her question, so straightforward and direct.

"I'm celebrating," Malin replies. "That you're here."

"You're really messed up."

"I'm not messed up."

"No, you're an alcoholic."

"What did you say?"

Tove sits in silence, poking at the pizza.

"Let's get one thing straight, Tove. I like a drink. But I'm not an alcoholic. Got that?"

Tove's eyes turn dark.

"So stop drinking, then."

"This isn't about that," Malin says.

"So what is it about?"

"You're too young to understand," and Tove's eyes flash with distaste and Malin wants to cut the shame from her own face, carve the words "You're right, Tove" in her forehead, then one of her hands starts to tremble and Tove stares at the hand, looking scared, but says nothing.

"How's school?" Malin goes on.

"Dad says you're . . ."

"What does he say?"

"Nothing."

"Tell me what he says."

Her voice too angry from all this tiredness, and the lamp above the worktop flickers twice before the light settles again.

"Nothing."

"You're ganging up on me, the pair of you. Aren't you?"

Tove doesn't even shake her head.

"He's turning you against me," Malin says.

"You're drunk, Mum. Dad was the one who thought I should come round."

"So you didn't really want to come?"

"You're drunk."

"I'm not drunk, and I'll drink as much as I like."

"You should . . ."

"I know what I should do. I should drink the whole damn box. You've decided to live with your dad, haven't you? Haven't you?"

Tove just stares at Malin.

"Haven't you?" Malin screams. "Admit it!"

Malin has got up, standing in the kitchen and looking angrily but beseechingly at her daughter.

Without changing her expression at all, Tove stands up and says in a calm voice, looking directly into Malin's eyes:

"Yes, I've made up my mind. I can't live here."

"Of course you can, why on earth wouldn't you be able to?"

Tove goes out into the hall and puts on her jacket. Opens the front door and walks out.

Malin downs her glass of wine out in the hall.

Then, as she hears Tove's footsteps on the stairs, she throws the glass at the wall and shouts after her daughter:

"Wait. Come back, Tove. Come back!"

Tove runs down Storgatan toward the river, past the Hemköp supermarket and the bowling alley, and she feels the raindrops and wind in her face, how nice the cold is, dissolving her thoughts and how the dampness in the air means that the tears on her cheeks don't show.

Bloody Mum. Bloody, sodding Mum. Only thinking about herself.

Dad's working tonight. I could have stayed at home on my own. I can do that now, I want to, I should have.

I hope he's at the fire station. Bloody Mum.

Her heart is thudding in her chest. Trying to get out, and her stomach clenches and she just wants to get away from the autumn, away from this shitty little city.

Up ahead, on the other side of the bridge, she can see the fire station. It's glowing in the light from the tall, yellow streetlamps.

She runs inside.

Gudrun in reception recognizes her, looks worried, asks:

"Tove, what's happened?"

"Is Dad here?"

"He's upstairs. Go straight up."

Five minutes later she's lying in the darkness with her head in her dad's lap on the bed in his room. He's stroking her cheek, telling her that everything will be all right. Then the light goes on and the alarm starts to howl.

"Shit," Dad says. "Probably another flood. I've got to go. I don't want to, but I've got to go."

"I'll stay here," Tove says, as her dad kisses her on the cheek.

Soon the room is dark and silent and she tries to think about nothing.

She sees herself standing on the edge of an immense plain in the darkness. She has no map, there are no lights in sight, but she still knows how to proceed. She just knows what she has to do, the certainty like a steady note inside her, entirely free of the sounds of childhood.

Her vision clouded by the cheap wine.

Malin is lying on her bed, listening to the raindrops drumming persistently on the window behind the blinds. She's tried calling Tove, but her mobile is switched off.

She closes her eyes,

Faces drift through her mind.

Tove. Mum. Dad. Janne.

Just go, Tove. Live where you like. I don't care.

She can't handle their mocking smiles so she forces them away and then sees Daniel Högfeldt's face, his lips are moist and she feels her crotch contract inside her jeans; the drink has made her horny, it's difficult to resist but not impossible, and then she sees Maria Murvall running through her closed room.

Fågelsjö.

The living and the dead, the soulless.

Jochen Goldman.

The thug whom Waldemar kept going on about back at the start.

Andreas Ekström's mother. Jasmin Sandsten's mother in another tragic room.

Jonas Karlsson. Were you blackmailing Petersson? Did you want to be like him? But seeing as there was probably only one killer, it can't be you. We checked, and you've got a cast-iron alibi for the night of the second murder.

Anders Dalström, Andreas Ekström's friend. Could he have found out who was driving and murdered him for the sake of his lost friendship?

Fredrik Fågelsjö. How does all this fit together? The threads of different lives singing in the darkness. Black birds squawking at them through the rain.

The bed, the world, spins round and round. What is it I'm missing? she thinks. What is it I'm not seeing?

How much wine have I drunk? Two glasses? Or five. I'm probably okay to drive. Of course I can drive. There won't be any patrols out at this time of night, will there?

You get out of your car in front of the castle, Malin.

A beautiful castle, but your drunken eyes can't tell.

It could never be my castle, but I wanted what I thought was there.

The green lanterns are hanging darkly along the moat, the imprisoned souls of the prisoners-of-war are whispering, their mouths glowing.

You were lucky on your way out here.

No mishaps, no pedestrians to hit, no patrols wanting you to blow in a tube.

I feel for you, Malin. You poor, wretched wreck of a human being, who can't even handle your love for your own daughter.

The doors to the castle are locked.

Malin has brought with her the bottle of vodka she bought at the same time as the wine box, drinking straight from the bottle as she walks round the castle toward the chapel.

The raindrops seem to be leaping from the skies as if from a burning building.

Her cotton jacket, the thin one that she for some reason put on, is soon wet through and cold, and she coughs, stumbling along the edge of the dark forest toward the building.

A son murdered and laid out naked upon the family vault. The upstart in the moat. Privilege. Denial. Degeneration, and a party one cold New Year's Eve. History like a pressure cooker for people's souls.

The door to the chapel is locked. She doesn't have a key, so she stands in the archway by the door, looking in at the icons, or the place where the body lay. She drinks from the bottle, two warming mouthfuls, missing the sweet, nuanced taste of tequila.

But the rawness of the vodka matches this moment better.

The forest behind the chapel seems to be moving. Evil is on the move, slithering, and all the windows of the castle seem to be lit up, skulls grinning in the recesses, laughing at all her shortcomings, well aware that the dead, and death, always win.

What am I doing here?

I'm searching for a truth. Fleeing from another.

She throws the bottle of vodka in the moat.

Full again.

The black water greedily swallows the bottle. No fish now.

There's a green glow from the cracks between the stones. Where does the light come from?

She can feel how she's losing her grip on the world, but the rain anchors her to reality, and she walks around the castle a few times to clear her head before getting back in the car to wait, listening to "nonstop music," a numbing racket that almost makes her fall asleep. She looks over toward the forest. Between the trees, scarcely visible in the darkness, the young snakes are there again. The shapes are there, but she can't hear their collective voice, if it's actually there at all. Maybe they've said all they wanted to say?

"I'm not scared of you," Malin shouts toward the forest. "Fucking bastard snakes."

She blinks, and the snakes are gone. All that's left is darkness, and she almost misses the slithering creatures, doesn't want to be without them. Then she hears the sound of a lawnmower, of feet trying to escape the blades.

She puts her hands over her ears and the sound disappears.

She feels almost sober a few hours later as she turns the key in the ignition and leaves the castle and the spirits and souls behind her.

She drives past the field where the accident must have happened. Stops, but doesn't get out.

The darkness and rain seem to shake figures out from the past, black souls that are still moving over the grass, the moss, and the rocks, trying to escape what they are.

She drives on.

Increases her speed.

On the approach to Sturefors she passes a warning triangle by the side of the road. A hundred yards farther on she sees a police patrol car, its lights on.

A uniformed officer she doesn't recognize waves at her to pull over.

She wants to put her foot down.

Follow Fredrik Fågelsjö's example.

Get away, but she stops.

The uniform raises an eyebrow when she winds down the window, an anxious look in his eyes.

"Detective Inspector Fors," he says. "What are you doing out at this time of night?"

He is a mask, Malin thinks. A talking mask, with thin skin stretched over his cheekbones.

The uniform frowns.

"I'm afraid I must ask you to blow into this."

56

An implacable Sven Sjöman is standing inside the door of his office, having just closed it hard behind him once he'd fetched Malin from her desk, where she had been sitting in her most respectable white blouse, which she had even managed to iron that morning. She doesn't know where Tove got to last night, she probably got the first bus out to Malmslätt. She hasn't checked with her or Janne yet, didn't want to wake them on a Saturday morning or answer any difficult questions, and if she hadn't got home Janne would have called. There was never any question of her staying over, even if Malin would have liked her to. Or was there? She hadn't spoken to Janne before Tove arrived, she took it for granted that they had talked to each other. I ought to call Tove, Janne—what if she didn't get home?

The look in Sven's eyes.

Have to deal with this first.

He knows I got caught.

And when she thinks about how Tove left yesterday she feels sick with herself, wants to disappear far away and never come back.

The clock on the wall of Sven's office says just after ten o'clock, no case meeting this morning seeing as they had one yesterday afternoon. Besides, it's Saturday. But obviously a working Saturday, what with two fresh, unsolved murders.

Sven looks at Malin for a long time before saying in a loud voice:

"I hope you appreciate what a fucking mess you've got us all into. Got yourself into."

Malin wants to get up and shout at him that she couldn't care less, that she isn't asking for special treatment, but she stops herself, thinks better of it. Right now she just wants to cling on to what she still has.

"I don't know what got into me."

"One point five parts per thousand, Malin. Drunk driving. The most obvious sign of an alcoholic. What the hell were you doing out there?"

"I'm not an alcoholic."

"You don't know what you are. Or what you're doing."

"So charge me, then. Report me."

"You don't know what you're saying. I'm not the only one risking my job for your sake."

Sven's voice lacks the protective undertone that's usually there, he's giving her orders now and expects her to take responsibility, do what she has to do.

The Breathalyzer turned bright red last night on the way back from the castle.

And the uniform and his colleague had looked at each other, made a call, as if something important was happening, as if they were trying to sort something out, then they told her they had spoken to Sven, and that they were both prepared to pretend nothing had happened. She had felt like telling them to go to hell out there in the cold, rainy darkness, but she had kept her mouth shut, in spite of how drunk she was, aware of the risk they were taking and that this must be utterly at odds with their sense of justice.

But the solidarity of the force is stronger, the sense of standing together. Of standing above the law?

"Everyone makes mistakes," one of the uniforms says.

They had driven her and her car home, saying it was what Sven wanted, and she had woken up on time with only a mild hangover, driven to the station, and sat at her desk, waiting for Sven to call her to his room.

"I was trying to listen to the voices," she says, and Sven goes over to his desk, sits down and looks at her.

"What voices, Malin?"

"The voices of the investigation. The ones you always talk about. They're there at the castle, the truth's out there, I know it is, I just can't hear the voices."

"I see, *those* voices."

"Yes, your voices. The ones you taught me about."

Sven mutters something, and Malin wonders if he's going to draw a comparison between her and Fredrik Fågelsjö, the drunk driver in their case, but it's unlikely that Sven would sink so low. He looks at her for a long while in silence before saying:

"We're not getting anywhere with the case."

"The rain's making the truth slippery," Malin says.

"What happened last night is history. I've spoken to Larsson and Alman. To them it's as if it never happened. But there's bound to be talk. And you need to keep quiet."

"Everyone here knows I drink sometimes."

"No."

"Yes, I could tell from the way they reacted last night. That they were getting confirmation of something."

Sven doesn't answer, just takes a deep breath and says:

"I need you on this case right now. You're the best I've got, you know that. If we weren't in such a bloody awful position, I'd suspend you, and you know that too. But right now I need you."

"Thank you," Malin says.

"Don't thank me. Pull yourself together."

"I will."

"No more false promises, Malin. Do you hear me? You only drive if you're stone-cold sober. And once this case is solved I'm going to make sure that you get treatment. And you're going to go along with it. Understood?"

Malin nods.

Looks around the room, a lost expression in her eyes.

When Malin is about to leave Sven's office he calls her back.

"That talk," he says, and she stops and turns round.

"What talk?"

"The one at Sturefors secondary school that you're supposed to be giving on Monday. Nine o'clock. You hadn't forgotten?"

Then she remembers. They discussed it several months ago, and she said yes, feeling a peculiar urge to go back to her old school.

"Haven't I got more important things to be getting on with? Maybe we could postpone it?"

"You're going to give that talk, Malin."

Sven looks down at a sheet of paper on his desk.

"And you're going to do it perfectly. Show the school kids a good example. They could do with it. So could you. Take the day off to-morrow. Take things easy. Get some rest. And don't touch the bottle."

Malin knocks on the door of paperwork Hades and hears a resigned "Come in."

Waldemar Ekenberg's tobacco-hoarse voice, then two other voices like faint echoes, a lively young woman and a man of her own age.

Paper from floor to ceiling. Black files and folders.

Enough for any brain to get lost in, to wither away in, and the room smells of damp and sweat and aftershave and cheap perfume, of weariness in the face of an impossible task.

In spite of this, the three officers are working feverishly, hunting through hard drives and files, and the calm but focused energy in the room cheers Malin up.

"Nothing new," Johan Jakobsson says without looking up.

Lovisa Segerberg shakes her blond head.

Waldemar looks up at her. What does his expression mean? Does he know, do they all know, about what happened last night?

No. Or do they?

Who cares?

"Anything else you need help with?" Waldemar asks.

"You mean, can I rescue you from Hades?"

"Exactly."

"Dream on."

"What about you two?"

"Me and Zeke?"

"No, you and the King."

"I'm about to talk to Zeke now. We'll see. We'll probably have a meeting this afternoon."

"If anything's come up," Johan says.

"Have fun," Malin says.

"Close the door behind you," Johan says.

"We don't want to lose any of the sweaty smell in here," Lovisa says with a grin.

Waldemar's nostrils flare, he seems to be trying to find a killer comment, and flashes a smile full of nicotine-yellow teeth before he says:

"Drive carefully, Malin."

Malin's mobile rings as she's walking back to her desk.

She answers, doesn't bother to check the display.

"Malin."

"Hello, it's me."

Ten days since she left the house, ten days since she spoke to him, and all she wants to do is hang up.

"Janne, listen, I'm pretty busy, can you call . . ."

She stops, the anger in his voice makes her lose the ability to put one foot in front of the other.

"No, Malin. You need to listen. How the hell could you just let Tove leave like that last night? What the hell did you say to her? What did you do to her? She was in pieces. She came down to the station and she was a complete bloody wreck. Hitting me is one thing, but messing Tove up like that . . ."

Words. She doesn't want to hear them. Doesn't want to think about it. Has thrust it aside until now."

"I . . ."

"Shut up! This is how it is: Tove lives with me. You don't come out here. If you want anything to do with her, you call, but be bloody careful about what you say. Those are the rules until you get yourself sorted out. Got it?"

Can he do that? Malin thinks. Yes, it wouldn't be hard to convince the authorities that I'm an alcoholic mother.

"Go to hell," she says. "All the fucking way to hell."

Tell me you love me, she thinks.

"Malin," Janne says, no anger in his voice now. "Pull yourself together. Tove needs her mum. Get some help."

Zeke isn't at his desk when she gets back.

Her hands are shaking, and she bangs them on the desk a few times to stop them and to get rid of the anger.

How low have I sunk? I let Tove vanish into the night. Into everything that might be out there. And then I got drunk.

She looks out across the open-plan office. Forces her thoughts and feelings aside. Reboots herself.

"Toilet," Zeke says when he comes back and Malin is sitting and waiting for him at her place at their desk. Waiting for them to get going with the practical business of the day, waiting to let work take over her mind and her feelings.

He looks at Malin, in the same way he did when she arrived at the station.

Amiably. Benevolently. But also anxiously. No irritation. Not a trace of it. Just sympathy. And she had turned away.

Zeke knows.

And he probably thinks the same as Sven. Let her finish this case, then she has to get help.

The look in his eyes is even more anxious now.

"Has something happened?" he asks. "You look . . ."

"Shut up. Let's get to work."

I don't want any help, Malin thinks. I just want Janne. Tove. Don't I?

Our life together.

Is that what I want?

The look on the face of Viveka Crafoord, the psychoanalyst, her words: "You're welcome to a session on my couch whenever you want, Malin."

Then Police Constable Aronsson comes over to their desk. A sheet of paper in her hand.

"I've just got this from the archive," she says. "It took a while, but they seem to have checked in all the corners now. The only thing they've found about the Fågelsjö family. Apparently Axel Fågelsjö attacked one of his workers sometime back in the seventies. Blinded him in one eye."

57

"He dragged me to the ground and whipped me. My back was stinging like it had been burned from the cracks of the whip, and when I turned round to get up the whip caught my eye."

Another voice in the investigation's choir.

Malin and Zeke are each sitting in an armchair in Sixten's flat in a block of sheltered housing, Serafen. From his living room he has a view of the Horticultural Society Park's bald treetops moving gently in the wind. The rain has stopped temporarily.

Sixten Eriksson. The man Fågelsjö beat up in 1973. The circumstances were described in the file they had received from the archive. Sixten had been employed as a farmhand out at Skogså, and managed to drive one of the tractors into the chapel. Fågelsjö lost his temper and beat him so badly that he was left blind in one eye. He was only given a fine and had to pay minimal damages to Sixten.

Sixten is sitting on the blue sofa in front of them with a patch over one eye, his other eye gray-green, almost transparent with cataracts. On the wall behind him hang reproductions of Bruno Liljefors paintings: foxes in the snow, grouse in a forest. The whole room smells of tobacco, and Malin gets the impression that smell is coming from Sixten's pores.

"It felt like I was inside an egg that was breaking," Sixten said. "I still dream of the pain to this day, I feel it sometimes."

The nurse who let them in told them Sixten was completely blind now that his other eye was afflicted by inoperable cataracts.

Malin looks at him, thinking that there is a directness about him, in spite of his darkness.

"Of course I was bitter that Axel Fågelsjö didn't get a harsher punishment, but isn't that always the way? Those in power aren't easily dislodged. They took one of my eyes, and fate took the other. That's all there is to it."

The court had given Fågelsjö no more than a fine, and showed understanding for his anger: According to the files, Sixten had been negligent with the tractor and had caused severe damage to the door of the chapel.

The old man couldn't have taken revenge on Fågelsjö by murdering his son so much later, that much is clear, Malin thinks. But Fågelsjö? He was guilty of extreme brutality then, so could he have done the same to his son?

"What did you do after that?" Zeke asks.

"I worked for NAF, until they shut the factory down."

"Did the bitterness pass?"

"What could I do about it?"

"The pain?" Malin said. "Did that fade?"

"No, but you can learn to live with anything."

Sixten pauses before going on:

"There's no pain that you can't learn to live with. You just have to transfer it onto something else, get it out of yourself."

Malin feels something change in the room.

The warmth is replaced by a chill, and an inner voice encourages her to ask the next sentence:

"Your wife. Is she still alive?"

"We were never married. But we lived together from the age of eighteen. She died of cancer. In her liver."

"Did you have any children?"

Before Sixten has a chance to answer the door opens and a young blond woman wearing the uniform of an enrolled nurse comes in.

"Time for your medicine," she says, and as the nurse approaches the sofa Sixten answers Malin's question.

"A son."

"A son?"

"Yes."

"What's his name?"

The nurse carefully closes the door behind her and Sixten smiles, waiting several long seconds before replying:

"He took his mother's name. His name's Sven Evaldsson. He's lived in Chicago for years now."

A bus struggles up Djurgårdsgatan, and behind the windows pale passengers huddle in their seats, their faces indistinct grimaces through the rain that has once again started to fall.

Malin and Zeke are standing in the rain, both of them thinking.

"Shouldn't those farmers have known about Fågelsjö's conviction? People ought to be talking about it still," Zeke says.

"Even if they knew, perhaps they didn't realize that we'd want to know," Malin says. "Or else they didn't want to talk about it. From their perspective, it's probably never looked impossible that the Fågelsjö family would get the castle back, in which case it probably makes sense to keep quiet."

As they're about to get into the car Malin's mobile rings.

Unknown number on the display. She answers in the rain.

"Malin Fors."

"This is Jasmin's mother."

Jasmin.

Which one of Tove's friends is that?

Then she remembers the woman in the room of the rehabilitation center in Söderköping, beside her daughter's wheelchair. The sense that her love for her daughter was boundless. If anything like that happened to Tove, could I handle it? The question was back again.

Raindrops on her face, pattering against her coat, the impatient look on Zeke's face inside the car.

"Hello. Is there something I can help you with?"

"I had a dream last night," Jasmin Sandsten's mother says.

Not again, not another dreamer, Malin thinks, seeing Linnea Sjöstedt's face in front of her. We need something concrete now, not more bloody dreams.

"You had a dream?"

"I had a dream about a boy with long black hair. I don't remember his name, but he used to visit Jasmin in the beginning, after the accident. He said they hardly knew each other but he'd been friends with Andreas, the boy who died in the crash. Jasmin's friends didn't know anything about him. I remember thinking it was strange that he kept coming, but he was friendly and most of them never came at all. I thought that the sound of people her own age might help her to come back."

"And you've just had a dream about him?"

Malin doesn't wait for Jasmin Sandsten's mother to reply, instead she's thinking that Anders Dalström, the folk singer from the forest, has got long black hair.

So now he's popped up in the investigation again. In a dream.

"Long black hair. You don't remember his name?"

"No, I'm sorry. But a very well-dressed young man without a face came to me in the dream. He showed me a film of the young man who used to visit Jasmin. A black-and-white film. Jerky and old.

"Wait a moment. I think his name might have been Anders. His surname was something like Fahlström."

58

Anders Dalström takes a sip of his coffee in the branch of Robert's Coffee attached to the Academic Bookshop, not far from Stadium and Gyllentorget. One of the showy American coffee shops that have successfully seen off the traditional old cafés. Latte hell, Malin thinks.

A lot of people, Saturday. Money burning a hole in their wallets.

The bookshop must do well in this sort of weather, when people are huddled up at home.

"I'm in the city," Anders had said when Malin called: They didn't want to drive all the way out to the forests outside Björsäter if he wasn't home. "I've come in to get some books. We could meet now if you like."

And now he's sitting opposite her and Zeke, wearing a blue hooded top and a yellow T-shirt with a green Bruce Springsteen on the chest. He looks tired, has bags under his eyes, and his long black hair looks greasy and unwashed.

You look ten years older than you did out at the cottage, Malin thinks. Is it right to disturb you again? But Malin wants to follow the threads of her conversation with Jasmin's mother, asking Anders about Jasmin.

"Why did you visit her? You didn't really know her, did you?"

"No. But it used to make me feel better."

"Better in what way?" Zeke asks.

Anders closes his eyes with a sigh.

"I was working last night. I'm too tired for this."

"Better in what way?" Zeke asks again, sounding firmer this time, and Malin notes that he's taken her place, asking questions that match her intuition rather than his own, perhaps.

"I don't know. It just felt better. It's so long ago now."

"So you didn't have any sort of relationship with Jasmin?"

"No. I didn't know her. Not at all. But I still felt sorry for her. I can hardly remember it now. It was like her silence was my own somehow. I liked the silence."

"And you didn't know that Jerry Petersson was driving the car that New Year's Eve?"

"I told you I didn't last time."

A bag of books by Anders's side, a few DVDs.

"What have you bought?"

"A new Springsteen biography. A couple of thrillers. Two films of Bob Dylan concerts. And *Lord of the Flies*."

"My daughter loves reading," Malin says. "But mostly literary novels. Ideally with a bit of romance. But *Lord of the Flies* is good, the book and the film."

Anders looks at her, staring into her eyes for a few moments before saying:

"Speaking of romance: You've probably heard it from other people, but there were rumors in high school around the time of the accident that Jerry Petersson was seeing Katarina Fågelsjö."

I can sniff out an unhappy relationship from a thousand miles away, Malin thinks. And I can pick up the smell of it here, here in Katarina Fågelsjö's living room, it's seeping out of this bitter woman's skin, and you want to tell us, don't you? You're the woman in the Anna

Ancher painting on the wall, the woman who wants to turn round and tell her story.

"I'll go and see her on my own. I might be able to get her to talk." Zeke had nodded.

Let her go to see Katarina. It might be dangerous, but probably not. "Go. Find out what we need to know."

White tights. Blue skirt, one leg crossed over the other. High heels, even at home.

Open up. Tell me. You want to, I saw your reaction when I told you what Anders Dalström had told us. About the rumors. The romance.

"You're mourning Jerry Petersson, aren't you?"

The perfectly balanced upholstery from Svenskt Tenn behind her back, Josef Frank's speckled, smiling snakes.

And Katarina's mask falls. Shatters into a tormented grimace and she starts to cry.

"Don't touch me," Katarina sobs when Malin makes a move to put her arm round her.

"Sit down again and I'll tell you."

And soon the words are pouring from the puffy, tear-streaked face.

"I was in love with Jerry Petersson the autumn before the accident. I saw him in the corridors at school, I knew he was off limits for a girl like me, but you should have seen him, Malin, he was ridiculously handsome. Then we ended up at the same party, at the headquarters of the youth wing of the Moderate Party, by mistake, and I don't remember why but we ended up sitting in the cemetery all night, and then we went down to the river. There used to be an abandoned pump house there, it's been demolished now."

Katarina gets up. Goes over to the window facing the river, and with her back to Malin she points, waiting for Malin to join her before she goes on.

"Over there, on that little island, that's where the pump house was. It was cold, but I still felt warmer than ever that autumn. Jerry and I used to meet without anyone else knowing. I was head over heels in love with him. But Father wouldn't have wanted anything to do with him. And that was that."

Then Katarina falls silent, seems to be trying to keep the moment alive, by keeping her memories to herself.

Malin opens her mouth to say something, but Katarina hushes her, giving her a look that tells her to listen, to listen to her, and not to herself.

"Then he disappeared off to Lund. But he didn't leave me. I kept an eye on him all those years, through my failed marriage to that idiot Father loved. I never forgot Jerry, I wanted to get back in touch, but I never did, I devoted myself to art instead, buried myself in paintings. Why, why, why did he have to come home again, why did he want the castle? I never understood. If he wanted to get back into my life, surely he could have just called? Don't you think? He could have just called, couldn't he?"

You could have called him, Malin thinks.

"And I should have rung him. Or gone out there. Ditched all my useless lovers. He was there, after all, maybe it was finally time to do something about our wretched, lingering love."

You always loved him. Like I've always loved Janne. Can our love ever end?

"Did Jerry ever meet your father?" Malin goes on.

Katarina doesn't answer. Instead she walks away from the window and out of the room.

Katarina is standing in front of the mirror in the bathroom. Doesn't recognize her own face.

Then she imagines that someone is holding pictures in front of her eyes, black-and-white pictures that were never taken by a camera but which somehow exist anyway.

Two young people walking beside a river.

A pump house.

Burning wood. And the voice is there, his voice, a voice she has been longing to hear.

"Do you remember how beautiful you were then, Katarina? That autumn? When we would walk together along the Stångå, taking care that no one saw us, how we would have sex in the old pump house, warmed by the fire we made in an abandoned stove. I would stroke your back, caress it, and we pretended it was summer, and that I was rubbing sun cream into your skin to stop it from burning."

New pictures.

Snow falling. She in her room at the castle. A figure walking through the forest in the cold. The closed doors of the castle.

"And then, against my will," the voice went on, "you wanted me to meet your father and mother. So I came out to the castle on the afternoon of New Year's Eve, like we'd agreed. I took the bus as far as I could, then walked through the cold, through the forest and past fields, until I saw the castle almost forcing the forest aside, on a small rise surrounded by its moat.

"I walked across the bridge over the moat.

"Saw the strange green light.

"And your father opened the door and I looked at him and he realized why I was there, and you came to the door, and he saw something in your eyes, and he shouted that there was no way in hell that someone like me was going to cross his threshold, then he raised his arm and knocked me to the ground with a single blow.

"He chased me away, over the moat, brandishing an umbrella, and you were shouting that you loved me, I love him, Father, and I ran, I ran and I thought you were going to follow me, but when I turned around at the edge of the forest you were gone, the driveway was empty, the door wasn't closed, but your mother, Bettina, was standing there, and I thought I could see her smiling."

Images of herself turning away in the castle doorway. Running up the stairs. Lying on a bed. Standing close to her father. Adjusting her makeup in a mirror.

Shut up, she wants to shout at the voice, shut up, but it goes on:

"I came to the party. You were there. Fredrik. He had drunk too much, was arrogant toward everyone and everything. It was as if I didn't exist for you. You didn't even look at me, and that made me mad. I drank, gulping it down, danced, fumbled with dozens of girls who all wanted me, I made myself unbeatable, I took Jasmin, who was in your class, just because it would upset you, I got behind the wheel of that car just to show the world who made the decisions, and that love really doesn't matter. I was in charge, and not even love could take that power away.

"And then, in the field, in the snow and the blood and the silence, I looked at Jonas Karlsson, begged him to say he was the one driving, promised him the world.

"And do you know, he did what I said, I got him to do it, and I re-alized deep down at that moment that I could have almost anything I wanted in this world, as long as I was ruthless enough. That I could make the lawnmower blades shut up.

"But not you, Katarina. I could never have you. Not the person you are.

"So, sure, in a way I was both born and died on that New Year's Eve."

Images of a car wreck. Funerals, a wheelchair with a mute body, a man with his back to her in an office chair, a steady stream of images from a life she had never known.

"And when I bought Skogså, I wanted to breathe life into what had died," the voice goes on.

"That was the very worst vanity, worse than any alchemist's.

"Soon I was standing in the very same doorway that I had been refused entry to for all those years. I walked bare-chested through the rooms, feeling the cold, rough surface of the stone against my skin."

The images are gone. All that is left is the mirror, her eyes, the tears she knows are there inside them somewhere.

59

Jerry rubs against the walls of a room illuminated by 103 candles in the chandelier hanging sixteen feet above his head. The stones are irregular and rough against his chest and back, like the surface of some as yet unexplored hostile planet.

The painting of the man and woman with the sun cream is hanging in front of him.

The rooms of the castle. One after the other.

The telephones. She's only a phone call away. He sits beneath his paintings and chants the number like a mantra.

It never occurs to him that she might be angry about what he has done, that she might think he has torn her family's history from their hands.

But he never dials her number. Instead he throws himself into the practical business that comes with a property like this, sorting out the tenant farmers and laborers of all different trades, visiting the whores he finds on the Internet, even in Linköping, often middle-aged women with an unnaturally high sex drive who may as well make a bit of money from satisfying their lust. He considers calling the young solicitor he bedded when the contracts were signed, but thinks that things might get a bit too close to home if he did that.

Some evenings and mornings he heads out into the estate. Drives through the black landscape, past houses and trees and fields, the field that seems to encompass the three beings that he is: past, present, and whatever is to come tomorrow.

He imagines he can see green light streaming from the moat and has green lanterns installed along it, as a response to the optical phenomenon down in the water.

He stands on the other side of the door, resting inside himself, waiting for a call, for a car he wants to come and pull up in front of the castle, but which never comes. He stands still, takes detours around the love he can never bring himself to open up to for a second time. That is the fear he can never conquer.

Instead he receives a letter through the post. Handwritten.

He reads the letter at the kitchen table, early one morning that autumn, when the skies have opened and seem to be raining corrosive acid onto the world of men.

He folds the letter, thinking that he needs to deal with this, cauterize it once and for all.

60

Push the bar up.

You're alone in the gym, Malin, if you can't manage it the bar will crush your throat and that'll be an end to all your problems.

To all your breathing. To all love.

One hundred fifty pounds on the bar, more than her own weight, and she pushes it up another ten times before letting it slip back into the supporting frame.

Janne. Now he's telling me what I can and can't do.

To hell with that.

But maybe he's right.

Tove. I want to say I'm sorry. But you're right to leave me alone for a while, aren't you?

How could I?

Her body wet with sweat. As if she's been running through the rain she can see through the little windows along the ceiling.

They've put up new wallpaper in the room. In place of the old vomit-green there is now an even worse pink wallpaper with little purple flowers.

This is a gym, Malin thinks. Not a fucking girl's bedroom.

She lies down on the bench again.

Ten more reps and she feels her muscles working, the effort sup-pressing every thought of drink. Rehab. Bollocks. I don't need that.

Every time she lifts the bar toward the dusty, blinding-white ceil-ing, she tries to get closer to the core of the investigation.

Lactic acid is burning through her body and she gets up, boxing the air, shaking life into mute, oxygen-starved tissue, and says as she punches:

"I. Am. Missing. Something. But. What?"

In the sauna, after first a long cold shower, then a hot one, she reads Daniel Högfeldt's latest article about the murders, the pages of the *Correspondent* hot on her fingers.

He goes through the connections between the murders and says that sources within the police are convinced they are linked, but that they don't know for sure yet.

In a separate article he gives a well-informed account of Fredrik Fågelsjö's failed financial investments, and how the family came to lose Skogså. He concludes: "Suspicion may now be focused on the Fågelsjö family, who some people claim would do anything to get the estate back."

He doesn't mention the family's new money, the inheritance they've received. But there are pictures of the houses they currently live in. Probably new photographs. The vultures never leave the be-reaved in peace.

Then a picture of Linnea Sjöstedt by her cottage tucked away near Skogså. Daniel reports her as saying:

"Of course they might have wanted revenge on Fredrik for losing the estate. It means everything to them."

Two hundred degrees in here.

Ten minutes and her body is shrieking, the sweat streaming from every pore, but Malin is enjoying the pain.

Nor has Daniel found out about Axel Fågelsjö's old conviction for actual bodily harm. Nor that Jerry Petersson was driving the car on that fateful New Year's Eve. That's good, maybe there are fewer leaks in the police station now. And Daniel is a decent person, really. He's never pressed her for information when she's been drunk, never tried to turn her into one of the leaks.

Malin stands naked in the changing room.

One message on her phone.

Daniel Högfeldt's number, by coincidence, and she assumes that he must want a session that evening. She calls the messaging service to hear what he had to say.

"Daniel here. I was just going to say that I've had an anonymous tip-off about your investigation. Call me?"

Daniel.

He doesn't usually give us anything. Keeps any tips he receives for himself. And these days people keen for money and media attention often call the papers with tip-offs and leads instead of calling us.

How did that happen?

"Daniel."

"It's me. I got your message."

"Yes, I just wanted to say that I got a tip-off about Fågelsjö over the phone. That it had to be the father and daughter who killed Fredrik. As revenge. That they're responsible."

"I can't deny that we've considered that."

"Of course, Malin. But this informant was particularly insistent. He sounded relieved when I said I was already thinking of writing about the connection."

"A nutter?"

"No, but there was something about him. Something that didn't fit."

"What was his name? Did you get his number?"

"No, no number came up. No name. And that's pretty unusual as well."

He's using this as an excuse to call me, Malin thinks.

He's got nothing. They get loads of tip-offs.

Anonymous.

About all sorts of things.

"I know what you're thinking, Malin. But this one was different. The fact that he was so insistent scared me."

"Did he have anything new to say?"

"No."

"Okay," Malin says. "You can come around to my place at nine o'clock tonight, then you can have what you want."

Daniel is silent.

Malin sees herself in the changing-room mirror, careful not to look at her tired face, looks instead at her toned body.

"You really are something, Fors, aren't you? I was thinking I could actually help you with your work for once."

"What, with that?"

"With the fact that it was a man and not a woman who called, for instance."

"Are you coming?"

The line breaks and goes silent.

He's coming.

Tell me you're coming. Then everything will be all right, if only for half an hour or so. That's enough.

Malin is lying on her bed in her dressing gown, waiting for Daniel to come, feeling the urge to have him inside her.

Nine o'clock comes.

Half past.

Ten o'clock. And she feels like calling him, but knows that such humiliation would be pointless, that he actually didn't want her and really was only trying to help.

In his own awkward way, with a meaningless tip-off.

Someone who wants things to be a particular way. Who wants to direct them to look in one direction when they ought to be looking elsewhere. The thought pops up again.

On the way home from the gym she called her dad.

He evidently hadn't noticed any Spanish police watching over him and Mum, but on the other hand he hadn't noticed his picture being taken either.

He told her that he and her mother were thinking of coming home for Christmas. Malin replied that Tove would be happy, but that they should expect fairly strained family relationships.

"Are you having a tough time?" Dad asked.

"No, there's just an awful lot of autumn at the moment," she said, thinking: Dad, we're fighting for our lives on my planet.

Are you Malin? Fighting for your life?

I think my father's doing the same on his planet.

Axel Fågelsjö.

Father.

I can see both you and him clearly, you're lying in your bed, and you've fallen asleep and are sleeping a dreamless sleep, a well-deserved rest after all that work trying to keep your impulses under control.

Axel is sitting at his kitchen table on Drottninggatan. He's taken his beloved shotgun out of the gun cabinet in the bedroom.

He smells the gun, I've seen him do that before, and I don't know why he does it. Now he's locking the gun away in the cabinet again.

I don't actually know what happened to me, Malin. I don't remember anything. That seems to be unusual, from what I've been able to gather from talking to other people up here where I am.

But that doesn't matter.

Because I've got you.

You'll be able to tell me what my fate was.

You talk of your fate, Fredrik, but what do you know, my silver-spoon boy, about fate?

There's no such thing as fate, just events which are the result of conscious actions.

When I ended up in the moat it was my own fault, no one else's.
In the most fundamental sense, I caused that event myself.
You imagine, Malin, that you're going to give me some sort of justice,
reparation after death. As if I could have any use for that?
I don't need anything from any of you.
I am already everything.

On Sunday a hard rain is lashing the ground, the people.

Malin stands in the window of her flat looking at the church tower, the way even the crows seem to be suffering in this wind.

She wants to hear Tove's voice, meet her, they could have spent the whole day together now that Sven has forced her to take the day off.

But she doesn't call her daughter, she does what Janne said, or at least what she thought he meant. She keeps her distance. Avoids her own reflection. If she were fourteen years old, she'd be slashing her wrists.

Instead she puts on her jogging clothes and runs twelve miles on various routes through Linköping. She sweats under the tight fabric, the city disappears before her eyes, and she feels her heart, feels that she can still trust its power.

Back home again, she calls the station. Waldemar Ekenberg tells her that nothing new has happened in the case.

She leafs through her papers about Maria Murvall. She prepares her talk at the kitchen table. The evening darkness settles outside the window.

Malin looks around the kitchen, thinking, I have nothing, I can't even handle Tove. And will I ever get the chance again?

61

There must be four hundred eyes, Malin thinks. And they're all staring at me. I hope the collar of my beige blouse is sitting as it should under this pale-blue lamb's-wool sweater, and why the hell am I bothered what this lot think of the way I look?

The hall of Sturefors School is full, pupils tapping at their mobile phones. Malin is standing behind a lectern, looking out over them, out at the hall she once sat in.

The head teacher, Birgitta Svensson, a woman in her fifties, wrinkled by smoking and dressed in gray, is standing beside Malin, takes a deep breath, and taps gently on a little black microphone with the fingers of one hand.

"Okay, let's turn off our mobiles now."

And to Malin's surprise they listen to her.

With a chorus of bleeps the phones are switched off, and the voices fall to a murmur until there is silence in the hall.

The smell of damp cloth. Of teenagers' sweet breath, of flaking plaster.

"Standing beside me up here is Malin Fors, a detective inspector with the police. She's going to talk to us about what the police do. Let's make her very welcome."

Wolf whistles. They all applaud, and when silence settles once more Malin loses her train of thought and isn't sure where to start, feeling a wave of withdrawal sickness course through her body, and she tries to focus on the clock on the wall.

It's 9:09.

She's supposed to talk for an hour, but about what?

The adolescents in front of her seem to know everything about the world, yet nothing at the same time. Calling them innocent would be a serious exaggeration, yet what do they know of violence? About human excess? Though a fair number must have seen more adult frustrations than they should have in their own homes.

Like Tove. My hand hitting Janne's mouth. How could I?

Silence.

No words seem willing to cross Malin's lips. A minute passes, then two.

The students are starting to squirm on their chairs.

"Violence," Malin says. "I work with what we usually call violent crimes. Rapes, and abuse."

She pauses again.

Sits it out.

"And murder. And as I'm sure you're aware, things like that do still happen in a peaceful city like Linköping."

Then the words flow by themselves, and she explains how a typical abuse case might be dealt with, about a few real cases, but none of the worst ones.

"We do our best," Malin says. "Let's just hope it's enough."

Her nausea remains subdued while she is talking, the adrenaline and concentration making her feel okay, but once the students start asking about the murders they are currently investigating, all the air goes out of her.

"Well, I think that's enough from me. Thank you," she says, stepping down from the stage before anyone has a chance to ask another question.

The whistling and applause start up again.

There's something ritualistic about the whole situation.

They would have applauded and whistled even if I'd been talking about the Holocaust, Malin thinks.

Outside the hall the head teacher comes up to Malin.

"That went well," she says. "You even got a few questions. That never usually happens. But I suppose they're excited about what's going on at the moment."

"It felt like they were listening," Malin says. "But as to whether they learned anything, what do I know?"

The head teacher takes Malin's arm.

"You shouldn't be so hard on yourself."

Malin wants to pull away, but the look in the woman's eyes is strangely intense as she looks into Malin's eyes and says:

"I'm sure they learned a good deal, and we're very grateful to you. Would you like a cup of coffee in the staff room?"

To her own surprise, Malin hears herself say yes.

Lovisa Segerberg is alone in paperwork Hades.

Waldemar and Johan have gone out for coffee.

She wonders whether to switch on Fredrik Fågelsjö's computer or look through one of the hundreds of folders they haven't yet had time to look at.

Instead she finds herself thinking about Malin Fors.

If it's true what the rumors say: that she was caught drunk-driving, but that it's been hushed up. That she's going into rehab as soon as the case is solved.

People are only human, and even police officers need a bit of slack sometimes. Otherwise there'd only be single-minded, cocksure officers left in the force, and no one wants police officers like that. Would the team cope without Malin Fors?

It would turn into something different, because Malin is the one who sets the tone. The person the others unconsciously lean on.

Maybe I should have coffee with her? Just us women. See how she feels?

Lovisa bats the thought aside and stands up.

Over on a shelf by the door sits a single black folder, apart from the others. God knows how it got there.

She pulls it down, then goes back to her chair.

Inside, three blank sheets of paper.

Beneath them an unfranked envelope, then some handwritten words on even whiter paper.

Lovisa feels time stand still as a warm sensation spreads through her body.

Could this letter be the thing they didn't know they were looking for?

Birgitta Svensson leans back on a green sofa and takes a bite of a dry, mass-produced almond cake.

Malin is holding her cup of coffee in both hands, the heat of the drink feels good against her palms.

They're alone in the staff room, and Malin thinks that it has a peaceful calm, a calm that smells of tea and coffee and books and paper.

"We only have one real problem at this school," Birgitta says, "and that's bullying. It's not a small problem either, but no matter what we do we can't seem to come to grips with it."

"Are there particular pupils responsible for it?"

Malin remembers the boys she encountered in connection with a murder a few years ago, and the way they terrified the whole of Ljungsbro School.

"If only it were that simple," Birgitta says. "No, it isn't just a few individual bullies here, it seems to shift the whole time. Someone who was the victim yesterday can end up as the bully today."

"What have you done to try to tackle it?"

"We've had speakers here. Group sessions. Individual counseling. But it's like a plague. Whenever we think we've finally solved it, something new happens."

"Maybe it will get better once this year leaves. The problem might resolve itself."

"But the school needs to function now. For everyone."

Tove.

You've never been bullied, Malin thinks. What would I do to anyone bullying you if you were?

Doesn't want to know.

"Last week," Birgitta Svensson says, "there was a boy in Year 8 who rubbed his cheeks with sandpaper in the woodwork class. It turned out that a big gang of boys in Years 8 and 9 had been tormenting him because his parents only have a rusty old car. Can you imagine? It was like it was okay to have a go at him, just because everyone else was. We couldn't identify anyone who was worse than the others, and no one felt responsible, they were all just 'joining in.'"

Birgitta Svensson makes quotation marks in the air with her fingers.

Then she leans forward, for the last bit of the almond cake.

"Sandpaper," Malin says. "He must have been feeling terrible."

"To be honest, he looked dreadful. Like he was wearing a mask of wounds."

Outside the school dining room there are posters from the Friends Foundation.

Encouragement to be friends with everyone, not to exclude anyone, to try always to see a person's unique qualities and characteristics.

A pipe dream, Malin thinks. Show any weakness and you can be sure that someone will bite.

Did Jerry Petersson show weakness?

Fredrik Fågelsjö?

Were they open and weak, if only for a matter of seconds, and then reality struck, biting them with its greedy jaws?

One of the posters shows a girl standing on her own in a corner. Five yards or so away stands a group of other girls. The text in the top corner of the poster says: "Everyone needs a friend. Could that be you?"

Malin heads toward the car, finally a break in the rain.

Inside her she can see Anders Dalström, and remembers what Andreas Ekström's mother said about him, that he seemed lonely, that Andreas could have been his only friend, and that Andreas looked out for him.

He visited Jasmin even though he didn't know her.

A tip-off from a male caller.

Lord of the Flies. Why that, of all films? The bullying film to beat all bullying films, surely?

The key in the car door, and twenty minutes later she's sitting in paperwork Hades with Zeke, Johan Jakobsson, Lovisa Segerberg, Waldemar Ekenberg, and Sven Sjöman.

In front of them on the table, in a plastic folder, lies a letter. Shaky letters written in black crayon.

The text: "I know all about New Year's Eve. It's time to pay. I'll be in touch soon. Be ready."

"So Jerry Petersson was being blackmailed," Sven says. "But who by?"

"Jonas Karlsson?" Waldemar says.

"Maybe," Zeke says. "But he has an alibi for the night and morning when Petersson was murdered. We'll check the handwriting, and see if there are any fingerprints on the letter. But who else could have known that Petersson was driving that New Year's Eve? He was the only one who knew, and according to him he hasn't told anyone."

"But Jonas has admitted that he likes a drink. Maybe he told someone when he was drunk?" Waldemar says, grinning pointedly at Malin.

"Jochen Goldman," Malin says. "He knew. And he seems to like sending letters. Maybe he needed money. What do we know about his finances? Really? We're just assuming he's absurdly rich."

"What about the Fågelsjö family," Lovisa says. "Maybe they were trying to blackmail Petersson into moving out?"

"Ah, yes," Sven says. "I've the call logs for the Fågelsjös' various phones. Nothing odd there. No calls to Jerry Petersson. I don't think they're behind this letter, it doesn't feel like their style."

"Do you remember that Petersson got a couple of calls from a telephone booth out at Ikea?" Malin says. "Maybe those calls are connected with this?"

She thinks about Daniel Högfeldt's informant, calling from an unknown number. A telephone booth? Difficult to prove without requesting Daniel's call log. And, because he's a journalist, practically impossible.

"We'll get Forensics to look at the letter," Sven says. "Maybe they'll find something. We'll hold back on talking to anyone about this until they've finished, then we'll have something concrete to go on if they find anything."

"I'd like to talk to Anders Dalström again, if that's okay," Malin asks.

"Why?" Johan asks.

"Just a hunch."

62

Malin accelerates and changes gear, thinking that maybe she should have brought Zeke with her, but she wants to explore this hunch herself, follow it wherever it leads her.

Zeke didn't protest, but she knows that Sven was assuming that they'd go together. If she's getting close to something, she might be exposing herself to danger, but what the hell does that matter?

If you investigate murders, you're always close to violence, but some things, some voices, can only be heard when you're alone.

The rain that's been falling on the way out stops when she arrives. The house in the forest looks abandoned, no light from the windows in the clearing containing the main building and workshop. The little clearing is actually a meadow, surrounded by dense mixed forest, and the whole site is reminiscent of a miniature Skogså, but with the pomp and power replaced by subordination and a palpable fear of the horrors that could be lurking in the darkness of the forest.

Anders Dalström isn't home, Malin thinks. Probably at work, in the old people's home. But doesn't he work nights?

She gets out of the car. Does up her black Gore-Tex jacket.

Anders's red Golf is missing from the drive.

Malin goes over the gravel and up the steps to the porch, where she peers inside the house and looks at the posters on the walls.

Quiet out here in the forest.

He probably wishes he had a girlfriend, or a family. The failed folk singer, what must it have been like, having to watch Lars Winnerbäck's success? Forty years old and working in an old people's home. Not much of a career. Does composing music out here in the forest give you peace? Was that why you moved here? Or are you bitter about other people?

But where are you now? Malin thinks. I only want to ask you some simple questions.

She knocks on the front door, rings the bell, but there's no sign of him.

She tries to look in through the other windows, but the curtains are drawn.

Oh well. The car's not there, after all.

She turns around and looks out at the forest, wondering where Anders might be. In the workshop? She walks over, but the doors are closed. Open them? No. Or should I? No, that would be too intrusive.

She looks over at the forest again.

He's watching her from the edge of the forest. The woman, the female detective. She's on her own. Why? He thought they always traveled in pairs, for security. Why did she go over to the workshop? Does she think the Golf's in there? It's at the garage. Is she looking for another vehicle?

Should I rush over to her?

What's she doing here, now? She ought to be looking elsewhere. But she's probably just here to ask some questions?

Now she's looking toward the forest, in his direction, and he ducks down, feels the wet fir needles and fallen twigs embrace him as long locks of hair fall over his eyes.

Did she see me? She can't have seen me. And what's she doing now? She seems to be taking a photograph of the sign on my door with her mobile.

Was that someone over there at the edge of the forest?

Malin isn't sure as she puts her mobile away. Anders Dalström could have been out in the forest hunting or picking mushrooms or something like that, and might now be on his way home. But he's seen me and doesn't want to talk to me.

Her pistol.

She's got it with her. She showed it at the talk that morning, aware that the sight of a real gun always arouses the interest of teenagers.

Something green amid all that gray.

She sets off toward the edge of the forest, crossing the waterlogged meadow, feeling her boots getting wet, but she wants to know what it was she saw.

Then a movement, something sliding away through the forest.

A person. A fox?

Impossible to tell. Malin pulls her pistol from its holster under her shoulder. Heads toward the forest, toward the darkness among the trees.

Anders Dalström is snaking through the forest, his long hair wet with rain.

She mustn't see me. What's she doing here? How could I explain why I'm trying to hide?

But he knows where he can go. There's a fallen tree just twenty yards in, and its exposed roots have left a hole, invisible if you don't know it's there.

I'm slithering like the young snakes inside me now.

Soaking wet. And cold, but none of that matters. Down into the hole. Hope the roots don't rock back into it. Into the hole, pull fallen branches over it. Stop breathing.

*   *   *

Where is he? Or whatever that was?

Malin checks the floor of the forest for tracks, but can't make out anything; the rain has beaten all the vegetation on the ground into a pulp.

The forest is silent and empty, except for the sound of her own breathing and the wind blowing through the treetops.

A fallen tree ahead of her.

She walks toward it.

Has someone been there? Is someone there? Then some heavy raindrops hit the back of her neck. She looks up. An owl is flying between the fir trees high above.

I must have been wrong.

No one here.

When Anders hears Malin's car start up and drive off, he carefully crawls out of his hiding place, hurries over to the edge of the forest, and reassures himself that he's alone again.

Then he runs over to the house.

He's weighed up his options, trying to understand what's happening, wishing it could still all be stopped, but at the same time wanting it all to be over, once and for all, for the snakes to be forced from his blood, to feel the calm that follows a raised hand.

The key in the lock.

Trembling hands.

It creaks, and he thinks about oiling the lock, ought to have done so long ago.

The door opens, and he runs into the living room and over to the gun cabinet.

He looks at the shotgun that he's keeping here for Dad, the one Dad hasn't been able to use for years, but which it would never occur to him to let his son use.

*   *   *

Malin is holding the wheel with one hand, and with the other she sends the photograph of the handwritten sign on Anders Dalström's door to Karin Johannison.

"Compare handwriting with blackmail letter. ASAP. Call me when you know. MF."

The rain fills the windshield in front of her.

Soon she sees the silhouette of Linköping ahead of her. The city seems to be sinking into its own sewers, a place that even the rats have abandoned.

63

Zeke is at his desk. His head slightly stubbly, black bristles sticking out in all directions like sharp quills.

"Did you get anywhere?" he asks as Malin sits down in her chair.

"I don't know," Malin replies. "Can you bear to hear what I'm thinking?"

"I think so."

Malin's mobile buzzes. Karin? So soon?

The message on the screen glows up at Malin: "I'll check at once. Karin."

Zeke smiles.

"From Karin?"

Malin smiles back.

"How could you know that?"

"Mysterious ways, Malin."

"Let's get some coffee."

They settle down at a corner table in the staff room.

"Well, let me start by saying that Christina Fågelsjö hasn't managed to find Fredrik's keys," Zeke says. "So it looks like he had them on him, and the murderer used his keys to open the chapel."

Malin nods.

"Anders Dalström," she goes on. "Andreas Ekström, who died in the car accident, was his only friend. He looked out for him, as Andreas's mum put it. Think about it. It's like his life stopped when Andreas died in the crash. What if he found out somehow that Jerry Petersson was driving? Maybe he met up with Jonas Karlsson in the pub and Karlsson told him the truth about that New Year's Eve but couldn't remember doing so afterward? Unless he found out some other way. He might have accepted that it was an accident, but that would all have changed when he found out that Petersson was driving. Petersson was drunk, after all, which makes it a serious offense."

"So Dalström decided he wanted revenge?"

"Well, possibly. Maybe he was bullied before Andreas turned up in his class. Maybe there's a load of pent-up violence inside him that started to leak out? But he'd probably have preferred to blackmail Petersson for money. Maybe he went out to Skogså that morning to put pressure on Petersson, and something went wrong and it got out of hand. And he ended up killing Petersson. What if Dalström felt that the violence made him feel stronger? That it gave him some sort of pleasure, and he found he couldn't stop once he'd started? That the aggression . . ."

Zeke is looking skeptical, and says:

"But why wait until now? Petersson had been living at Skogså for eighteen months. And even if Karlsson only let the cat out of the bag fairly recently, Dalström doesn't look like the vengeful type, Malin. He doesn't seem energetic or courageous enough to blackmail anyone for money. Besides, I thought he seemed pretty good-natured."

"Maybe," Malin says. "But the victims of bullying, if that's what he was, are often said to have a propensity for violence when they grow up. And what do we really know about him?"

Zeke nods.

"That might be true," he says. "But what about Fredrik Fågelsjö? How do you explain that? Or was someone else responsible for his murder?"

"I've been wondering about that," Malin says. "What if Anders Dalström murdered Fredrik for the simple reason that he wanted to divert attention away from himself and toward the family instead? After all, they had good reason to be pretty upset with Fredrik. That might explain the call Daniel got from an insistent informant."

"So it's Daniel now, is it?"

"Shut up."

"Okay. But what call?"

Malin tells Zeke about the conversation, but he just raises his eyebrows.

"It's still too vague," he says. "Could anyone really commit two murders on such flimsy grounds?"

"People have killed for less. And he might have developed a taste for violence after the first murder. Maybe violence gave him the outlet he needed. And the different methods could be explained by the fact that he felt more confident once he'd got away with the first one?"

"So you're seriously suggesting that Anders Dalström carried out what looks like a ritual murder of Fredrik Fågelsjö just to save his own skin? And all because he's discovered some sort of necessary violence inside himself?"

Malin nods.

"Is that really enough, Malin? The body was lying naked on the family vault. We haven't seen many cases worse than that."

"There's still a piece of the puzzle missing," Malin says. "Maybe I'm completely wrong. It's like I'm having trouble thinking straight. Too much shit floating about."

"There's still a slim chance that it was the Fågelsjös. Fredrik could have murdered Jerry, and Axel and Katarina could have had Fredrik killed. Or Goldman might have sent a hit man. Or it could be something else entirely."

"I know," Malin says.

"And Anders has alibis. He's supposed to have been working on the nights of both murders."

"I'll call and check again," Malin says.

"Let's go in person," Zeke says. "Make sure they check properly."

The staff nurse in the Björsäter old people's home shows Malin and Zeke into the nurses' office, tucked away in a corner of a well-lit room with a view of a recently planted forest of fir trees. There's a colorful embroidery on the wall, presumably made by the residents in occupational therapy.

"No," the nurse says, "Anders isn't working today. He mostly works nights."

Malin nods.

She paces restlessly up and down the small, windowless room, looking at the bottles of pills lined up behind locked glass doors.

"I did call and ask before," Malin says. "But we'd like to ask again: Was he working the night between Thursday, October 23, and Friday, October 24? And the night between Thursday and Friday last week?"

The nurse pulls a folder from a low shelf.

Opens it and checks carefully, as if to demonstrate that she is taking Malin's question seriously.

"According to the roster, he was working both nights."

"According to the roster?"

"Yes, sometimes they swap without telling me. It's against regulations, but as long as everything works . . ."

"Could you do me a favor?" Malin says. "Can you check to see if he swapped shifts with anyone on either of those nights?"

The nurse nods.

"Yes, but I'll have to call the other night staff. Most of them will be asleep now. Is it urgent?"

"Yes, it is," Zeke says.

Five minutes later the nurse holds out her hands in defeat.

"No answers from any of them. They're all asleep. Can I call you back later this afternoon?"

"Yes, please do," Malin says.

"Do you have any idea where Anders might be?"

"He wasn't on duty last night. But he's probably at home."

"I was there an hour or so ago. He wasn't there."

"Have you tried his mobile?"

"No answer," Malin says.

"No? You could try asking his dad. He lives in sheltered accommodation in the city. His dad's blind, Anders visits him fairly often."

"Which home is he in?" Zeke asks.

"Serafen."

Serafen, Malin thinks.

The same place as the blind Sixten Eriksson whom Axel Fågelsjö beat up. Malin and Zeke exchange glances.

"Do you know his father's name?"

"Sixten," the nurse says. "Sixten Eriksson."

64

Sixten Eriksson is sitting on the sofa in his room at Serafen, staring into his darkness, unable to see the cheap reproductions on the walls. The smell of tobacco is even more pronounced than it was last time.

He doesn't want to face us, Malin thinks, even though he can't see anything.

She and Zeke had discussed the possibilities in the car on the way to Anders Dalström's house after their visit to Björsäter.

"That definitely gives him another motive," Zeke had said.

"Getting revenge for what happened to his father by murdering the son of the man who committed the offense."

"But why now?" Zeke asked.

"Maybe he's got a taste for violence, like I said, if Petersson's murder was a blackmail attempt that got out of control. If you've killed once, you can kill again. You've crossed a line. And maybe he thought he could confuse us even more, and that would help him get away with it."

"Don't you just love human beings?" Zeke said.

"And no one knows where he is."

Anders wasn't home this time either. They've already called the station. Sven said they'd put out a call for him to be brought in, seeing as they needed to talk to him even if it didn't lead to anything.

And now Sixten Eriksson's darkness. On his own. No sign of Anders here either.

"I made up the bit about Evaldsson. Sven, too," Sixten says. "Anders took his mother's name, Dalström. I don't know anything about what he might or might not have done, but I'd never set the police on him no matter what's happened. Of course I'm protecting him, I've always protected him."

"Do you think your son could have murdered Fredrik Fågelsjö in revenge for what happened to you?"

Malin tries to make her voice sound curious, gentle.

But Sixten doesn't answer.

"Could he have murdered Jerry Petersson? What do you think?"

Zeke aggressive, pushy.

"Pain needs a way out somehow," Sixten says.

"Has he said anything?" Malin asks.

"No, he hasn't said anything."

"Do you know where he might be?"

Sixten laughs at Zeke's question. "If I knew where he was, I wouldn't tell you. Why should I? But he comes here fairly often. Aren't children funny, no matter what their parents do to them, they still come running back for love and reassurance."

Malin and Zeke look into the old man's blind eye and Malin thinks that it can see more than hers right now. His clouded lens seems to possess a certainty about how this autumn's dark drama will end, that the man in front of them has delved deep into hate and evil through his own suffering.

"So you used to hit him?" Malin asks. "You used to beat Anders when he was small?"

"Do you know what it's like, not having any depth of perception?" Sixten asks. "Pain in your nerves that burns right into your brain, the whole time, day and night?" He goes on: "I hope Axel

Fågelsjö is suffering all the torments of hell right now, now that his son is dead. He can finally get his share of this life's pain."

"Did you ask your son to kill any of the Fågelsjö family? Fredrik? Axel?"

"No, but I've thought about it. I can't deny it."

Searching through the shelves. My hands, Dad used to hit them with a ruler.

Do you see my eye, boy?

What do I need?

Anders Dalström is moving through the aisles of the ironmongers' store in the Ekholmen shopping center. The kebab he's just eaten is gurgling in his stomach.

Rope.

Masking tape. The other people are looking at me, what do they want? The rifle's in the car. I'm going to put an end to all this, and it will be a relief, the police will find him and wonder, utterly confused.

I'm going to kill him. After all, it started with him, didn't it? Maybe Dad will be pleased?

Anders feels that the last of the snakes will soon be leaving him. Everything will be fine again, the way it should have been. Andreas, he thinks, can you see me now?

I'm going to get rid of the root of all this evil.

He pays. Gets in the car, heads off toward Drottninggatan.

Some voices are like the crack of a whip, Malin thinks. They cut right into your most vulnerable areas.

"Jochen Goldman here," the voice says for a second time.

Bastard.

Malin feels the phone against her ear, the rain on her hand as she stands in Djurgårdsgatan outside Serafen.

But she also feels a peculiar warmth when she hears his voice. A warmth in completely the wrong parts of her body.

His suntanned face by the edge of the pool. Hardness and softness in men like him and Petersson.

"What do you want with me?"

With her free hand Malin opens the car door, sinks into the seat, holds the phone tight against her ear, listening to Goldman's breathing.

"The photographs," she goes on. "You took those photographs of my parents and sent them to me, didn't you? You got someone to take them."

"What photographs?"

She can see Goldman's smile before her. The game it implies, we can have a bit of fun, can't we, you and me?

"You know which ones."

"I don't know anything about any photographs. Of your parents? Why would I take pictures of them? I don't even know where they live."

"Are you in Sweden?"

"Yes."

"Have you been in Linköping?"

"What on earth would I want to go there for?"

"Did you send Jerry Petersson a blackmail letter? Were you trying to get money out of him?"

"I've got more money than I need. If that's actually possible."

The skies have opened again. Hail, little white grains, are drumming rhythmically against the body of the car.

"Are you listening to Negro music?"

"Hail," Malin says.

"If I wanted anything done in Linköping, you hardly imagine I'd go myself?"

Inferences, intimations.

"What do you want?"

"I'm at the Grand in Stockholm. I've got a suite. I thought maybe you'd like to come along. We could have a nice time. Drink some champagne. Maybe take some pictures. Just the two of us. What do you say?"

Malin clicks to end the call.

Shuts her eyes.

She's not sure that Jochen Goldman really exists. That her parents exist. That there's ever any explanation whatsoever for anyone's actions.

They drive past Axel Fågelsjö's door on Drottninggatan. Neither of them sees the long-haired figure slide through the door like a shadow.

Jochen.

You and your nasty little games. You still got me in the end, didn't you? You never forgive any transgression. Even though you commit a fair number yourself.

I'm drifting over the plain and the forests now, over the castle and the field where the accident happened, I'm drifting over tenant farmer Lindman's house, see his Russian wife quickly packing her bags, so quickly, heading for another man in another place, taking half, more than half, of what Lindman has, just as she planned right from the start.

Lindman.

I was the one who fucked his first wife when she was up in Stockholm for a conference. I found her at the bar in Baldakinen, and the way she screamed up in the office on Kungsgatan . . . Probably couldn't bear the smell of manure after that.

I was contacted. Like the blackmail letter promised.

I remember that the phone ringing in advance of the conversation summoning me to the Ikea parking lot reminded me of those screams. As if the unassuming ringing wanted to burst my eardrums.

65

LINKÖPING, SEPTEMBER

Petersson is standing beside his Range Rover in one of the central rows of the almost empty parking lot outside Ikea in Tornby, listening to the rain drumming on the car roof, and the persistent, relentless sound of the drops reminds him of the phone ringing, calling him here. The parking lot must have space for a thousand cars, but on one of the first properly rainy nights like this it's almost empty. The retail lots glow in the darkness: Ica Maxi, Siba, Coop Forum.

In the distance he can see the copper-green spire of the cathedral, the numbers on the clock shining through the veils of mist and low dark clouds of the evening.

"Wait outside the car. I'll be there at eleven o'clock."

Petersson looks at his watch, wipes the rain from his eyes, knows how to handle this.

Then he sees a car turn into the carpark, a red Golf that pulls up alongside him, and a man the same age as him gets out.

Is that you, Jonas? Petersson thinks. Jonas Karlsson, you who saved me long ago.

No. Not Jonas, someone else.

Instead of waiting for the man in the green jacket to start talking,

Petersson leaps at him, forcing him up against the door of the Range Rover, taking a stranglehold of his neck and snarling:

"What the fuck do you think you're doing? Whoever the fuck you are. Do you think I'm going to take this sort of shit from anyone?"

And the man in the green jacket sinks, his body slumping in fear, and he says:

"I didn't mean anything. Sorry. I didn't mean it."

"What you wrote about that New Year's Eve is wrong."

"Yes. I was wrong."

"How did you hear about it?"

"A letter."

"Who from?"

The hand gripping the man's neck getting tighter, his voice getting weaker.

"I don't know. But the letter was postmarked in Tenerife."

Jochen.

"And who are you?"

"Someone who got in your way. You didn't even notice."

The man in the green jacket says his name, and Petersson searches his memory, but nothing springs to mind. With all his strength he throws the man in the green jacket to the ground. Kicks him, screaming: "Who the fuck are you?"

And the man groans his name again, says: "Andreas Ekström was the only friend I ever had."

Jochen.

Punta del Este. I should have kept my mouth shut. God knows how you got hold of this tragic loser. But if you want to you can find out anything, can't you?

More kicking. Hitting soft flesh beneath the green jacket, and it feels good.

"And now you want money, do you? My money, is that it? Stay away from me. Otherwise this is going to turn out really fucking badly."

More groaning, the rain like a solid monochrome mass in the air.

Petersson leaves the man behind him, in the rearview mirror he sees him writhing on the tarmac, trying to get up.

Back home in his big, empty castle he brings up a number on his mobile phone, wants to call the woman who is waiting to hear his voice.

But the phone call is never made, and remains as inaudible whispering inside Petersson's head. Instead the sound of rotating, hungry lawnmower blades takes over, the drumming of feet on the grass, feet that can never carry their body far enough or close enough.

66

Axel Fågelsjö hears the doorbell, vaguely, like a cry for help from an already long-forgotten dream.

Who the hell can this be? he thinks as he walks through the sitting room, past the portraits of his ancestors.

The police again? Can't they leave me in peace? Alone with all my mistakes and inadequacies, with all the love I've lost.

Those damn journalists? He'd had to unplug his phone and disconnect the doorbell. But now he's put them back in. He thought they'd got tired of him, the fourth estate.

Grief.

For you, Bettina, for our son. That's all I've got left now.

I want to be left in peace with it.

The doorbell sounds shrill now. A salesman? A Jehovah's Witness?

Fågelsjö looks through the peephole, but there's no one there.

What the hell?

He looks again.

The stairwell, empty and silent. He unlocks the door. Is someone after me now? he has time to wonder before the door flies open, hitting him in the forehead and making him stagger backward.

Lying on the parquet floor, he finds himself staring into the barrel of a rifle. He sees long black hair and a pair of eyes full of longing, desperation, and loneliness.

*   *   *

The house in the clearing is still silent and dark.

Now that daylight is no longer lighting up the façade it looks even more anxious, as if it were on the point of collapsing under the weight of all the sorrows it has been forced to contain.

Malin and Zeke stop the car. Anders Dalström's red Golf is still not there.

They get out, and Malin takes a deep breath, trying to work out if there's anyone apart from them there.

"He isn't here," she says. "Where the hell could he be?"

They go up the steps, look through the window in the front door.

A computer is flickering on the table in the living room.

Malin feels the door handle. Unlocked.

"We can't go in," Zeke says. "We need a warrant."

"Are you kidding?"

"Yes. I'm kidding, Fors. The door's open. Obviously we suspect a break-in."

They go inside.

The gun-cabinet in the living room.

Malin goes over and finds it unlocked. A solitary shotgun inside. Rifle ammunition on the floor, but no rifle.

Has he got another gun? Malin wonders, then says, "Wherever he is right now, he could be armed."

She goes into Anders's bedroom. The blinds are closed and the room is dark and cold, damp.

A film projector has been set up on a bench, reels of film scattered across the floor, unrolled.

A film is sitting in the projector. Without thinking, Malin switches it on, and on the white wall she sees a boy moving across a grass lawn, running, screaming soundlessly as if he's running from something, as if there's a monster holding the camera, ready to catch him if he trips or runs too slowly.

Then the boy stops. Turns toward the camera, trying to look beyond its lens, cowering as if preparing to be hit, the black pupils of his eyes like little planets of fear.

The reel comes to an end.

Zeke has crept in behind Malin, put a hand on her shoulder and says: "I could have done without seeing the look in his eyes."

They leave the room. In the kitchen is a computer, its screen showing the online telephone directory, and Zeke reads out loud:

"Axel Fågelsjö. 18 Drottninggatan. What the hell is he up to?"

"Axel Fågelsjö," Malin says. "Do you think he's going straight to what he thinks is the source of the evil? The man who beat up his father and turned him into an abusive parent?"

Zeke's face is half illuminated by the glow of the screen, raindrops glistening on his head.

"So you're sure now?"

"Yes, aren't you?"

Zeke nods.

"Should we call for backup at Fågelsjö's apartment?"

"Yes, we'd better," Malin says.

"I'll call," Zeke says, and Malin hears him talking to the duty-desk, then he gets put through to Sven Sjöman.

"We think it checks out," Zeke says, and Malin can hear him trying to sound urgent and factual. "Things have been moving quickly, we haven't had a chance to call. Karin's comparing the handwriting."

Silence.

Probably a mixture of praise and cursing from Sven. They should have called earlier, once they found out that Sixten Eriksson was Anders Dalström's father.

"Who knows what he's thinking," Zeke says. "He's probably pretty desperate by now."

Once they get outside again Malin heads over to the workshop.

The door is ajar. Zeke is right behind her.

Is he in there? She pulls out her pistol. Carefully kicks the door open with her foot.

An old, black Mercedes.

She peers inside. Silent, empty.

"That could be the black car Linnea Sjöstedt saw," Zeke says.

Malin nods.

The next minute they're back in the car again.

Their speed seems to blur the forest and the rain into one single element. Is Anders Dalström already inside Axel's apartment with him? Or is he somewhere else entirely?

Jerry Petersson.

Fredrik Fågelsjö.

Was it your arrogance that finally caught up with you? Your actions? Your vanity? Your fear? Or something else?

Sven Sjöman and four uniformed officers are inside the apartment on Drottninggatan. They picked the lock. The apartment is empty, no sign of Axel Fågelsjö, and no signs of a struggle.

Malin and Zeke arrive fifteen minutes later.

"Good work," Sven says to Malin as they are standing in the middle of the sitting room looking at the portraits on the walls. "Bloody good work."

"Now we just have to find Anders Dalström," Malin says. "And some concrete, conclusive evidence."

"We'll find it," Sven says. "Everything points toward him."

"But where the hell is he?" Zeke says. "And where the hell is Axel Fågelsjö?"

"They're together," Malin says. "I think they've been together much longer than either of them realizes," she goes on. Thinks, If Axel Fågelsjö is in Anders Dalström's hands, it's my job to rescue him. But is it really worth me worrying about him? How can I have any sympathy for someone I find revolting in so many ways?

Then her mobile rings. Karin Johannison's calm, assured voice at the other end:

"The handwriting on the sign on the door and the blackmail letter are the same. The same person wrote the letter."

67

ANDERS DALSTRÖM, IMAGES FROM A LIFE

There are no explanations.
They're pointless, and no one can be bothered to listen to them.

But this is my story, listen to it if you want to.

Father.

Your one working eye behind the lens of the camera, you say the pictures will resemble the way you see the world, with no depth of perception, and without any real hope. Did I inherit your hopelessness, your diffidence about life?

You must have been the most bitter and frustrated person on the planet, and you took that anger out on me, and I learned to creep out of the way, to disappear from the flat in Linghem and stay away until you calmed down.

People would see me, and there was talk about how you beat me and Mum because of your bitterness about your lost eye, your agony.

I saw you, Father, behind the camera, and I would run to you in spite of your anger, but I hesitated, instinctively, and I took that hesitancy with me in my dealings with other people.

At school I was alone at first, then they started getting at me, and none of the teachers could be bothered to care. They hunted me, hit me, mocked me, and I would shrink into the corners. One day, in Year 4, they pulled my clothes off, and I ran across the playground naked through the snow, and they chased me in front of a thousand eyes, and they kicked me when I fell.

They pulled me into the school building.

They forced my head into a toilet full of excrement and urine.

They did this over and over again, and in the end I didn't even try to escape. They could do what they liked, and my subordination made them even angrier, wilder, more bloodthirsty.

What had I done? Why me?

Because of the slouched shoulders you gave me, Father? The ones we have in common?

Stop, someone shouted one day, and then a muscular, confident frame was attacking the hunters, hitting them, giving them nose-bleeds, shouting, "You're not going to attack him again. Ever."

And they didn't.

I had finally gained an ally.

Andreas. Recently moved in from Vreta Kloster.

On his very first day at school he made me his. I've never under-stood why he wanted to be my friend, but maybe that's just what friendship is like; just like evil, it suddenly shows up where you least expect it.

I lived through Andreas during those years, and his family would sometimes open their home to me, I remember the smell of fresh-baked buns and raspberry syrup, and his mother who used to leave us alone. What we got up to? The things boys do. We turned our little world into a big one, and I never really came home anymore. You couldn't reach me, Father, thanks to Andreas.

Your bitterness didn't get hold of me—unless it actually did after all? Yes, it had probably already taken root.

You hit me, and I tried to make my way to whatever I thought was beyond the beatings, to what had to exist beyond the beat-ings.

Music. I found music, don't ask me how but it was inside me.

Deep inside, and Andreas pushed me on, bought me a guitar with the money he earned picking strawberries one summer.

But then when we started high school something happened. Andreas pulled away, he wanted other people besides me, he dropped me as the world grew, but I never stopped hoping, because he was my friend, and I never managed to get close to anyone else in the same way.

He used to trail after Jerry Petersson, the coolest of the cool. And he used to fawn over the posh kids as well.

They weren't even on my radar, not in my dreams. I knew I could never be like them.

And then Andreas died one New Year's Eve.

Maybe I gave up then, Father?

I escaped into music.

And I sang at that last day of school, a song about what it's like being born in Linköping and growing up in the shadow of all manner of dreams, how we tried to drink the anxiety away in the Horticultural Society Park on those last evenings of high school, and I must have struck a chord, because the applause in the hall seemed to go on forever. I was asked to sing it twice more, then that evening everyone wanted me to sing it on the grass in the park, even the posh girls.

You weren't there in the audience in that hall with your camera, Father.

I started working in the health service, I rented a cottage in the forest to have space to write, and ended up staying there. I must have sent a hundred demo tapes to Stockholm, but I didn't even get any replies to my letters to Sonet, Polar, Metronome and the others.

Year followed year. I got a job in the old people's home in Björsäter. Often there were just two of us at night, we took turns sleeping, and nights suited me fine, they let me avoid other people. And you still hit me when you got the chance, even though you were almost blind from the cataracts in your eye.

I could have hit back, but I didn't.

Why not? Because then I would have been like you. Violence and bitterness would have turned me into you.

Then Mum died and you ended up in a home, completely blind now and your camera fallen silent forever. Your fury a calm fury, your bitterness a gentle tone, your life a wait for death.

Sometimes I would read articles about Petersson, about how successful he was.

And it was as if something grew inside me, an invisible egg that grew bigger and bigger, until it cracked and out poured millions of tiny yellow snakes into my blood. They wore all my tormentors' faces. Yours, Father, those of the boys in the school playground, even Axel Fågelsjö's. I knew very well who he was, what he had done to you.

I wanted to get rid of the snakes. But they slithered wherever they wanted.

Then Jerry Petersson moved back. Bought the castle and the estate from Fågelsjö, and I got a letter, God knows who from, telling me the truth about that New Year's Eve. It had never occurred to me that Jerry Petersson might have been driving. There were black-and-white photographs in with the letter, of him standing in the field, standing still with his eyes closed, as if he was meditating.

So I wrote my own letter, but my nerves let me down in the parking lot. He who had everything and who had taken everything from me, he stamped on me like I was an insect again.

But I crawled back up.

I swore to stand up for myself, he wasn't going to break me and Andreas again, I'd demand money from him, even though I had no idea what I would do with it.

So early one morning I got in the car and drove out there.

The snakes were hissing, I could almost see them crawling inside me, see their leering faces mocking me.

I waited for him in front of the castle, with a heavy stone in my hand to protect myself, and one of father's knives in my pocket. Violence imprinted in the wooden handle he had held so often, with the

Skogså coat of arms branded on it—he must have stolen the knife when he worked there.

I had a piece of paper in my hand.

The snakes were seething.

Slithering within me. And they were fury and fear rolled into one.

I knew that something had reached its conclusion. And that something else was about to begin.

68

I look down on the earth, all the different worlds that history has given this city and the land around it. I see the rain lashing the trees, the grass, the moss, and the ancient rocks, and I know that there's a lot left to come. I see a car approaching a castle at dawn one day, a black figure waiting beyond a moat.

That's me I can see, heading toward my imminent death, but I don't know that, and by the time I do know, obviously it's too late. But now, in this moment that can encompass all time, I can feel the steering wheel tremble in my hands.

69

Jerry looks ahead through the fog, gripping the shaking steering wheel. The Range Rover carries him over the ground.

Who's that waiting up ahead? Is that you, Katarina, finally come back to me?

Or is it someone else? Some obstinate bastard? Tell me it's you, Katarina. It's you, isn't it?

It isn't you, Katarina.

It's never you.

I get out of the car and see Anders Dalström in front of me, his face desperate, his black hair wet, he's holding a stone in one hand. He refuses to give up, and I fix my gaze on him, but nothing happens, he doesn't back down.

"I want five million," Anders yells, and I laugh and say, "You're not getting anything. I'll crush you like a little rat if you don't leave now. It'll be worse than in the parking lot."

Anders holds out a note with his free hand.

"My account number," he yells, and the rain makes the ink on the note illegible, and I laugh again.

He gives me the note.

"Five million, within a week."

An amused grin crosses my lips, but then I get bored, crumple the note, and toss it onto the gravel, not giving a damn about Anders and his damn stone.

Anders picks up the note with his free hand and puts it in the pocket of his jacket.

I turn to walk away, then hear a howl from the depths.

I see something black coming toward me, feel a sudden pain, and I fall. Then decades of cumulative fury are sitting on top of me and it burns and burns and burns in my stomach and Anders Dalström crawls away from me and I feel my brain, my thoughts vanish into pain.

I crawl across the gravel, the pain in my head and my guts feels like the final pain of all, spreading through my whole body like an ancient wind.

He's killing me, I manage to think, as I crawl under the chain around the moat, and I imagine I see a stone hit the surface of the water.

Is that blood running over my eyes?

I'm the boy again, I'm the man. I'm with Katarina beside calm water, possibly a river, and I anoint her back with oil and she whispers words of an extinct language in my ear.

The wind owns me now. And I fall, I've stopped breathing by the time I hit the water in the moat, and at last the shiny blades of the lawnmower have fallen silent and I open my new eyes.

70

"I killed your son," Anders Dalström screams, "and I'm going to kill you!"

He's tied Axel Fågelsjö to a chair, and he watches as the old man tries to pull himself free, a peculiar mixture of loathing and resignation in his eyes, the fear they betray, the fear that comes of not knowing what's happening.

"The same way you killed my father."

"I've never killed anyone."

"You killed him."

Anders can see Fågelsjö trying to say something else, trying to shout, but no sound comes out of his mouth.

He pulls a scrap of cloth from his bag, ties it tightly around the old man's head, letting it slip deep into his mouth, it feels good to pull it tight, see the pain in his eyes, feel the waves of calm flow through his body.

He wanted to give the old man an explanation.

Force him to listen to it.

"What sort of father do you think he was after you killed him? He hunted me with that camera, hunting me and trying to destroy me, as if he hated me for the life I still had ahead of me, as if I *were* his pain."

Fågelsjö squirms on his chair, trying to get loose—unless he wants to say something? Ask for forgiveness?

Hardly.

And Anders punches him in the cheek with a clenched fist, feels the pain spread through his knuckles and hands, and the violence is nice and soft, makes the evil disappear.

So he punches again, and again and again. The snakes move, the boys in the school playground, Dad's blows, the snakes have their faces now, the excrement in the toilet, the pain of never experiencing any reliable love.

Pain, pain, pain.

All the pain of the world. All the world's fury gathered in those blows. The fury that must have given Jerry Petersson forty stab-wounds to his torso. How many will I get?

Who is he? Fågelsjö thinks.

Bettina, who is he?

His confused talk. About snakes, and faces, but at the same time, in the middle of all the madness, he seems to know what he wants, who he is.

Against his will, Fågelsjö gives in to his fear again and tries to get free, wants to run, escape, but he's stuck fast, won't get any-where, so he may as well take the blows, try to make sense of this, and if it's true that he killed my son, he'll get what's coming to him, I promise myself that, I promise all those who have gone before me.

The room.

It's beautiful and familiar, one of my rooms, no one else's.

Bettina. Your ashes are scattered in the forest.

He's stopped hitting me now, just sitting on a chair by the wall and he seems to be gathering his strength to say something.

*   *   *

"Listen, old man."

Anders gets up and goes over to Fågelsjö in the middle of the cold room.

"What you did to me, to my dad, would be reason enough for me to kill your son."

He puts his fingers in Fågelsjö's nostrils and twists them upward, and Fågelsjö grunts with pain. Anders feels like pulling his nose right off his face, wants to feel warm blood on his fingers, feel the last cold-blooded, blind creatures slithering out of him.

"And do you know what?" he shouts. "I like using my body to show how powerful I am. Violence has spawned me, can't you understand that?

"I took him outside his house. Beat him to death there, then I drove him to the chapel.

"I want you to know that.

"What did you care about me? What Dad did to me when the pain in his eye and in his head took over?"

Then Anders strikes again, but he gets scared when he feels the old man's chin against his knuckles.

The snakes are moving again. There are more than ever and they're swimming through his veins, drinking his blood.

He's mad, Fågelsjö thinks, as he tries to escape the pain by remembering, by keeping his consciousness clear.

For a moment he thinks that he would actually like to be beaten to death by this maniac, because then I can finally be with you, Bettina. I was with you, in the forest, on the morning of the first murder.

So hit me.

Let me go to the woman I love.

And Fågelsjö knows who the young man in the room is now.

The son of that hopeless farmhand whose eye he blinded.

It was a shame, but these things happen.

He was an oaf, and maybe he got what he deserved.

And Fredrik? Did he get what he deserved?

No one tells me, or anyone in my family, what we deserve or don't deserve.

Then he strikes again. With the butt of the rifle now. Burning pain, and I feel my teeth come loose, and my eyes feel like they're going to burst from their sockets.

What happened to the farmhand? He sat in silence during the trial, I remember that, but what happened to him after that? Could he have been in pain, the way I'm in pain now? He was blinded in one eye, but that's hardly a handicap worth making a fuss over, is it? Maybe he was bitter, but life is much easier if people know their place, no matter what that place is.

A knife now. A knife, and he shows me the coat of arms on the handle, Skogså, before he cuts my cheek.

It stings, and I scream.

Bettina, can I come to you now? Are you proud of me? I don't want to end up in the chapel, I want to be with you, in the forest.

What does a castle mean, really? A few acres of forest? Memories that no one cares about?

I'm going to put an end to this, Anders thinks. I'm going to do what I like, just as he has always done.

His face is yours, Father.

Are you one and the same?

But there's no reason to hesitate. They never did when they managed to catch me in the school playground.

Blood is running from Fågelsjö's cheeks, and Anders wants to drive the knife into his fat gut, but he can't, something's holding him back, whispering "no" into one ear. He throws the knife into the corner and puts his fingers in Fågelsjö's nostrils again, blocking them, then puts his other hand over his mouth, pressing the rag hard, and he knows that the old man can't breathe now. That he must be screaming for air in there, and the cocky, arrogant look he had in his eyes just now is gone, replaced by something else, maybe some sort of primeval fear.

Monochrome flickering.

Something slithering over my body. It will be gone forever.

Someone's whispering something. Is that you, Andreas? Are you there?

Give me air.

I want more.

I want to see you, Bettina, Fredrik, but not just yet. Katarina. Where are you?

I've done wrong, I admit it, let go, forgive me, I've done wrong, but don't let it end now, I want more life, I'm scared, I can feel the heat licking my ankles, I'm trying to scream for forgiveness, scream that I can love you and everyone else, that you have to let go, that it's your only hope, and blood is pouring but you carry on, pressing your fingers deeper into my nose.

And I want air, give me air.

71

"**M**um?"

Tove's voice a hammer blow to her heart as Malin opens the door on her way out of the block on Drottninggatan.

Zeke beside her, restless, wanting to run to the car.

"Tove."

Can't talk now, darling.

A quick run-through in Axel Fågelsjö's apartment just now.

Where can Axel Fågelsjö and Anders Dalström be? In all likelihood, together.

Sven: "If Anders took Fredrik to the castle, he may have taken Axel Fågelsjö there as well. Zeke and Malin, get out there at once. Talk to Katarina Fågelsjö and anyone else connected to this. Dalström could be a danger to the public, we need to get hold of him as soon as possible."

"Mum, I was wondering if I . . ."

Malin hears her daughter's voice as she's running toward the car, not taking in what she's saying, instead, "Tove, I've got to go."

She clicks to get rid of Tove, but a moment later she wants to call back, has to apologize for the way everything turned out the evening she came around, when she just let her disappear, and she's the world's worst mum and sorry, because it isn't so damn easy being human.

On the other side of Drottninggatan the Horticultural Society Park lies dark and cold and the rain is boring down from the sky now, restricting their visibility ahead, and she wonders what Tove wanted, knows she ought to call back, maybe she needs me now, but instead Malin says:

"Okay, drive. Fast as you can. Quick!"

The car's headlights are eager searchlights heading along the rain-tormented tarmac of Drottninggatan.

Malin's mobile rings again. Tove? Not this time. Another number on the display.

"Malin."

"Johan Stekänger here."

The solicitor. Jerry Petersson's executor. The man who found Fredrik Fågelsjö.

"I wanted to tell you that the castle was sold yesterday. For twice as much as Petersson paid for it. Petersson's father accepted the offer."

"Who bought it?"

"I'm afraid . . ."

"There's nothing to stop you telling us."

"I . . ."

"Now!" Malin says. "Otherwise I'll be on your backside like a tick from hell for the rest of your life. So, who bought it?"

"Axel Fågelsjö himself, who else? We signed the contracts yesterday, and he got the keys to the front door as a symbolic gesture. We've put all of Petersson's possessions in storage, and the art's gone to Bukowski's auction house. He laughed at that business with the keys, said he'd kept several sets. And I don't think Petersson ever changed the locks."

*   *   *

"He's bought back the castle," Malin says.

Zeke keeps his hands on the wheel, staring ahead at the road as they drive out of the city, out into the dark countryside.

"That was quick work."

"An old fighter," Malin says, as they head toward the castle way above every speed limit.

They must be there.

Fields.

Forest.

What's on the move out there? What is it that clouds people's minds? What drives them to do things that there are hardly any words for? Like the honor killing they'd investigated before this case.

What makes a person not answer a call from her daughter? Malin shuts her eyes, sees Tove on the floor of that room with the madwoman bent over her. Sees a rape victim on a chair in a dark corner of a godforsaken room in a godforsaken hospital.

Tove Fors.

Fredrik Fågelsjö.

Anders Dalström.

Jerry Petersson.

I know what unites you.

I can do something for you, Tove. For me. For us.

If I can't manage to love you, who on earth could I manage to love?

They're the first car on the scene, and the castle rises up from the black earth, an ark for all the feelings human beings have ever felt.

The green lanterns are glowing, spreading green light over the water in the moat. Unless the glow comes from the water itself?

No car in front of the castle.

Malin runs up to the door, yanks at it, but it's locked.

Shit.

They aren't here.

Zeke comes up behind her.

"Doesn't look like they're here," he whispers, and Malin wonders why he's whispering.

"Damn. I was so sure."

Silence around them, except for the rustling of the forest.

"He could have locked the door behind them with Fågelsjö's key," Malin says.

"Let's go around," Zeke says.

And they circle the castle, over to the chapel, deserted and shut up. The rain patters on their jackets, and Zeke is moving stiffly in front of her.

They're walking in silence.

Where's the car? Malin thinks. They must be here.

They turn a corner, and they can hear a car, maybe one of the patrol cars, coming up the drive, and now they can see light, a thin strip of light seeping out from the shutters on one of the cellar windows.

They look at each other.

Nod, wipe the rain from their faces, run to the front of the castle, the gravel and stones crunching under their feet.

They see three uniformed officers getting out of a patrol car.

"The door," Malin shouts. "They could be in there. In the cellar."

A moment later the uniforms are throwing themselves at the door, but their efforts are wasted.

"This is impossible," one of them shouts, and Malin orders them back, draws her pistol from its holster, and ignoring the risk of ricochets she kneels down at the side of the steps leading up to the doorway and shoots off the black-painted iron lock, probably several hundred years old, emptying her magazine, and the lock falls from its chiseled hole onto the stone steps.

Malin is first inside.

Rushing through the rooms.

The kitchen like a shiny white slaughterhouse even in the darkness.

She rushes down the steps into the cellar, expecting to see Axel

Fågelsjö down there together with Anders Dalström. But what will the scene look like?

The cellar is dark and cold, and she's having trouble breathing, she can feel the others behind her, their fear, their footsteps drumming rhythmically on the stone floors. She crouches as she goes through the passageways, kicking open the door to what must once have been a prison cell. Was this where the Russian prisoners of war were locked up before they were walled up in the moat?

They go through one, two, three rooms. All empty.

Then a fourth door.

Light coming from behind it.

Malin presses the handle.

What am I going to see?

She opens the door.

72

Is he still here?

Bettina, is that you?

No, but is he still here?

What was it he said?

I didn't understand.

Someone's coming now, is he coming back?

He took his stinking fingers out of my nostrils, but the rag is still in my mouth. He didn't cut me again.

Ropes around my ankles and wrists. I try pulling this way and that, and I know he's going to come back, I want to see you, Bettina.

Or do I?

I want to stay. I know what I've got to do, I can feel the light returning to my eyes now, I heard a door open, is that death or life coming in?

Spare me.

I'm a good person.

The room is bathed in light from a spotlight in the ceiling.

Malin sees him.

He's sitting still on a chair in the middle of the room, blood running from his head and nostrils.

Axel Fågelsjö.

Alone. No Anders Dalström.

Fågelsjö. Not so imposing now, and Malin thinks that it makes little difference if he's alive or dead, yet she still hesitates in front of him, approaching him slowly, is he dead, alive?

Fågelsjö seems to be melting into the stone beneath him, his blood seems to be sucked up by the castle walls, and she can feel the heartbeat of history, pumping a strange music through her veins.

Standing right in front of Fågelsjö now.

She puts an arm on his shoulder.

He squints. His eyes seem to clear.

Malin waves the others into the room. No one else there, where's Anders?

Fågelsjö jerks.

Coughs, wants the rag out of his mouth, and Malin looks around again, nothing, and she puts her pistol down on the stone floor, Zeke breathing heavily behind her.

Then she takes the rag from Fågelsjö's mouth as a uniformed officer cuts the ropes tying his wrists and ankles.

He throws up his arms, as if with some peculiar, newfound power.

Kicks his legs.

His bloody sweater shudders, and Malin can see the fat moving beneath it.

Then he moves, and stands up.

Looks down at Malin.

"The bastard didn't have the nerve," Fågelsjö says. "He didn't have the nerve."

He probably did have the nerve, Father.

But he couldn't, didn't want to.

I see you sit down again, defenseless, and not long ago you were experiencing the most profound of all fears, the feeling that is the only thing that exists on the boundary where life and death meet.

You were there just now, and now you've been called back, but have you learned anything, Father?

I don't think so.

I shall be buried in a few days' time, Father, but you don't care about that, or do you? The family vault is ready out in the chapel.

There's so much I don't know about you, Father, and now Malin Fors and Zacharias Martinsson are standing by the door, they're talking to their boss, wondering: Where is Anders Dalström?

You're close now, Malin, but this drama isn't over yet. There are still a few more moments of obscurity and clarity to come.

You've found the knife, with the coat of arms on the shaft, the knife that perforated my body. Karin Johannison will let you know within a few days that it was the knife that inflicted my wounds.

I'm tumbling around in my space, amused as I am by this relentless desire for events to play themselves out, come to a conclusion, so that a new beginning can finally have its beginning.

There's some justice in the position I'm in. I destroyed friendships, and many other forms of love, and I never took responsibility for that.

But where is he now, Anders Dalström?

You know, Malin. You know.

Malin is crouching beside Fågelsjö, who has sat down on the chair again, when she sees Waldemar Ekenberg and Johan Jakobsson coming over from the direction of the stairs.

Fågelsjö is carefully but firmly wiping the blood from his face, breathing slowly, saying:

"He didn't have the nerve. The bastard. But he knocked out several of my teeth."

"Did he say anything as he left?"

"No."

"Do you have any idea where he might have gone?"

"No. Where would someone like that go?"

The man before her looks huge on his chair, the look in his eyes tired but sharp as he says:

"When animals are about to die, they go to places they've been before, places that are important to them."

"Did he have a rifle?"

"How else do you think he got me down here?"

"So you were here when he arrived?"

"No, I was at home in the apartment, but I was about to come out here when he arrived. It was time to come home."

Malin jumps up and runs over to Zeke without paying any attention to Johan, Sven, or Waldemar.

"Come on!" she yells. "I know where he is."

Zeke follows her without asking, and they rush toward the car over the moat where the water seems to be frothing with green bubbles. The rain is pounding the ground and soon they are in the Volvo, carrying them faster and faster through the darkness of the estate, imagining that they can see the spirits of those who have gone before them, drifting anxiously outside the car windows.

They sit in silence.

Behind them other cars with flashing blue lights.

But no sirens.

The sound of wind and rain and engines dominates the forest and fields.

They pass Linnea Sjöstedt's cottage, a dull glow coming from the windows.

They pass the building where the party took place that New Year's Eve, turn once, twice, three times, and then the sharp bend by the field where Jerry Petersson and the others rolled over and over and over, bodies flying through the air, the winter night must have been shattered by the sound of metal crumpling, bodies breaking, beyond any hope of repair.

A car some way out in the field.

White, almost transparent rain in the beams of light from the headlamps.

And at the boundary of light and darkness stands a man with a rifle in his hand.

73

Lights and sounds.

Cars, spraying cascades of color.

I couldn't kill the old man. But I could kill his son, I had that much in me. And it felt wonderful.

I did it.

I didn't mean to kill Jerry Petersson, but can anyone say he didn't deserve to end his days like that?

It's time for me to go. This is it. And this is a good place, Andreas, isn't it?

If you're here, show me, because in that case I'll stay. And stare straight into the yellow faces of the snakes.

The lights.

The cars.

Shouting and people, that person moving toward me like a black silhouette over the waterlogged meadow.

I can't see the person's face.

But I know it isn't you, Andreas.

Out of the car.

"I'll take this on my own, Zeke."

The figure out in the field seems to be shaking, just like in the images of his life. His long black hair like a whip in the wind.

And in his hand the rifle. A sporting rifle.

Malin has drawn her pistol for the second time that day.

Close to their prey now.

Evil, confusion, fear, all within sight.

He's holding the gun along the side of his body.

The others take cover behind the cars, Sven's voice, anxious, concerned, but full of certainty: I can't stop her from doing this, and now she's walking toward the man in the field, and the closer she gets, the clearer his contorted features become, the torment in his eyes. It's as if he can't see me, Malin thinks. As if he's alone in the rain and wind, and his gaze seems to be searching for something he's been missing for a long time.

I can't see anything but darkness.

Can only feel the sharp slithering of the snakes inside me, can only hear their whimpering. Feel Dad's blows, hear their shriek as they chase me.

You're not here, Andreas.

That's enough for me, there's nothing more for me to do here, and the cold rain that has pressed through all my clothes will never stop, nor will the darkness.

I'm looking at the lights and the person coming toward me, she seems to be shouting, but I can only hear an agitated rumbling, as if she wants something important.

But I ignore her. Instead I put the barrel of the rifle in my mouth, and caress the trigger the way your finger often caressed it, Dad, before your eye was destroyed.

I see her in front of me.

But I can't see you, Andreas. You're not here.

*   *   *

He's raised the gun to his mouth.

His finger's on the trigger, careful yet without any uncertainty.

"Don't do it," Malin shouts. "It won't make anything better."

As she shouts a powerful wind sweeps over the field, somehow making a rattling sound.

He's going to shoot, Malin thinks.

But Anders Dalström doesn't pull the trigger, instead he meets her gaze, and his eyes become calm, reassured by what is about to happen, and Malin shouts again:

"There's another way, there always is," and time becomes compressed and she sees Janne and Tove standing in front of her. They're sitting watching television in the house out in Malmslätt, waiting for her to come back with her love, that must be it, they must be missing that. I want to understand, she thinks, what it is that stands between me and the love that I feel.

"Don't do it."

My voice a prayer now.

Don't do it.

There's always another way.

"Don't do it," she shouts at me. I can hear it now.

But I want to do this, and I look out into the darkness, and I see a car roll and spin, and the world tumbles into nothingness, it ends.

Tell me, why should I stay?

The barrel is cold and hard. A taste of gunmetal and iron.

I'm going to do it now.

And her mouth moves, but no words come out, but what is it I can hear, whose voice, and what's it saying?

Do it. Do it.
You weak fucker. Do it!

Pull the trigger and put a stop to this.

Of course I was driving, but what difference does that make? You had no life before that, and afterward you had a reason to believe in your own misery, and you never moved on from that.

Hopeless.

So do it, do it, do it, do it now, now, now!

Away, away, away.

Anders Dalström wants to wave his arms in the air, wave the disembodied voice and everything it's saying away, even if it's saying the words he most wants to hear.

Do it.

"Sit still. I've got the ruler. Hold your fingers out."

"Get him, get him."

Do it.

I will, I will, but have I got the nerve?

Go away!

I want to do it myself.

Do it, says the voice, don't, says another, don't do it, and whose face is that in front of me?

He's staring into thin air, as if he's focusing on something just in front of my face, Malin thinks.

I know what you're looking for, she thinks, says, "He's here. He wants you to stay."

And Anders stands still, stops shaking, just as if the film of his life had come to an end, then he moves his mouth, but Malin can't make out his words, the noises coming out of the gap around the barrel are aimed at someone else.

His finger on the trigger.

Darkness like a wall behind him.

What's that in the darkness?

*   *   *

Andreas? Is that you, are you there?

Is that really your face floating in front of hers? In her face? In place of her face?

What are you saying?

"Anders, it's me, but so much more," the voice says now.

"I'm the one you need to listen to. No one else.

"And I don't want you here.

"No.

"You're not done yet. The snakes will go. I promise.

"The life you'll lead might not be easy or enviable, but it will be your life.

"You can see my face now. It's me. Isn't it? So take the barrel of the rifle out of your mouth. Otherwise I'll disappear again."

It's you, Andreas.

And you're telling me not to do it.

I'm going to listen to you. How could I do anything else?

Don't do it.

The blades of the lawnmower are finally silent, nothing chasing me anymore, and one day, some day, love will come to me again, the love I sought and fled from.

So don't do it.

For my sake. For Katarina's. For everyone's sake.

Malin sees Anders slowly take the barrel of the rifle out of his mouth, then with a quick jerk he throws the rifle out into the boggy ground of the meadow, then he puts his hands in the air and looks Malin right in the eye.

What can you see? Malin thinks.

Me?

Someone else?

She aims her pistol at the man in front of her.

Feels the rain running under her collar and down her back, hears the sound of steps behind her.

Then she sees two uniformed officers go over to Anders, force his arms behind his back, with gentle smiles.

An arm on her shoulder.

Zeke's voice in her ear:

"You're crazy, Malin. Crazy."

Epilogue

*A*nyone who looks and listens can hear us.

> *We're all here, all us boys who have been captured by time.*
>
> *We're drifting around you, together.*

We are everywhere and nowhere.

We have the same voice, Jerry, Andreas, and Fredrik, we're a choir beyond your understanding.

The man in the prison cell down there is alone, he's about to go to court to be sentenced.

At the same time, he can never be alone, because he knows who he is, why he did what he did.

A murderer can be enviable. How odd is that?

But there's a lot that's odd.

And there are few people who look and listen.

There are few who have the nerve to believe.

Malin looks around the room. There's an institutional atmosphere to the study center that's been turned into a treatment home for alcoholics who have crossed some sort of boundary for respectable behavior.

Six weeks here.

Sven Sjöman was immovable.

"I'm taking you out of active service. You're on sick leave, and you're going to go to this treatment center."

He put the brochure on his desk, the nasty little pamphlet turned to face her.

Like an advert for an activity holiday.

Yellow-painted residential blocks around a white-plastered turn-of-the-century house. Birch trees in bloom.

Snow outside at the moment, the rain of late autumn transformed into beautiful crystals.

"I'll go."

"You've got no choice if you want to remain a detective."

She called Janne. Explained the situation, like Sven wanted her to, and he didn't sound surprised, maybe he and Sven had spoken to each other.

"You know you've got a problem, don't you?"

"Yes."

"That you're an alcoholic?"

"I know I can't handle drink, yes. And that I've got to . . ."

"You've got to stop drinking, Malin. You can't have so much as a drop."

Janne had let her see Tove. They met for coffee out in Tornby, then they went to H&M to get new clothes for both of them. In the café Malin apologized, said she's been acting completely crazy recently, told her she was going to get help, as if that was news to Tove.

"Do you have to be gone so long?"

"It could have been even worse."

Malin had felt like crying, and she could see Tove holding herself together. If that was what she was doing.

It was as if a grown-up were sitting opposite Malin, a familiar stranger, someone who had changed, and they were sitting in the midst of retail mayhem trying not to be sad together. Of all the things a mother and daughter could do together, they were doing this.

Tove had said, "It'll do you good, Mum, you need help."

Do fifteen-year-olds say things like that?

"I'll be okay, you've got to try to get better."

Sick, in Tove's eyes. But there is something sick about a parent who abandons their child.

"I'll be home before Christmas."

But this place.

Sitting in groups and talking about how much they want a drink.

Having individual sessions with someone who can't get her to open up.

Admit that she's an "alcoholic."

Missing Tove so much it's driving her mad. Feeling so ashamed she wants to turn her skin inside out. Trying to find ways to bear the shame.

Hugs outside the house in Malmslätt when she dropped Tove off. Janne behind the illuminated kitchen window.

"Be careful. Don't let anything happen to you. It would kill me."

"Don't talk like that, Mum, don't say that. I'll be fine."

Malin doesn't miss Janne. Not missing missing him is the best thing about being here.

Who wants to sit around talking about their destructive behavior? Their patterns, the things that trigger the thirst. Their memories.

Leave my memories the fuck alone.

Don't want to, don't want to, don't want to know.

Dreams about a faceless boy. About secrets.

Lies. Told to your face by well-meaning people. Sleepless nights, dreams about snakes being chased by lawnmower blades through sewers full of blue-stomached rat corpses.

This all ends for the dead, but not for me. Unless perhaps it does?

The images in the dreams are black and white, as if filmed on an old Super 8 camera, and sometimes there's a boy in the pictures, a boy running over different grass to the lawn in the film on Anders Dalström's bedroom wall.

Yesterday I sat with the others. I said the words straight out: "I'm an alcoholic."

Dad phoned me here.

He had heard from Janne where I was, why I wasn't answering my phone at home or my mobile. He didn't sound worried, just relieved, him too.

"You weren't doing too well when we met."

What are you hiding from me? The two of you. What is it I don't know? Are you and Mum going to carry your secret to the grave?

Are you hiding the reason I'm sitting here in a room in a treatment center in the middle of the forest staring at a washed-out rag rug?

Malin curls up on the bed against the wall. Pulls her legs up and thinks about Maria Murvall, how she's sitting on another bed in another room.

What does this world want with us, Maria?

I'm going to be home by Christmas. I'm going to handle not drinking. We'll have a nice, peaceful Christmas. I've got to stay calm.

The sofa in the television room is covered with green fabric.

Malin is alone there, none of the other women with the same problem as her seem to be interested in what's going on in the world.

Anders Dalström's trial starts today. The interviews with him, him saying it was like he had snakes inside him, and that they had somehow disappeared from him when he killed Jerry Petersson. He talked about calm. The sort of calm he wanted to experience again, and which made it easy to kill Fredrik Fågelsjö, but that the snakes refused to listen to any violence against Axel Fågelsjö.

Börje Svärd's wife, Anna, died earlier in the week, finally allowed to stop breathing, and Malin called Börje but got no answer, and she hasn't tried again. But she knew he was going to keep Jerry Petersson's dog, whatever its name was.

She takes a sip of the tea she's just got from the kitchen.

Looks out of the window, the same darkness as before.

Then the start of the evening news, a female voice and pictures:

"The man who admitted murdering two people in Linköping this autumn, as well as the kidnap of a third person, was killed today during an attack in Linköping District Court. A man who has been identified as the victim of the kidnapping and the father of one of the murder victims had somehow managed to smuggle a sawn-off shotgun into the courtroom and . . ."

Malin feels faint.

She spills tea in her lap, but doesn't feel the heat as she concentrates on the screen.

Pictures from the courtroom.

A commotion.

She hears the shots. The screams.

Then Axel Fågelsjö's face, pale scars on his cheek.

His head held down against the floor of the courtroom by two police officers.

His face expressing conviction, determination, isolation, and grief.

A face, not a mask.

You did it, Malin thinks. And I understand you.

The monster above Tove. Ready to strangle her.

If a parent doesn't protect his or her child, who else will?

My task is to protect Tove.

There's a place in this world for me as well, Malin thinks. She feels that everything's going to be all right.